D0099072

INTO THE DIM

JANET B. TAYLOR

HOUGHTON MIFFLIN HARCOURT
BOSTON   NEW YORK

www.hmhco.com

The text was set in Adobe Caslon Pro.

Library of Congress Cataloging-in-Publication Data
Taylor, Janet, 1967–
Into the Dim / Janet Taylor.
pages cm
Summary: Sixteen-year-old Hope Walton travels back in time
to help rescue her mother, a member of the secret society
of time travelers, who is trapped in twelfth-century
England in the age of Eleanor of Aquitaine.
ISBN 978-0-544-60200-7
[1. Time travel—Fiction. 2. Secret societies—Fiction.
3. Families—Fiction. 4. Love—Fiction. 5. Great
Britain—History—Henry II, 1154-1189—Fiction.] I. Title.
PZ7.1.T386In 2016
[Fic]—dc23
2015008455

Manufactured in the United States of America
DOC 10 9 8 7 6 5 4 3 2 1
4500578095

For Phil: Who always, *always* believed I could . . .
{{45888}}

CHAPTER 1

Everyone in town knew the coffin was empty.

I think that's what packed the pews — the pure curiosity of the thing. They didn't come for love or admiration. Nope. They came for the show. They came because it was big news. A juicy scandal that jolted our small southern town like spikes of summer lightning.

Hometown boy Matthew Walton was finally laying his wife to rest. By the time my mother's funeral began, it was standing-room only.

Though it was only midafternoon, I was already drained. Sweat bled through the back of my shirt, gluing me to the wooden bench. As the inept fan buzzed overhead, a quick, darting movement caught my eye. A small bird flitted among the rafters. Trapped. I knew exactly how it felt.

As the priest droned a pallid eulogy, venomous whispers began to surge from the hushed crowd behind me. The hateful words oozed up to corrode my skin, exposing muscle and tendon and jittery nerve endings.

"*. . . hate to speak ill of the dead, but we're all thinking it.*"

"Personally, I couldn't stand the woman." "That Sarah Walton. Always thought she was so much better than the rest of us." "Yeah. Snooty bit . . ."

The voices trailed off as the priest wound down. But the quiet round of chuckles that followed made my teeth shriek, like biting down on tinfoil. My throat ached with the urge to scream. To tell them how they were all vapid, backward simpletons, just like my mom always claimed.

Of course, I'd yell into their outraged faces. *Of course she thought she was better than you. Because she was. She was better than all of you put together.*

My mother was far from "snooty." She simply couldn't tolerate these small-town divas with their sly prejudice and malicious gossip. She'd rejected them long ago, and they'd never forgiven her for it. But she was brilliant and brave and . . .

Gone.

The word slammed around in my brain, keeping time with the bird's desperate circling. I could almost hear its fragile heart, beating so fast it was bound to rupture.

My hands clenched in my lap. My legs strained with the effort of staying in my seat. God, I wanted to see their shocked expressions when I shot to my feet, spun around, and—

I flinched at a sudden thump. The bird, in a bid for freedom, had crashed into the false security of the stained-glass window. It tumbled to the floor in a heap of floating feathers. My heart stuttered, and the rage dissipated on a wave

of exhaustion. My fists relaxed. The urge to scream subsided as I stared at the crumpled creature lying so still on the
ground. A life snuffed out in an instant, just like that.

The eulogy ended. Jaw set, I followed my dad's stooped
form to our place near the altar. As his narrow shoulders
hitched, I finally let my gaze drift to my mother's beautiful,
empty coffin. I sidled away, gulping. Pain pinged my temples. An iron band tightened around my scalp. Squinting
against the pain, I focused on the details. Burled walnut,
mahogany inlay, brass handles, and the casket's manufac-
turer discreetly embossed in the lower left corner: JOHNSON
& SONS.

The words roared out of nowhere, a newspaper article I'd
seen years before began to scroll through my mind in neat,
orderly rows.

*Johnson & Sons have manufactured fine quality caskets locally
since 1921, when Johannes Johnson immigrated from—*

My hands twitched. *Not. Now.*

I struggled to concentrate on something else before the
words overwhelmed me. Before they became too big for my
skull. I tried to look somewhere else, anywhere else, but my
gaze kept drifting back to the flower-draped coffin.

Roses, lilies, and a huge spray of reeking blue carnations
that Mom had always called by their Old English term, "gil-
lyflowers." *The Gillyflower. Queen Elizabeth Tudor's favorite
blossom. She surrounded herself with them at court . . .*

The information swelled, marching across my vision
in glowing green columns. The genus and origin of each

type of blossom, followed by dates and significant events of Elizabeth's reign. The words expanded until details of every European monarch since Charlemagne flowed before my eyes in a translucent overlay of glowing green columns.

August 12, 30 B.C., Cleopatra, Queen of Egypt, committed suicide.

1775, Russian czarina Catherine the Great defeated the Pugachev Rebellion.

On and on it went, until the chapel and the mourners — the real world — filtered away. I felt myself swaying, listening only to the symphony of knowledge in my head. Then, cutting through the din, the sound of my mother's voice, low and incessant.

A true photographic memory is extremely rare, Hope. It is imperative that we devise a way to keep your mind organized. People with your kind of eidetic abilities must learn to contain all that information, to tamp it down, or it will overwhelm you. Concentrate. Stay firmly grounded. Focus only on what is right before you.

My training kicked in. I shoved back the mass of useless information, spooling it down into the mental image we'd come up with. A battered gray filing cabinet, like the one in Mom's office. In my head, I slammed the door for good measure and glanced over at my dad.

He hadn't noticed. That was no surprise. Pasting on a smile, Dad heaved a quiet sigh as curious mourners began to thread their way toward us for handshakes and awkward hugs.

Firmly grounded. Focus on what's right before me.

Yeah. 'Cause that's so much better.

The endless line passed, leaving behind a sickly odor. Too many flowers mixed with a crap-ton of cheap cologne. My gut began to rebel as Dad turned to me, brown eyes owlish and distracted behind thick frames. When he couldn't quite meet my eyes, a last phrase — a straggler — loosed from the billions I'd tucked neatly away. It curled and flapped like a ribbon set loose on the wind.

A miasma arose. The decaying bouquet of a doomed queen's garden.

Who wrote that? The answer came to hand like a well-trained dog. *Oh, right. It was —*

"Well, thank God that's done and we can all get back to our lives," my grandmother said as she marched toward us. "Though I still say it was a ridiculous waste of money to buy a casket, Matt. You could've had a nice little memorial service, but —"

"Hope and I needed closure, Mother," Dad said. "Leave it alone."

Beatrice "Mother Bea" Walton gave a nod to the petite, round-faced woman who had moved to stand at my father's side.

"Stella, honey," she said, "would you be a dear and go make sure the car's ready?"

"Of course, Mother Bea. Happy to." Stella proffered a tremulous smile before rushing off to do my grandmother's bidding.

My father's new girlfriend was a nice lady. A librarian. And one of the few people in this town my mother had genuinely liked. I didn't blame her for jumping at my grandmother's command. Everyone from the mayor to the bag boys at the grocery hopped to when Beatrice Walton issued an order. I was always mildly surprised when they didn't bow.

I didn't really blame Dad for being with Stella either, though it had only been seven months since Mom died. When he'd fallen apart, Stella had been the one to pull him back together. She'd tried to befriend me, too. But I didn't want a friend. I wanted my mom.

After Stella scurried off, my grandmother directed her words at my father, her son the scientist. Her youngest, her pride and joy until eleven years ago, when he'd gone against her wishes and married my mom, taking on five-year-old me in the process.

"I assume you'll get Hope registered at the high school come the fall," Mother Bea said. "No more of that silly homeschooling, now that your wife's gone."

Mother Bea never called my mom by name. Just "your wife." I shot a look at Dad. He wouldn't look at me. But when he nodded to my grandmother, a cold dread began to spread through my veins.

High school? Actual high school? This was a joke. Had to be.

When I was younger, I'd begged to go to "real" school, but Mom wouldn't hear of it. *And waste your talents on that inbred travesty they call an education system? Hardly.*

Now they meant to thrust me into that world of Friday night football games, pep rallies, and "good ole boys" with decapitated Bambis in the back of their mud-spattered pickups?

The very thought filled me with horror.

"And the letter?" Mother Bea was saying. "You've explained about the letter?"

Ignoring her, I turned to Dad, confused. "What letter?"

For an instant, he only glared at his mother. Finally, he forced a sickly barely-there smile and reached for my hand.

"Hope," he said, "a few weeks ago, I received an email from your mother's sister, your Aunt Lucinda. She's invited you to spend the summer with her in Scotland. Isn't that wonderful, honey? You'll get to meet your mother's people. I've told her you would come, of course, and—"

"What?" The word bounced against the walls of the empty chapel like the poor, doomed bird. "What are you talking about?"

"W-we"—my dad stuttered over the word—"that is, Stella and I, feel that it would be good for you to get away, honey. You need to heal. We all do. And . . . well . . . we've planned a little trip ourselves. A—a cruise. So I thought . . ."

He trailed off, helpless in his betrayal. Mother Bea gleamed with triumph as he reached into a pocket and pulled out a crumpled piece of paper. He smoothed it out, and pressed it, limp and damp, into my hand.

Dear Matthew,

As I've already offered my condolences, I shall not do so here. This letter is, instead, in reference to your daughter. I wish to request that Hope come spend the summer with me, here at Christopher Manor. As you are aware, the manor is located in a lovely area of the Scottish Highlands. I feel its pastoral landscape could be soothing to Hope. As there are other young people who live at the manor, she will not lack company of her own age.

Attached you will find the pertinent information regarding the first-class ticket I have selected. I look forward to hearing from you.

Sincerely,
Your sister-in-law, Lady Lucinda Carlyle

Postscript: Please inform Hope that I also believe there are insights she might gain at her mother's childhood home which would not be feasible for her to discover in her current circumstances.

My lungs constricted as I let my eyes rise slowly from the paper to stare at my dad, the man who'd raised me since I was five years old. The only parent I had left.

My voice came out so small. "You're sending me away?"

"No!" he exclaimed. "No, it's not like that, Hope. It's just that now—"

Before he could say more, the pale-lipped funeral director arrived to usher us out to the waiting limo. I jammed the paper into my own pocket as the two of us slipped inside. Deciding to ignore the fact that my dad wanted to get rid of me, I turned to him on the wide leather seat. I had more urgent issues to deal with.

"Dad." I tried to infuse calm into my voice as we pulled out behind the flashing police escort on our way to the gravesite. "Please. Please don't bury that awful . . ." I had to stop. Swallow. "What about the video?"

"Not this again." He mumbled as he leaned back against the stiff seat, closing his eyes and pinching the bridge of his nose.

With a sharp exhale, he nudged the glasses back into place and turned to face me. "Sweetie," he said. "I know you think you saw something. And I believe you. I do. But we researched it for weeks. None of the U.S. or foreign networks recognized your description of the news footage."

"I know what I saw, Dad."

He scraped a hand across his mouth. I recognized the gesture as poorly-disguised annoyance. I'd seen it before, though not often. Once, when I'd accidently deleted his paper on 'Karenia Brevis,' the organism responsible for red tide in the Gulf of Mexico. And again at eight, when I'd scribbled Socrates's speech to the Athens jury in permanent marker on his office white board.

"This isn't easy for me, either, Hope." His voice was

hushed and so, so sad. "But we have to face facts. Your mother was inside that lecture hall when the earthquake struck. No one on the lower floors survived. It's been over seven months now, honey, and I . . ."

His jaw flexed. A lone tear escaped and rolled down my father's cheek. "It's time to let her go."

After the quake, I'd become obsessed with the news. I didn't sleep, I barely ate. The extra pounds I'd always carried around had melted away as I pored over each picture, every article, hundreds of hours of news footage. The video had aired only once, on one of the satellite channels in Dad's office.

Most people wouldn't have noticed.

I wasn't most people.

With crystal-clear recall, my mind never stopped replaying the ten-second clip.

The girl's body lay only a few yards from the collapsed university high rise. She'd obviously tried to run when the building came down, but an immense beam had fallen, crushing her beneath its weight. The footage had panned over her mangled corpse for only an instant, but it was all I'd needed. The neon-pink flyer crumpled in the girl's limp hand was ripped and bloody and coated with white dust. I could make out only the first few words, written in Hindi, then in English.

Today's lecture series with renowned author and historian Dr. Sarah Walton is can—

That was it. That was all. But I knew, I *knew*, what that last word really was.

Not *can. Canceled.*

For some reason, my mother had canceled her lecture that day. She had not been inside that tower when the earthquake brought it down.

Ecstatic at first, my father had contacted the American embassies in Mumbai and New Delhi. Then every hospital, shelter, and rescue organization. But as the days and weeks dragged on, he'd slowly let the hope and faith that we'd find her just slip away. When I refused to let it go, his look had turned from pity to concern.

"Hope." He spoke carefully over the limo's purring engine, as if to a small child. "We've been over this so many times. If Sar—" He paused, took a deep breath through his nose. "If your mother was alive, she'd have contacted us. If she was injured, someone else would have. They've identified all the survivors. I'm so sorry. But, sweetheart, it's time to move on."

I threw up my hands. "Oh, you'd love that. 'Cause if she's dead, you can stop feeling so guilty about hooking up with Stella."

Since the day my mom—the sun around which we both

revolved—went supernova, Dad and I had existed in a kind of wobbly orbit. Two orphaned planets. Polite, unfailingly cordial, but never quite synchronized.

"Bet you wouldn't just throw me out like this if I was your *real* daughter," I muttered, staring out the glass at the trees whipping past.

My dad flinched, hand pressed to his heart as if to keep it from stopping.

I hadn't cried when he made me go with him to pick out the coffin. I'd remained stubbornly mute while Dad and the funeral director made all the arrangements. During visitation the night before, I heard my grandmother whisper how I was an unnatural, cold child.

None of it had touched me. It wasn't real.

It took the horrified, wounded look on my father's face for it to finally break through. I heard it happen, a quiet snap deep inside.

"Dad?" I choked. "Daddy? I'm sorry. I didn't mean it. I didn't. It's just that I—I can't . . ."

"I know, sweetie." He pulled me across the seat to wrap me in his arms. "I know."

The tears came then. Because he was right. They were all right. My mother was dead, and I had been so stupid.

CHAPTER 2

I'D LISTENED IN ON THE KITCHEN EXTENSION WHEN MY dad took the call all those months ago. The man from the Red Cross sounded so apologetic. His proper speech and Hindi accent made the words almost soothing. The search for survivors was called off, he'd explained. Explosives had been set to bring down the rest of the dangerous, mangled mess that had once housed the university lecture halls. Anyone still missing was now presumed dead.

I think Dad even thanked him before hanging up.

Now presumed dead.

The phone had tumbled from my hand as the files in my mind blew open and began to flood with images of death by crushing. Death by suffocation. The walls closed in around me as pain blasted through my brain. Unbearable, unspeakable pain. When my father rushed into the kitchen seconds later, I was curled on the floor, screaming in agony.

I'd had them before. Cluster migraines, the doctors called them. Brought on by my unusual mental "gift," and exacerbated by severe claustrophobia. They weren't dangerous, but when my brain—with its photographic capability—took in too much stimuli, it simply couldn't cope.

Though the shrinks could diagnose the headaches all day long, they'd never been able to pinpoint the exact source of the horrific, breath-robbing nightmare I'd suffered my entire life.

After Mom died, the dream had gotten so much worse.

In it, I'm trapped inside the belly of a great tree. A dank, cold place in which the living wood tries to consume me. Where fat, leggy creatures drop down from the blackness above to roam through my hair and skitter across my face.

For months after Mom died, I woke up every night, biting back screams, my sheets sweaty and tangled around me. They'd recently subsided to only once or twice a week. Though now when the nightmare came, I stayed awake the rest of the night, too afraid to fall asleep again. Without the comfort of her voice or her cool hand to smooth the hair off my clammy face, the monsters always returned.

In the end, I did nothing as they lowered the shiny, tenant-less casket into the ground. Back in our own car, Dad pulled up in front of the house, but didn't get out. His hands tightened on the steering wheel. "I won't force you to go," he said. "But Stella and I will be gone for a few weeks. We're taking a long drive west, then up to Seattle, and the Alaskan cruise is for two weeks. It's something she's always wanted to do."

I managed not to roll my eyes, but it was a close thing.

"You can, of course, stay with your grandmother."

I blinked at him. He knew I'd rather live in a cardboard box and take showers with the hose than stay with *her*. A woman who'd never, in all the years I'd known her, shown me one ounce of kindness.

"No, thanks," I said, though it left me with decidedly few options. It wasn't like I had a friend I could stay with.

Or a friend.

"Yes, well . . ." He sighed. "I'm sorry, honey, but those are your choices. It's your call, though I think the trip would be good for you. We can get you a mild sedative from Dr. Miller for the plane ride." He squeezed my knee and smiled, as if that was the answer.

A mild sedative. Just the ticket. That would take care of the massive panic attacks that would surely come when I was alone forty-thousand feet above the Atlantic Ocean.

"I've forwarded you the email from Lucinda," he said as he got out of the car. "I never met her, but she and your mother were very close, you know. Promise me you'll at least think about it."

I snorted. *Sure. No problem. I'll just hop on a plane. Easy-peasey.*

Unlike a normal person, I wasn't worried about crashing. I'd researched the chances of that, and they were infinitesimal. No. It wasn't splatting into the ocean and cracking into a million pieces that made my teeth itch. It was being trapped inside that suffocating metal tube.

As I walked across the porch, the memory zipped into place.

My mom was a prominent historian and author of a dozen popular biographies. Universities all over the world paid her very well for her lectures and book-signings. She'd tried for years to take me along on her circuit. She'd begged, cajoled, promised me a great time. A little over a year ago, I'd finally agreed. We planned it for months. We'd fly into London and rent a car, and I'd actually get to see some of the historical places I'd spent most of my life studying. I wanted to go so badly, I could taste it. Then, three days after my fifteenth birthday, we went to the airport.

It was an unmitigated disaster.

I tried. I tried so hard to make myself get on that plane. In the end, my mother had boarded alone, while I vomited quietly in my dad's back seat, the claustrophobia-induced migraine splitting my skull in two. After that, no matter how much she begged, I wouldn't even discuss it.

Alone in my bedroom, I slumped in my battered desk chair, staring down at the smears of red graveyard mud that tracked across the frayed carpet. The muted clink of dishes rose up through the floor. Below, I could hear the muffled voices of people who'd followed us home. Done with the whole mourning thing, they were busy stuffing their faces with casseroles and neighbor-baked pies.

She's gone. She's really gone. And now Dad is leaving me too.

But ten hours on an airplane? Impossible.

The area inside a typical Boeing 747 is 1,375 square feet. The average size of a small house. Not so bad, right? A house. Plenty of room. No big deal.

But if you're in a house, you can go outside. You can step out and breathe the air. If you want—if you need—to.

Panting, I lowered my head to my knees as tiny jets of agony began to pulse across my scalp. An invisible band slowly tightened across my chest as sweat gathered at my hairline and across the back of my neck.

When black spots appeared at the edge of my vision, I knew I was seconds from hyperventilating. Grinding my teeth, I forced myself to perform the breathing technique Mom and I had practiced over and over, when everything became too much. When the vast quantities of information that never, ever left my brain just kept expanding.

In . . . two three. Out . . . two three. That's right, Hope. There you go. Slow and easy. Just keep counting.

When my breath had normalized, I sat up and turned back to the computer. The subject line in the forwarded email read, "Invitation from your aunt."

Aunt. I scowled at the four black letters. *Yeah, right. Might as well say "Invitation from a total stranger."* My mom and her only sister *had been* close, that was true enough. They'd talked on the phone every week. Sometimes for hours. But Mom always claimed her sister was something of a recluse. She never visited. And in all those years, she'd never asked to speak to me. Not once.

I tapped ragged fingernails on the wooden desk. I didn't need to read the letter. I'd committed it to memory in that one, quick glance. *As I've already offered my condolences, I shall not do so here.*

I grunted. *Wow. What a sweetheart.*

My gaze snagged on the postscript.

I also believe there are insights she might gain at her mother's childhood home which would not be feasible for her to discover in her current circumstances.

"Insights?" I muttered. "What's that supposed to mean?"

I stood and paced to the window. Even here, in my own space, I felt suffocated. I shoved the sash open, but the muggy June air only made it worse.

Frustrated, I slammed it back down. Wrapping a fist in the nubby curtains, I started to jerk them closed, when a blaze of blue caught my eye. Our neighbor's massive hydrangea bush.

I flinched away from the window as the memory sliced me apart.

The annual Walton Fourth of July picnic was mandatory. Only imminent death excused attendance. That year, Mother Bea had hired a professional photographer, who'd spent the day snapping candids. Twelve, chubby and awkward, I'd spent my day ducking out of them.

As the sun waned, my grandmother had perched in her favorite wicker chair before a great wall of blue hydrangeas to begin formal portraits. When the photographer called for the grandkids, Dad towed me toward the plethora of cousins. Stifling a sigh, I'd arranged myself near the back. Mother Bea's perfectly permed gray head swiveled, scanning her progeny. When the photographer raised his huge camera, she gestured for him to wait.

Without bothering to turn, my grandmother made the announcement. "I'd like for these to be blood kin only," she called. "Hope, you understand, don't you, dear?"

Stung—stunned—it took me a second to get it. After I slunk away, my grandmother ordered the obviously disconcerted photographer to proceed. Several of my cousins snickered as waves of hot embarrassment baked my face. Of course it wasn't a secret that no Walton blood flowed in my veins. But never before had I been singled out that way.

Left out that way.

In the tangerine glow of a perfect sunset, I'd watched the mob of tanned, golden-haired kids cluster around their matriarch. Uniformly big teeth gleamed as they grinned on cue. I stood alone, a pale, dark-haired stain against a gleaming white column.

My mother's reaction was predictably fierce, and the next day, after my lesson in Empirical Russian, she'd informed my father that she and I would attend no more family functions.

My mom despised her mother-in-law and everything she stood for. She would never have wanted me to stay.

I sank down in the desk chair. Tears blurred the screen as, hands shaking, I typed in the two-word reply.

"I'll come."

CHAPTER 3

I woke just as the plane taxied into Edinburgh Airport. Dad had been right about the sedative, though I was fairly sure Dr. Miller, a kindly, old-school pediatrician who'd treated my myriad ailments since I was six, might've upped the recommended dosage just a smidge.

The first, lighter round of meds had kicked in just as I boarded and strapped in. Somehow, I had stumbled to the right gate in Atlanta. Then I'd spent the next ten hours passed out, drooling, and—based on the mutters of the disgruntled passengers around me—snoring like a bear with a sinus infection.

Before I left, I'd tried to research my aunt's home, Christopher Manor. There was little to find. Only a few faraway photos posted by hikers traveling through the famous Scottish Highlands. And a stern warning that—unlike a lot of other grand Highland estates—it was not open to the public.

"Your aunt's right sorry she couldn't be here to welcome you herself, lass." Mac, Lucinda's lanky, balding caretaker, had explained when he met me at baggage claim with a little, handwritten sign. "Urgent business, you understand."

All this way. And she wasn't even here?

Still drowsy and more than a little grumpy, I hadn't said much on the long, dark drive from Edinburgh. But when we pulled up the gravel drive and parked in front of the massive, imposing mansion, I couldn't help but gape.

Floodlights illuminated five or six stories of golden stone that glowed against the night sky. Square Norman towers stood sentinel at each corner, giving the manor a boxy look. There were no storybook turrets that I could see, but the crenelated tops of the walls and towers made it easy to imagine long-ago kilted archers defending the house against rival clans.

"The house nestles right up against the mountain," Mac said as he saw the direction of my gaze. "She's a right good old girl."

I nodded, still mute with awe. I couldn't tell how far the mansion stretched out behind. But judging by the distance to the hump of the mountain in the near distance, it had to be enormous.

Inside, the house was dark and silent. Only the soft glow of wall sconces set between grim-faced ancestors lit our way as we trudged up two flights of wide, carpeted steps. The scents of stone, lemon polish, and musty drapes cascaded over us as I followed Mac's knobby shoulders down a narrow hallway.

Only a small bedside lamp lit the room where Mac

deposited me and my bags. With a groan, he laid my suitcase on a nearby table before pointing out a thermos and covered plate. "My Moira wanted to wait up for ye," he said. "But I told her we'd be sore late getting in. Still I swear she'll take a broom to these old bones if ye don't eat at least two of her famous jam sandwiches."

At my very-polite thanks, his grin widened, making his small blue eyes disappear into a fan of wrinkles. "Aw, Lass," he said, "You've had a hard row to hoe. But it's right pleased we are to have you here. Now, you get yourself some sleep. The others will be rarin' to meet ye come the morn."

Still druggy and exhausted, I climbed up the three wooden steps to the bed and, fully clothed, passed clean out.

The clack of footsteps woke me the next morning. I cracked one crusty eyelid to see that pearly dawn light now puddled on the floor of my new bedroom, brightening as I watched. Groaning, I glanced at the ornate bronze clock on my bedside table.

Not even seven, yet. Who the hell is wandering around at this ungodly hour? And in heels, no less.

I pulled the quilt up to my chin and burrowed deeper into the feather mattress.

Without warning, the bedroom door flew open with such force, it smacked against the paneled wall. I shot up, heart hammering. Before I could blink, a dainty, elf-faced girl with an upturned nose and short spiky hair the startling shade of a blue Slurpee bounded into the room. In a short skirt and peasant blouse — and sporting the highest platform heels I'd ever seen — the girl scampered up the steps to the bed and settled herself beside me, wriggling like an excited puppy.

"Cheese an' rice." A toothy grin lit her entire, freckled face. It was infectious, and I had to force my own lips not to respond. "I thought you were going to sleep away the morn."

My mouth felt lined with cat fur, my brain pickled from sleep. I shoved my hair out of my face and scooted back until I was pressed against the puckered velvet headboard.

She followed my gaze to the half-open door. "Shh. I'm supposed to let you sleep, but you look fine to me. I'm Phoebe, by the by," she said. "Mac's my grandda. You met him last night, I hear. He and Gran help Lu run the estate."

"I'm—"

"You're Hope," she said, giving me a blinding grin that went all the way to her hairline. "I know. Everyone knows. We're so excited you're finally here."

"That's, um . . . good?" I managed before she hopped to the floor.

"I'll put your things away while you get ready."

I winced as the bubbly girl began yanking clothes from my suitcase and jamming them into a massive ancient dresser. When a pair of too-large sweats emerged from the jumble, she cocked an eyebrow at me.

"They're my mom's," I said as I slid from beneath the covers. "I just—"

"You don't have to explain to me. I sleep in one of my da's old shirts. I know it's nutters, but sometimes I can still smell him. We lost him when I was but a babe. Still . . ."

Her smile wobbled as she swiped a hand beneath her nose. "It's pure natty, but I don't care. Gran and I had a huge row when she threw it in the bin and I fished it right back out."

It was so weird to watch someone else handling my things. I'd never had a friend back home. No one to wear my clothes without asking or ruin my favorite sweater or share stories about boys. When I was younger, I dreamed of having a friend like that, but Mom always claimed being around "empty-headed" girls my own age would only distract me from my studies.

Stifling a groan, I eased out from under the covers and stumbled to the center of the room, taking a first real look at my new surroundings.

Holy cow, I'm living in freaking Hogwarts.

Turning in an idiot circle, I gawped at the shabby opulence. Dusty ostrich feathers topped yards of midnight-blue velvet that draped the immense canopy bed. A high, scalloped ceiling was complete with plaster cherubs. Stuffed bookshelves lined each side of an honest-to-God marble fireplace. I inhaled, tasting book glue and the ghosts of long-ago fires.

Phoebe cheerfully slammed the last of my things into a

drawer. "Pure awesome room, aye? It was your mum's, you know. Sarah's."

I could see it. My mother as a young girl, curled on the tartan loveseat, strawberry hair tucked behind her ears as she frowned down at a leather-bound book.

Phoebe tactfully ignored me, humming under her breath as she heaved my empty suitcase over to a closet. I noticed her eyes were an exact replica of her grandfather's. Small. Blue. Smiling.

Before setting the frame on a bedside table, she studied the only photo I'd brought. Me and Mom, lying on a bed of autumn leaves, brown and gold bits tangled in our hair as we grinned up at my dad.

"Gads," she said. "You don't look anything like her. Sarah, I mean. You're exotic, like some gypsy girl, with that dark hair and those great gray eyes of yours." She tilted her head, studying me. "But then, you're adopted, aye? Lucky, that. They say I look just like my mum. And you couldn't know, but that's pure unfortunate."

I couldn't help but grin at her comically tragic expression. A stud pierced one straight, rust-colored eyebrow, which I assumed meant that beneath the dye, she was likely a redhead. The silver stud winked in the light as she babbled on in an accent so thick, I had to concentrate to understand.

"I met her—Sarah—when she was here in the fall. She came before . . . Well, she was in an awful hurry then, wasn't she?"

"You saw my mom?" The words tangled in my mouth

until I almost couldn't get them out. "But . . . she never . . . I mean, I thought she went straight to India. Are you sure it was *last* fall? When, exactly?"

The girl's mouth snapped shut, eyes widening at the obvious mistake.

My mind whirled, trying to take it in.

Mom had left home only once last year. The final time, nearly eight months earlier. *Why hadn't she mentioned going to Scotland?*

"So, uh . . . you haven't met Collum yet," she bumbled on. "Just so you know, my brother can be a bit of a wank, sometimes. Though if he acts like that to you, I'll give him—"

Phoebe winced as a distant voice called up the stairs.

"Bollocks!" she groaned. "If Gran catches me, I'm done for. Don't mention you saw me, aye?"

"But," I called after Phoebe as she fled the room. Feeling as though I'd been buffeted about by a tiny, blue tornado, I whispered to the now-empty room.

"But why would she lie to us?"

CHAPTER 4

AFTER A QUICK SHOWER IN A CLAW-FOOT TUB WHOSE HAND-held sprayer spat rusty, lukewarm water, I wound my way down the curved stairs and through a series of rooms. High ceilings soared over scarred wooden floors lined with tatty vintage rugs. Scruffy antique furniture was clustered in comfy arrangements before fireplaces mounted with crossed swords or family crests.

I followed the sound of clinking dishes until the heavenly scents of baking bread and frying eggs overcame the odors of stone and age. My stomach rumbled as I paused in the long dining room to watch a spider swing between the prongs of a huge deer-antler chandelier. Judging by the spotless gleam on the massive table beneath, I didn't think the impressive web would be there long.

Two voices penetrated the nearby door, the source of the delicious smells. When I heard my name, I shamelessly pressed against it to listen.

"What did ye think of her?" a woman's voice spoke. "Will the lass be able to handle such a thing?"

I recognized Mac's gravelly rumble. "The child barely spoke, my love. She was exhausted, and most Yanks get a bit fankled when they first see the manor, even in the dead o' night. All I know is that Lu believes her capable."

"Lu believes in her because she's Sarah's daughter." The woman sounded unsure. "She's had no real training, and 'tis a hard task for one not raised to it."

I couldn't make out Mac's reply, though I heard the woman's response well enough.

"I hope that's so. I worry about the poor lamb. We've so little time to get her prepared."

I frowned. *Get me prepared? For what?*

I didn't like the sound of that at all. But I probably wouldn't learn much lurking in the shadows. Exhaling, I pushed into a bright, homey kitchen. Next to a flour-dusted island, Mac and the woman stood in a loose embrace. A thick, graying braid swayed across her back as he rocked her gently, her head tucked under his chin. My throat swelled, watching them. When I was little, I'd once come upon Mom and Dad in the same pose, swaying to music only they could hear.

Mac's blue eyes opened, and I realized I'd been right about Phoebe. The eyes were identical.

"Why, look who's come to join us, darlin'." He released the woman, grinning at me, and I realized he'd passed his blazing smile along to his granddaughter too. "Welcome to Christopher Manor, lass."

Within a few seconds, I learned the round-faced woman was Moira, of the jam sandwiches. That she was Mac's wife and Lucinda's best friend and business partner for more than thirty years. That she and *only* she ran this house, and that I was too thin and needed fattening up. Despite her bulk, Moira bustled around the kitchen with the grace of a ballerina.

She hustled me toward one of the benches that lined the long, scuffed but scoured kitchen table. Soon she was smiling down at me as I scarfed up steaming eggs and two pieces of warm bread slathered with fresh butter and strawberry jam.

When Moira offered a large ladle of baked beans, Mac chuckled at my horrified expression. "Aye, I understand you Yanks don't appreciate the bean for breakfast?"

"Well, they're mostly a supper thing for us. Thanks, though."

"Pity that." Mac smothered his own breakfast with a hearty portion. "Ye don't know what you're missing."

I scanned the room, wondering where the girl had gone.

"If you're looking for Phoebe"—Moira settled onto the bench next to me with a groan—"I've sent the little minx to the village. She knew she wasn't to speak to ye till Lu's return."

"Our granddaughter's a bit on the curious side," Mac explained through a mouthful of food.

Moira snorted. "Curious—that's an understatement if ever I've heard one, John MacPherson."

"Hope"—Mac wiped his mouth with a yellowed linen napkin—"Phoebe's a good girl, and I hope ye'll take to her. She's high-spirited, but she has the biggest heart in the Highlands, she does."

"With the biggest mouth to go along," Moira muttered, though a fond smile softened her words. "Our grandson, Collum, has gone with Lu. Ye'll meet him when they return in the morning. Collum's a . . . serious lad. As different from his sister as night is from day."

I laid my fork down, careful not to look up from my plate. "Speaking of Phoebe," I said, "she mentioned something about my mother being here in the fall. But how could that be, when—"

Mac stood abruptly and hurried to open a door that led out onto a mud porch. "Och, look a' the time. I must away to the west barn. One of the ewes is near her time."

He thrust long arms into a faded vest and plucked a houndstooth cap from a peg on the wall. "Moira will show ye the house. If this rain lets up, I'll take ye out on the horses later. I hear ye're a fine rider."

Moira snatched up my empty plate as he left. I stood and offered to help. At the sink, I turned toward her. "Moira, about my—"

She shooed me from the kitchen before I could finish the sentence, telling me she'd come for me once she'd finished up in the kitchen, and we'd take a tour of the house. I paused in the doorway and turned to face her. My utter confusion must've shown, because her apple cheeks rose as she gave a soft sigh.

"Child," she said, "let me offer ye some advice my old mum used to give me." When she smiled, her eyes nearly disappeared behind the full cheeks. "A drop of patience can yield an ocean of reward. Now, I admit, I often have a hard time following it myself. But I'm offering it to ye anyway." She cocked her chin toward the door. "Now scoot."

The rear of the house, which apparently contained more parlors, a billiards room, and a grand ballroom, was sealed off. Locked up due to heating costs, Moira told me during the tour. After viewing innumerable bedrooms, most shrouded in ghostly dust covers, I was relieved when Moira pushed open a set of wide double doors saying, "And finally, there's the library, o' course."

Moira reminded me of my dad's grandmother, the only member of his family who never treated me like some kind of fungus that had invaded their family tree. Memaw died when I was ten. Like her, Moira was all round curves and sweetness, a person who solved life's problems with hugs and a tin of sugar cookies.

I liked Moira, except that all during the tour, whenever I opened my mouth to ask about my mom, she diverted the conversation with a quirky comment on this ancestor or that piece of furniture.

I swallowed down my latest attempt as we stepped inside the cozy room, the sights and smells a balm to my jangled nerves. Tall mullioned windows. Muted yellow light. Aged leather and old paper. The library smelled like Shakespeare. It smelled like my mom.

I breathed it in, walking over to pull a book from one of the floor to ceiling shelves. *The Royal Forests of Medieval England,* by Charles R. Young.

I'd read it, of course. The words were installed in my memory files along with billions of others. If I needed them, I could bring them up by chapter or page number.

"Ye'll find most of the best history books ever written on these shelves, my lamb," Moira said. "And you're welcome to any you care to read." She paused, head tilted as she studied me. "I understand ye've the gift of memory?"

Some gift, I thought as I slid the book back.

"Yes, ma'am," I said. "When I see or read something, it . . . well, it just kind of sticks."

"What a blessing that must be," Moira said as she cupped my cheek. "Your mother told us you were a very special girl. It's happy we are to finally have you here, and to welcome you into our family."

Family.

I nodded, my throat too tight to speak.

"Now"—Moira linked arms with me and towed me toward the marble fireplace, above which hung a huge painting—"may I introduce Lord and Lady Hubert Carlyle. Your many-times great-grandparents. And with them is their son, Jonathan."

Hubert was a stern-looking guy with a walrus mustache

and heavy jowls. His wife looked as if she'd been sucking on lemons. But the young Jonathan's hazel eyes danced with mischief. I liked him immediately.

In the portrait to their right, Jonathan was older. He was situated behind a beautiful, seated woman whose shiny dark hair was replicated in the two little girls kneeling before her. One hand on his mother's shoulder, a gangly, adolescent boy stared out with his father's sparkling eyes.

"Jonathan's wife, Julia," Moira said. "And their children."

"Oh . . . the little girls are so cute," I grinned at the youngest girl's chubby cheeks.

Moira stared up for a long moment. "Aye." The word came out as a croak and she had to clear her throat before continuing. "Aye. They certainly were."

The far side of the fireplace held a smaller portrait of a round-faced couple. The woman had Moira's merry eyes and round chin. "These are my own ancestors on my mum's side, James MacPherson and his wife, Edwina. James was Hubert's estate manager. Mac is also distantly related to the two, this part of Scotland being riddled with MacPhersons, ye know."

I wandered around the welcoming room, touching this and that, until I noticed a heavy silver frame on a small table tucked into a far corner. My eyes widened. I couldn't believe it.

"Hey, Moira," I called, picking up the photo. "Is this my mom? Wearing a toga?"

Moira slid a pair of reading glasses off her graying hair.

She squinted in the low light, then muttered, "I thought I'd put this one away."

She reached to take the picture from me, but I pretended not to notice. Her mouth tightened, but she said nothing as I tilted it for a better look.

She sighed. "Yes, that's Sarah. And Lucinda beside her."

Aunt Lucinda looked a lot like my mom. Smooth hair, in a shade of ripe apricots. Broad at hip and shoulder. Same long nose and close-set eyes the color of faded denim. But even though Lucinda was smiling in the picture — and dressed for a frat party besides — her erect posture seemed too stern, like she was preparing to rally the troops.

Mom was squashed between her sister and a guy with freckles and a blaze of red hair. The boy had his arm around Mom, squeezing her to him. While Lucinda looked to be in her twenties, the other two couldn't have been much older than I was now. Hair wrapped around her head in elaborate braids, her shockingly slim body draped in folds of white linen, and gold sandals laced up bare calves, my mom grinned madly into the camera. So young. So happy. I'd never seen her look like that.

Moira peeked around my arm. "That's Collum and Phoebe's da, our son Michael, there with your mum. I'd always hoped . . ." She paused, frowned. "Well, but he was young and stupid. Ended up marrying a local girl, didn't he? Fiona, the children's mum, wasn't worth a hill of beans. Took off with another man soon after Phoebe's birth. I ask you, what kind of woman leaves a young lad and newborn behind for a father to raise? If things had been different, he and Sar—" Her voice cracked as she traced a finger over the happy-looking young man. "Oh, but Michael did love those babes." She gave a small sigh. "He's been gone nigh on twelve years now."

"I'm so sorry, Moira," I said, feeling a rush of sympathy for the funny girl, Phoebe. At least I still had my dad.

She waved me off, and I stared down at the photo, still incredulous. "So *my* mom actually went to a toga party."

"Not exactly," Moira said.

Suuure.

At the edge of the frame, a pretty, olive-skinned girl with high cheekbones and jutting chin stood slightly apart from the others. Dark braids twined to her waist, like slender snakes. She was the only one not looking at the camera. Instead, her black eyes were narrowed on Michael MacPherson and my mom snugged up together. While the rest practically danced off the photo, the brunette glowered. Though she was dressed like the others, there was something different about her. The longer I stared, the more I could almost feel the rage and jealousy flow off the picture.

"Is the black-haired girl Fiona?" I asked. "'Cause she doesn't look too happy in this picture."

Moira stiffened and plucked the picture firmly from my

grip. Mouth tight, she glared down at the dark-haired girl, and I got the impression she wasn't Moira's favorite person. "No," was all she said.

Moira thumped the frame onto the table, picture side down.

"And this is the end of the tour, I'm thinking."

With a decisive step, she moved off toward the door. I didn't follow at first, only watched as she flitted around the room, clicking off the small, mismatched lamps and casting the library into shadow.

"Hey, Moira? I—"

"Och, but this place needs a good dustin'," she cut me off, reaching on tiptoe to swipe a finger across the edge of an upper shelf.

When Moira glanced back to see me standing still and alone in the center of the room, her pursed mouth softened. "Come along then, my lamb," she said, "'tis time for tea."

CHAPTER 5

WHEN MAC WOKE ME FROM A NAP A COUPLE OF HOURS later, I felt drained—a wrung sponge left to dry on the sink. My limbs dragged as I moved the book that lay open on the bed beside me, a biography of Eleanor of Aquitaine someone had left on my bedside table, and followed him to the stables.

Outside, the lowering sun shot streams of gold through heavy clouds as I trotted through the stable yard astride a sturdy gray mare named Ethel. A fragrant breeze blew past, ruffling my clothes as I stared, astounded by the brutal beauty of the land around me. Beyond the yard, the valley spread out like a rumpled green and purple quilt, with the vast moor just beyond.

Behind us, the fortress-like Christopher Manor guarded the sheep and cattle that roamed between it and the charcoal roofs of a small village. The town lay at the foot of the valley, on the opposite side, nestled between craggy, twin mountains rubbed bald by millennia of wind and rain. A river bisected the gorge and disappeared into the heather and gorse of the moors.

"The uplands look flat," Mac warned from his perch on a wide gelding. "But 'tis full of dips and hidden burns—those are streams, mind—that cut through the heather before joining the river. Ye'll come on them sudden-like, especially once ye get closer to the big mountain, so keep our girl here to a nice, easy trot." The lines in his weathered cheeks deepened as he smiled. "Ethel likes to run, so ye'll have to hold her back."

I pivoted in the saddle. "I can go alone?"

The horse danced under me, eager to get moving. When I stilled her with heels and reins, Mac nodded in approval.

"Seems ye handle yourself well enough."

Every girl of good family should sit a horse well. My mom's approving voice spoke in my memory.

I'd adored my weekly riding lessons, the only nonacademic hobby my mother had ever allowed. At eleven, I'd never been near a horse before. Yet that very first day, my instructor, Mr. Waterman, told Mom he'd never seen a child take to riding like I did.

Look at her go. It's like she was born to it, Miz Walton.

Watching me, Mom frowned, though I'd blushed to the roots at the old man's praise. Used to feeling awkward and klutzy, from the moment I climbed in the saddle it was like my hands and feet took on a mind of their own. On the horse, I'd felt graceful for the first time in my life. The smells and the movement of the horse and leather beneath me was familiar, like returning to an old friend. It felt wonderful. It felt right.

After Mom died, Dad never mentioned the lessons. I could've said something, I suppose. But it hadn't seemed right without her. So I'd kept quiet, and the one activity I had loved slid to the wayside.

"I'm away to the south pasture to check the flock." Mac walked his horse over to the gate and leaned down to open it. "Ye'll have but a few hours of peace, lass. I'd enjoy them if I were you. When Lu returns tomorrow, things may become . . . different."

He frowned, as if he wanted to say more.

"Mac?" I nipped at a cuticle on my free hand. Moira's warning echoed in my head, but I had to try one last time. "When was my mother here last?" I trailed off as his eyes cut away.

He clucked to his gelding, who ambled over until our knees almost touched.

"Lass," the word came on a sigh. "I don't pretend to understand what you've suffered. You've been through the wringer, and that's the truth of it. But I'm knowing one thing for certain." He placed a rough, careworn hand over mine where they gripped the reins. "Our darlin' Sarah loved ye more than life itself. And she did her best by ye. And so too will all of us here. Ye can take to the bank, aye?"

My throat closed. "Yeah," I whispered.

"Away with ye now," he sniffed, and wheeled his horse. "But be careful, aye? And dinna be too long. Moira'll have my hide if ye miss supper."

"Thank you, Mac."

With a backwards wave, he moved off toward the opposite fence.

The horse responded to the barest pressure of my knees as she trotted down the long valley and out onto the magnificence of the Highland moor.

Ethel splashed through the narrow burn, which twisted and turned upon itself, growing deeper and faster the closer we got to the huge mountain range that bordered the uplands to the north. These were higher, misty and still snow-capped, even in June. Weaving through clumps of gorse and thistle with ease, the mare wended her way around the waist-high boulders that sprouted up like mushrooms.

When I loosened the reins, Ethel's powerful muscles bunched and elongated under me. Strands of hair lashed my face as the wind whipped past. The roar of the river ahead pounded and my body began to relax, to move in rhythm with the horse's gait.

A pitted boulder appeared before us. I jerked on the reins, but Ethel apparently had a different idea. She raced straight toward the rock. My mouth opened in a scream that turned to a shout of pure joy as we soared over it.

With the horse pounding beneath me, I felt alive. I felt free.

A glint of reflected sunlight caught my eye. I reined up, squinting across the brush at a figure on horseback that had emerged from behind a large clump of rock. He—pretty sure it was a he—held something to his face that winked in the weakening sun.

Binoculars? Is someone watching me?

When I clucked at Ethel and headed toward him, the man veered his horse and raced off in the opposite direction. Curious now, I nudged the mare into an easy canter. Ahead of us, the stranger galloped away. Every once in a while he glanced back, as if gauging the distance. He was looking behind him when they crested a steep hill. His horse—apparently not in the mood for a jump—planted its hoofs. The rider went flying over the animal's head, disappearing from view as the now-riderless horse shied and galloped away.

"Oh. Crap," I said, and kicked my heels hard into Ethel's flanks.

I dismounted beside a steep riverbank. Below, the clear brown water dashed against the boulders, drowning out any other noise.

"Hey!" I yelled, but the guy had disappeared.

When I edged closer, the damp earth of an overhang

crumbled beneath me. Arms pinwheeling, down the slope I went, crashing through mud and brush, before I fetched up—panting—at the pebbled edge of the surging river.

I saw him then, tangled in a patch of undergrowth at the water's edge, like a piece of driftwood. He was sprawled face-up across a flat rock, clothes splattered with mud, laces of his brown hiking boots floating in the swift current. He wasn't moving.

My jeans wicked up the frigid water as I splashed through the shallows toward him. His head lay cocked at an angle that hid his face. I couldn't tell if he was even alive.

"Oh God oh God oh God." A crimson ribbon of blood trickled from his dark hair to stain the mossy rock.

"Hey," I called. "Hey, can you hear me? Are you okay?"

The stranger's ripped shirt lay open beneath a crumpled camp jacket, revealing a terrible scrape across a tanned chest. His visible hand hung bruised and still, the long tapered fingers dangling in the water.

What if he's dead? What do I do?

Dread dug sharp claws into my spine as I splashed to his side. His chest moved up and down.

Thank God.

I carefully shook his shoulder. "Hey! You all right? Wake up. Can you hear me?"

Nothing.

My mind raced as I tried to decide what to do. *Stay with him so he doesn't roll off and drown? Ride back to the house and*

*call 911? Do they even have 911 here? Dammit, why didn't I
bring my phone?*

An expensive-looking camera hung around his neck. The
source of the glint I'd seen. The display screen had brightened to life when I shook him. When I saw the image it
displayed, my mouth dropped open.

"What the hell?"

"Not bad, eh?" I nearly toppled over as he muttered in
a voice creaky with pain. "Of course, it likely won't win
any prizes. But you have to admit, the composition's quite
lovely."

I didn't respond as I jerked the camera toward me and
scrolled through the images. He was right. The light, the
setup, the arrangement of each image highlighted the stark,
breathless beauty of the Scottish Highlands. It wasn't the
background that freaked me out, though. It was the subject.

Every photo—more than a dozen—was a close-up of me.

My eye twitched. "Who are you? Why were you taking
pictures of me?"

Dark, damp hair was plastered over his forehead, though
with blood or water, I wasn't sure. I could see now that he
was around my age. Sixteen. Seventeen, maybe. He gave a
little groan as he scraped the hair back and turned his face
toward me.

Then, he opened his eyes.

Behind a fringe of black lashes, his left eye was a soft
green, like sunlight on moss. The right, the brilliant blue of

an October sky. As I stared down at him, the world warped around me.

The rush of water grew muted and distant. *My nose and chest filled with the stench of . . . smoke? Yes. Wood smoke, tinged with a sickly sweetness of charred meat. Somewhere, a fire crackled and popped like bacon in a pan. Screams. The thump of hooves. A winey scent of overripe apples.*

"Hello?" a voice called from far away. I clung to it like a lifeline.

The river's gurgle returned, and I suddenly realized I was standing in the middle of a swift current, gaping down at a complete stranger.

"I know what you're thinking, love." The words came out husky, his accent more blue-blood than Highlander. "You're wondering how someone so strong, so handsome, and so obviously endowed with athletic ability could've gotten himself thrown from a bloody horse." He winced as he sat up and swung long jean-clad legs over the side of the rock. "The answer is quite simple, really."

His camera still in my hand, I yanked on the strap. He groaned when it jerked his head forward. I tilted it to read the brass plate bolted to the side. PROPERTY OF BRAN CAMERON. IF FOUND, PLEASE RING . . . When I let go, the heavy camera struck against his chest with a satisfying thwack.

Edging a few steps back, I asked through stiff lips, "Why were you taking pictures of me, *Bran Cameron*?"

At first I thought he was ignoring me as he examined the

blood smeared on his fingers. "Forgive me, won't you? I'm, uh . . . feeling a bit off."

With a moan, his head dropped into his hands.

"Crap," I grumbled, torn between irritation and pity. "Are you okay?"

And what the hell do you do if he's not, Walton?

Bran raised his head and gave me a wobbly grin. One of his canines was crooked. Oddly, it made me feel better, because the rest of him looked as if he'd been drafted by an architect. All clean lines and straight edges. He wasn't beautiful, the nose a bit too long, the lips sculpted instead of full. Though his jawline was sharp enough to cut glass, it was his eyes I couldn't look away from. Those peculiar, mismatched eyes.

"I know you." The words tumbled out before I could stop them.

"I don't think so, love." He peered at me. "I can assure you if we'd ever met, I'd remember. I have an uncanny ability to remember pretty girls."

Pretty? Me? Yeah. Sure.

His trim eyebrows waggled. "Unless of course you attend St. Sebastian Academy down in Kent? I admit, I've snuck past their fences a time or two. And I may have had a pint or three beforehand. So if we did, as you Americans like to say, 'hook up,' I wish to offer my sincerest apology for my poor memory."

Blood boiled into my face. In my sixteen years on this

earth, no guy had ever, *ever* flirted with me. The redneck boys where I was from preferred girls like my cheerleader cousins. Size two. Blond. Busty. Brainless.

"As you so astutely observed"—from his seated position, he gave a comical bow—"I am Bran Cameron. And, yes. I was photographing you. Though in truth, I was out stalking."

At my look, he chuckled. "Not in any depraved way, I assure you. I was merely hunting for the Highland stag. Some use guns to stalk. I prefer electronics." He gave an exaggerated shudder that almost made me smile. "Less blood and entrails, that way. Then I saw a lovely vision on a horse and, well . . . I couldn't resist." He shivered. "And now that we are properly acquainted, would you mind terribly helping me off this rock and out of this bloody cold water?"

I realized I was just standing there, gaping at him like a moron, while his lips turned blue with cold.

"Oh." I held out a hand. "Yeah, okay."

He took it, pulling himself to his feet. Strong fingers squeezed mine as he bobbled, then steadied. My eyes were level with his chin. I focused on that, instead of his eyes.

Back on dry land, I noticed blood pulsing in a steady stream down his neck, staining the collar of his jacket. I hurried over to Ethel and retrieved a scarf I'd tied to her saddle.

"Here. You're bleeding."

Looking up into his odd eyes, once again the disturbing

sensation of familiarity rolled over me. When I stumbled, Bran steadied me before I could tumble headlong into the river.

I was blinking too fast, trying to rid myself of the bizarre feeling, when he said, "I'm sorry, but did you tell me your name?"

"Hope," I managed. "My . . . I mean, I'm Hope Walton. And I've got to go." I eased out of his grip and quickly moved to untie Ethel's reins from the brush.

"I don't mean to be a bother," he called, "but earlier you said you knew me from somewhere." When I turned, he was close. Right beside me. "Do you?"

"Do I what?" I edged away, nervous at the intense look on his face.

"Know me."

"No." The word tasted like a lie, though I couldn't explain why. "But then again, I'm not one of those slutty St. Sebastian girls."

He laughed out loud at that. Then groaned as he pressed the scarf against his head.

"Actually," I said, "I just got here last night, so we couldn't have met. I-I've barely been out of my hometown before. See, it's my first time overseas. I'm here visiting my aunt, and . . ."

Shut up, Walton. Why are you babbling like an idiot to this stranger?

I shoved the reins over Ethel's head and tried to mount,

but my knees felt shaky, and my wet foot slipped from the stirrup. Ethel took a nervous step, confused at my signals. Bran grabbed her bridle, and when I glanced over to thank him, I saw that his lingering smile had vanished.

"Your aunt," he said flatly. "Yes, of course. Lady Lucinda Carlyle."

"You know her?"

He didn't answer, and the blinding grin he turned on me seemed forced. I managed to make it onto Ethel's back, but I didn't leave.

"I want to thank you for rescuing me, Hope Walton," Bran said. "And, no, I am not acquainted with your aunt. I only know that this is her land." He reached up and tugged on a thin leather cord around his neck. A silver medallion popped out from beneath his collar, which he absently brushed against his lips. "Say, might I ask a favor? I realize rescuing me from certain death is enough of an imposition, but I should like to ask anyway."

Still uneasy, I shrugged. "I guess?"

"Would you mind terribly keeping our running into each other today to yourself? You see, this is private property, and I should hate very much to be fined for trespassing."

"I won't say anything."

"Brilliant." Bran pressed the wad of purple fabric to the side of his head with a hiss. "And. This might be utterly presumptuous of me, considering the circumstances," he said, "but would you care to go for a proper ride sometime? I'm not a native, of course, but I've spent time in these parts.

And I know some breathtaking spots you simply must see. Before you say no," he said, raising a hand in oath, "I solemnly swear *not* to brain myself on a river rock. Or sneak photographs without your express permission."

"Oh," I said, "I don't . . ."

His rueful expression was so exaggerated, a giggle bubbled up from my chest. It felt creaky and rusty from disuse as it passed my lips.

A sudden crack of thunder split the sky and echoed down the valley toward us. Ethel quivered and pranced beneath me.

I glanced up to where Christopher Manor crouched at the head of the valley. Ominous gray clouds rolled in over the mountain behind it, pulsing with bursts of lightning. Unlit against the odd, stark light of a purpling dusk, the manor appeared dark and somehow menacing. I shivered as I turned back to Bran, the wind cold against my back.

Thunder rumbled again from the dark clouds, making Ethel strain against her bit, eager to be off. I wondered idly what Moira would think about me sneaking off to meet some trespassing stranger. I decided I didn't care.

"Okay," I said. "That would be . . . I mean . . . yes, okay."

This time, Bran's smile was genuine. "Then I shall look forward to it. *If* that cantankerous beast over there doesn't throw me again and break my neck . . ." He made a face at the gelding, now peacefully grazing several yards away. "I will be here the same time each afternoon." He executed a funny, formal bow. Till then, Mistress Walton. I must say, it was surprisingly pleasant to meet you." His lovely, mismatched eyes widened a bit. "Surprising considering the *situation*, I mean."

I nodded, biting back a grin as the mare took off like a shot.

Under a crack of thunder, I thought I heard a shout. "See you soon, Hope Walton."

The heavens opened as Ethel and I raced back toward the stable. Pebbles of rain drilled into me, stinging my face. My thighs chafed against the inside of damp jeans as I held on tight.

I should have been miserable. But I barely felt it.

CHAPTER 6

JET LAG BLOWS.

At least it was morning. Sort of, though according to the bedside clock it was hours till daylight. But Lucinda would be back today. I'd finally get some answers, which was good, 'cause I was really tired of all the secrecy.

The night before, Phoebe had obviously still been banished, since only Mac, Moira, and I shared the quiet dinner of lamb, curried peas, and something called Spotted Dick, which sounded horrifying but was actually a delicious, rich cake filled with currants and covered in a thick custard.

I'd expected to crash hard, to sleep off the wearying hours of flight and disappointment. My brain apparently had a different agenda, however, and I only managed a few fitful hours of sleep. As I flipped and flopped in the ridiculously lavish bed, my thoughts drifted to the boy from the river. Bran Cameron. I'd kept my promise. Hadn't told a soul about his trespassing. He wasn't hurting anyone, after all.

And he wants to see you again. I twisted over and buried my face in the down pillow. *Let's just hope he forgets the way you stared like a moron when you saw his eyes.*

What the hell was that *about, anyway?*

The antique bedframe creaked as I flopped back over. Staring up at the deep blue canopy, I wondered how long it had been since someone inspected the aging wood that supported all those yards of heavy velvet.

I scrambled out of the high bed as if it were on fire and wrenched on my ratty flannel bathrobe. I needed a good old, dry history book. That's just the ticket to take my mind off things.

As I crept downstairs in the quiet of predawn, a step groaned beneath my weight. When no one emerged to order me back to my room, I went on, keeping to the edge of the steps. Generations of grumpy-looking Carlyles and MacPhersons glared at me from their gilded frames as I descended.

"Problem?" I challenged a snooty matron with a poofy bun and squinty eyes. When she didn't answer, I flicked her painted nose. "That's what I thought."

Only two lamps now illuminated the once-cheery library. Shutting the doors behind me, I reached for the nearest bookshelf, then froze.

Is that . . . music?

I skirted back and forth across the room, pausing occasionally to listen. Still barely audible, the music seemed to grow a bit louder as I weaved my way toward the rear wall. Next to a faded tapestry, I leaned in and placed my palm against a bare spot on the wall. Through the heavy wood paneling, I felt the definite thump of bass notes.

A puff of air that smelled like dirt and wet stone whiffed across my bare legs, ruffling the hanging's embroidered sheep in their woven pasture.

I grinned, and peeled the weighty fabric aside, revealing the hidden door behind it. It stood slightly ajar, held open by a bronze spaniel someone had placed in the crack as a doorstop. An enormous padlock splayed open and dangled from its hasp.

Please. I prayed as I grasped the crystal doorknob. *Please don't let this be the room where they hide the deformed cannibal cousin. 'Cause it's just too damn early for that.*

I jerked the door open to find . . . brooms. Nothing inside the deep closet but exactly what you'd expect. Brooms and mops and, oh — how thrilling — a shelf of dusting supplies. I let my head roll back to stare at the ceiling. Nothing but a stupid, ordinary broom closet.

Disgusted, I started to ease the door shut, then hesitated, certain my senses were playing tricks. Nope. The music was definitely louder here. And, at the very back corner, a thin strip of yellow marred the perfect darkness.

Using my new buddy "Brassy the Wonderdog," I propped the door open, then reached in and tentatively poked at a slick, wooden broom handle. It didn't move. Didn't budge, in fact. I began to tug on one after the other, until I realized they were — each and every one — fastened to the back wall. Bolted, as if they were only a display.

Then I saw it. The stray cotton strand of an upside-down mop that was pinned, snagged in the seam of light. When I yanked hard on the knotted thread, the entire thing—brooms and all—opened noiselessly toward me. Music poured over me, washing up a set of wooden steps that led downward into the shadows.

I grinned. "Gotcha."

One seemingly endless flight down, I emerged into what appeared to be the manor's cellar. The space was enormous. A low, barrel-vaulted ceiling was supported by a row of stone pillars that curved away into a shadowy darkness.

I shivered in the chill. My slippered feet whispered on the paving stones as I wove through the detritus left behind by two centuries of Carlyles and MacPhersons. Modern light fixtures mounted at intervals to the rough brick wall cast shadows on the swept-clean path. Muscles tense, I breathed in musty air and the rich, mineral smell of earth.

All right, I'm under the ground. Under. The. Ground. Those pillars probably hold the weight of the entire house on their shoulders. What if they collapse? What if it—

I shut that thought down before it could fully form. Forcing myself not to turn and flee back up the stairs, I moved along the wall, following the music. At a modern doorway, an odd, alien light filtered out from beneath, glowing green on the stones. It was quickly muted when I opened the unlocked door and a series of fluorescent bulbs buzzed to life overhead.

If the library was all dusty rugs, antique lamps, and the solace of old books and leather, this room was its polar opposite. The gleaming, white-tiled floor showed not a speck of dirt. Towering ultramodern glass-doored cabinets ran along the entire length of the left wall, directly across from three large, curtained booths.

Here, the music — that I now recognized as heavy metal — battered at my eardrums. Bracing my hands over my ears, I approached a department-store-quality mirror. Three pale, wild-haired reflections glared back at me.

Yeesh.

Snatching the tartan stretchie I found in the bathroom off my wrist, I raked my medusa curls back into a high ponytail and searched for the source of the punishing sound.

The eerie glow had come from the far side of the room, where the biggest monitor I'd ever seen was mounted to the wall, connected to a series of massive computers. I quickly reached out and flipped down the volume on a set of huge desk speakers.

My ears rang in the glorious silence. Finally able to think straight, I stepped back and stared up. Hundreds of green lines streaked across the screen from one side to the other, all of them intersecting only in the very center. Every so often, a line flashed from green to red in a pattern I couldn't begin to interpret.

The curved desk was littered with empty cups and dirty dishes. An executive chair was pushed back as though someone had left in a hurry. The screen saver on the lone desktop monitor shifted. A slide show of the blue-haired Phoebe. First grinning and backlit by the sun. Then looking down, her gaze gone soft and sweet as she held a newborn lamb in her arms.

Either she liked to look at herself—a *lot*—or whoever ran this operation had a major thing for her. When I touched the mouse, her image faded to reveal an Excel spreadsheet with thousands of numerical notations.

A piece of paper was taped to the edge of a shelf just above the desktop. Handwritten on it were the words *"The universe is big. It's vast and complicated and ridiculous. And sometimes—very rarely—impossible things just happen and we call them miracles."* The Doctor.

Doctor? My gaze flicked to the picture beside it that showed a plain-faced, floppy-haired guy sporting a bow tie. He didn't look like any doctor I'd ever heard of.

Shrugging, I checked out the other taped-up printouts. Pictures of Einstein. Steven Hawking. Isaac Newton. Leonardo da Vinci. In the center hung a large glossy photo of a young Nikola Tesla.

Alongside the wall monitor was a large rectangular black board. On it, digital lines of yellow text flipped by so fast, even I barely had time to commit them to memory.

Antwerp 111713.21
Istanbul 041099.12
Brighton 071817.07

Vienna 111938.18
Boston 011788.06

I studied the strange panel for a long moment. I'd seen one for the first time only two days before.

"An airport arrival and departure board?" I whispered, frowning as the letters unscrambled and replaced themselves with astounding speed. "Why? What is it tracking?"

Some of the lines changed more slowly than others. One, near the bottom, reappeared again and again.

London 121154.04

A bundled series of color-coded wires ran along the wall. On this end, they spread out, terminating at the backs of the powerful computers. The other ends disappeared through a small hole in the bricks, near the door.

I stepped toward the row of tall cabinets. A series of black cords emerged from the side, plugged into several wall sockets behind them. As I cupped my hands to peer through one of the frosted glass doors, I felt a hum, then a click and hiss as pressure from my hands caused a magnetic latch to release. The door swung open.

What. The. Frick?

Going down the row, I pushed on each door, until they all gaped open. Until I could see that inside each and every one hung a variation of the same thing.

Costumes. Very expensive, very authentic costumes.

Organized by era and size, each lot labeled with three-by-five cards pinned to one sleeve.

LATE EIGHTEENTH. FR. COURT GOWN. W-SZ 6

300 B.C. SENATORIAL CLASS MATRON. W-SZ 14

EARLY TUDOR. MERCHANT CLASS. M-SZ 40L

Pull-out bins of matching hats and shoes lay beneath each set, along with stacks of coins from the corresponding era.

There must be hundreds of thousands of dollars worth of stuff here, I marveled as I thumbed a pile of ancient gold coins.

My fingertips traced the ivory lace of a frothy gown more ruffles than dress. A cowgirl getup with red leather boots. A scratchy wool cape trimmed in white fur. A starched white apron covering a severe black dress labeled LATE SEVENTEENTH. AMERICAN QUAKER. W-SZ 12.

The last cabinet held shelves of wigs secured to dummies' heads, the hair colors ranging from ebony to auburn to a silvery blond, their strands bundled in neat mesh nets.

I nipped at a ragged cuticle until I tasted blood. *Okay. Costumes. Hidden staircases. Underground computers.*

The puzzle pieces rattled around in my head. No matter which way I turned them, nothing would click into place.

Cursing under my breath, I started shutting cabinets, hiding the evidence of my snooping. Just as the last one closed, a vibration pulsed up from the floor beneath my feet. It rolled up through my body.

Earthquake? Here? Oh God. Gotta get out. Gotta run. Move!

I couldn't. My body froze up as the files in my mind whipped through everything I'd ever read about earthquakes in the British Isles.

Uncommon. Little damage. The largest on record was a 6.1 on the Richter scale, back in 1931, and . . .

The colorful wires trembled as the vibration increased. A dozen of the lines on the monitor flashed to red. The airport board flipped by so fast, it made my eyes water. I opened my mouth to scream.

Then, abruptly, it all stopped. Everything went blessedly quiet, but oh, I was so done with this.

Whatever little scheme they had going on here, they could keep it. All I wanted was some answers about my mom, then I was outta here.

Peeking out into the wide, empty cellar, I rushed toward the stairs. The instant my foot hit the bottom step, I paused, trying hard to hear over the blood careening through my veins.

Oh. No.

Above my head, moving inexorably toward the hidden closet, came the clomp of heavy footsteps, and the unmistakable sound of whistling.

CHAPTER 7

THE CHEERY TUNE DREW CLOSER. ADRENALINE SPARKED on my tongue with a metallic tang.

I didn't know these people. But I had a strong hunch they wouldn't like it if they knew I'd been rummaging around in their bizarre secret . . . lair or whatever this was.

Breathless, I glanced back toward the long cellar that arced off into shadow.

Hide.

It was my only thought when I flew toward the far end, tripping as my slippers slapped the rough stone. I rounded the bend and skidded to a stumbling halt. Huge and round, blocking my retreat, stood the metal door of an enormous vault.

I had no time to analyze why there was a bank-size vault hidden beneath my aunt's home.

The rattling of brooms echoed toward me down the empty space. Frantic, I began punching random numbers on a back-lit keypad. When nothing happened, I slapped desperately at the small dark display panel rooted in the stone above it.

Oh crap. Oh crap. Oh crap. How am I gonna explain—

A red light sprang to life beneath my palm. I jerked my hand back just as the panel turned green. Words scrolled across the panel. HOPE D. WALTON. IDENTITY ACCEPTED.

A metallic click sounded deep within the vault. I had to leap back to avoid getting smacked as the heavy door swung open on greased, noiseless hinges.

My jaw dropped. No time to wonder why the security system recognized me. A heavy tread now stomped down the wooden stairs at the other end of the cellar. I had no idea if they could see this far into the cellar or not. But I wasn't taking any chances. I bolted inside and grabbed the metal bar on the door's interior. I pulled. At first, it wouldn't budge. I jerked and heaved until finally the heavy steel swung back toward me.

Uhh . . . wait.

Too late. I couldn't stop the momentum. The door shut. The locks engaged with an ominous snick. And I was trapped in a cold cocoon of utter darkness.

Oh God. No air. No air. No air.

My diaphragm seized, smooshing my heart into a tiny space. It slammed in my throat like a captive bird trying to escape its cage. My lungs refused to work. Green dots throbbed at the edge of my vision.

Nearly retching in panic, I no longer cared if I was caught.

I beat on the door, screaming for someone—anyone—to let me out, but my voice only echoed off the metal, swallowed by the black space and empty stone. For seconds—hours, maybe—I smashed my fists into steel, until my split knuckles ran sticky with blood.

My knees smacked the stone floor. A chill bled through the thin fabric of my robe as I tried to hold on to reason. I snatched at it, but it trickled through my fingers like sand. I lost my tenuous hold. White-hot pain seared through my brain as fear took me. In that instant, I was back inside the nightmare tree.

I lay curled inside the trunk of the hollowed-out tree. Outside, the snow-shrouded ground of a forest clearing sparkled silver with moonlight. Claw-like shadows skittered across the ground as a howling wind whipped the bare branches. I was little, and all alone except for the doll in my lap.

"Don't be scared, Elizabeth," I whispered to her painted face. "He'll come back for us. He promised."

A crack from overhead. I flinched, knowing what came next. It happened every time, but knowing didn't help. I couldn't stop it. An enormous, laden branch from high above gave under the clinging weight of ice and snow. It cascaded to the ground, bringing other thick branches with it. Everything went dark. I froze as something scurried across my hand. I cast my doll aside, shoving at the obstruction, but it wouldn't budge. I clawed at the thick wood until my hands bled. When something heavy and leggy dropped down into my hair, I began to thrash and shriek, ripping out handfuls of curls.

Only one thing had ever reached me once I was trapped in the nightmare tree. My mother's voice, leading me out of the darkness. Only she had ever been able to banish the fear and the frost.

Mom.

As I thought of my mother, a warm tendril began to thread through me. My mom was infuriating and stubborn, yes. But also tough and certain in everything she did. She made me feel safe. She made me feel loved. And *she* would never cower here, like a mindless pile of quivering goo, just waiting for rescue.

No.

She would find a way out. Nothing—nothing—ever scared Sarah Walton.

I stood on Jell-O legs and reached out. Blindly, I traced my way around the smooth edges of the vault door. When I touched rough stone, I kept going until my fingertips revealed the smooth plastic and reassuring bumps of a light switch.

I threw an arm over my eyes when a series of hanging fluorescent bulbs buzzed to life. My eyes adjusting to the glare, I stared around at the wooden crates and draped objects that filled the small chamber, which had been carved into bedrock. Booths of smoky glass stood on either side of the vault door. The right one was empty, but the left held a large object suspended on a rod with wires set into stone.

I blotted my stinging knuckles on my robe, then reached out to touch a card affixed to the glass.

ARTIFACT 5419. TAPESTRY 182 x 283 CM.

CREATED: FLANDERS/LONDON, 1153. ACQUIRED:

AT AUCTION, BATH, 1789. LC, MM1, CM.

Tapestry. Okay. So the second set of numbers are obviously dimensions. Roughly six feet by nine. The rest . . . some kind of code, maybe? Or was it the year? But why would anyone hide a priceless, nine-hundred-year-old artifact all the way down here?

The hermetically sealed door on the front of the booth hissed when I pulled it open. Muted light blinked on inside and cast a sheen over the silky drape covering the object. When I stepped inside and tugged on the slippery cloth, it whispered to the floor, making the horizontal rod sway back and forth. I blinked, my brain unable to parse what it was seeing. My vision tipped sideways. My shoulders hit the cool glass wall as I stumbled back, stunned.

It was a tapestry all right, the colors faded from smoke and wear. And it looked old. Very, very old.

Against a garden backdrop, two blond women in pink gowns stood on either side of a third, seated woman. The blondes stared into the distance, vague and forgettable.

But it was the red-haired woman in the middle who robbed my breath. Her ice-blue twelfth-century gown rippled across her knees, creating the illusion of motion. An opal pendant rested in the hollow between her collarbones. Blue eyes I knew as well as my own peered out of a wide, freckled face. She wasn't willowy like the others, and you couldn't quite call her pretty. Her jaw was too square and the features too strong. Her angry gaze burned through the weave as if she wanted me to feel her rage. The weavers who'd created this work of art had gotten it right. Down to the oblong mole on her neck and the Fourth of July burn scar through one auburn eyebrow.

All the air whooshed from my lungs as I stared into my mother's face, woven into an object that was nearly nine hundred years old.

CHAPTER 8

My fingers reached up to trace the coarse fabric of her cheek. "Mama?"

"What in blazes are *you* doing here?"

I whipped around so fast, my neck cracked. A man, dressed in a dark blue uniform that looked to be from the American Civil War, stood scowling at me from the doorway of the booth.

Shocked by his sudden appearance, not to mention the bizarre costume, I could only gape at him. I knew the door to the vault hadn't opened. I'd been facing it the whole time and would've seen it. Heard it.

So where on God's earth did he come from?

"How did you manage to find your way in here?" he said with an incredulous head shake. "You know Lucinda's going to have a right fit when . . ." He trailed off, and rolled wide-spaced eyes toward the ceiling, as if I was an irritating toddler caught playing in her mommy's makeup. "Come on. Get out of there."

"I—" The words dried in my throat. What could I say? *Yeah, I've been prowling around in your little freak show. And someone better tell me what the hell is going on here.*

As his lips tightened in annoyance, I committed bits of him to memory. A little older than me. Broad, sturdy features. Handsome enough, even with the scars of an adolescent bout of acne. The military cut of his straw-colored hair. The perfect posture. The strong jaw clenched in annoyance. Everything about the guy screamed control. Discipline. And irritation.

He also looked vaguely familiar. An image popped into my brain. A face from one of the pictures in the library. Though this guy was blond, his eyes hazel instead of blue, the resemblance to Phoebe's dead father, Michael MacPherson, was unmistakable.

So, this must be the famous Collum.

"You know what?" I shot a thumb over my shoulder at the hanging. "Don't worry about what I'm doing here. I just want to know what the hell *that* is supposed to be."

"That"—a muffled voice spoke from behind a stack of crates—"is why I invited you here, Hope."

The boy's frown deepened when the voice commanded, "Bring my niece out, Collum. Since she's here anyway, we might as well finish it."

Finish it?

Oh, I so did not like the sound of that.

When the muscular Collum reached for my arm, I backed

out of reach. With a disgusted snort, he stepped back out of the way. I paused, unable to make my feet move.

"Come on out, Hope," called the shadowy voice, which, based on the "niece" reference, could only belong to my Aunt Lucinda. "There's no cause for alarm."

No cause for alarm. Sure. You only caught me breaking into your secret hidden vault thingy.

But the truth was, my aunt's voice didn't sound angry. Just very, very tired.

Deciding to go on the offensive, I shoved past the boy and out of the booth. "Where have you been? I came all this way, and you . . ." My voice trailed off as my aunt stepped around the stack of crates and I took in what she was wearing.

Okay. No.

From the ruffled parasol slung over one shoulder to the wide taffeta skirts of her 1860s-era gown, my forty-eight-year-old aunt looked like a stocky, banana-yellow version of Scarlett O'Hara.

"Yes, well." Blond ringlets from an obvious wig waggled around Lucinda's plump face as she cleared her throat. "I suppose you have questions."

"Questions?" I choked.

She went on as if I hadn't spoken. "Though I didn't expect our introduction to be quite this abrupt, I suppose it might as well happen this way." She didn't smile as she extended a hand. "I am Lucinda Carlyle. Your mother's sister."

A velvet drawstring bag dangled, heavy and bulging, from her wrist as she extended a hand. When I pointedly ignored the proffered hand, she sighed and let the arm drop back to her side.

My tongue like a slab of cold meat, I asked, "What is all this? Why is my mother's image woven into a nine-hundred-year-old tapestry? What am I doing here?"

Collum muttered, "That's a good question. Why *is* she here?"

Before anyone could speak, the vault door buzzed and swung open. Moira, wrapped in a plaid bathrobe, her graying hair ensconced in a phalanx of pink sponge rollers, rushed in. Hectic spots appeared on each round cheek as she wheezed. "Hope Walton, how in the name of Mary and Bride did ye get down here? Get back to yer bed this instant!"

Lucinda, in her belled skirts, laid a hand on the flustered woman's arm. "Let it be, Moira."

Moira deflated slightly, though she still puffed with aggravation. "Are ye fine then, Lu? Did everything go as planned?"

"Yes. Quite well, in fact. I think the senator will be most pleased."

Lucinda pulled the bag from her wrist and passed it to Moira. A grin passed over Moira's lips as she took a quick peep inside. The bag made a muted metallic clank as she set it on a nearby crate.

I gawped in disbelief as everyone around me acted as

though it was perfectly normal for grown people to prance around in the middle of the night dressed like extras in a bad movie.

"Go back to bed, Moira," Lucinda leaned her parasol against a bumpy covered object. "You too, Collum. I'll explain things to Hope after I get out of this blasted costume." She gave an irritated tug at the low neckline. "We'll be up in a while."

Moira shook out the fabric bundle she carried under one arm. "Nonsense. I'll stay too. Ye'll need help with the corset. Besides, ye must be exhausted."

"You're too good to me," Lucinda said. "Hope, you'll help as well, won't you?"

I stared from one to the other, my mind whirling so fast, it flipped into blankness. I found myself nodding.

"That's settled, then," Lucinda said.

When we entered the costume room, a guy was sitting at the computer desk, his enormously broad back turned toward us.

"Hey, Lu. Col," he said before wheeling around in his chair. "How'd it go with—?" He sprang to his feet. "What's *she* doing here?"

Computer boy was a titan. At least six and a half feet tall, with skin the color of an autumn acorn. Twisted, finger-length dreadlocks stuck out in all directions as if he'd been tugging on them. He topped the freckled Collum by a head, and his beefy proportions mirrored many of the professional football players my dad so admired. He should have been formidable. Yet behind a pair of gold-framed glasses, the boy's brown eyes seemed bashful as they fixed on me.

"Oh no," he groaned, slapping a hand the size of a small ham to his forehead. "Lu, I only left the watch room for a tic to get . . . something. I—I thought she was asleep."

Though he towered over her, the boy visibly shrank under my aunt's scrutiny.

"Yes, Douglas." Aunt Lucinda flicked a look at the mangled remains of a sandwich lying near the desktop monitor. "I see that."

"Douglas Eugene Carlyle." Moira's scorching tone made the big guy shrink even further, until his head looked like it wanted to crawl inside his shoulders. "How could ye leave the door untended, lad? The poor lamb is likely scared out o' her wits."

Collum strolled over and gave Douglas a sympathetic clap on the shoulder. "Bad timing, mate."

Douglas reached up and swiped at a smear of mustard on his cleft chin before he bowed his head in shame. "Gor, Lu. I'm pure sorry for it."

Lucinda nodded and patted him on the arm. "No harm done. It's likely better this way, actually." She grunted. "Introductions, then, I suppose. Just because we're weary doesn't mean we should neglect the niceties. Hope, this is Douglas Carlyle, my ward, and your cousin . . . of sorts. His father—my cousin Charles—and his mother, Yourna, were killed in a car accident when Douglas was only seven. He joined our family and has lived here with us ever since."

I met the boy's kind eyes. His hand swallowed mine in a gentle, warm grip. "Call me Doug," he said, smiling. "And it's pleased we are to have you here at last."

"And Collum MacPherson you met informally." Lucinda gestured to the laconic boy, who barely glanced at me as he slipped off his officer's cap and tucked it under one arm. "Collum is Mac and Moira's grandson. Later today, you'll meet his sister, Phoebe—"

"Too late," Moira muttered.

"Ah, naturally." Lucinda and Moira exchanged a wry look before Lucinda went on. "Well, in any case. May I present Sarah's daughter, and my niece, Hope Walton, lately from the United States."

I felt like my eyebrows had disappeared into my scalp by then. Even leaving aside the whole costume thing, my aunt's so-proper introductions were too bizarre to bear, especially buried as we were in some freaky high-tech burrow secreted deep beneath the ground.

"Um . . . hi?" was all I could manage before I spun on Lucinda. "What—"

Before I could say another word, Moira had hustled my aunt away into one of the curtained booths. Fabric rustled, and I heard the snap of hooks being undone.

"Hold your water, Hope," Moira ordered as she emerged, carrying a huge bubble of yellow taffeta. "Ye'll get your answers. But let your auntie change first. She's pure tired."

Moira began to bustle about, humming under her breath as she tucked the various costume accouterments away in the tall cabinet. Doug crept back to his computer. Only Collum acted as if anything unusual might be going on. He passed his gun belt and officer's coat to his grandmother, but his cold hazel eyes stayed focused on me. Dressed in a tight gray T-shirt, his Union-blue pants tucked into black boots, Collum's muscles bulged as he leaned against the wall, arms crossed.

If he wouldn't scowl like that all the time, he'd actually be kind of cute.

Ignoring him, I marched over to the booths just as the curtain was whisked aside. Lucinda emerged swathed in a soft navy tracksuit, a terry-cloth turban wrapped around her head.

"Much better, Moira," she said. "You were right, as usual."

When I wouldn't move out of her way, Lucinda stared into my face, her turbaned head tilted. A look of something like pity creased her eyes as she studied me. "Yes. Yes, you're absolutely right. It's time you knew."

For one split second, I longed to stop her. To walk away and go on with my broken little life. I straightened my spine and stared right back. I'd come way too far to chicken out now.

"This will be difficult for you," Lucinda said without dropping her gaze. "You were brought up in a household of logic, Hope. Of academia and rationality. And your mother's descriptions of your eidetic abilities are quite astonishing. In the end, however, Sarah decided your phobias had grown too intense for you to bear those secrets she wanted so desperately to share with you."

My face burned at the casual way she brought up my issues . . . problems . . . whatever, but I disregarded this. "What are you talking about?" I said. "My mother didn't have *secrets*."

Doug wheeled the desk chair over and offered it to Lucinda, who skirted around me to sit. Pinching the skin between her eyes, she exhaled long and deep. "Hope, I want you to know that my sister's decision to keep all this from you is not something I agreed with. We argued about it. Often. In the end, I honored her wishes. Unfortunately, we've now come to a place where that is no longer an option."

Lucinda let out a long breath and squared her shoulders before continuing. "Prepare yourself, Hope. It is now time for you to set aside what you think you know of this world. For there are things in it which are not easily explained."

CHAPTER 9

I stood mute while my aunt and Moira held a brief, private discussion, after which they marched out the door. Lucinda gestured for me to follow.

I had no choice. I scurried after them as they moved along the cellar and back through the still-open vault door. Behind me, I heard the two boys follow.

"Lu," Moira fretted, "ye look pale. Couldn't this wait till morning?"

Lucinda murmured something I couldn't hear as we wove among the high stacks and cloth-draped objects. Near the rear wall of the stone chamber, we stopped. Lucinda waved Doug forward, where another security layer was embedded in the stone.

"In the year 1883," Lucinda said as Doug keyed in a code, "after a late night of brandy and cigars, my great-great-grandfather Hubert Carlyle, along with his estate manager, James MacPherson, and Dr. Carlos Alvarez, a family friend, went down to view the excavations of Huberts's new wine cellar. The room in which we currently stand. Construction had ceased, due to the family's waning funds, but Hubert wanted his friends to view the progress."

There was a grating sound. A section of stone the size of two men began to slide back into the rock.

"The excavations," Lucinda continued over the noise, "had left this back wall unstable. No one was injured in the rock fall, but the collapse did reveal something quite odd." Lucinda gestured toward the now-open portal. "An ancient stone staircase."

"And too bad for us it wasn't an ancient escalator," Doug mumbled, pushing through the door.

As he helped Moira and Lucinda through, I glanced down at a dust-covered glass case. Tacked to the front was another of the innocuous labels.

ARTIFACT 3624. TRANSYLVANIAN REGALIA.

ACQUIRED: CARPATHIA, 1573. LC, MM1, MM2.

I read it again. My gaze tracked over the hundreds of boxes and crates, all with similar labels. On the far wall I could make out the top of a jackal-headed statue. And weren't those sword hilts sticking up from the packing material in that open crate?

The shock was wearing off now, and a piece of the puzzle clicked into place.

LC, MM1, MM2.

Lucinda Carlyle. Mac MacPherson. Moira MacPherson.

Archeologists? Art dealers? Are these some kind of black-market antiques?

None of that jelled with the period clothing or the computers. I was still missing something. Some vital element.

"Oy," Collum's shout from the opening made me jump. "Get a move on, yeah?"

We descended in a single line down a set of ancient steps carved into the very bedrock of the mountain. Each one was worn in the middle with age and use. As we moved down and down the switchback path, I trailed my hand along the cold stone, feeling rough, rudimentary chisel marks beneath my fingertips.

Wire-caged light bulbs hung at intervals, clipped to the same bundle of colored wires I'd noticed in the computer room that tracked along beside us.

Even with Moira and Collum's flashlights lending support to the scant pools of light, the darkness began to press in on me. The air thickened with the damp, elemental scents of earth and stone. The walls warped, and the already low roof loomed over my head.

Too dark. Too close. It's going to collapse. We'll be buried alive. I gotta get out. I gotta go.

I flinched when a dislodged pebble skittered past me down the steps.

"Wait." I braced myself against the wall and tried to suck

in the dense air. "Wait. I don't . . . It's too . . . Can't . . . breathe."

Collum turned from the step just below me. The light from his flashlight splashed across my face, and his irritated expression changed. He took my hand in his own callused one. For the first time, he sounded almost decent.

"Listen to me," he said. "Close your eyes and hold on to my shoulder. The passage opens up just below. Not much farther now. You can do it."

"Yeah. Close my eyes. That'll help." I'd meant to sound sarcastic, but without any breath behind them, the words emerged raspy and pathetic.

Cold sweat trickled down my back. Behind me, Doug said, "He's right, Hope. Nothing to fear. This passage has been here a good long time."

Collum secured my clammy hand on his shoulder and turned, tugging me down another step. "That's right. Come on. You're safe. Just like that. Keep going."

Collum had been nothing but a jerk to me since we met. But the warmth of his sturdy shoulder beneath my hand felt good, and after a few seconds I was able to force my feet down one step after another.

By the time we came to a final bend, my thighs trembled with effort, but I could breathe almost normally. Lucinda disappeared and I heard a click. Diffuse light glowed in the tunnel below us. The air here smelled different, like the wind after a lightning storm.

"All right," Lucinda called. "Bring her in."

Collum turned to face me in the arched entrance, blocking my view of whatever lay beyond. His freckled features hardened. I guessed he'd met his niceness quota for the day.

"Listen, Lu's having a rough go of it right now," he said. "I don't want you causing her any more grief. So you just listen to what she has to say. Got it?"

At my sullen nod, he stepped back. "Now don't move off that step."

With that, he moved aside, leaving me to gape at what lay hidden deep within the Highland mountain.

The oval-shaped room had started life as a cave, no doubt. But at some point in the mythic past, the place had been transformed. Overhead the stone ceiling soared up and disappeared into shadow, while carved symbols and ancient runes danced across the walls.

Celtic? My brain quickly shuffled and sorted through pages and images of all the ancient languages I'd ever studied. In an instant, my vision was overlaid with glowing translucent lists. *No, I decided. This writing is older than Celtic. Much older. I don't know what that is.*

More of the electric lights had been strung up along the walls, though I could see carved stone holders where torches had once hung. Embedded in the floor were tiny bits of colored stone. A mosaic, woven in a distinct pattern. At its middle, I recognized the elongated figure eight, the symbol for infinity, but not the meaning of the three wavy lines that bisected it.

The room's incredible beauty seemed alien there, in what

had to be the heart of the mountain. But that's not why my jaw dropped with awe. Equidistant from the center of the figure eight stood two pyramidal machines. Each taller than me, they were topped with silver, mushroom-shaped caps.

I knew them at once. Or, at least, who must've created them.

"Tesla," I whispered.

Doug nodded in approval. "You're right, Lu. She's smart."

The bundle of colored wires were secured to the floor, their ends attached to the back of the buzzing, clicking machines. Tiny filaments threaded out of holes in the sides of each mechanism, snaking up the walls and terminating in hundreds of round silver discs a couple of feet above our heads.

Wanting a closer look, I stepped down, then yelped as a prickling electric sensation flowed up from the soles of my feet. I shot a look at Aunt Lucinda, who was watching, as if waiting for my reaction. Out of the corner of my eye, I saw Collum smirk as I scrambled back onto the steps. The feeling vanished.

"What," I gritted, chafing at goose bumps that had erupted all over my arms, "the mother-loving hell was that?"

"You can come down, Hope," my aunt called. "I assure you it's perfectly safe."

"Yeah," I said. "Excuse me if I don't take your word for it."

With a glance to Moira, Lucinda approached the closer of the two machines. "You were correct in your assumption.

This is an original Tesla design. I understand you were once quite intrigued by the man?"

I huffed at that.

While most girls probably obsessed over singers or movie stars, I'd been infatuated with famous historical figures. And Tesla . . . well . . . he was amazing. A genius. More than a genius, really. When I was ten, I'd papered my room with pictures and articles of the troubled inventor. I'd always felt an odd kinship with him. Like me, Tesla had a photographic memory. Except unlike the vast array of historical facts and figures that lay dormant and useless in my own brain, Tesla had spun magic out of his incredible mind, creating some of the most impressive inventions ever known. Alternating current. The tesla coil. The man had invented lasers and robots in a day where people still traveled by horse and buggy, for God's sake.

Yeah. Intrigued. You could say that.

And if what they claimed was true, I was standing in a room with one of his original inventions.

Wow.

"They look like mini versions of Wardenclyffe Tower, don't they, Hope?" Doug chimed in.

From the way he was beaming at me, and based on the large photo taped to his desk, I knew I'd found a fellow fan.

"Yeah, I've seen the pictures. It was supposed to transmit power wirelessly," I said. "But it didn't work. What are these? Prototypes?"

Lucinda cleared her throat. "Not exactly. Earlier I

explained how my ancestor Hubert Carlyle and his friends found this chamber, quite by accident. When they experienced the same sensations you just felt, Hubert contacted his son Jonathan, who was attending university at Oxford. On a recent trip to Paris, Jonathan happened to have become acquainted with a young inventor named Nikola Tesla. Jonathan wrote and entreated his new friend to come investigate."

"Alternate power source," Doug put in. "That's what Tesla thought at first. He was keen on finding a way to harness it."

"But . . ." I glanced around the chamber, empty but for the machines and the people scattered about. "What kind of power? From where? I don't understand."

"They didn't either," Moira said. "Not then, anyway."

Aunt Lucinda approached and held out a hand. I hesitated, gnawing at my cuticles until I nipped into tender flesh. Ignoring her outstretched hand, I stepped down onto the floor. I felt it immediately, like an invisible current. As we walked the perimeter of the room, stepping carefully between the wires, the power seemed to flow from every direction at once.

The lines beside Lucinda's mouth deepened. "Tesla's machine did not work as he'd hoped. Oh, it harnessed the power here, no doubt. But in a way they could never have dreamed."

Collum snorted and leaned against the wall. "Aye. No one could've predicted that, could they?"

When Lucinda gestured to Doug, his wide face lit with

glee. "Oh, I've been waiting forever to show this to someone new."

He flicked the switch on a small metal box lying near the door. When it kicked on, white smoke blasted from holes in the top.

"Don't worry," he called over the hiss. "This is just a fog machine. Helps you see it better."

It?

A fan blew the heavy mist toward the ceiling. Soon, I could smell it. Damp and cold and vaporous. He clicked it off. "Okay. That's enough. Get the lights, will you Coll?"

The lights went out. And so did all the air in my lungs. Above our heads, laser beams seared across the room in the exact pattern I'd seen on the computer screen upstairs. Lines of brilliant neon green, with a few flashing red in a continuously changing pattern. Hundreds of them, all intersecting at the very center of the chamber, like a psychedelic spiderweb.

"What is this place?" I whispered.

"The first time it happened," Lucinda said quietly as she stared up, "was in 1888, during a soiree to celebrate the engagement of Jonathan Carlyle to Julia Alvarez, Dr. Alvarez's daughter. Tesla had given up and moved on, but the three men — Hubert, MacPherson, and Alvarez — filled with whiskey and swagger, decided to operate the machines for themselves. Jonathan and Julia followed their fathers down the stairs, worried that in their drunken state they might come to harm. The young couple arrived just in time to witness the three men, standing directly in the center of the symbol, being surrounded by a whirling cyclone of rippling power. Julia was struck dumb with horror, but Jonathan acted quickly to power down the machines."

"When everything settled," Moira spoke. "The three men were gone. Vanished into thin air."

I flinched as the lights clicked on. The lasers dimmed, though I could still see a phantom glimmer through the remnants of the fog.

"They didn't die, you know." Collum gave a cool shrug. "Only took a bit of a holiday."

"What?"

Collum waved a hand at Lucinda. "Lu, put the poor thing out of her misery, won't you? We've got work to do."

As she approached, my aunt's tired features looked so like my mother's, it made my throat ache.

"I'm sure that in the course of your studies, you've likely read how there were some ancients who believed in lines of power that thread through the earth," she said. "That they often erected monuments where those lines supposedly crossed. Standing stones, cave markings, and the like. This cave was one of those places. Though we believe the language is far older, the closest translation of the carvings you see here is ancient Gaelic. *Slighe a' Doillier*," she said. "The Dim Road. We just call it the Dim."

The Dim. Soundlessly, my lips formed the words. A horrifying idea rippled just below the surface of my mind. My mother's face, trapped within the tapestry's weave. *Costumes. Computers. Tapestries. Machines.*

"Aunt Lucinda." My voice sounded very small against the rock. "What happened to my mom?"

Lucinda spoke in a voice so bland, she might've been reading the weather forecast. "In rare places around the world, these ley lines intersect in huge concentrations. Here — amplified a thousandfold by Tesla's machines — they create a passage into the past."

"It works something like a miniature wormhole, see," Doug started, but Moira shook her head, quieting him.

I stared at the machines, stupified, as Lucinda finished. "Yes, Hope. My sister is alive. But she is also lost. In London, as far as we know. In the year of our Lord 1154."

CHAPTER 10

No.

Logic battled with a crazy, hopeful notion that tried to rise inside me. My aunt's words, so matter of fact, banged around inside my head like manic pinballs.

Impossible.

"I don't . . ." I managed. "I don't want to hear any more."

"Carlyle, MacPherson, and Alvarez had disappeared off the face of the earth," she went on as if I hadn't spoken. "Julia was distraught, convinced that the machines had somehow vaporized them. Jonathan convinced her not to speak of what they'd witnessed, until he could get in touch with Tesla. The only person with whom they shared their secret was MacPherson's son, Archie. Who would've believed them, after all? They would've been thought mad."

Pressure built inside me at each word. Soon I'd shatter and there'd be nothing left of me but a red smear on stone.

"The men reappeared," Lucinda continued. "Suddenly and without warning, exactly seventy-two hours later. Just popped back into existence in the exact spot from which they'd vanished. Jonathan and Archie saw it with their own eyes. Jonathan writes of it in his journals. How bedraggled and ill they were. How MacPherson had bled from the eyes and ears. Yet all three men were still very much alive."

Taking a breath, my aunt delivered the final blow.

"When the men returned, they told their wives and children an unbelievable tale. On oath, all three swore they'd been swept along by an unfathomable force and cast back through time itself. And," she said, "they did not return empty-handed. They were in possession of a leather bag of freshly minted, four-hundred-year-old coins. A sword. And a fine jeweled dagger. Artifacts they claimed they 'found' and which they eventually sold for enormous profit."

This was so far beyond imagination, it was laughable. My mother had raised me on a foundation of hard facts, historical evidence, analytical thinking. It was absurd to think she'd actually believed this fairy tale. This science fiction.

"Despite the danger," Lucinda was saying over the noise in my head, "they tried it again. And again. Before long, they'd amassed a great fortune with the artifacts they 'acquired' while on these journeys. Tesla knew, of course. For a percentage of the proceeds, he kept it to himself. He eventually modified the machines to calculate the general era in which they'd arrive. Even with that rudimentary method, they could prepare. Costumes. Money. Weapons. Of course we now use a much more sophisticated and exact system, thanks to Douglas here."

Doug ducked his head at the praise, but when he looked

over at me, his gaze was sweet and open. "See, Hope, you can't control the Dim, really. It opens when it pleases. All you can do is monitor the patterns of the different lines. That's what the computer program keeps track of. The device . . . amplifies the power of the lines. They are symbiotic. One won't work without the other."

The airport board upstairs.

Antwerp 111713.21

Istanbul 041099.12

Brighton 071817.07

Not codes. Dates.

London Dec 4, 1154.

My back went cold.

Lucinda's faultless posture drooped. She stumbled back suddenly, as if too exhausted to go on. Moira made a sound of dismay. Collum was there in an instant to keep Lucinda upright. When Lucinda tried to wave them both off, Moira mumbled a few, quiet words in her ear. Finally, my aunt nodded, and the two boys helped her sit in a straight-back chair.

Moira moved to my side. "Eventually," she said in a calm, steady tone, "as men tend to do, Carlyle and Alvarez argued. Alvarez split from the others after he secretly found a similar location high in the Andalusian mountains of Spain. He persuaded—or more likely threatened—Tesla into building two new machines, and then he began his own exploration."

Collum spoke, his upper lip curled into a sneer. "Alvarez's

descendants and the people who work for them call them-selves the Timeslippers, if you can believe it."

"Aye," Doug said with derision. "Original, right?"

I spun to face Lucinda. Her eyes were closed and she was scrubbing a hand over her mouth, as if her next words tasted bitter.

"The Timeslippers are now led by Carlos' great-great-*great*-granddaughter. A woman called Celia Alvarez. I understand you saw her photo in the library."

"I did," I mumbled. "She—"

I thought back to the expression on the black-haired woman's face. Bitter. Angry.

"Hope," Moira said. "Celia and your mother were once the best of friends. Sarah loved her like a sister. It was Celia who contacted your mother in India. I don't know what Celia told her to convince her to go. But I believe Sarah thought she could still reason with her. Unfortunately, she was wrong."

Sweat popped out on my face, despite the chill. The room began to spin, slowly but relentlessly, around me. Large as it was—the room suddenly seemed to contract, to press in until every atom of oxygen was squeezed from my cells.

I took a step back, heading for the stairs, but Collum fol-lowed.

"Oh, you can tell yourself we're mad if you like," he said. "Scuttle back home to your books. Continue to cower in your house and act like the poor wee broken thing you are."

I whipped around, my face on fire.

He came closer, his voice gone gritty. "But you know the truth now, and you can't unlearn it. If you leave, you'll always wonder what would've happened if, for once in your life, you'd had the courage to do something brave. You'll always wonder if you missed the one shot you ever had at being more than just a scared little girl."

My gaze flicked to the Tesla devices behind him.

"We are Viators." Pride infused Collum's voice as he gestured to the others, who were gathering behind him. "That means—"

"Traveler," I snapped, meeting his gaze. "Yeah. I know my Latin. I know what it means. But even if this ridiculous"—my hands flapped, encompassing everything in the cavern—"is real, I don't know what you expect *me* to do."

"Sure you do, silly."

I spun around to find Phoebe standing just above me on the stairs, wearing fluorescent blue jammies that matched her hair. Her grandfather was at her side, his lanky figure wrapped in a flannel robe, his own sparse strands mussed from sleep. Mac gave me a reassuring wink and moved to stand between his wife and Lucinda.

As I remained rooted to the spot, Phoebe gave me a friendly nudge. "No reason to go all barmy on us, Hope. It's no biggie, really. We're just time-traveling thieves is all."

"Phoebe Marie MacPherson!"

"Just messing with her, Gran. We don't steal anymore. Or at least not much."

She gave an exaggerated wink, making Lucinda growl.

"Jeez, Lu, I'm only teasing the girl." Phoebe brushed past to snuggle under Doug's arm. His gentle eyes fixed on me as he hugged her to him.

Lucinda spoke. "I'll admit, some of our ancestors were not what you'd call lily white in their dealings. My own father—unbeknownst to most of the world—was the source of almost every rare coin traded or purchased over the last thirty-five years. But I stopped all that when I took over." She shot a grumpy look at Phoebe. "The Viators no longer profit from any artifacts acquired during our journeys. For the last twelve years, our focus has narrowed, and become more concentrated."

Collum tensed at that but didn't speak.

"All you need to know at this time," my aunt continued, "is that the Timeslippers"—she grimaced, as if the word tasted foul—"have always viewed themselves as our rivals. They also have no morals. No compunction when it comes to preserving the proper timelines. And since Celia became their leader, she has recruited some very unsavory characters. We believe they're trying to locate something that could endanger us all. An object which might have the ability to control when and where the Dim will open."

"We begged Sarah not ta go." Moira worried at the knotted belt of her robe. "But she wouldn't hear it. She . . . she felt she owed it to Celia to persuade her to give up her preposterous quest."

"It's not preposterous," Collum shot back. "The Nonius

Stone is real. And if Celia gets her hands on it, there's no telling what she'll do."

The Nonius Stone.

The name was familiar. If I wanted, I could burrow in my memory and pull up the information. But the stairs were empty at my back now. I could run. Leave this place and go home.

I didn't move.

"Well, this is all of us, Hope," Lucinda said, spreading her arms wide. "We Viators. Excepting your mother, of course."

The only sound came from the rush of my own blood in my ears, and the chatter from Tesla's machines. I studied each person in turn. Their faces wore identical, earnest expressions. Something wrenched apart in my chest. This was no deception. No elaborate joke. They were serious.

"It was an ambush," Collum said, his hands in fists. "Celia laid it, and now your mum's trapped there. Alone."

My eyes burned, but I clenched my jaw and forced my shoulders back. An insane urge to laugh bubbled up inside me as I realized why Lucinda had sent for me. I needed to hear it, though. They had to say the words.

"Why am I here?" I asked in a flat voice.

Phoebe's friendly, animated face was grave when she spoke. "The Dim'll open in six days," she said. "One of its weird quirks is that it won't allow a person to go back to the same place and time more than once. It's been tried in the past. But the Dim knows, somehow. Doug says it recognizes the person's genetic pattern."

Doug took up the explanation. "When someone tries to return again to the same point in space and time, The Dim just shuts down, see. All the lines turn to green. We don't know why, though I believe it has something to do with the Dim disallowing a paradox to occur. For instance, you could cross your own path. And, oh, all kinds of awful . . . Well, let me show you." He whipped out a small notebook and began sketching a series of intersecting lines.

Phoebe laid a hand on his arm and stepped out from the others.

"Listen, Hope," she said, her small blue eyes locked with mine. "Lu, Gran, and Mac already went back to look for Sarah a few months ago. Though they didn't find her, they found clues. A noblewoman, new to town, had recently joined the baroness's household in Baynard's Castle in London. No one they spoke with knew where the woman came from. And the baron and his family had left town for their castle in the country. There wasn't time to go after her. But they did find out the woman's name. Sarah de Carlyle."

My mother's name felt like a slap. I lurched back, but Phoebe grabbed my hand, her gaze locking me in place.

"The Dim won't let them go again, see? And Viators never travel with just two, cause if one gets hurt"— her face scrunched into a frown—"or worse, the other person would be all alone. That leaves you, me, and Collum."

She took a deep breath and exchanged a quick look with the others. Lucinda nodded, and Phoebe squeezed my limp hands between her small, cold ones.

"We're going after your mum, Hope," she said. "The three of us. And this time we're going to bring her home."

I nodded thoughtfully, as if all this was perfectly ordinary. *Sure. I get that. Want me to travel through time with you? No problem. I'm on it.*

My feet were backing up the stairs. I forced them to stop as my vision filled with the image of Mom's face in the tapestry. She'd looked so angry. So scared.

My head jerked as a detail I'd registered, but had no time to examine, pricked at me. The hoop of embroidery she'd held in her lap seemed to magnify in my mind. The stitched words had been tangled in vines and flowers, and written in a language only a scholar would recognize.

I knew it, though. Aramaic. It was one of the many my mother had taught me.

Find me, it said.

My cunning mother had sent her sister a message through a thousand years, just hoping she would find it and come for her.

I nearly tripped as I stumbled down the step. "Th-the embroidery," I gasped.

The others were arranged in a semicircle around me. Together. Bonded. Only I stood alone. Lucinda was nodding, almost smiling.

"Yes, we know about the message," she said. "And I'm very pleased. Your mother prepared you well, Hope. You have more knowledge of history, and archaic languages, than many learned professors could absorb in their lifetime. Do you now understand why? You've been training for this since you were four years old. We need that knowledge. We need you."

The last time I heard my mother's voice was the morning she left us forever. She'd been pacing, the rising sun painting her bedroom pink and gold. I'd gone to apologize for being such a brat to her the night before, when she'd dared suggest I go with her. I paused in the hall outside when I heard her arguing with someone over the phone.

Of course I want to tell Hope the truth. A pause. *Oh yes. Last night. And she got so angry.* The female voice on the other end grew louder.

As I hid in the dusky hallway, I watched Mom's restless shadow flit across the wall. Her heels clacked as she roamed the room.

Listen, I—I don't know what else to do. Hope's just so fragile. I assumed she'd grow out of it as she got older. As she assimilated into . . . well . . . but it just gets worse. Though her mind is the most astonishing I've ever known, the phobias and anxieties she's racked with are—

The voice on the other end of the line cut in. On the

wall, my mother's shadow covered her eyes. *Yes, and I take full responsibility for that. But I wouldn't change it. Not ever. You weren't there. It wasn't even a choice. I will never regret taking Hope from that awful place.*

I'd startled at that. Oddly, I had no memory whatsoever of the Eastern European orphanage where my mother had found me when I was four. Was the voice telling her she should've left me there?

Still, she was saying, so that I had no time to process the comment, *I've begun to think it might be kinder to keep all this from her. If the thought of a plane ride practically incapacitates her, how do you suppose—?* The voice spoke. Mom sighed and said, *I know, but she's my* daughter. *And I'm beginning to believe she may never have the strength to bear the truth.*

I remembered creeping away, the apology still captured in my throat. *So she thinks I'm a weakling? Fine,* I'd decided. *Let her think it. Who cares?*

Anguish, bitter and dense as lemon peel, nipped at the back of my tongue as I realized it was my fault that Mom went on that trip alone. If I hadn't been such a coward, if I'd gone with her, maybe none of this would have happened.

My throat clicked when I swallowed. I took a step toward them, my eyes dry and flinty as they locked on my aunt's. "So when do we leave?"

CHAPTER 11

AFTER WE'D CLIMBED BACK UP THE STAIRS, MOIRA ordered us all to bed.

"Rest," she said, shooing us to our rooms. "That's what is needed now. We can discuss all this further after everyone's had some sleep."

Back in my room, the girl who glared from the silvered bathroom mirror looked like she'd been through a natural disaster. Pale, chapped lips. Dark curls frizzed and matted. The skin under my eyes like bruised fruit.

Mom's alive, I mouthed to the mirror. *Alive.*

Unable to bear the fear in my own eyes, I averted my gaze, splashing my face with cold water until it ran down my chest, drenching my nightgown. Wet and shivering, I burrowed beween the sheets, praying sleep would erase the dread that slithered over my skin.

After a few hours of disturbing dreams, it was time for my first official lesson. Time Travel 101.

"It was easy after that."

Seated around a long table in the library, a modest, brilliant Doug fended off the others' praise. "No, no. Tesla was the visionary, not me," he explained. "It was his idea to use alternating current that could read the pulses from the Dim, then use a crosscurrent to interrupt the flow at specific times. My program merely amplifies his readings, pinpointing the time and place and giving us more time to prepare."

Doug was obviously eager to have a fresh audience. So far, he hadn't noticed my lack of enthusiasm. For one thing, most of his intricate scientific explanations were way out of my realm of knowledge. And for the other, every synapse in my brain was taken up by thoughts of my mother. Of what might be happening to her in that other world in which she was trapped.

"See, Hope," Doug said, oblivious, "when the ley lines are interrupted in a certain sequence, it creates an opening. A vacuum. As I mentioned last night, it's easiest to think about it like a small wormhole. Here, let me show you."

When he snatched a piece of paper and began scribbling more numerical equations, Phoebe jumped into his lap and planted a kiss on his wide mouth.

"Enough, love," she said with her lips pressed against his. "You'll make poor Hope's head explode."

Doug grumbled a bit, but plopped the notebook down on the table to snug Phoebe comfortably across his lap. I grinned at the sight of his brown cheek resting on the top of her crazy blue hair.

My gaze drifted past to the torrents of rain sheeting the window. An image of Bran Cameron's face wavered before me, somehow watery and indistinct, as if the features were blurry. All but the eyes. Those odd, mismatched eyes stayed clear and sharp.

It's pouring buckets out there. No way he'd come today. Besides, I chided myself, *it's beyond selfish, thinking about some boy when you just found out your mother's still alive. Sort of.* I tapped a fingertip idly on the glossy table. *Still . . . if he came, and I didn't show, that would just be ru—*

The slam, as Collum dropped a huge stack of books on the table in front of me, brought me halfway out of my chair. The top one slid off into my lap. *Court Life Under the Plantagenets: Reign of Henry II,* by Hubert Hall.

"Quit daydreaming," he said. "You've got a lot to make up, so get busy."

I thumbed through the stack, shrugged, and pushed them back across the table. "Already read them. What else you got?"

"Read them again. You may know a lot, but there won't be any reference books or computers where we're going."

"I don't *need* to read them again." His attitude made me mulish. "I know what they say." I flipped open a book at random, glanced at the page number, then stared at him as I recited the words. "Page sixty-seven. Paragraph three."

As I delivered the dry, dusty facts of the 1154 coronation of King Henry II and his wife, Eleanor of Aquitaine, the words tumbled effortlessly from my tongue. But the subject drew me back to another voice that warmed in admiration whenever she spoke of her favorite person in history.

Eleanor of Aquitaine was a brilliant and powerful woman, Mom had lectured, poking the crackling logs in our little-used fireplace. *She was a champion of women's rights even then.*

On a rare impulse of mischief, I'd piped up. *Yeah, and I read that when she went on Crusade with King Louis of France, she showed her boobs to the troops.*

Blood rushed to my face. Daring words from an eight-year-old. My mother had laughed, though. Throaty and genuine.

Yes, she said. *That is true. But perhaps not her most notable accomplishment.*

When she smiled at me, eyebrows raised, pride had bloomed across my chest. I grinned back, so thrilled to contribute to a subject my mother loved.

Wanting—needing—more of her approval, I sighed. *Oh, Mom, wouldn't it be neat to travel back in time and meet Queen Eleanor in person?*

My mother froze with the poker shoved deep in the fireplace. A log popped. A glowing ember landed on the carpet, but she didn't react.

After a moment, she stood and kicked the coal back into the hearth. *Yes. Well.* She cleared her throat. *You never know what is possible in this world, Hope. But now I think it's time to resume your Greek lessons. Begin writing out your verb tenses.*

I looked up and realized the others were staring at me.

Without realizing it, I'd recited seven pages from memory. Doug stood and clapped in admiration, while Phoebe gaped, open-mouthed.

"That's bloody brilliant, Hope," she said. "And you can do that with anything you've read?"

"Interesting." Collum's wide mouth curled into smugness. God, I wanted to smack him. "Then why don't you tell us what you know of King John's treasure?"

"Hey, mate," Doug said. "I don't think—"

"No," Collum said. "She knows everything, right?" He turned to me. "Then you'll know this tale. The one where a poor farmer who lived near the Wash in Lincolnshire found the lost treasure of King John in 1573?"

I blinked at this abrupt change of topic. "What?"

"What do you know of it?" he demanded.

Though my brain was fizzing with everything that'd happened, it sharpened now. As they always did when presented with a history question, my thoughts quieted and focused. I flipped through my imaginary files for everything I'd read of the lost treasure of King John, youngest son of the medieval King Henry II and Eleanor of Aquitaine.

John had been a bad king. His barons turned against him, forcing him to sign the Magna Carta, which took away most of his power. It was said that after losing countless battles with the French on his own soil, the feckless king was on the run. On October 12, 1216, John and those of his men who were still loyal were fleeing with all the riches of the kingdom through the eastern part of England. His train was attempting to cross a dangerous, boggy area of mud flats and marshes located between Northampton and Lincolnshire. The king himself had crossed safely, but it was raining, and an unexpected tide came in. Some were sucked down into pools of quicksand. Others washed away in the surge. Dozens of John's people, horses, wagons, gone in moments. Worst of all, at least from John's perspective, all of England's greatest treasures, including the crown jewels, were lost forever.

Puzzled by the question, I told them what I knew.

"But I don't know what *you're* talking about," I said. "What farmer? King John's treasure was never found. It's one of the world's great mysteries. Treasure hunters still search for it today. I've read about it a hundred times."

Phoebe's eyes blazed as she glared at her brother. Collum wouldn't even look at her. He only stared at me in smug amusement, as if I was the only person not yet in on a joke.

"Sure." He shrugged. "That's what they say. *Now.* But up until twelve years ago, the books told a very different tale. They spoke of a farmer who, while plowing his land in 1573, accidentally came upon John's treasure. Apparently being a deeply superstitious man, he waited until he was dying to tell his son what he'd found. The son was a patriot and was hugely rewarded when he dug up the whole thing and handed it over to his queen, Elizabeth I." Collum's eyes bored into mine. "So you don't know everything. Because twelve years ago, history was *changed,* when the Timeslippers went back and—before the farmer could tell his son—took matters into their own hands."

"Obviously"—I whipped around to see my aunt striding angrily toward us, Moira in tow—"obviously," she repeated, "we tried to stop them. We failed in that task."

"Th-that's impossible," I whispered.

"No, lamb," Moira sighed as she placed an ornately carved box on the table. "Unfortunately, it is not. Once we learned of the Timeslippers' plans, we sent a team back to intercept them. But by the time we arrived, Celia's father and his men had already murdered the farmer's entire family and stolen the treasure."

I felt suddenly ill. My breakfast of toast and eggs gurgled in my gut.

"And upon our return," Lucinda said, "history had changed to what you now know to be true."

The implications of it made my brain ache. "But how?" I blurted. "I mean, okay. So it changed in the books. But what about people's own memories? The ones who knew the truth?"

"Even our own people's knowledge of the event had altered," Lucinda said, sitting down heavily in the chair opposite me. "No one but Mac, Moira, and I knew the truth of what had really occurred. The others had difficulty believing us. Fortunately, the Viator journals are always stored in the Dim's chamber. Those had not been modified. They—

along with our own eyewitness accounts—were the only proof we had."

Though she perched arrow straight on the edge of her chair, my aunt's face looked drawn and horribly wan beneath what I now realized was obviously a blond wig.

What's wrong with her? 'Cause it's obvious something's going on.

"It was my first decision as leader." She spoke in a flat, tired voice. "My father had recently been stricken with a heart attack and was bedridden. My entire life, he and I had argued over the morality of profiting from objects taken from the past. I wanted to return them." Her lips curved into a bitter grimace. "Father never took me seriously, of course." Her voice took on a deep, gravelly tone. "'What will you do, Lucy? Walk up to old Vlad Dracul with his crown, then wave from the stake as he impales you for thievery? No? Then leave well enough alone.'"

"Your intentions were good, Lu," Moira interjected. "We all knew that."

Lucinda shrugged off the comfort. "Yes, but who did Father blame for what happened next?" Her gaze dropped to the table. "And rightfully so. It was my fault Michael—"

"Lu," Moira insisted, "that was Celia, and you know it. Besides, old Roderick was already so ill. What happened had nothing to do with—"

"No!" Lucinda jolted from her chair. "He said it himself, the night he died. 'Have a care with your decisions, daughter. I might have acquired a few trinkets over the years, but I never lost a man under *my* watch.'"

When my aunt met my startled look over the tabletop, she blinked, coming back to herself in an instant. Her shoulders straightened, but I could see what it cost her.

Moira cleared an obstruction from her throat. "Shall we go ahead and show Hope the lodestones, then?"

I watched the high color recede from Lucinda's face as she eased back into her chair. "Yes," she said, waving a hand at the box. "You're right, of course. Please . . . proceed."

Moira unlatched the tarnished brass handles, Aunt Lucinda flipped open the heavy lid and reached inside. A long swirl of silver spooled out. Even in the watery light from the windows, a riot of rainbow colors shimmered in the black stone, set into a pendant that swung from the end of the chain.

"Hope," she said, "you'll recall what I said about James MacPherson. That he was quite ill when he and the other two men returned?"

When I nodded, she went on, her faded blue eyes fixed on the dangling necklace. "It was more than illness," she said. "The man was unconscious for days. When he finally woke, he'd lost partial use of his left arm, and his face drooped on one side for the rest of his life. Dr. Alvarez also suffered a much slighter version of the illness, while Hubert Carlyle showed almost no signs."

Lucinda laid the pendant carefully on the table and placed

the other objects from the velvet-lined box beside it. A thick man's ring and two matching bracelets.

"At first, they could not comprehend why the voyage affected MacPherson so much more than the others. By process of elimination, they came to realize that Carlyle and Alvarez each had on their person one thing which MacPherson did not. Or at least, not in the same manner, exactly. Can you guess what that was?"

Moira reached behind her thick braid of black and silver and unclasped a necklace. She laid it beside the others. Hung on a slender chain was a gold ring set with a tiny white chip. The answer seemed fairly obvious.

"Opals," I said. "They're all opals."

"Very good." Lucinda nodded her approval. "Hubert Carlyle was wearing this ring." She pointed out the heavy band lying on the table. It was set with a rare black opal, like the one in the pendant. "Carlyle's wife had given it to him on the occasion of their twentieth anniversary. He never took it off." She touched one of the twin cuff bracelets, which held smaller, though similar, dark stones.

"Opals had become popular again, thanks to Queen Victoria. Dr. Alvarez happened to have these very bracelets in his pocket that night, as he'd planned to present one to his wife and one to his daughter Julia to celebrate her engagement to Jonathan Carlyle."

She nudged Moira's contribution with a finger. "James MacPherson, fortunately for him, always carried his dead wife's wedding band inside his sporran. Had he not," she said, "he'd have died then and there. Though his stone was of lower quality, it saved his life and brought him home."

"The stones act as a sort of homing device, you see," Moira said. "No other jewel will do. Not diamonds nor sapphires nor emeralds. Only the opal."

"I've studied the molecular compositions, but"—Doug shrugged his huge shoulders—"no definitive results. All we know is that the finer the stone, the less the journey affects you."

Phoebe nodded emphatically. "Without them, the Dim either kills you, makes you really sick, or leaves you behind. You don't ever want to be careless and lose your lodestone. I mean, look what happened to Sarah." Her face fell. "Cheese an' rice. Hope, I'm so sorry. I didn't mean . . . See, I know how you feel, 'cause—"

Collum cut her off. "Sarah's wasn't lost," he said. "It was stolen by that she-wolf Celia."

"Collum is likely right about Celia," Lucinda said. "My sister was anything but careless. She'd never lose something so precious. Still, you shall take the extra bracelet with you for her use, when you—"

"How do you know she's not dead?" I blurted out. "I mean, how can you possibly know that?"

Moira reached across the table and squeezed my clenched fist. "We have proof—of sorts—that she was still alive several months ago. The tapestry you saw below was sketched in September of 1154. A few weeks ago, we traveled to a much later year and purchased it from a baron who was selling off his father's belongings."

"And this timeline to 1154 is remarkably stable," Lucinda said as she gathered up the jewelry and placed it back in the box. "When Mac, Moira, and I went back to search, we talked to several people who knew of her. That was less than a month after she disappeared, but Sarah is there, Hope. We know she is."

Doug spoke up. "I know it's really hard to take in. See, Hope, once the Dim opens to a place, time flows in the exact linear fashion in both timelines. So the same eight months or so have passed there as have passed here."

Eight months. My mom had been lost in that horrible, barbaric time for nearly eight whole months. Sure, she apparently knew what she was doing. But even I knew the odds weren't great that a lone woman could survive long in an era when plague and dysentery, brutality and war, were commonplace. An era when even the smallest nick could be fatal.

I caught my aunt's gaze. Though she hid it well, I could feel the thread of doubt twining through her.

No matter what Aunt Lucinda claimed, my mother might already be dead.

CHAPTER 12

THAT NIGHT, PHOEBE AND I SAT CROSS-LEGGED ON MY mattress, scarfing filched lemon bars that flaked, buttery and tart, on my tongue.

"Here's something I don't get," I mumbled through a mouthful of crumbs. "Why can't someone just travel back to last summer and tell my mother not to go?"

"I wish," Phoebe said, nibbling at the pastry. "Be simpler, yeah? But the most recent year the Dim has ever opened to is around ninety years ago. Doug thinks it has something to do with not allowing someone to cross paths with their younger self. That things could get royally messed up if you met yourself." She swiped a dusting of powdered sugar off her upper lip.

"I guess I can see that," I said, chewing thoughtfully. "Like, if you could go back willy-nilly, whenever you wanted, you could tell yourself not to marry someone. Or, hey, you could tell yourself to buy stock in Apple or Microsoft."

Phoebe snorted. "I'd tell myself to write Harry Potter. Be richer than the bloody queen."

"That's a good one," I agreed. "I'd invent Facebook."

In moments, we were howling with laughter, spraying lemon crumbs everywhere as each idea grew more outrageous than the next.

God, it felt amazing to laugh. To laugh until I cried, until the muscles in my sides ached. Muscle that hadn't been used that way in a long, long time.

Phoebe sobered suddenly, wiping at her eyes. "I think you should know something." She glanced at me sidelong. "You remember Collum mentioning something about Celia, and a thing called the Nonius Stone?"

"Yeah."

"Well, see, there's this story about it, aye? It's supposed to be, like . . . the mother of all opals. Lu and Collum believe it's real. And they think Celia's after it. That she wants it to gain control of the Timeslippers' device."

The Nonius Stone. My hands twitched as I visualized my fingers filtering through the neatly organized files in my mind. I took a huge bite of the pastry, head tilted in concentration.

There. There was the passage I'd read.

The Roman philosopher Pliny the Elder spoke of how, in 35 B.C., Mark Antony had become entranced by the colored lights that moved within a marvelous stone, known throughout the Roman Empire. He wanted to present it as a gift to his love, Cleopatra. The owner—a Roman senator named Nonius—refused to sell, claiming the "jewel of the night" was everything to him. When Antony threatened him, the wealthy senator disappeared. He left everything behind—his family, his fortune—fleeing with only the clothes on his back. And the great jewel.

"But, it's just a legend, right?"

"Could be," she said. "But Coll is obsessed with finding it." Phoebe fiddled with the pastry in her hand, spilling crumbs on the quilt. "It's our da, see? He got left behind too. A long time ago."

The bite I'd just swallowed stuck halfway down. "Your dad? But . . . Moira said he died."

Even as I spoke, our conversation in the library rewound in my head.

No. What she said was: *He's been gone.*

"Well, it's likely," Phoebe said. "He was injured. And it was twelve years ago. I was four, and Collum seven. A long time." She sighed as she plucked at the crumbs on the quilt. "See, Lu had shut everything down after the King John thing happened and her father died. But no one beats my Gran when it comes to research. She learned that in 1576 a great jewel had been sold off by a tiny convent near the Wash. Apparently, it was found in the pocket of a young girl who'd fled to the nuns shortly after her whole family was murdered."

"One of the farmer's family survived the attack?"

Phoebe nodded, her small eyes gone round. "Aye. Betsy Fortner. She didn't live long, though. But the nuns found something sewed into her skirts. The Viators decided it must be the Nonius. That the Timeslippers had missed it, somehow. Lu sent a team back to investigate."

The hair on the back of my neck prickled.

"Who?" I could barely whisper the word.

"My da," she said in the same hushed tone. "Your mum. And Celia Alvarez. *She* was still a Viator then. Had been since she ran off from her own family when she was fifteen or so. Claimed she hated her father. That he beat her. Asked Lu and Sarah's da to give her refuge." Phoebe made a face. "'Course I don't really remember much about what happened the night they returned, but Collum does, and it hits him hard sometimes."

"What . . ." I coughed to dispel the choking sensation. "What happened?"

Phoebe stared off, dredging the memory from a deep, dark place. I wondered how much was actual recollection, or if it was that she'd heard the story so many times, it had inserted itself as memory. She picked up the last lemon bar, brought it to her mouth, then set it back on the china plate, uneaten.

"All I recall," she said, "is Mac waking us in the wee hours. Collum was in a rage, 'cause they wouldn't tell us what was happening." She paused to swipe at her eyes, smudging black streaks into the vivid blue hairline. "Da was everything, yeah? See, he'd got our mum knocked up when they were just kids. Seventeen or so. They were married for a few years, but Gran says they were never happy. Fiona hated everything about the traveling, too. Refused to have anything to do with it. She lit out right after I was born. Mac called and told her what had happened to Da. She never even came to see us. Not that I care."

She shrugged, as if being abandoned by her mother meant nothing. But when her mouth twisted, I put a hand over hers.

"It's okay." She sniffed. "Truly. I have Collum, and Gran and Mac, don't I? And Lu, o' course. But Da . . ." She leaned back on the plush pillows. "Anyway, they sat us down and told us he was gone. I didn't know what that meant. Not really. But Collum? Oh, he was in a state like you've never seen. Wanted to go get him, right then and there. Couldn't understand when they told him it was impossible."

I could see it. The solemn, round-faced little boy I'd seen in the photos, confused and furious when he learned the only parent he had left was gone.

"What about my mom?" I asked. "What did she say about it?"

"I never saw her. They told us later that Sarah had left in the night. Celia, too. She went straight back to the Timeslippers, and that was the last we ever saw of *her*, thank God. Gran says your mum up and moved to Oxford. They didn't even hear from her for a long while. And by that time, she'd adopted you, married your dad, and moved to the States."

I frowned. My mom just *left*? Took off in the middle of a disaster, leaving her family alone to deal with the aftermath? That didn't sound like her at all. It didn't make sense.

"And it was all for nothing, anyway," Phoebe said. "Wasn't even the Nonius Stone. Just a bloody big emerald."

She went on, her voice getting raspier as she spoke of what happened. How all she knew was that on their return to the location where the Dim would take them back, the three Viators were attacked. Michael MacPherson had been injured in the fight, and the thieves had absconded with all but two of their lodestones. Apparently, there'd been a fierce argument about which one of them would be left behind.

Phoebe stared down into her lap. "When the Dim began to open, Da ran into the forest, sacrificing himself so Celia and your mum could come home."

"Oh my God," I breathed. "That's awful. Your dad must've been really brave staying behind like that."

She smiled through the tears. "Aye. He was a hero for sure. We're always hoping the Dim will open to that time again, but it never does. Collum's convinced if we find the Nonius Stone, we could use it to control the Dim. That maybe with the great stone, Doug could program it to open to when and where we want. That we could find Da and bring him home."

"Would that work?"

"No idea." She shrugged. "But Coll believes it."

"Jeez. No wonder he hates me," I whispered. "He's waited so long, and it's *my mom* we're going after."

"Nah." My new friend picked up a lemon bar, her sunny

personality back in a blink. "It's not that. Ever since Lu assigned him to this team? Forget it. *He's* the leader. The big boss man. He's just acting like a git now 'cause you're smarter than he is and he knows it." She squeezed my hand with her sticky one. "But he'll work like the devil to bring Sarah home. Don't worry about that. He takes this mission very seriously."

As she hopped down off the high mattress, scattering crumbs all over the shiny wooden floor, I followed, my mind working through this new information.

Phoebe dropped onto the floral loveseat, and unfolded a worn leather bundle she'd brought along and tossed it onto the cushions. Nestled inside lay a trio of lethal-looking throwing knives. She selected one of the slim blades and began sharpening it against a whetstone.

"From the day Da was lost, Lu started hunting the Nonius Stone, determined to get him back. You heard Lu," Phoebe said. "She blames herself. So now we follow every lead, no matter how obscure. And Collum's even worse." Sparks flew from each agitated stroke as she resumed, apparently unsatisfied with the results. "The only one who doesn't travel is my Doug. And it's not fair. He would be a bloody amazing traveler, but for the epilepsy, see? Got it from a head injury in the car accident that took his parents."

"Oh, that's awful," I exclaimed. "The poor guy. He was with them when they died?"

She twisted the stud in her brow, frowning. "Aye, it's bad,

Hope. And he's convinced it'll get worse, that one day his beautiful brain will get all scrambled. He swears he'll leave before he'd let me see him like that."

Sparks. The grinding of steel on stone. The smell of wood floors and metallic shavings. The sweet, tart taste of lemon bars that coated my throat as my heart sank.

A wave of protectiveness washed through me for Phoebe and her kind, brilliant boy. My chest ached at the thought of something happening to Doug's exquisite mind. And what it would do to my new friend if it did.

"Aw, but when he gets all maudlin like that, I just tell him to bugger off," she said, sniffing. "He's not getting out of marrying *me* someday over some little thing like that. Still, the travelin' is too dangerous for him. If he were to have an attack while we were away, well . . ."

Phoebe set the whetstone aside and tested the blade's sharp edge against the pad of her thumb. She smiled grimly at the thin line of red that appeared. Teeth sunk in her lower lip, she took aim and, with a flick of her tiny wrist, sent the blade spinning across the room to bury itself in the paneling.

CHAPTER 13

Soon enough, I learned they were all skilled with some kind of weapon. Not only could Phoebe pin a fly to the side of the barn with her knives, she'd been trained in martial arts since she was a kid. In astonished awe, I watched the petite girl grapple both Doug and Collum to the ground over and over.

"You could learn this, Hope," she called. "Doesn't matter how small you are. Aikido uses your opponent's own momentum against them." Phoebe demonstrated a few moves, her small hands and feet flying as she once again dropped her sweating brother to the mud-slick ground of the stable yard. "Of course, if that doesn't work"—she patted the knives at her side—"you just stick them with your blade."

Collum's weapon of choice was a short, wide gladiator sword that had belonged to his father. Watching him and Mac spar left me clenching and breathless. Even Doug was astonishingly fast with his staff, a six-foot piece of rock-hard oak.

No surprise to anyone, especially me, I was clumsy and

awkward with any weapon they tried to put in my hands. After days stuck inside while the skies shed buckets onto the mountains and moors, I'd discovered the only place I was of any use at all. The library. And even there, practically every time I opened my mouth, Collum shut me down. It was getting old.

The rain had finally stopped. I peered down the misty valley toward the river and wondered if Bran Cameron would be there today.

Even thinking about the possibility that he might be there — *could* be there — made my face go hot. It was a stupid hope, I knew. But I so needed a little normal in my life just then. Not that meeting up with a boy was normal. Not for me. But I'd take what I could get.

As I watched, Phoebe flipped Doug for the third time. The massive boy landed on his back with a whoomp that shook the ground. He lay still, gasping. Eyebrows waggling, Phoebe held out a hand. "That's six to two," she said. "Done, then, are you?"

With a move quicker than I would've imagined possible for someone his size, Doug rolled to his feet. And in one smooth motion, he'd hauled Phoebe over his shoulder and — both of them giggling madly — carried her off into the house.

Mac and Collum had finished their earlier battle. The older man was now watching as Collum eviscerated a leather-bound, straw-filled dummy that hung from a beam sticking out the side of the stable wall.

Earlier, I'd tried to chuck a few of Phoebe's knives at the

figure. The few that had miraculously struck had bounced off and splatted to the ground.

"Nice work, lad," Mac called as he sheathed his blade. "Old Angus will need some stitchin' up ere we use him again, I bet."

He strolled toward me, the crow's feet around his eyes deepening as he called over his shoulder. "And take it easy on our lass here. Remember, this is all new to her."

Mac's hand was gentle as he clapped my shoulder. "Ye're doin' fine, lass," he said in a voice for me alone. "Ye're smart as a whip and twice as tough. 'Tis a lot to take in, I know. But Collum's a good lad. Ye'll be right safe in his care."

Mac headed inside, leaving only me and Collum in the muddy yard. A fact I wasn't totally thrilled about.

The Highland mist swirled down off the far mountains and writhed across the moors like a mass of angry spirits. Exhausted from three eighteen-hour days of endless study, costume fittings, and practicing the twisty medieval dialect, I turned away to head inside. If I hurried, I could change out of the long practice skirts Collum had insisted on and be headed out on Ethel's back in ten minutes.

Collum moved to block me, dropping a knife at my feet.

"Not yet," he said. "You didn't do so well earlier, and everyone should know how to use a blade. We're going to a brutal time. You won't be able to fend off an attacker by quoting passages at him, so pick it up. We aren't leaving this spot till you know how to use it."

I frowned down at the slender stiletto. Nothing mattered

more than finding my mom, but Lucinda had already lectured us time and time again to have as little contact as possible with the "natives." So why he thought I'd need to use a blade was beyond me. I wasn't an idiot. I knew where we were headed was a dangerous place. But I'd already managed to nick myself three times with the miniscule eating knife I'd been rehearsing with — no forks in the twelfth century — so how the hell did he suppose I'd do with an actual weapon?

Grumbling under my breath, I retrieved the knife and balanced it gingerly on my open palm. The color of aged ivory, the hilt was carved with whorls and odd symbols. I smoothed a finger across the satiny surface.

"That's bone," Collum said, "with a canny sharp blade. Got it off a count on a trip to 1823. It'll do for you. Now grip it like this."

Collum wrapped his rough palm over mine, showing me an underhand grip.

"Okay, okay," I said. I slapped at the full skirts. "But let me go change. I've tripped on these stupid things a dozen times already. If I don't get some jeans on, I'll end up gutting myself. "

I was hoping for a laugh. A chuckle. God, even a twitch to break the guy's unrelenting intensity. But Collum's expression never wavered as he looked skyward. "And will you be wearing *jeans* where we're going? I can't be with you every second. You have to be able to defend yourself. But if you're not going to take this seriously, then —"

"Fine," I muttered. "It's just that I'm really not into the

whole piercing, slicing, mutilating thing. You have to admit that's not something a normal person learns."

He nodded slowly and slid his own knife back into its sheath. "Aye. All right, then. I understand."

My shoulders slumped in relief. "Great. So I'll just concentrate on—"

He moved on me so fast, I stumbled back and fell flat on my butt. He danced away, smirking.

"Oh, that's just great," I groused as cold thick mud soaked through layers of material.

He held out a hand to help me up. I ignored it. "I got it."

I jerked to my feet, then bent over to kick up the knife. Before I could blink, Collum slapped it to the ground and crushed my hand in his iron fist. The pain sent me to my knees.

"Going to quote at me from your wee books, now?" he said. "Terrify me with a nice factoid?"

"Collum." Irritation warred with a growing alarm as he squeezed harder. "Let go of me."

"I thought you didn't need any help."

I twisted and squirmed, scratching at his arm. But his biceps felt as hard as the wood of Doug's oak staff.

Collum shrugged, taunting in a voice I didn't like at all. "Aw, poor wee lass has lost her knife. Course, you say you can't stab anyone anyway. So it wouldn't have done you much good. Guess that means you're helpless, then."

"All right, *all right*. I get it," I said. "I'll practice with the freaking knife."

He let go so abruptly, I nearly toppled sideways. "Good. Now—"

As if my hand belonged to someone else, I whipped his own dagger from his belt and cracked him on the side of the head with the wooden hilt.

Collum staggered back, stunned. My nerveless hand dropped the knife to the ground.

Oh crap.

He gaped at me as he reached up to rub at his temple. One side of his mouth twitched. Then, as I stared in complete and utter shock, Collum threw his tawny head back and roared with laughter.

When Collum MacPherson laughed, he did it with his entire body. Heaving and bellowing, he held his sides and just let go. Like his sister's, Collum's laugh drew you in, and soon the two of us were leaning on each other, wheezing and gasping for air.

"That's my girl," he managed when he could finally speak. "Now, that's what I wanted to see. Looks like there's some spirit behind that wally, whinging facade o' yours after all."

Before I could decipher his words and decide whether I was insulted or oddly pleased, he clapped me on the back with such enthusiasm, I stumbled forward.

"Good show, Hope." He nodded, still chuckling. "Good show. Now pick that up and let's go again."

CHAPTER 14

"THEY SAY THE HIGHLAND EAGLE MATES FOR LIFE."

After days of being trapped by weather, and enduring every kind of time travel lesson imaginable, I'd finally gotten a chance to sneak away. When I arrived at the river to find Bran Cameron waiting for me, I'd tried to play it cool, hide my excitement. But with my cheeks still hot from two hours of stabbing practice and the breathless flight on Ethel's back, I doubted he bought it.

After a long, twisting ride up a mountain path, we'd tied the horses and made our way to the edge of a great drop-off. Legs dangling, we stared out at the green and purple valley that sprawled out before us. In the distance, a lone mountain rose up above Christopher Manor, dwarfing the huge house. I stared, suppressing a shiver as I thought of what lay at its stone heart.

The wind gusted through the valley, driving the pair of enormous eagles higher as they rode the currents, performing an intricate dance.

"They're beautiful," I said, turning to Bran. "I've never seen eagles before."

A pulse of quicksilver hit when his gaze dropped to my mouth.

"Yes," he said. "They bond right out of the nest, you know. And stay by each other's side until one of them dies. The other usually succumbs soon after. Grief, they say."

I thought of my dad and how much . . . smaller he'd seemed without my mom. He'd withdrawn from everything. Especially me. At least until Stella came along.

Staring at the birds, anger began to bubble inside me.

"But how could they just give up like that?" I shifted, rocks digging into my thighs. "What if the eagles have babies? They just let them die? I mean, sure it's tragic, but kind of selfish, too."

"I agree. Just because they can't be with the one they love, they wither away and die? Seems like cowardice to me. Sometimes one has to muddle through, even if one isn't happy. Isn't that what life really is? Simple perseverance?"

I shrugged. "Yeah. No matter how bad it gets, you just keep plodding along. Maybe you're numb, but I mean . . . what else can you do?"

"Well"—Bran cleared his throat—"this is titillating conversation. Dead birds. A numb existence. What else can I bring up to liven the moment? Starving children? Crippled puppies?" He tilted his head, examining me through long lashes. "You know, I'd almost given up on you."

"Chores," I squeaked. "My aunt . . . She has lots of chores for me."

He nodded. "Oh. Well, that I quite understand. My mother is the queen of *chores*."

Sitting on a mountaintop alone with a strange boy should have felt odd. I'd never spent any time alone with a boy, if you didn't count my snot-nosed cousins. My mother thought dating a bigger waste of time than having friends.

Not that the opportunity had ever come up.

Still, I felt strangely comfortable sitting there next to Bran, like we'd known each other for a very long time.

"You know," I told him, "before I got here, the only thing I knew about Scotland was from crusty old history books. Oh, and from *Braveheart,* of course. My dad loves that movie, though Mom hated it."

"Oh yes. Most Scots detest it. Makes their national hero look like a bloody outlaw. William Wallace was actually a very educated man. More of a politician than a grimy rebel. No murdered wife, either." He cocked an eyebrow. "Had a pretty mistress, though. Does that count?"

I scrunched my nose. "Disappointing. The dead-wife story is way more romantic."

The breeze whipped around us, playing backdrop to the symphony of crying birds and the soprano tinkle of sheep bells in the meadow below. I closed my eyes, letting the peace of it flow around me.

"So," Bran said, "what kind of duties does an American girl such as yourself perform all day, down there in that big house?"

My serenity flattened.

Oh, not much. Just what any normal sixteen-year-old girl does. Memorize a million books about the twelfth century. Practice speaking with a medieval accent. Learn to stab people.

And then, of course, there's the whole traveling-through-time thing.

On the way up the mountainside, Bran told me he was out of school for the summer, and on holiday with his London-dwelling mother. He hadn't offered anything further. I was okay with that. Of all people, I understood that everyone had their secrets.

"Not much," I finally said, staring down at the sheep. "This and that. My aunt likes projects. What about you? What does Bran Cameron do when he's not out stalking?"

Twirling a twig of heather between the palms of his fine-boned hands, he huffed. Instead of answering, he said, "And what is your view on knees?"

"Knees."

"Yes, knees."

He grinned so wide the crooked eyetooth showed. A glowing warmth started to fill me when I saw that smile.

"Absolutely. On Saturday, you see, there is a festival a couple of villages from here. It's a small event to be sure, but the lads throw huge stones about, and there will be plenty of greasy food. Plus, bonus . . ." He waggled slim eyebrows. "I always wear a kilt to these events and thought it best to ascertain your opinion on knees. Just in case you feel unable to restrain yourself when you see mine."

Never had a boy asked me to go anywhere with him. Ever. I'd figured this ride would be it. Just his way of paying me back for saving his life. But now, maybe . . . possibly . . . this almost-beautiful boy was actually asking me out. I had no precedent. No idea what one said in this type of situation. So, like the loser-nerd I was, I found myself blurting, "Y-you mean like a date?"

"No, Hope," he said, tucking back a grin. "I don't mean like a date."

"Oh." Disappointment. Embarrassment. By the cartload. "Sorry. I—"

I started to turn away, but he grabbed my hand. My skin felt like it was melting as I stared down at the inch of ground between us.

"I don't mean *like* a date," he said. "I mean exactly a date. You. Me. Greasy food. Knees."

One adorable sideways smile later, and my heart started doing klutzy somersaults inside my chest.

Then, like some celestial being had judged my happiness undeserved, his words penetrated, and my grin smeared away. "Wait," I said. "Did you say Saturday?"

At his nod, I continued, trying to hide my misery. "I can't. I'll be, um . . . away that day. For a few days, actually."

His hand sprang open, releasing mine. For an instant, his gaze sharpened before he shrugged and turned back toward the view. "I see. Well, if you're busy, you're busy. More knees for me, then."

"I'd love to go. Really. It's just that—"

"It's quite all right." He threw a rock off the ledge, watching it tumble end over end into the valley below. "Actually, now that you mention it, my mother likely has some things for me to attend to this weekend."

"Not fun things, I'm guessing."

He laughed, though now it sounded flat and humorless. "No."

"Maybe when we both get back?" I suggested.

"I'd like to think that would still be possible," he said.

I blinked at the phrasing, and at the way his features had turned solemn. I knew the chances were pretty slim. *If* I even survived all this, and *if* we found my mother still alive, we'd likely leave as soon as possible. How that would go over back home I didn't want to think about. Not yet.

As I stared down into the valley, something brushed the side of my face. I held very, very still as Bran Cameron tucked the strand of heather behind my ear. Its soft blossoms tickled my cheek, and the sweet, earthy fragrance filled my senses.

My lungs squeezed to half their normal size as I turned to look into his mismatched eyes.

"Uh, Bran?" His name tasted like a piece of toffee that melted too fast on my tongue. "Can I ask you something?"

"Of course."

"Your eyes," I fumbled. "They're so strange."

His eyebrows shot up. "Not used to making idle conversation, I take it?"

My mouth dropped open in horror. I rushed to apologize. "I didn't, I don't mean strange as in weird or anything. It's just that I feel like I've known someone with eyes like yours, but I can't remember who. Which is totally bizarre for me, because I have this memory thing, and . . ."

I trailed off as something fired behind his eyes. It was snuffed out so quickly, I wondered if I'd imagined it. He turned away, his gaze tracking a pair of lambs that had wandered away from the flock. "I assume it's a family trait. Though I can't be certain."

"You didn't get them from one of your parents?" I said. "Because I thought heterochromia was hereditary."

"It's possible." He shrugged. "Never met the people."

Bran's arms went up in a lazy stretch that exposed a strip of trim, tanned stomach. I gulped and tried not to stare. Despite the casual words, a tightness formed around his eyes.

"You're adopted?" I sat up straighter. It was disconcerting: I'd never met another adopted kid. My dad's family—particularly my grandmother—always acted as if not having "Walton blood" was a disease. At Bran's admission, for the first time I felt less . . . alone, somehow.

I'd never been very curious about my origins. I'd decided long ago that if my birth parents had just thrown me away like that, why should I care?

Only once, after a fierce argument, I'd stormed to my room, determined to locate my "real parents." I knew the name of the Eastern European orphanage where she'd found me. But the only thing I could find was a grainy black-and-white photo of a charred building that had burned to the ground the year I was adopted.

"I am too," I said to Bran. "Adopted, that is. And you know, it never bothered me until recently."

"Why is that?"

I didn't answer at first. Instead, I watched as the lambs' mother nudged them back toward the rest of the group. "Not sure," I mused. "I guess it's being here with my mom's family. They're all so tight. And there are all these ancestors hanging on the walls. I swear to God they glare at me like *Who are you and what are you doing in my house?*"

Bran snorted. "Try spending five minutes around my mother's mum for any length of time. At least the portraits don't tell you that to your face." He tilted his dark head, peeking at me from the corner of his eye. "Do you remember anything? About your life before, I mean?"

"Nope," I said. "But I was only four or so. You?"

Bran's lips parted. The tendons in his neck tightened. His fine-boned fingers tightened into a fist.

"No." He bit off the word. "I was but an infant. Had a stepfather for a while. Gave me his name. Nice chap, but he didn't stick around long. Not that I blame him."

Silence taut as a rubber band stretched between us. I could all but feel the anger boiling beneath the surface.

"So," I said, hoping to cut the uncomfortable tension, "do you have siblings?"

His shoulders loosed, and a different smile from any I'd seen before split Bran's face. He gave an emphatic nod. "Tony," he said. "My brother. Oh, he's a great lad. Sweet. And smart as a whip. I love him as much as I would if he were my own blood." Like a cloud muting the sun, the smile faded. "I don't see him much. He's only twelve, and even though he's her real son, Mother won't often allow him to come home."

I noted the emphasis on the word "real."

"Why?"

Bran's sleek black eyebrows drew down over those Crayola eyes. His mouth opened, then snapped shut as though the words he was trying to dredge came from a faraway place. "Tony's young." He gave a careless half-shrug. "Too young to be of much use to my mother. Not yet anyway. And she places little value on anything that isn't useful."

I decided I didn't much like Bran's mom. Not if she treated a twelve-year-old kid that way. And certainly not when talking about her made Bran's mouth go all hard like that.

As if it could sense our change in mood, the wind shifted direction. Cold tendrils filtered through the mild evening air, bearing aloft the heavy smell of rain. In the distance, a bank of ominous clouds boiled over the top of a mountain, devouring its peak. As Bran squinted at the gray-white mass, I could see an unease lurking behind his eyes. He turned back to me and plastered on a smile. But it didn't touch his eyes. Unlike the ones before.

"Rain's coming. Shall we go?"

Standing, he dusted off his palms. I grabbed the offered hand. He pulled me to my feet, but as I stood, I realized one of my legs had gone to sleep. Bran steadied me as it crumpled.

I'd never been this close to a boy before and I wanted to freeze the moment. To bank it against the frightening, unknown void that my life had so recently become.

I memorized the rasp of his calloused palm on my bare skin. The bleating of sheep and the rush of wind as it curled around us. When I breathed in, I could smell him. Bran Cameron. Clean cotton and fresh-cut wood. Saddle oil and sun-warmed skin that somehow reminded me of toasted marshmallows that dissolved melty and delicious on your tongue.

"Hope." Bran's voice sounded oddly husky as I opened my eyes and looked up into his. "I want you to know that I—I've truly enjoyed today. It . . . This . . . was real. For me at least. Don't forget that."

Me? Ever forget *this* day? Unlikely.

Before I could utterly embarrass myself and beg to stay just a little longer, a crackling came from the underbrush behind us. Our heads whipped toward the sound as a large, rust-colored deer tiptoed out. A gangly, spotted fawn followed, nosing under his mother's belly.

Bran's grip tightened on my wrists. Bound together, we didn't move a hair as the doe raised a slender head and blinked at us with lashes so lovely, they seemed fake. Eventually, sensing we were no threat, her velvety ears twitched. She bent to nibble at the tough grass. The baby shifted with his mother's movements, struggling to stay attached. Spellbound, we watched him totter on spindly, impossibly thin legs.

Bran turned to me with a joyous grin. At the motion, the doe's head shot up. In a flicker of white tails, both animals were gone.

I exhaled, ready with a joke about Bran's camera and how he wasn't such a great stalker after all. But the words died when his hypnotic eyes searched mine.

"So beautiful," he whispered.

He meant the deer—I knew that. But for an instant . . . a tiny space in time . . . it almost felt like he was talking about me.

"Camera." I blurted. "You . . . no camera."

When he grinned, I wanted to tumble off the side of the mountain.

"I wish," he started, then shook his head.

We were so close, I could smell mint toothpaste and sun-kissed skin as his breath brushed across my lips.

My eyes closed. Adrenaline shot through every cell in my body. Everything else fell away. My chest tightened. But this wasn't fear. Well, it was. But not scary-frightening. No. Scary-exhilarating. Scary-wonderful. *He's going to kiss me. My very first kiss.*

Bran's chest moved in a quiet sigh that I felt more than

heard. His hands tightened on my skin. My breath hitched, and I barely had time to think, *Ohh . . . this is it,* before he stepped back and let his hands drop, the moment lost forever, except in my imagination.

CHAPTER 15

Doug's shy, baritone laugh filled the library as I practiced walking . . . again. I was getting better, though the gown I was using while Moira finished our actual costumes was way too long.

"The trouble is," Doug said, "you're swinging your arms like an ape. Women don't walk that way in the past. Here, Hope. Let me show you."

The big guy pressed his palms together at waist height and made a curiously graceful turn about the room. "See? Don't use your arms to balance. Just kick the hem out as you walk."

Phoebe snorted. "No way, babe. I'm asking Gran to take our hems up. Hope will trip a million times if she has to do it like that."

"She can't let her ankles show." Doug dropped onto a squishy sofa beside her. "You either, come to that. You'll drive the lads crazy. Or else they'll jail you for a harlot." He sighed in false annoyance. "Then I'd have to go crack some medieval skulls. And who has the time?"

Phoebe leaned over and kissed the tip of Doug's long nose. My throat tightened as I watched them exchange a tender grin. At first glance, they didn't seem to work as a couple at all. Phoebe's tiny delicacy against Doug's brawn. But when he told me the story of how they'd met, I realized I'd never met two people more perfectly matched.

"It was my first day at school after Lu brought me to live at Christopher Manor." Doug's hands had flown over the keys of his laptop as we sat alone together in the library. I'd never seen anyone compartmentalize so completely, doing three or four things at once with absolute precision. "Well, ye'll notice there aren't a lot of people here with my skin color? My mum was from Senegal, see, and while in Edinburgh there were plenty of kids like me, here . . ." He shrugged. "Add in that I was already a foot taller than anyone else in my year, and, well, I caught the attention of some of the older lads."

Phoebe entered. She stayed unusually quiet as Doug spun his tale. But she stood behind him, her fingers curled around his shoulders as he typed.

"They surrounded me on the playground. I was crying, missing my mum. Big as I was, it didn't occur to me I could've beaten them senseless."

"And that's the truth of it," Phoebe interjected. "Could've smashed them to pulp had he not been so gentle."

"All of a sudden," Doug said, "this tiny creature comes wading into the crowd, braids flying, yellow lunch box swinging in a mad arc. Let's just say some of those brats lost their milk teeth that day."

He smiled at me over her head. "She passed me a note in class the next day. It said 'Will you marry me? Check yes or no.' Of course, I checked yes so hard it tore the paper."

"Made you fall in love with me, though, didn't I?" Phoebe said.

"Aye." He tugged her into his lap. "I guess you did at that."

They giggled together, their warmth so genuine, it flowed over me like a summer wind. I turned away, knowing I'd never experience a love like that. One built on that kind of shared history.

My mind flipped back to those moments at the river when Bran Cameron and I had said goodbye. The entire ride down the mountain, I'd felt like an idiot for being disappointed. I mean, why on earth would someone like Bran Cameron kiss *me?* He was just being nice because I'd helped him. That was it. Still, when we parted, he'd stared down at me with an odd look I was still trying to interpret.

The next day, Lucinda, Mac, and Moira left for Edinburgh on some business they wouldn't share, while Phoebe and Doug traipsed down to the village for lunch and some alone time. Collum? Who knew where *he* was. Probably eviscerating some poor, innocent target dummy with his big, shiny sword.

Just before they left, Lucinda had entered the library, where I lay sprawled on the tatty leather sofa, idly skimming through yet another description of the coronation of Henry II and Eleanor of Aquitaine.

"Here," she'd said, placing a stack of leather-bound books on the long table. "Read through these while we're gone. I believe they may answer some of your questions and give you a better background on what the early Viators faced."

When she was gone, I realized my aunt looked even worse than before. Drawn, and so, so pale.

Unsettled, I moved to the table and began thumbing through the journals. They began with Jonathan Carlyle, son of the Viators' founder, and my mom's great-grandfather. Though difficult to follow at first, I was soon tearing through the looping Victorian script.

January 1895. Tesla's machines are a marvel. To think technology could come so far. Julia understands it better than I. My darling bride has an acute mind, while mine is that of a plodding historian. Nikola believes his alternating current disrupts the strange power flowing through the cavern below, causing the cyclonic rift. He is less certain of the opal's significance. Yet after MacPherson's illness, we dare not travel without one.

Had we only known. I can hardly bear to render this account. I do so now only to warn future travelers.

My father, Dr. Alvarez, and Julia's brother, Luis, were due back. Three days is all the time this majestic power will lend. I was almost to the cavern when I heard the cries and the rush of the dark cyclone.

As I entered the cave, the sight before me was unimaginable. My father, on his knees with a rucksack clenched in one hand, weeping like a child. Julia's father, on his feet, Luis clasped to his breast. And I—I can barely put to page what I saw next.

I'm ashamed to admit my knees went weak. For though Julia's father held on to his son desperately as he howled his grief, from the waist down my beloved's brother was simply gone, as if a cosmic force had ripped him in half. Blood rained down from Luis's lifeless torso. And, as I looked on in utter horror, his entrails slithered out upon the tiles. I heard Julia's tread upon the stair, heavy with our first child. I could not let her *see such a terrible thing. I could scarcely stand it myself. What awful power do we play with?*

I frowned as I turned to the next entry, dated five years later. From what I could tell, Dr. Alvarez had already left the group, who now called themselves Viators. Julia's idea, and something of a joke to the early travelers. At first, Jonathan spoke only of the advancements his friend Tesla had made with the machines. A ticker tape now sprouted from the back of one of the mechanisms, which displayed the pulses in the lines of power. Matching the pulses with a log of their previous travels, they could determine the general place and era in which they would arrive.

I skimmed through several volumes. Jonathan eventually regained his sense of humor and wonder at the sights they encountered, and I fell again under his spell as he described what they'd seen and the riches they brought back.

Partway through 1910, the handwriting changed. Blots of ink now dotted the pages. Some of the lines were smeary and smudged, as if they'd gotten wet. My gut knotted as I deciphered the cramped writing.

On a journey a hundred years into their past, husband and wife — along with their friend Archie McPherson — found themselves near a tiny, secluded loch only a few miles from their current home. Though they'd traveled there to see a local baron about some kind of painting they hoped to purchase, the three were delighted when they arrived in the year

1801, close to the exact spot on which—a hundred years in the future—they would build a holiday cottage. As the sun shone down on the trio, they decided to play hooky and simply enjoy the beauty of the as-yet-unspoiled countryside.

March 17, 1910. I report the account, Jonathan wrote, *to warn of the evil we've unleashed. I shall not look upon my Julia's face again until I can repair what we have broken. She has left, claiming she cannot bear to be near me without thinking of them. Our precious girls. We played God that day. And now we suffer for our sin. I must find it. This mysterious opal Tesla believes is the key. I must find the stone and get them back. For I think Julia shall die without them.*

Even blurry and dotted with water marks, Jonathan's words made my mouth go dry. My tongue stuck to the roof of my mouth and I was desperate for a drink. But I couldn't pull myself away. I had to finish it.

My Julia had looked so merry that morning. In her peasant's gown, she was as beautiful as the day we wed. I played the gallant, casting my cloak on the ground for her to sit upon. Afterward, Archie and I stripped to our undergarments and went splashing into the loch, shouting like children at the cold.

It was she who first pointed out the young saplings near the water. In our own time, the trees had grown gnarled and ancient. An eyesore. "You know," Julia mused as we munched on freshly picked blueberries that burst in our mouths like a gift from summer herself, "that is the very tree from which our impetuous Penelope will fall."

Penny's arm had never healed right, and I'd always resented those blasted trees.

"Well, then." I stood and in amused retribution wrenched one of the infant trees from the ground. Not to be outdone, Archie did the same to its sister, who'd dared drop a hornet's nest on us during a summer picnic three years later. "That's done for them, I'd say."

Julia, do you remember how you kissed me then? With the summer sun bright on our hair and the sweet juice on our lips?

I will never be that warm again. Oh, that I could take it back. Holy Father, let us take back that one reckless moment.

Home. Thrilled as ever to be safe and of sound limb in our loving house, we flew upstairs, *caring not that we had played truant, without thought to our mission. If only we had gone on that long walk to the baron's home instead of dripping water on the carpet, all of us sun browned from our lazy follies. With Archie following, Julia and I called out to our children.*

The next few lines were too smeared to read. I skipped ahead, though a cold foreboding crept up my legs as I perched on the edge of a deep leather chair.

My mother and our Henry met us at the top. Our son had grown tall and straight as a sword over the summer. Oh, how his young face lit to see his mother so sunburned and jolly. He lived for the day I would take him on his first journey, two years hence, when he turned sixteen.

"Wherever are the girls?" Julia asked, puzzled. Unusual, their absence. Normally they were first to greet us, begging to view the trinkets and treasures we brought back. Bubbly Catherine, who at twelve already cared far too much for boys and pretty dresses. And Penelope. Only ten and already a little scholar.

"Yes," Archie called. "I've brought Penny a fern to identify."

"Father!" Henry's face, aghast and suddenly pale. My mother's hand flew to her mouth.

"What's happened to the girls?" I demanded. "Tell us."

It couldn't have been serious. Only three days had passed, and surely they would have informed us at once.

"Are they ill?" My voice sounded hollow, as if it came from the bottom of a well.

"But, Father . . . Mother?" I remember, quite clearly, hearing the tremor in my son's voice. "Why would you say such things, when my sisters have been dead these two years?"

I flinched at the sound of a door closing nearby. Someone was back, but I had to know what happened. I traced a finger over the bottom of the page where the lines had been crossed out with such vehemence, the thick vellum was ripped. I had a hard time swallowing as I turned to the slashed, crabbed writing that followed.

Archie rode for the loch as if the hounds of hell were at his heels. Julia and I stayed behind, begging my mother for an explanation.

As she spoke in a tight, choked voice, my mind whipped back to the day, two winters past, when my sweet girls—skating alone on the frozen loch—had fallen through the ice.

"No!" Julia insisted. "No. They pulled themselves out. I remember it well. A small incident, nothing more. They were but wet and chilled. Stop this insanity! Why do you keep shaking your head at me like that?"

My mother lost the ability to speak and fled our chamber in tears. When Archie returned, his face was the color of chalk. I wanted to pull him aside, but Julia wouldn't have it.

Our friend tried to be brave as he explained that the trees we'd pulled from the earth in that previous time were gone. Those mighty oaks did not exist in this time. I stumbled *backward as though he'd struck me when he whispered, "The roots, man. Don't you remember? The roots had weakened the ice near the shore. The girls were able to break free and wade to safety because of the roots. Without them, the ice was too thick near the edge, and . . ."*

I fell to my knees before my beloved as the truth struck home. "Forgive me," I whispered. "May God forgive us all, for we've killed our sweet girls."

I sat back hard in the chair, hand covering my mouth.

"Read it, did you?"

I jumped up. I hadn't heard Collum enter. Tears blurred his features as I gulped. "I—I can't believe it. It's so awful. Those poor people."

I glanced at the portrait next to the mantle. Jonathan's family, still whole and happy. I tore my eyes away, unable to bear looking at the faces of the cheerful little girls.

Collum didn't move from his spot near the fireplace, lit even in summer against the chill evenings. "Read the rest," he said quietly. "It's on the last page."

Hesitant, I picked up the book and flipped through a series of blank pages until I reached the final one, written in Jonathan's looping scrawl. It held only a few words.

Mea culpa. Mea culpa. Mea maxima culpa.

"My fault," I whispered, translating the Latin phrase. "My fault. My most grievous fault."

And just below.

Must find the Nonius Stone. Tesla says it's the only way.

I turned back to Collum, but he was frowning down into the flames. I knew what he was thinking. The Nonius Stone. If his father was still alive, it was the only thing that might save him.

"But doesn't this prove that anything we touch could affect the timeline?" I asked.

"Unlikely," he said. "Other than this, and the King John treasure debacle, we haven't found that to be the case. The Carlyles were too close to their own time. And on their own property. Plus, they made a deliberate change. But it doesn't mean we aren't very, very careful."

At my horrified expression, he sighed and replaced the poker. Sitting, he scooted his chair close, until our knees were almost touching.

"What if I mess everything up? I mean, I have no idea what I'm doing, Collum. What if—"

"Hey," he said, shocking the tears away when he took my cold hands between his own. His level, serious gaze captured mine. "You'll be fine. You're smart. Smarter than anyone I've ever known. And Phoebe and I will be with you. I—we—will keep you safe."

"But—"

"No," he interrupted. "We need you, Hope. And that's the end of it."

Collum withdrew a soft, worn handkerchief. With gentle swipes, he dried my cheeks. Then, as if startled by his own kindness, abruptly stood.

I shivered and watched him go.

CHAPTER 16

Just before dawn, in the chamber deep beneath the mountain, everyone said their goodbyes. No fog machine this time, though it was cold enough that our breaths streamed out to twine above our heads and snag briefly on the neon strands.

"It's a go," Doug huffed as he pounded down the steps. "Lines 212, 486, 510, on the latitude. Lines 101, 419, 771 on longitude. Fits with the location. Forested area several miles outside London. Same sequence as when you all went before, Lu, so the date checks out."

"You have your lodestones?" Moira's eyes brimmed as she snipped a thread here and checked a seam there. "Phee? You know how forgetful you are."

"Gran." Phoebe jangled the bracelet on her wrist before pulling her grandmother into a fierce hug. "Hope has her necklace, and Col his ring. And we've the extra bracelet for Sarah. Don't worry about us. We're good, aye?"

I squeezed the lump of the opal pendant concealed

beneath the ruby bodice of my gown, reassuring myself it was still there.

Standing alone, I shifted my weight from one boot-clad foot to the other. Ran a finger over the intricate black embroidery bordering the round neckline. Tugged at the scarlet ribbons that laced up the sides and cinched the cream-colored sleeves to the bodice. The long folds of midnight-blue wool that made up the skirt swished around my stockinged legs as I forced my knees to stop shaking.

Once we . . . arrived, we'd walk a thin line. Not draw attention to ourselves, yet appear wealthy enough so that doors would open for us.

As I huddled inside my warm cloak, my teeth chattered. Collum strode toward the center of the chamber and gestured for me to follow. "Ready?"

"Ready as you can get to travel through time, I suppose." I muttered though paralyzed lips.

Collum looked like an extra in a Robin Hood movie, with his father's gladiator sword strapped to his side and the thick leather belt cinched around a cobalt-blue tunic. He gave me a quick once-over that gained me a grudging nod of approval. I reached for the water skin of toughened hide that hung at my hip, attempting to wash away the taste of ancient stone and ghosts.

"You should know"—Collum flicked a glance from under his blond lashes—"the journey itself can be a bit unsettling. Particularly your first. But we'll be there with you on the other side, so try not to panic."

Still quaking like underdone egg custard, I managed to mumble, "Sure. Yeah. No problem."

"It's time," Lucinda called.

Doug wrapped Phoebe in his massive arms, so that her feet dangled inches from the ground as he rocked her gently back and forth. Bran Cameron's face flickered through my head as I watched, and allowed myself an instant of self pity.

If Collum and I looked like kids playing dress-up, Phoebe was utterly transformed. Since spiky blue hair might draw some attention our way, my friend now wore an auburn wig, braided and coiled behind her head. The eyebrow stud was gone, of course, and her small, pointed face was blotchy as she took her place next to Collum and me. Doug's whiskey-colored eyes stayed fixed on her as he escorted a sniffling Moira to the steps.

Mac's face crinkled as he approached. "You stay close to Collum, lass," he said to me. "And bring yerself home safe, aye?"

Mute, I could only nod.

With a final squeeze, he dropped my hand and joined Lucinda and Moira on the staircase. Only Doug now remained in the chamber, checking his watch and reviewing the dials on Tesla's machine. My stomach was doing backflips, and I wasn't sure I could hold down the breakfast Moira had forced on us an hour earlier. Collum's hands shook as he worried the opal ring on his finger. Seeing him nervous made it better. And worse.

Lucinda's gaze fixed on mine. *Bring her back,* she mouthed.

I managed to nod, but fear was starting to take over as purple electricity popped and crackled around the mushroom tops of Tesla's machines. Building. Growing. Condensing.

No. I—I don't want to do this. I want to go home. Please. The words died before they reached my tongue, my body frozen in place.

"Okay, guys," Doug yelled over the increasing whine. "The sun will rise at 0750 on December 6. That's when the pattern will repeat. I'll power up the machine at that exact moment to bring you home." As he looked at Phoebe he tapped two fingers to his heart. "You'll be there? Promise?"

"On my lunch box," Phoebe croaked.

Doug smiled though his face had gone bleak and scared. "Good. Then I won't worry a bit." He took a breath. "Here we go. Three . . . two . . . one."

A click as Doug flipped the toggle switch on the back of the master machine.

No. No. No!

Too late.

The two beams blasted toward us, meeting just over our heads in a cataclysmic clash.

Funny, I'd almost grown used to the low pulse of energy that flowed through the chamber. The interruption, the sudden absence, shook me to the bone. It grated along every nerve ending. Doug bolted for the staircase as the incredible power of the ley lines—blocked from their natural flow by Tesla's current—began circling us.

The vortex of energy whirled higher and higher. I couldn't see the ley lines. Not exactly. But I could feel the power rage around the unnatural disruption that encased us, angry and immutable.

A sound like the cracking of the earth's crust screamed in my head. I clamped my hands over my ears, desperate to block it. Warm blood drizzled from my nostrils. "Oh God!"

"Don't fight it," Collum called over the noise. "Makes it worse. Relax and let it take you."

Phoebe's freckles stood out in 3-D. She pulled me close to yell in my ear. "Don't worry. Gran claims it's like childbirth. Afterward, you barely remember the pain."

Sweat slicked the back of my neck. *Childbirth? Oh sweet Moses. I want out. I can't do this. No way. No freaking way. Let me . . .*

Out.

I was wrenched upward and into a darkness so dense, it seemed to leech the blood from my veins and peel the skin from my flesh. Tumbling, falling—endlessly falling—through a living entity of blackness. It surrounded me. Choked me. The nightmare tree rose up before me. Black spiky branches reached down to stab at me. They snatched me, hoisting me high into an inky sky. I crashed through the branches, frozen wood slamming into my flesh as it stuffed me into its mouth. I was back inside. Things crawled in my hair and down the back of my dress. I shrieked. I screamed and sobbed and fought. But no one could hear me.

Then my descent halted sickeningly. Before I could orient

myself, I was hurtling backwards. Faster and faster. My hair lashed at my face. My stomach heaved as colors and spears of light surrounded me. Shades of plum and green and yellow. The colors of death and decay.

Faces appeared and disappeared. Fat-cheeked babies that morphed into crumbling skulls in an instant. Millions of faces. An unending stream of shrieking mouths on either side. I closed my eyes, or thought I did. But death was everywhere.

I scrambled for something—anything—to hold on to. But there was nothing. I was nothing. A microbe. A grain of sand on a beach surrounded by a dry ocean.

Then, the pain, as I slammed through what felt like the world's largest plate-glass window. Except I was the one who shattered into a million pieces.

Blood boiled in my veins. My joints flexed into unnatural poses. The pain . . . Oh God, the pain.

Help me. Help.

Everything sped by in swirls of green and white and brown. Cold air washed my skin. Seared my lungs.

My lungs! I'm breathing.

I filled my chest with the glorious taste of air. Blessed oxygen raced to my starving cells, and slowly I became aware of cold, hard earth beneath my back.

I cracked an eyelid. Stark, rosy light sliced into my skull, and I squeezed it shut again. Groaning, I rolled to my side and puked till I thought I might die.

When the heaving slowed, I peered through watering

eyes to see Collum crawling across a bare forest clearing toward me. A strange purple light flickered over him, dissipating as I watched. Closer to me, Phoebe lay splayed on the ground, the same lavender haze fading from her skin. As I inched across the cold earth, the last remnants of the tinted light arced off my fingertips, then disappeared.

When I reached my friend, I swiped at the blood beneath my nose and shook her. "Phoebe! Can you hear me?"

She moaned and began to stir. I rolled her away just in time.

"Ugh." Wiping her mouth, she scooted away from the disgusting mess, moaning, "Hope? You all right, then?"

I collapsed onto my side, arms no longer able to hold me up. "Yeah. Though it would've been nice if someone had warned me"—I shuddered as my gut gave a final twinge—"about the rotting baby heads."

Phoebe peeked through one bleary eye. "Uh . . . rotting baby heads?"

"No one's experience is the same," Collum explained, his voice hoarse. "That's why we didn't warn you. But the first time is always the hardest. The next time won't be quite so bad."

"Well, jeez," I muttered. "Thank God for small favors."

CHAPTER 17

FINALLY RECOVERED ENOUGH TO STAND, WE RETREATED from the eerie glade and began to slog through the snow-laden, primeval forest. New sunlight glittered pink and gold on chittering limbs. I breathed in the forest scents of ice and wet wood and stillness. So fresh and clear, I tried not to think about how no one in a thousand years had tasted air like this.

I looked back only once. The little rise, surrounded by a perfect circle of ancient oaks, pulsed with a sleepy power. Nothing littered the bare earth inside. Not a weed. Not a leaf. Not even a fleck of snow, as though it didn't answer to natural law.

"According to the research, the locals believe this part of the forest is haunted," Collum said, noticing my look. "Which is good for us."

I'd read about places in the woods where even today people didn't venture. I wondered if some of those dark areas were nodes, other places where ley lines crossed. Maybe the spooky feelings people reported were the unseen power of the earth warning them away.

Collum forged ahead, breaking a trail. I followed, zombie-like. Sure, my cheeks were already burning from the cold. And snow squeaked under my boots. And I could hear the birds waking in the dawn light. But none of it seemed real. How could it?

"I know how you feel." Phoebe's breath puffed out in a white cloud as she stomped along beside me. "Bloody bizarre, right?"

I snorted. "You could say that."

"Well, I cried like a baby the first time, so you're doing better than me."

I *felt* like crying. But Collum had set a brutal pace, and it took all I had to keep up.

At the rutted road that twisted through the frigid forest, we hitched a ride with a farm family headed for London. It took a lot of coaxing, and some coins had changed hands. But soon we were perched on a wagon laden with winter root vegetables. Collum did all the talking at first. But gradually I joined in. When the "thees," "thous" and "wherefores" sprang naturally from my lips, I felt a pang of gratitude for my mother's insistence that I master all those archaic languages. Still . . .

If you'd just told me, Mom, maybe it would've been different. Maybe I would've been different.

We had so little to go on.

My hands tightened on a basket of turnips. *Well, I'm here now, aren't I? And I'm coming for you.*

Collum rode up on the wooden bench beside the farmer. I began to chat, carefully, with his wife. Phoebe stayed quiet, still uncomfortable with the twisty medieval dialect. Two ratty-haired children perched atop a crate of wormy apples, casting shy glances our way.

"'Twill be our last trip to town before the roads close for winter," the woman offered. "But my John just had to come see the new king crowned. Wanted the little ones to see it too."

She sighed and settled her thin frame more comfortably against the hard wagon bed. "I pray to all the saints this winter won't be hard as the last. We lost our good milk goat. And our youngest babe."

The young woman's prematurely weathered face never changed as she spoke. Phoebe and I exchanged a look, marveling at a time when the loss of livestock and a child were uttered in the same breath. In this era, however, losing a goat would likely cause more suffering. She could always have more children.

We rested as best we could, jouncing along the nearly impassable road. One of the children, a little girl with a perpetually runny nose, crept closer and was soon fussing with Phoebe's braids. I shut my eyes, the sun winking in orange patterns against my lids, and listened to the cadence of the conversation going on up front.

The sway of the wagon lulled me, and I must've drifted

into a sort of fugue. Tiny nuggets popped up like bubbles in my drowsy mind.

A man's voice, speaking urgently as his strong arms set me on the ground. A whiff of burning that coated my tongue. Shouts. Screams. Someone grabbed my hand, and I began to run.

My eyes popped open. The half dream dissipated, leaving me shaken and strangely hollow. I lurched across the wagon and eased down beside Phoebe. Our feet dangled from the back.

She glanced at me sidelong. "You all right, then, Hope? You look pale as milk."

"I'm fine."

Phoebe raised a skeptical eyebrow, then uncapped a leather flask and handed it to me. "Here, take a drink. It'll help."

I took several long gulps. The slushy water we'd filled from a clear spring burned my throat. "Thanks." I croaked.

"Look"—Phoebe nudged my side—"I know it's hard, yeah? This is my third journey, and it still feels like a dream. Or like I'm inside a play. But you get used to it. I promise."

I snatched another look at the family, the little girl now snuggled in her mother's lap, the older boy at her feet. It struck me suddenly that these people were *dead.* Only dust in the ground in our own time. And yet there they were. The father chatting quietly with Collum. The mother stroking her daughter's hair. How could anyone ever get "used" to something like that?

When we emerged from the forest, the farmer halted. I rose to my feet. Phoebe pulled herself up beside me. Everyone, including the family, gaped at the sight of the walled medieval city lying before us in the distance.

London. 1154.

Wow.

Distant bells chimed the hour, I thought I counted ten peals, though there were so many ringing all at once, it was hard to tell for sure. Tendrils of smoke rose from a thousand fires to coat the sky above the city in a smoggy cloak.

The farmer drew his son up onto the slatted boards between him and Collum. "There she is, boy." The man smoothed his child's rumpled hair. "Londontown. And our good King Henry there to greet us."

"I pray on catchin' a glimpse o' the new queen," the wife said. "Do ye know, we hear she went on Crusade with her first husband, that Frenchie king." Her voice lowered. "They say she rode with her tatties on full display to entertain the troops."

"I heard that too." I agreed, tucking back a grin.

For the first time, the historian in me woke and squirmed with excitement. I was here. I'd traveled through time and space. The possibilities stretched out before me—so many worlds, so many famous people and events.

My jaw dropped as something occurred to me. My mother was a renowned historian, with prestigious awards for her academic publications. Her lectures were booked up months in advance. Reviewers wrote how Sarah Walton's lectures painted such vivid pictures, it was as though she'd seen the history with her own eyes.

I snorted. *Kinda cheated there, didn't you, Mom?*

And now I was seeing it with *my* own eyes. London on the eve of one of the most famous events in English history. The coronation of its greatest royal couple, Henry II and his infamous wife, Eleanor of Aquitaine.

I shook my head. *Unbelievable. Freaking Eleanor of Aquitaine.*

Her fame had endured over a thousand years. Born in 1122 to the Duke of Aquitaine, her only brother had died young, leaving Eleanor the richest heiress in Christendom. At barely fifteen, she'd been married off to the weak and overly pious French heir, who within two weeks would become King Louis VII. By all accounts the marriage had been cold and loveless. Two daughters. No sons. Fictional accounts claim Eleanor and the fiery future king of England had fallen in love at first sight. But it was likely only good politics when she divorced Louis and quickly married Henry.

Still, Eleanor and Henry had been happy for a long time. The eight kids that followed proved that. Until it all came crashing down when Henry hooked up with "Fair Rosamund" Clifford. That did not sit well with the prideful queen, and Eleanor had eventually sent her sons to war against their own father. In punishment, Henry had imprisoned his rebellious queen in a remote castle for sixteen years.

Well, I guess no marriage is perfect.

A squirmy feeling oozed over me. What would happen if—no, when—we brought Mom back? How would my own mother react when she found out another woman had already taken her place?

CHAPTER 18

THE TRAFFIC THICKENED AS WE NEARED THE TOWERING stone walls. The massive construction of gray stone and mortar stretched its strong arms to encase the city like a protective father.

I squirmed in anticipation as we waited in the long line. At the gate, guards searched some of the wagons, but mostly they just waved people through. Fine carriages rolled past us and were admitted with flourishes and deep bows.

Apparently, even in this time, rich people got all the perks.

Everyone relaxed when we were waved through with little more than a glance. Once through the thick gate, we emerged into a fairy tale.

A very stinky, very grungy fairy tale.

The thatched roofs of two- and three-story buildings leaned precariously out over twisting, rutted lanes. Dirty snow still clung to shadows and roofs. The smell caught me off-guard at first, and I had to cover my nose. Rotting garbage and raw sewage. Wet wool and manure. Every so often, the sweet stench of decaying meat. I didn't want to think what kind. All of it overlaid with a pervasive pall of wood smoke that hung in incremental layers in the air around us. As I sucked in the mélange of odors, I frowned. It was bad. Really bad.

"Be glad it's winter," Phoebe said, noticing my expression. "Bet it would knock you to your knees in summer."

I wrinkled my nose. "Right."

The feeling eventually faded as we lurched deeper into medieval London. Vendors shouted wares on every corner. Rags and copper pans. Hot potatoes. Boots. A strong, fishy odor wafted by as we passed a man crying, "Oysters! Get yer oysters here!"

Phoebe and I exchanged a glance. Oysters were one of the things we'd been warned against. Not that I'd ever dream of eating one. They were riddled with typhoid.

Phoebe gave her upper arm a significant rub, where she— like Collum and I—sported brand-new typhoid boosters. I'd had my initial shot two years earlier, when my mother first spoke of taking me on some of her more remote lecture tours. Apparently I'd also been inoculated for smallpox. Though at the time, I'd had no clue. Doug claimed Lucinda had pulled some strings for that one, since the disease was eradicated in our time. I remembered thinking it odd that the "nurse" had come to our house, then had tea with my mother afterward.

Staring now at the crowds and the filth, I was suddenly and deeply grateful for the shots.

Horses and wagons clogged the streets leading to the center of the city. The smell of wet horse and unwashed people grew thicker as we slogged ever forward through the straw-covered muck.

"You don't think about them having traffic jams in the Middle Ages," I said to Phoebe when we stalled for an over-turned cart.

A beefy, red-faced baker doffed his cap to us as we jounced past. We both laughed when his equally rotund wife jabbed him with her twig broom.

At the edge of the great market that packed the yard before St. Paul's Cathedral, we parted ways with the family. Mud squelched under my boots as I gaped up at the famous church. In this time it wasn't yet Christopher Wren's elegant, domed marvel I'd seen in so many photos. That wouldn't be built for hundreds of years. Still, the cathedral's high stone walls and square Norman towers were imposing.

Hundreds of tents and ramshackle booths crammed the vast area before the front entrance. People clogged the straw-strewn, muddy aisles, wrapped to the eyeballs in dark cloaks and nubby scarves. Somewhere, a hammer banged rhythmically on steel. Voices and laughter carried across the space as men tipped horn flasks to their lips and warmed their hands over fires set in iron barrels. Women haggled with vendors. Everywhere people had gathered into loose circles to watch the dozens of performers. Acrobats flipped a woman into the air. A monkey crept into the crowd to steal a farmer's hat. A dwarf offered odds on any newcomer who'd chance wrestling with his burly partner.

It was overwhelming and deafening. The most disgusting, the most beautiful, sight I'd ever seen.

"Wow," I breathed, trying to look everywhere at once. "I mean . . . wow."

Collum's lips twitched as he and Phoebe exchanged a grin. "Aye," he said. "I know."

I jerked as something damp and wooly brushed against my fingers. Glancing down, I saw a dingy sheep nibbling at my cloak. The smell of moldy, wet blankets floated in a cloud around us as a young boy smacked the animal with his crooked staff. It ambled on, unconcerned, joined by a dozen bleating cousins.

"It's like a flea market," I said in wonder, "except instead of tube socks and cheesy artwork, they're selling armor and live sheep."

Phoebe's eyes flicked from one ramshackle booth to the next. "Ohhh, would you look at all this stuff."

"Oh no." Collum snatched the back of Phoebe's cloak as she darted away. "I know that look. Don't even think about it. We're going straight to Mabray House."

Lucinda, Mac, and Moira's previous, unsuccessful trip to London a few months earlier had provided us a place to stay, a rented house, not far from the square. And Moira had tracked down the merchant who'd brokered the deal for the tapestry. For a few coppers, he'd given up the nobleman's name. Unfortunately, the merchant told them, the baron lived far out in the country, nearly to Wales. They'd had no time to get there before the Dim came to take them home.

My mother had last been seen at the massive Baynard's Castle, near the Thames. Historically, Baynards — a private residence of that noble family — was the most elegant castle in London, shadowing even the Tower and Westminster Palace, which had stabled horses and barracked soldiers during the recent civil war. Research claimed Henry and Eleanor had taken it over upon their arrival, gathering their nobility there, while the royal palace of Westminster was made livable again.

Yet the man who'd commissioned the tapestry was named Babcock. Not a member of the wealthy Baynard family at all, as far as we could tell.

Why some stranger would commission a tapestry of my mother in the first place, we didn't know. But with the king and queen's arrival, it was a good bet he'd be back for the coronation. No nobleman would take the chance of snubbing his new monarch.

The big problem was getting inside. Our first choice, posing as the children of a wealthy merchant, held less risk but might open fewer doors. The backup plan involved forged papers that proved we were the children of a minor lord from the far north of England. Moira's intensive research had located a real baron who did indeed have three children and was known to have been something of a hermit.

The second plan was dicey, though. If the nobleman had decided he'd better head down to London to meet the king, or if one of his neighbors knew him or his children by sight, we could end up in a crap-storm of trouble.

"So this house Mac rented . . . ?" I squinted at the rows of two-story wattle-and-daub structures that lined the narrow streets. Each lane twisted and crooked off with little sense of direction. "Do you know where it's located, exactly?"

Collum ignored me as he squinted at one path after another.

"I know we couldn't bring the map," I pressed. "But if you're having trouble, I got a glimpse of it, and—"

"I'll find it."

Phoebe grunted. "Coll, you should listen to Hope. She's got a bloody photographic memory . . . *Hello*. Then we wouldn't have to spend half the day searching."

"Don't say 'bloody,'" Collum said distractedly. "It's not yet in use. And I said I'd find the house, so quit gawking at me. Belongs to some Finnish merchant who rents it out by the year. Comes with a couple of servants to maintain the upkeep too." He set off into the market. "Let's go. We need to get settled. Seventy-two hours, then we have to be back at the clearing. Sunrise on the third day." He glanced up at the smoggy sky. "And this one's half done over."

✦

"The number three has always had significance to the ancients," Doug had told me a few days earlier as he fiddled with the computer keyboard before the great monitor. "Jesus rose on the third day, and so on. But there's one immutable rule. Exactly seventy-two hours from the moment you arrive, the pattern in the ley lines will repeat. I'll power up the device at that exact moment, and the wormhole will open to bring you back. If you miss that window, there's no telling if or when the pattern will come again. You must be back within a few feet from where you started. And you must, *must* be wearing the lodestone."

✦

I trudged after Collum, but a chill raced up my back, thinking about what had happened to Julia Alvarez's brother. According to the journals, the man had lost his stone while carelessly hopping a stream. Though his father had wrapped him in his arms, without a stone on his person Luis Alvarez had been ripped in half trying to get home. If for some reason we didn't make it back to the glade by sunrise on the third day? Poof. Left behind. Just like Michael MacPherson. Just like my mom. I groped for the lodestone snug beneath my bodice and clutched it tight.

At a stall selling braided whips, I felt a tiny twinge of satisfaction when I saw our fearless leader had stopped to ask for directions.

He waved us over. "I have it. Let's get moving."

"Coll," Phoebe wheedled. "Can't we at least grab a bite first? I'm starving."

Collum rubbed the back of his neck. "All right. But make it quick and don't go far." He dug into the leather bag at his belt and handed each of us a few copper coins that resembled squashed, miniature pennies.

Phoebe grinned and gestured for me to follow. "Let's go before he changes his mind. I'm getting some of that meat. Oh, it smells amazing. I just hope it's not goat. I hate goat. Tough as a boot."

At a cooking stand, a man in a filthy apron carved hunks of bloody flesh from a swinging carcass. He threaded strips onto metal skewers, barely letting the flames lick, before sliding them off into the gloved hands of waiting customers.

"No way," I said. "I am not touching that. I'm going to see what else they have."

I edged away, grateful for some space in which to process all this. A heavenly whiff of cinnamon drifted across my path. I followed it to a booth manned by a stout kerchiefed woman who slid a wooden paddle into a round clay oven, then dumped a load of lumpy pastries on the counter.

"Apple tarts here! Get them while they're hot."

In moments, I had one of the steaming pastries in hand. It was sticky with honey, and as I took a huge bite, the dough flaked on my lips. Bitter, scalding juice ran down my chin. I gasped and glanced around for the napkin dispenser.

That's when it really hit me.

No napkins.

No napkins, 'cause there's no paper. There's parchment, scrubbed and scraped animal hide. But even that's for scribes, priests, and the very rich. No newspapers. No Post-it notes. No magazines or notebooks.

Oh God. No toilet paper.

I had a sudden, horrifying realization of what it meant to be "on the rag." Bits of pastry flew from my lips as a hysterical bark of laughter popped out. My gaze lit on a tiny girl who crouched nearby, staring at me through a tangle of filthy blond curls. Raw sores pocked her thin mouth. She shivered in tattered, stained clothes.

Her crusty eyes were fixed on the food in my hand.

"Here." I forced down the bite in my mouth and held the rest out to her. "You can have it."

She hesitated, her wild eyes roving all around before she snatched the pastry and bolted. Without a word, she crammed half of the steaming thing in her mouth. Shivers danced across my skin as I saw a gang of rough little boys skim through the crowd after her as she raced away. Suddenly, I didn't want to be alone anymore.

"Phoebe?" My voice sounded screechy.

I turned and scanned the crowd for my friends. People with dirty hair, pitted faces, and brown teeth blurred around me as I tracked back the way I thought I'd come. The jumbled market looked the same in all directions. I began to shove through the crush of reeking strangers, stumbling over my long skirts.

"Collum." Terror rose in me, hot and fast. "Phoebe!"

I froze, immobile. My friends were gone.

CHAPTER 19

LOST. ALONE. AND WALLED IN BY A MASS OF PEOPLE WHO were long dead, I nearly lost it. What I *wanted* to do was shut down, curl into a tiny ball, and start rocking back and forth in the mud.

Get ahold of yourself, Walton. You're okay. They probably went to the house. That's it, just keep walking. You'll be fine.

Gritting my teeth, I moved out to the street. A quick glance at the smoggy sky didn't help. I *thought* my path had taken me east of the market, but I couldn't be sure.

The houses in this area loomed larger than those near Westminster. The streets were wider, cleaner. Here and there, solid-looking three-story buildings had been constructed of new stone, instead of straw-infused mud and wood. A squeak of ropes came from overhead, and I looked up to see a servant hauling in laundry from lines strung across the road, between upper floors.

"Hello," I shouted. "Please? Can you help—"

A crack ricocheted through the empty street as the shutter slammed.

"... me." I whispered to the empty air.

Loneliness crashed over me, and suddenly all I wanted was to go home. Not some rented hovel in this godforsaken place. Not my aunt's spook-house of a manor. *Home* home.

Really? The voice inside me sneered. *And what would you do there, huh? Stay with Mother Bea? Bow down and just take all her abuse until your dad and Stella come home? Then what? Could you face it? Waking up every morning of every day for the rest of your life knowing you could've saved your mom if you hadn't been such a coward?*

I knew there was only one answer to that question.

Straightening, I inhaled, filling my lungs with smoke-tinged air. My eyes closed instinctively as every map of medieval London I'd ever seen began to reel out from the files in my mind. My fingertips twitched as I discarded one after the other until the one Collum had been studying appeared. I blinked, the map now layered across my vision like a translucent film.

Mabray House. I pivoted to the left. *That way.* Steadier, I marched off down the muddy street. Then I heard the scream.

❦

"I assume," Lucinda had said over cups of strong, sugared tea. "That you've heard of the Grandfather Paradox? The theory which posits that a man traveling through time cannot affect major events of the past, even if he tries to do so?"

She took a sip of the steaming liquid. "Ah. Good. Well,

as you now know from Jonathan's journals, there are limits to that theory. But allow me to reiterate anyway. If a man wished to go back in time to kill his own grandfather, it would not be possible. Nature would find a way to prevent such a deed, since if he killed his ancestor, the man would not exist to travel back in the first place. Do you see? Now, when it comes to the native people, we are very careful what we do . . . And even more cautious with what we do not do. By the tenets of the Grandfather Paradox, if you are foolish enough to interfere with the course of events, it means you were destined to do so. Do you take my meaning?"

As my aunt's spoon clinked in her cup, I'd tried to process this new information. If someone was supposed to interfere with past events, did that mean they were destined to be in that place and time? My brain twinged, trying to wrap itself around the implications.

"When Celia was with us," Lucinda went on, "she claimed the Timeslippers were trying to push the boundaries of the Grandfather Paradox. Fortunately, the Dim limits them as well. Like us, they cannot force it open to a specific time or place. However, with Tesla's designs, if they locate the Nonius Stone, that could change.

"It's why we must find it before—" She gave a sudden, violent yawn. When it passed, my aunt had peered at me through watering eyes. "Forgive me. I seem to be a bit fatigued."

"That's okay, Aunt Lucinda," I said. "You don't have to—"

"But I do," she said. "So let these words be your guide, Hope. No matter what you see or hear. No matter how badly you may wish it. Do not interfere with — or interject yourself into — any situation that is not of your direct concern."

As she rose to unsteady feet, I'd brushed off her warning. "Don't worry about me, Aunt Lucinda. Danger . . . it's not really my thing."

I let my head roll back on my shoulders until I was staring up at the smoky London sky. Blowing out a breath, I marched over and pounded on the nearest door. "Hello? Help! I think someone needs help out here!"

Nothing.

The cry came again. Louder. More insistent.

"Crap." I groaned. "Crap, crap, crap."

The image of the map faded as I headed toward the sound. At the mouth of the next alley, I crouched behind a pile of straw-lined crates. The sounds of a struggle came from the far end, in the deep shadows cast between two houses.

What am I doing? This is none of my business.

Splintery wood dug into my cheek as I peered around the stack. At first, all I could see were the backs of two men in the black and silver livery of the city guard. Under the control of the London constable, the guard were *supposed* to watch over the citizens, keeping them safe.

Dark cloaks whipped back and forth in the wind that swirled down the passage, bringing the aromas of manure and filthy snow. I couldn't see her. The girl. The men had her pinned against the dead-end wall. Though she sounded calm, she was obviously in a bad spot.

"Please," she said, "just let me go. I do not wish for trouble."

The larger man bent toward her until his head was low enough that I could see the pale part in her brown hair. "Oh, but we like trouble, don't we Charles?"

"Aye, Eustace," he replied. "Trouble sounds just about right."

My jaw clenched. My blood turned to slush.

"Eustace Clarkson"—the girl's voice was louder, though still steady—"my grandfather sent me to deliver this medicament to our new lady queen. I'm sure Her Grace would not wish you to tamper with her servant. If you release me, I shall make no mention of this to her. Or to Captain Lucie."

The boy turned to his friend, and I saw his profile. Bulky. Cropped platinum hair, so light his pink scalp peeked through. A murky pale-gray eye narrowed.

I should run. I should just run away right now.

"You dare threaten me?"

I flinched as Eustace slammed a palm onto the wooden boards next to the girl's face. "It sickens me that our king would allow a Jew to even enter his palace, much less tend his queen."

The muscles stiffened across my back. A burn of anger began to edge out fear as I saw him flash a cruel grin.

Charles cleared his throat nervously. "Eustace, oughten

we get back to our duties? We do not wish to be at odds with Captain Lucie. He could have us dismissed from the city guard. Or worse."

"William Lucie." Eustace spat at the girl's feet. "That piece of shite. Thinks he's better than me because he's the son of the Castellan? He's only a bastard Richard Lucie got off some serving whore. We'll say we were trying to control the crowd. They'll never know we left to chase this one down."

Charles spoke haltingly. "Aye, but Sir Richard claims him as his son, and William is good with a sword. If she tells him—"

"Shut up!" Eustace roared. "Rachel here knows better than to open her pretty Jew mouth, don't you Rachel?"

"Master Eustace." Rachel's voice was so magnificently composed, I found myself rooting for her to spit on him or kick him right where it counted. "If you leave me be, I shall say nothing to Captain Lucie. But let me pass, for Queen Eleanor will not appreciate being made to wait for her draught."

I tensed, ready to back away. If they didn't let the girl go, I'd just beat on doors until someone came and make *them* help her. It was the smart thing to do.

Snarling, Eustace reached down and rucked Rachel's russet skirts up to the waist, baring white legs. She flailed at him, but Charles—apparently forgetting his fear of this Captain Lucie—snatched hold of her thrashing fists and pinned them above her head.

"You know," Eustace purred, "I always wondered what a Jewess had between her legs."

Oh, that's it.

I scrambled to my feet. "Stop it! Leave her alone!"

As they whipped around, my hand slapped over my mouth. I wanted to rip the words from the air, stuff them back down my throat, and scuttle away like a scared rabbit.

Oh sweet Moses, what have I done?

Eustace Clarkson's sword pinged against the stone wall as he ripped it from its hilt. I fumbled for the dagger in my boot, slicing through my skirts as I withdrew it. Eustace advanced down the alley toward me. I backed up as his gaze raked down my body.

Letting go of Rachel, the red-haired, bucktoothed Charles hooted, "Stand down Eus, it's just a wench. A pretty wee black-haired one at that. Now we can each have one."

"Well, well. And so we can." The nasty grin on Eustace's pitted face sent a sharp new fear through me.

Something Phoebe had once said shivered through me. *Be mindful, Hope. Men in the Middle Ages think nothing of rape. In most cases, it's not even a crime.*

At the time, it had seemed ridiculous. But as Eustace sheathed his sword and took another step in my direction, the horror of it suddenly seemed all too real.

Rachel, seeing her shot, took it. She darted between the men and bolted toward the street. As she ran, her enormous golden eyes locked with mine.

Run, she mouthed.

CHAPTER 20

I DIDN'T WAIT TO ASK QUESTIONS.

Rachel shoved the pile of crates over to buy us a few, precious seconds. Her yellow veil billowed behind her as we sprinted through the narrow streets.

"This way," she called.

Heavy footsteps pounded behind us, but I didn't look back. All my attention was focused on not tripping and stabbing myself with the knife still clenched in my hand.

Rachel ducked through a low doorway. The pungency of worked leather. Boxes of scraps and barrels of nails. A cobbler's shop. The owner's eyes went wide as Rachel muttered something to him in a language I thought was very old Hebrew. The man thrust his chin toward the curtained back of the shop.

"Come," Rachel huffed. "There's another way out."

In the tiny rear living quarters, a woman sat on a neatly made bed, nursing a baby. I had a second to register the aromas of fried garlic and onions before racing after Rachel toward the open door of a rear entrance.

I misjudged the door frame's height. My forehead

slammed into the low, wooden beam. Green and white sparks bloomed through my sight. The blade dropped from my suddenly nerveless hand. Two beats later, the blinding pain hit and I nearly went to my knees.

Rachel panted. "We cannot tarry. You know not what Eustace Clarkson is capable of. We must away."

I couldn't leave my dagger behind. Collum had given it to me. Had *trusted* me with it. I bent and groped for it through a nimbus of agony. I nicked my thumb but managed to snatch it up before Rachel dragged me out the door.

A crash, angry yells, and a cry of alarm sounded from inside the shop. Rachel slammed the door shut and wedged a stone in the jamb to slow them. With a firm grip under my elbow, she hauled me with her. At the entrance to the street, I heard the door crash open behind us.

Close. Too close.

Rachel gasped when a cloaked, hooded figure darted toward us from the mouth of the shadowed, narrow alley. I skidded into her back, almost knocking her over. I knew what she was thinking. *Trapped. We're trapped.* But when the person quickly shoved past us, Rachel wasted no time. She grabbed my arm, wrenching me out onto the main street. The ring of swords colliding sounded behind us, and I could barely keep up as Rachel hustled us away. Through a haze of red pain, something about the way the stranger had moved — agile, fluid — niggled at me.

My vision tripled and blurred as Rachel led me down one winding street after another.

When I faltered for the third time, she paused, her face going ashen as she panted. "Oh, I am sorry, mistress. You are bleeding. I — I didn't realize. May I take your blade from you? I'd hate for you to faint and fall upon it."

When I swiped at my eyes to clear them, my fingers came away slick with blood.

"No," I said, "I've got it." Blinking, I blindly fumbled the blade back into its sheath.

Rachel scraped back strands of her chestnut hair before scanning my face. "We should get you home at once, mistress. Where do you live?"

Through pulsing throbs, I told her of Mabray House, and where I thought it was located.

"I know it well." Rachel nodded. "But we must stop that bleeding first."

She guided me to a stack of crates draped with fishing net. Layers of silvery scales littered the muddy ground, reflecting the wintry sky in a dull rainbow. The pain and pervasive stench of rotten fish made my gut roll and heave.

Kneeling before me, the girl's golden-brown eyes examined an area high on the left side of my forehead. "Forgive me, mistress, but you look quite the horror."

Murmuring to herself, she reached into one of several leather bags hanging from the belt circling her narrow waist. Tipping a corked bottle onto soft cloth, she deftly cleaned away the blood and wound a long strip around my head. A fresh green smell of herbs and cut grass soothed the nausea but did little to ease the agony firing through my skull.

"Oh, but you must be in pain, mistress. Back at my grandfather's shop, I have the black poppy. It would help, though it be a far walk."

Black poppy? That was opium. Pure and undistilled. Like taking a shot of heroin. Tempting, but I wasn't quite to that point yet.

"N-no thank you," I managed. "Just give me a minute, please."

It was more than a minute. But eventually my pulse slowed. The pounding receded enough so that I could at least see again. I exhaled long and slow, then turned to Rachel. "Thank you."

"You look better," she said, her anxious expression clearing. "Mistress ah . . ."

"Hope," I told her. "Hope Walton."

"Well, Mistress Walton, I am Rachel bat Judah. And I thank you for saving me." She offered me a hand up. "I think you are new to Londontown, yes?"

I smiled. *Oh, you have no idea.*

I noticed she'd replaced the yellow silk veil. Her gown was lovely, made of fine, moss-colored wool, with amber sleeves that draped elegantly over her slim white hands. As she leaned down to pick up a dropped cloth, a chain of interlocking gold links popped out from inside her bodice. At the end swung a circular pendant set with an opal. A big one.

"It's good to meet you, too, Mistress Rachel." I tore my gaze from the pendant. "And I thank you, too."

We started down the street. Though wobbly at first, I soon got my feet back under me as we strolled across an open, cobbled area. There I got my first real look at the mighty Thames, and the famous London Bridge. The traffic increased as we neared the river. People lined up to cross the rickety wooden passage, while wagons and horses boarded flat-bottomed ferries that crossed dozens of times a day.

"Mistress Rachel!" A rangy soldier in his early twenties thundered up on a sorrel gelding. He dismounted in a leap and flew toward us. I lurched back, ready to run. Then I saw Rachel's expression.

Chain mail glinted on the boy's arms. A hood of the metallic rings draped from the back of his neck over a knee-length surcoat emblazoned with three gold lions on a bed of scarlet.

He looked Rachel frantically up and down. "God's bones, I heard you were running through the streets as though chased by demons. What happened?"

"William." She breathed his name.

The look that passed between them stretched like a piece of taffy, sweet and long. William's eyes ate her up. Their bodies swayed toward each other, as if magnetized. Lined up with a dozen others, waiting to cross the bridge, an old man in a pointed yellow hat grunted and frowned at the two of them. Rachel's gaze broke first. Her eyes darted toward Yellow Hat, and she took a careful step back.

I had to admit, William was cute in a medieval boy-next-door way, with wide-set blue eyes and a nose that looked as though he'd broken it more than once. Rachel became suddenly interested in the cobbled ground. In the late-afternoon light, her cheeks flared red.

A Jewish girl and a Christian soldier in the Middle Ages. Uh oh.

Yellow Hat kept eyeballing them and tugging on his impressive beard.

"Hello," I said to break the awkward silence. "I take it you're William?"

The soldier tore his gaze from Rachel as if he just realized there were other people on the planet.

"Mistress Hope Walton." Rachel hurried to introduce me, hands fluttering. "May I present William Lucie, newly made a sergeant in the queen's service, and . . . my friend."

Something like a growl came from Yellow Hat. Rachel turned and dropped a hasty curtsy in his direction. "Good morrow, Master Yeshova," she called. "Fine weather today, is it not?"

He grumbled a reply but turned back toward the shuffling line.

"Captain Lucie"—Rachel's tone turned carefully formal—"Mistress Walton is new to London. When she became injured, I simply offered my assistance."

Her eyes pleaded with me to go along.

"Yes," I agreed, getting it. "Yes. I fell and hit my head. Rachel here helped me."

William studied me. When his tense features relaxed into a gentle grin, I got it. I understood why Rachel loved him. And oh, it was glaringly obvious he loved her, too. I felt the gentle pulses of electricity just standing near them.

For one instant, my thoughts turned to that moment on the Scottish mountain when Bran Cameron had skimmed the twig of heather behind my ear. I'd thought . . . but, no. That was stupid. I shook my head to dislodge the memory and smiled at William and Rachel.

William Lucie bowed in my direction. "Mistress Walton, if I can ever be of service—"

A wagon driver yelled for us to move on. William glanced toward his horse, his brow crinkled with conflict.

"Go back to your duties, Captain Lucie," Rachel said softly. "We are fine."

The soldier bit down on his lower lip and leaned toward her. When he noticed Master Yeshova's critical observation, he turned his movement into a courtly bow.

"Be careful, Mistress Rachel," he said. "I worry when you roam the streets alone, especially with all these ruffians in town for the coronation."

Rachel's chin lifted. "I can well care for myself, sir."

"I know," he said. "But I would not see harm come to you."

William dragged his eyes from Rachel and bestowed one of his lovely smiles on me. "Well met, Mistress Walton. You won't find a better friend than Mistress Rachel."

He mounted and rode away, his horse's hooves clip-clopping on the cobbles. I looked at Rachel, brows raised. But all her attention was fixed on the retreating boy.

CHAPTER 21

IN THIS SECTION OF THE RIVERFRONT AREA, MANY OF THE large houses boasted stone walls with inset gates that protected the small interior courtyards. The evening air smelled better here, and the streets appeared cleaner.

I shivered as we strolled down the cobbled street, the sharp evening air penetrating cloak and gown to press frozen fingertips along my skin. My cheeks burned with it as the neighborhood around us quieted. In that odd, purplish nonlight of dusk, everything looked surreal and dream-like. Almost too clear to be real.

"So," I said, breaking the awkward silence that had fallen since we left William, "you deliver medicine to the queen?"

"Oh yes." Rachel nodded."My grandfather was once a great physician. In his youth, he studied at the University of Salerno. When our people were forced out of France, they fled here. Though in England he is only allowed to be an apothecary." She frowned at that. "Her Grace's old physician was too ill to travel to England. But Grandfather was once a classmate of his, and recommended him highly to the queen. Today, my *saba* tends an old widower who is near the end. Her Grace knows me, since I've gone with him before, so he sent me in his stead."

I liked her grandfather immediately, a guy who chose to take care of a poor old man instead of a queen.

"What's wrong with Her Grace?"

Rachel chuckled. 'Tis but indigestion. Though she bellows as if she were dying. She's large with the king's second child, you know." Rachel lowered her voice confidentially, but her white teeth gleamed as she grinned. "Do not speak of it, but I heard her confess to Sister Hectare that she worries she'll belch in the archbishop's face when he lays the crown upon her brow."

As we walked, my new friend kept up a running commentary. But all I could think about was my mom, and how she might be close and I'd never know it. She might even live on this street, or just around the corner.

What if she's miles and miles away from here? Or . . . or worse?

"Mistress?"

I was startled out of my stupor. "Please," I said, forcing a smile, "call me Hope. After all, you did save my life today."

"After you stopped Eustace Clarkson from taking *my* honor." Rachel shuddered inside her cloak. "Things have been worse for my people since Will — Captain Lucie — left the city watch for the queen's service. He protected us. Now, for some reason, Eustace has set his sights on me." Her lips thinned in disgust. After a moment, though, she shook herself, as if trying to cast off the horror of what she'd endured. "So, you must be in London for the coronation, then?"

"No. Yes." I stumbled on the uneven stones. I didn't fall, but my boot heel splurched down dead center in a cold pile of horse poop.

Perfect.

I fumbled for our cover story. "We came from the country so my brother can handle some of our father's business. While we're here, however, I hope to find my cousin. Sarah de Carlyle. I know she was in town a few months ago, but . . ."

I trailed off as an insidious hopelessness snaked through me.

How will we ever find her in three days? This place is too big. There're too many people. It's hopeless.

We stopped in front of a green-painted gate set into a rock wall. The words MABRAY HOUSE was chiseled into a flat stone. My stomach coiled into a knot.

Oh God, please let them be here.

"You know," Rachel mused, "I could ask Captain Lucie about your cousin." She tilted her head in thought. "I must make haste now, as I am very late delivering the queen's evening draught. But if you wish, you could come with me when I revisit the queen on the morrow. I do not know your cousin, mind. But the castle servants know everyone. They might be of help."

I blinked at her. The castle. Someone there was bound to have news of her. I beamed at Rachel. "Yes! That's awe—

I mean yes. That would be most welcome. I'm so sorry I made you late. But I would love to go with you. Thank you. Thank you so much."

Rachel grinned and moved as though to embrace me. She checked herself, the smile dropping from her lovely face as she stepped back.

"For-forgive me," she muttered to the ground.

It took me a second to get it.

"No." I reached out and squeezed her in a quick hug. "I don't care what religion we follow. We're friends now, aren't we?"

As I let go, Rachel ducked her head, but not before I saw a tear glimmer behind her lashes. I began to feel lighter than I had in months. I had a lead on my mother, thanks to Rachel. A cold breeze gusted, bringing with it the smell of smoke and sewage, fish and tar and ice. The smells of the medieval world.

Rachel started as a distant bell rang in the gloaming. "Curfew soon," she said. "I must away."

After promising to come by and fetch me in the morning, she hurried off into the vicious London streets. As I watched her go, I thought about what I'd endured in only one day here. I realized Rachel was the bravest person I'd ever met.

Through the gate, I passed an herb garden gone to seed. In the cobbled courtyard, I stared up at the thatched roof and shuttered windows of the half-timbered house. Torches flamed on either side of a green front door. As I raised a hand to knock, the door jerked inward.

Light streamed from behind the familiar form, casting his features into shadow. A profound relief turned my knees to jelly.

"Collum" was all I could manage to say.

He stepped out onto the stoop, arms folded across his chest. His normal irritated demeanor seemed like play time at Chuck E. Cheese compared with this. He squinted, glaring at me. "Where," he asked through stiff lips and clenched jaw, "the bloody *fuck* have you been?"

My head reared back as if he'd slapped me. Before I could respond, before the angry words could leave my lips, he reached out and snatched me to him. Strong arms wrapped me up, pressing me against his chest as he rocked me back and forth, murmuring into my hair. Shocked into an exhausted, melty state, I sighed and let my bruised head rest against him.

As if the embrace caught him by surprise, his arms dropped abruptly to his sides and he stepped back. "Get inside," he said, his eyes scanning the street beyond the gate.

Inside a low-beamed front entrance hall, Collum's eyes lingered on the bandage wrapped around my head. Some of the anger that raged in his eyes softened. "What happened?"

I tried to explain, but the words jumbled on my tongue.

When I swayed, he scooped me up, carrying me like a child past a set of stairs that led up to a second level, and into a larger room where he deposited me in a high-backed chair near a central fire pit. "Jesus, you're a right mess." He thrust a pewter goblet into my hands. "Drink."

Firelight flickered off moldering tapestries. Cobwebby beams disappeared into the shadows above as the swirl of alcohol, cinnamon, and cloves rose up to envelop my face. I clenched the cup, letting the heat soak into my frozen fingers.

"Do you need a doctor?"

"No." My voice came out raspy. "I'm okay. I just—"

We both looked up at the sound of feet pounding down the steps. Before I could blink, Phoebe flung herself at me so hard, I nearly dropped the cup.

"Great fuzzy sheep balls, Hope! We feared you were dead." On her knees at my feet, she looked up into my face. "We looked and looked for you. Collum just got back from searching. I stayed here the last hour, hoping you'd show."

"That's enough," Collum interjected. "She's here now. Give the girl some air."

Phoebe gave my legs another painful squeeze before she stood. Though Collum still looked disgruntled, I grinned up at both of them, feeling stupidly grateful to have real friends for the first time in my life.

When I took a huge gulp, the spicy, pungent liquid scalded my throat.

Phoebe chuckled at my expression. "Mulled wine." She plucked the goblet from my fingers and refilled it from the pitcher warming on a flat stone near the fire. "With cinnamon and cloves. There's beer, but" — she made a face — "it's sore bitter. And when I asked Hilde for some boiled water, she looked at me like I was mental. Told me I could keep the bath water when I was done washing if I liked."

"Who's Hilde?"

"Housekeeper. Comes with the place. Wait till you meet her. Gah, she's a piece of work, that one. And just get your knickers out of that twist, Collum MacPherson. Hope'll tell us what happened when she's ready. Gads, what happened to your head? Oh! You must be starving. Come on."

She tugged me to my feet, chattering as we walked across the flagstone floor toward a wide doorway. I noticed Collum staring at me, his normal dour expression returned.

"Don't mind him," Phoebe said. "He was worried witless, and don't let him tell you different. I knew you'd find your way, though, with that epic brain of yours. But Collum insisted on searching. Kept yammering, 'No man left behind.'"

I giggled at her spot-on impression.

"Tell you true, we were both scared. Almost as bad as when this horrible Spanish Inquisitor bloke tried to arrest Gran for heresy." She patted my hand. "Now, let's get you something to eat. You look fair dreadful."

"Gee, thanks." My hand went to the bandage. My hair poofed over it like a mushroom cap.

Thank God the mirror isn't common yet.

Collum followed at our heels, grumbling under his breath as we passed into a room with a long, ornately carved dining table. Another central pit blazed, sending out tendrils of heat.

Weariness pulled on me like gravity. My feet tangled in my skirts. Stumbling, I caught myself on one of the massive, faded wall tapestries. I looked up to see an ancient ship being dragged down by an enormous kraken while the tiny figures on board screamed in terror.

I knew exactly how they felt.

"Sit. Sit." Phoebe guided me into one of the two carved armchairs near the fire and bustled to a chunky buffet near the far side of the room. The pain was back, and my eyeballs now pulsed with each boom of my heartbeat.

"Here you go." Phoebe handed me a fresh cup of wine, sloshing a few drops of thick red liquid onto my lap. "Tell us, are you all right?"

"I'm fine." I managed a wobbly smile. "Just a headache."

I slumped against the high back of the chair and studied the smoke curling up from the crackling flames. It slithered over blackened beams that crisscrossed the low ceiling, before finding its way out a hole in the roof.

Phoebe pushed open a door near the back of the room and called, "Hilde? Can you bring some food in for my sister?"

The next few swallows went down way better than the first. Warmth spread out from my gut, and I started talking, leaving nothing out. When it was over, I slumped deeper in my chair.

"You took too much risk," Collum spat. "What is the number one rule, eh? Do not interfere with the locals."

"What was she supposed to do, Coll?" Phoebe said. "Let that git rape the girl?"

He mumbled something into his cup.

"That's right," she chastised. "You'd have done the same thing, and you know it. So hush. Hope got us a lead on Sarah. Thanks to her, we have something to go on. Good job, Hope." She saluted me with her cup and took a long, thoughtful draught.

Collum grabbed my shoulders and stared at me intently. "Still," he said, "from now on, you will listen to me, stay *near* me, and follow my rules, understood? You could've been attacked or robbed or." His jaw worked. "Or worse."

My teeth started to chatter at the thought of what nearly *did* happen. I set the cup down quickly before he could notice, and glanced around desperately for some way to hide my shaking hands. A basket of raw, cottony wool sat on the floor beside me. A thin, rounded stalk of wood with a circular base lay on top of the fluff. I picked it up, tied a piece of the wool to the top of the stick, and began rolling it between my palms. A slim strand of attached wool stretched out of the raw material. I twisted. The thick warp of wool began to thin. My hands moved faster and faster as the events of the day blurred in my head.

Never let your hands lay idle, child. A soft, comforting voice filled my mind, bringing with it an odd sense of nostalgia. *Not too quickly, or you shall tangle it.*

"Hope!" Phoebe's voice jerked me back to the smoky room.

I blinked to see her and Collum both gaping at me. No, not at me. At the bundle of wool thread now wrapped around the stalk of wood in my hands. Somehow, I'd turned the messy wad into a lumpy strand of undyed yarn.

"That's brilliant," Phoebe gasped. "You know how to spin wool in the old way? Even Gran can't do that. Sarah taught you, then?"

I stared down at the objects in my lap. My heart was beating too fast as I hurled the spindle, with its untidy new thread, back into the basket. "N-no," I spluttered. "I've never . . . I mean, she didn't . . ."

A door banged open on the far side of the hall. A dumpy woman with apple cheeks and a wide apron waddled toward us, grizzled gray hair peeking from beneath a white cap. She would've looked like the kindly old grandma in a storybook but for the sneer curling her nearly toothless mouth. A skinny girl of eleven or twelve with a long brown braid over each shoulder trotted in her wake, toting a packed tray.

The woman's piggy eyes matched the muddy color of her serving dress. They flicked over us and landed on me. "That her, then?" she said to Collum. "The sister you was looking for?" Hilde paused to drop a perfunctory curtsy before adding, "Milord."

I tensed as Collum's gaze pinned me to the chair. "Aye. Our sister." He made a vague gesture in the woman's direction. "Hope, this is Hilde, the housekeeper. The girl is her granddaughter, Alice."

Hilde took in my stained skirts and bandaged head. "Supper was served long ago. Old Mab has gone to her bed."

I lifted eyebrows at Phoebe, who mouthed, *The cook.*

"Oh, that's okay," I replied, "I can fix my own—"

Hilde cut me off. "No one messes about in Mab's kitchen. Alice, serve the bread and cod." She barely glanced at the girl, who struggled with the heavy tray. "Cold, mind you. I know the archbishop has granted an indulgence to eat meat during the week of the king's coronation. But this house will not break the holy Advent fast for the sake of frivolity."

I rose and hurried over to the girl, attempting to take the wobbling tray before it crashed to the floor. Hilde intercepted me and snatched it from the girl's hands. "Get back and scour them pots, girl. Praise be the saints, you ain't got the sense God gave a goose."

As the girl scuttled past, Hilde cuffed her on the side of the head. The girl whimpered. Phoebe shot to her feet at the same time as I rounded on the old woman.

Collum moved to block the two of us, though his eyes narrowed on the hateful woman. "That will do, Hilde. Good night."

The housekeeper's jaw moved, as though chewing a nugget of undigested food. Oh, how I wanted to smack her.

"This household attends early mass," she said sourly as she slammed the tray onto the table. "We do not break our fast until after." She turned, speaking only to Collum. "I suggest you take your sister to hand, milord. You'd do well to get a tighter rein on her from now on. There are unclean elements roaming this city, and I hear the new king invites even more of them. Until the Godless Jews are scourged from this land, decent *Christian* folk are not safe."

With a harrumph, the odious little woman stomped from the room.

Phoebe looked at me, teeth bared. "Told ya she was a piece of work."

CHAPTER 22

IN THE DARK, SLIMY SKITTERING THINGS CREPT OVER ME, BUT I was too weak to brush them away. My shredded fingertips were bleeding and numb from trying to claw my way out of utter blackness.

A tiny, waking part of me knew I was having the nightmare. I even knew where I was. The small bedchamber at Mabray House. Snuggled under heavy quilts in the narrow bed, Phoebe snoring next to me. I tried to fight my way out of the dream. But it sucked me under like a whirlpool of tar.

A scrabbling sound from outside. A glint of moonlight. Hands reached in. Frosty fingers grasped my wrists.

I jolted awake. Shivering and sweating all at once, I gasped pallid clouds into the air. I eased from under the covers and snatched up the flask on the bedside table. I took a huge slug, then choked.

Wine. *Ugh. How are these people not all drooling alcoholics?*

Still, I downed it, and by the time I woke again, Phoebe was up and gone.

The young girl, Alice, had brought up my gown, all

cleaned and brushed until it looked good as new. Poor thing must've worked all night. Despite the ice that rimmed the wash basin, I managed to clean up and dress myself.

Thanks to Rachel, today we might get closer to finding my mother.

What if she's there? What if we just walk in . . . and there she is?

I knew it wouldn't be that easy. Still, I couldn't help the tiny beacon of hope that lit inside me at the thought. And as I hurried down the stairs, I felt better than I had since we'd arrived.

Halfway down the steps, raised voices filtered out from the dining hall. I paused just outside the half-closed door.

". . . flighty and doesn't understand the risks." Collum's rumble. "We lost a half a day chasing after her. We didn't even have time to search for this Babcock. Running off like that! She'll end up getting us all—"

"Just stop," Phoebe said. "Hope's doing her best. And as a matter of fact, it's *you* who's acting dodgy. You're up to something, Collum Michael MacPherson. And don't try to deny it, because I know you too well."

I filled my lungs and stepped through the door. Collum turned his back to me, but not before I saw the high color in his cheeks. Phoebe crossed the room quickly and took both my hands in her smaller ones.

"You look better today," she said. "And that bruise on your head? Well, it just brings out that purpley tint in those lovely smoke-colored eyes of yours."

"Thanks, I guess?" I made a scrunchy-face at her, then turned to narrow an annoyed glare at Collum's back.

You think I'm flighty? Whatever. Who got us in the castle? Phoebe motioned to the long table set at the front of the room. "The gorgon brought out some kind of fishy stew even I won't touch. But there's bread and cheese. You hungry?"

"Starving."

The bread was gritty and the cheese smelled a bit like feet, but I gobbled both down anyway. I sniffed at the cup Phoebe handed me and grimaced. "Beer?"

She shrugged. "It's that or nothing. I think old Hilde's a bit miffed that we didn't go to mass this morning."

Hilde stomped into the room. "Milord," she muttered, "someone at the door. Says she's here for *her*."

The housekeeper pointed an accusatory finger at me. By the crimson patches on her nonexistent cheekbones, I knew who it must be.

"It is a *Jewess*." She snarled the last word. "Right on the front stoop. Claims she has business here."

"That's because she does," I snapped as I stood, slammed the beer down, and hurried toward the entry hall.

Rachel was shivering outside the front door, muffled head to toe. Snow lay in a thick layer on her shoulders. She'd obviously been standing there a long time.

"Hilde," I asked through clenched teeth, "how long did you leave my guest standing in the snow before you told us she was here?"

Hilde's florid face darkened.

"Do not concern yourself, Mistress Hope," Rachel protested. "Truly. 'Tis no trouble."

"Yes, it is." I glared at the servant. "We should've been told immediately. You let her stay there and freeze on purpose, didn't you?"

Hilde sniffed. "Jews don't feel the cold like Christians."

"Ugh," I said. "You horrible old—"

Rachel interceded, her delicate cheekbones flaming under her hood. "Mistress Hope, perhaps we should away. Queen Eleanor will be expecting her posset."

Hilde flashed me a defiant leer, turned on her heel, and disappeared into the house.

"That was blood—" Phoebe flicked a glance at Rachel and cleared her throat. "That was brilliant, Hope. I'm glad you told the old cow off. Totally worth it, even if we end up with spit soup tonight."

Phoebe stepped forward and enveloped Rachel in one of her exuberant hugs. "I'm Phoebe. Hope's sister. Are you sure you wouldn't like to thaw by the fire, Mistress Rachel?"

Rachel, rattled by the unexpected embrace, shook her head. "No. I—I am not allowed to cross your threshold, Mistress Phoebe, and we must be on our way to Baynard's Castle. Her Grace will be especially anxious today and will need her medicine more than usual. Tonight she'll stay inside the Tower, where I cannot enter, and on the morrow, the coronation."

Collum bowed in Rachel's direction. "I am Hope's

brother, Collum. And as my sisters say, you are welcome here anytime."

Rachel's nodded her thanks and glanced at the sky. "Shall we go?"

As we gathered our cloaks, Collum moved in front of me, eyes narrowed as he peered down into my face.

"What?" I stared back as I wrapped yards of scratchy wool around my neck.

He tapped two fingers against his lips, studying me for a moment. "Nothing. Just try to stay out of trouble."

"Come on, you two," Phoebe called from the stoop.

I hurried out the door, ignoring an uneasy, anxious feeling. Our plan to get into the castle had been flimsy at best. Now we were headed straight to the queen's apartments. If there was anywhere we'd find information about my mother, it would be there. In a moment, Collum followed, and the four of us headed out into a London covered in a new blanket of fluffy white.

CHAPTER 23

THE SUN BLAZED IN SLIVERS FROM BEHIND THE NOW-emptied clouds, glimmering on thatched roofs and the snow that blanketed the ground, covering the mud and muck. London spread out before us, looking like something from a storybook.

Magical.

"It is, isn't it?"

Though I didn't realize I'd said the word aloud, I only nodded while Rachel went on quickly. "On days like this, when the city is so clean and new, I sometimes imagine things aren't so ugly beneath."

Up ahead, Collum howled as Phoebe dumped a handful of snow down the back of his tunic. Rachel and I exchanged a smile. When my new friend tripped over something beneath the snow, I snatched her arm. The pendant I'd seen the day before swung out on a chain between us as she steadied herself.

"Your pendant is lovely. An opal, is it?"

Rachel grimaced. "Yes, though I care not for it. My father

bids me wear it. He is a goldsmith, you see, so it is good advertisement. The stone was a gift from the man I am promised to."

"Promised to?" I said, confused. "You mean William?"

Shocked, she stopped in her tracks.

"Oh no, mistress." Rachel's wide eyes skittered all around to ensure no one was near enough to hear. "Captain Lucie is but a friend. I—I am to wed another. A cousin in Spain, an arrangement made when I was but a child. Once the coronation celebrations are done, my father is taking me to him."

Her head bowed, she fingered the pendant. "This opal is my betrothal gift. My—Isaac's—family trades in rare and valuable stones." Her eyes fixed on the street before us. "It is a good match."

"Oh," I said. "Oh. Well, yes. Yes, I'm sure it is."

I didn't know what else I could possibly say to erase the troubled look Rachel tried so hard to hide. I knew that girls in this time had no choice whatsoever in where they lived or who they married. I knew that love rarely entered the picture. Even grown women were nothing but property, their lives dictated and their fates decided by men.

I quickly changed the subject. "So your father is a goldsmith?"

"Yes," Rachel, obviously relieved, answered. "In fact, on the morrow, my father—along with other leaders of my community—will present their majesties with a special coronation gift. Father is quite pleased with himself. A rare specimen of opal arrived only weeks ago, and he's worked day and night to set the jewel into the hilt of a fine dagger. It's meant to represent the Jews' bond with the new king."

Collum, who obviously had ears like a bat, stopped short and was staring at Rachel as we caught up. His broad cheek-bones, which always looked slightly wind burned, had gone scarlet with cold or excitement.

"Mistress Rachel," he said, hazel eyes intent on the pendant, "I hear that some of the finest stones have a name. Does the one in your father's possession happen to be named, by any chance?"

Phoebe joined our huddle, shifting from foot to foot as people streamed around us toward the castle.

"Well, yes. I believe it does. Father called it the . . ." Rachel frowned, thinking. The three of us leaned toward her as if pulled by a thread. Tendons bulged from Collum's neck, willing the word to come. "I am sorry, but I cannot recall," she said. "The Notharius, perhaps? Something akin to that?"

Air oozed from Collum's lungs as he stepped back. "I knew it."

Phoebe let out a whoop that startled a nearby clerk, causing him to drop his stack of scrolls.

As we continued tramping through wet snow, Collum murmured under his breath to me. "If it really is the Nonius, that would explain why this particular pattern kept repeating."

"What pattern?" I asked, forgetting my irritation at him.

"The ley lines. They kept repeating the sequence to this

exact time and location. It's pure unusual for them to do that. It has to be the Nonius."

"Yeah," I said, "but it's not like we can get to it, right?"

He huffed and stomped ahead. Guess I'd rained on his parade.

As we approached the gate, Rachel moved slower, hunched against the cold like an old woman.

When the guard waved us in with barely a glance, Rachel relaxed. "The first few times I came here alone," she said quietly, "the guards were not kind. But after the queen's companion, Sister Hectare, had a word with them, I've had less trouble."

We bypassed the steps to the main entrance and passed through a servant's portal. In the vast kitchens, steam rose from enormous pots of boiling liquids. The roof of the high, circular room was layered with smoke from dozens of open ovens set into the walls. At floor-level, the miasma of sautéed onions and roasting meat, simmering sauces, and bubbling soups made my belly gurgle. Servants in splattered aprons yawned as they diced vegetables or plucked feathers from seemingly every kind of fowl known to man. Huge, plump geese dangled from hooks, their blood draining into buckets on the stone floor. Everywhere were headless ducks and chickens. We dodged a young boy carrying a wicker basket filled with the limp carcasses of tiny, delicate larks.

We shuttled out of the way as two boys struggled to heave the ravaged carcass of an enormous boar onto the stained wooden block.

"Pork pies for supper tonight, lads," a servant with a face like a bulldog called. Noticing Rachel, he leered. "You wantin' a taste, Jewess? Oh, I forget. Already had you some, didn't you? That delicious stew I brought up for you and the maidservants last week."

He guffawed, elbowing his partner in the side.

Rachel blanched. But like a true lady, only raised her chin and moved steadily across a covered breezeway connecting the kitchens to the main part of the castle.

"He did that on purpose?" I asked, lips stiff in anger. "Put pork in your soup?"

"Yes," she said. "One of them brought a stew up to feed the queen's servants after Her Grace went to dine privately with the king. I was hungry and they claimed 'twas beef. I should have known better. After I'd eaten a few bites, the boy crowed and told me to enjoy my Jewish hell, as I'd just eaten swine."

Collum growled behind me and turned back toward the smirking kitchen boy. Rachel laid a hand on his arm.

"Please, Master Collum," she said. "There is no need. It is far from the worst insult I've borne."

"But how could they do that to you?" Phoebe complained.

"'Tis but the way of things." Rachel shrugged as she led us up a dingy staircase to an elegant landing. Another, broader flight led down to the decorated entry hall.

"Master Collum," Rachel said. "If you and Mistress Phoebe will kindly go down to the Great Hall, we shall meet you there. They are serving breakfast, and by the king's decree all are welcome today. Last eve, I asked permission only for Mistress Hope to attend me in the queen's chambers."

I could see Collum gearing up to argue, but after a glance at Rachel's face he nodded.

"For God's sake, be careful this time," he hissed, his hand gripping my arm in warning as Phoebe headed reluctantly down the steps. "While you're inside, Phoebe and I will ask around about this Babcock. See what we can find out. You do the same, but don't take any unnecessary chances. Is that understood?"

"Yes." I jerked out of his grip. "I'm not an idiot."

He stared down at me, eyes impenetrable as they searched my face. "I know that," he said. "It's just . . ."

Turning my back on him, I stomped after Rachel, grumbling under my breath. I guess I wasn't quite over being pissed at him after all.

When I caught up with her at the door to the queen's chamber, I forced my jaw to unclench, then let out a long breath as I tried to focus on Doug's instructions of how to glide like a proper lady.

I suppose I'd expected a palatial chamber, with the queen perched atop a gilded throne. This was Eleanor of Aquitaine, after all. As Henry II proclaimed about himself, in my mom's favorite movie — or, well, the actor Peter O'Toole, who was playing him had proclaimed — "He married out of love, a woman out of legend."

But when we entered the low doorway, and I stared at the faces packed into the stifling, tapestry-lined chamber, I hoped—prayed—that my mother would just pop out of the crowd and we could go all home.

Even in winter, the room was sweltering. Three enormous copper braziers radiated heat upward in undulating waves. The chamber was packed with women, their long gowns like a jewel-toned flower garden. I bobbed on my tiptoes, scanning the room.

Nope. Not here.

I swallowed back the pang of disappointment. It wasn't like I'd really expected it to be that simple. And yet the back of my throat burned.

Rachel frowned. "Are you all right, mistress?"

I nodded, unable to speak as we were motioned to a far corner. Blinking hard, I focused on the room.

A few bored lute players plinked in the opposite corner, and a steady stream of black-clothed clerks toted armloads of documents for the queen's signature. Rachel and I stood against the wall. As small groups split and re-merged, I caught partial glimpses of a very pregnant woman seated behind a desk, feather quill in hand.

Everyone was standing, except the queen and a child-size nun seated on a nearby stool. Despite my frustration, I gasped.

"It's her." I grabbed Rachel's arm. "Eleanor of Aquitaine."

Rachel smiled indulgently. "Yes. Our new queen is a rare woman indeed," Rachel whispered. "And next to her is Sister Hectare, the queen's closest companion aside from Amaria, her former nurse." Rachel's eyes went soft as she watched the tiny nun. "Sister Hectare is a wise and kind woman."

Hectare was the oldest person I'd ever seen. Rheumy eyes, a veined nose like a toucan's beak, and wrinkled-parchment skin that draped from her face and neck like swags of melted wax. She looked as though she might keel over dead at any second. And yet, as Eleanor met with this guest or that, she often leaned in to consult with the old woman.

From the corner of my eye, I saw a tall, black-robed figure, a priest, enter and approach the queen. The genial chatter died away as he glided serenely forward to bow before the desk.

CHAPTER 24

"So kind of you to *finally* join us, Thomas." The queen's voice was throaty and rich as she spoke in the imperious French of the nobility. "Sister Hectare, isn't it thoughtful of Thomas to take time out of his very busy day to answer a summons from his queen?"

The priest spoke from a low bow. "My apologies, Your Grace. I was with His Grace, the king."

"Naturally." Eleanor sounded amused, though I thought I could hear strain beneath the courtly manners. "You've kept my Henry much occupied since our arrival. I do believe the two of you have become thick as thieves."

The priest started to murmur a reply, but Eleanor stood, interrupting him. "Of course, before we came to England, *I* was His Grace's closest companion."

Standing, Eleanor of Aquitaine was taller than most of the women. She was still swathed in a swirl of gossamer nightclothes, though it was nearly noon. Auburn waves frizzed down her back in the humid air, defying the rule that a married woman must cover her hair. White skin smoothed across sharp cheekbones and high, arched brows.

"Since His Grace the archbishop introduced you two," Eleanor went on, "I've barely seen Henry. Do you not find that odd, Thomas? A queen who must make an appointment to see her own husband?"

I sucked in a breath. I knew the priest now.

"No way," I whispered incredulously, forgetting my medieval speech for a moment. "That's Thomas à Becket."

Rachel looked at me sidelong from beneath her dark lashes, hesitating only an instant before her eyes flicked back toward the priest. Her delicate nostrils flared. A look of loathing passed over her usually placid features as she stared at the man who was murmuring smooth apologies to his queen. "Yes," she said. "That is he, indeed." She bit off the name. "Becket."

I could only stare at the infamous priest. Thomas à Becket. Soon to be Henry's chancellor, then archbishop of Canterbury. The person who inserted himself between Henry and Eleanor, causing a rift that widened through time until it ended in a devastating war between Henry and his sons. In less than ten years, Henry and Thomas would turn on each other too. A battle of church against state would begin, ending only when Henry inadvertently caused Thomas's murder inside Canterbury Cathedral. A deed still spoken of a thousand years later as one of the most notorious crimes in history.

Thomas à Becket. One of the most powerful men in England. Or at least he soon would be.

"He despises my people, you know," Rachel confessed under her breath, barely contained fury in her voice. "Becket had my cousin arrested a few weeks ago on a false charge." Her arms contracted around her slim body. "Horse theft, they claimed. His wife, Anna, was in childbirth, and he was trying to get home to her when his own mount went lame. The Christian family who loaned him their horse wished to testify on his behalf, but Becket threatened them somehow." Her voice lowered to a hiss. "Abram died in prison two weeks later. Head injury. They claim it an accident, but we all know the truth."

I glanced back at the clergyman's aesthetic features. Nothing I'd ever read about Becket implied that kind of cruelty. Just went to show you how wrong the history books could be.

I touched her arm in sympathy. "Rachel, I'm so sor—"

"Shhh." Rachel began fumbling in the basket hanging from her arm as a wimpled servant appeared before us, carrying a steaming silver goblet.

Removing a twist of burlap from the smallest satchel at her belt, Rachel untied the piece of twine and—with practiced movements—tapped in a few grains of reddish powder. She took the cup from the servant and swirled the contents. When my new friend went to pass the goblet back, the sour older woman hesitated, as if she didn't want to touch anything Rachel had handled. Sneering, she reluctantly reached out.

But as she did, the queen called, "No, Wilifred, let the girl approach and bring it to me herself. Her friend as well."

Rachel hurried forward. I shuffled after her. Our skirts displaced layers of fresh rushes that covered the flagstone floor. Rose petals and twigs of lavender and rosemary, interspersed within the straw, sent up the smell of summer as we crushed them beneath our boots.

Women in colorful court finery made a pathway for us. I searched every face as we went, but my mother had not miraculously appeared.

A few feet from the cluttered desk, Rachel dropped into a low curtsy. I followed, though my legs shook so they could barely hold me. We stayed there, heads bowed, for a long moment, until a pair of gold and jewel-encrusted slippers appeared in my field of view. Peacocks and golden lions.

"You may rise."

Rachel rose. Swallowing hard, so did I.

My breath left me in a silent whoosh. The statuesque woman before me wasn't beautiful. Her nose was too long, her mouth too narrow, and a deep cleft split her square chin. But the strong bones of her face would never age, and as I squirmed, her pine-forest eyes studied me. In that moment I understood why people still worshiped this queen, even a thousand years after her death. There was strength and a fierce intelligence glowing behind those wide-set eyes.

"Good morrow, Rachel," the queen said. She took the cup and propped herself against the front of the desk. Back arched, the bulge of her pregnancy pushed out toward us, flagrant and round as a basketball against the draping, periwinkle robes. "I thank you for bringing my tisane. This prince is strong. He kicks as though he were already riding into battle, without regard to his mother's digestion. But that is men for you, no?"

A titter from the crowd as Rachel mumbled a reply.

Eleanor shot the liquid back in two long draughts. "Ahh, no one makes a medicament like the Jews. Do you not agree, Thomas?" Eleanor smoothed a hand over her belly as if to say, *You can't do this for your king, can you?*

I tensed. For a moment, I'd completely forgotten about the priest.

At the edge of my vision, I saw Thomas Becket's slash of a mouth tighten. The first crack in his cool façade. "I do not, Your Grace. I trust my health to Christ alone. Not some heathen concoction."

Eleanor leaned backward over the desk, whispering theatrically to the elderly nun. "The good father prays away *his* wind, Hectare. Oh, that I could rid myself of mine so easily."

I couldn't help it. The chuckle just popped out.

Becket stiffened and turned to me for the first time. "You understood your queen just now?"

Oh no. I gave an involuntary nod. The queen had switched to Latin and I hadn't even noticed. *Stupid.*

The priest's dark brown eyes narrowed on me. "Clearly the girl is no Jew, as she wears not the yellow veil," he said in crisp Latin. "How is it that you consort with our Hebrew *brethren*" — his lip curled at that — "yet can speak the language of your betters and Holy Mother Church?"

"I — my mother taught me, Father." I dropped my gaze to the floor, but he crowded me. His fingers dug beneath my chin, raising my face to his.

"Your speech," he said, moving closer until his stale breath washed over me, "it is odd. And I do not know your face. What is your name? Tell me at once."

Thrown off by the menacing tone, I completely blew any shot to use my aristocratic, fake identity as I blurted out my own name. "H-Hope, sir . . . F-Father. Hope Walton. I —"

Becket inhaled sharply and drew back. His hand fumbled for the bulky silver cross at his chest as his thin lips mouthed my name silently to himself.

With an abrupt half turn toward the door, he shouted, "Guards! Seize this girl!"

Two uniformed guards began hurrying toward us. I didn't even have time for my utter confusion to turn to fear before the queen held up a hand, stopping the men in their tracks.

"Halt," she told them, though her intense eyes sharpened on me. "Explain yourself, Thomas."

"She is a spy, Your Grace," Becket spluttered, crossing himself. "An agent of the French. I've had it straight from a trusted friend who warned me to watch for a young girl who speaks with an odd accent and knows all manner of languages. A girl with hair as dark as night and eyes the color of a stormy sky. She even gave me the traitor's true name. An unusual name for a simple merchant's child, do you not agree, Your Grace?"

When Eleanor didn't answer, he went on. "I shall see her jailed. A few hours under the ministrations of—"

"No," Rachel exclaimed at the same time I gasped, "That's not true."

"You lie," Becket sneered. "She understood you, Your Grace. You spoke in Latin just now, and she understood. Explain *that*."

Fear was beginning to eat away at my reason. The stifling room closed around me, and I had to force myself not to run. Everyone was staring at us, mouths open in shock.

The tiny nun stood and limped around the table. She tugged Eleanor down to whisper in her ear. The queen nodded, eyes narrowing on Becket, before turning her attention to me.

"Yes, girl," the queen repeated in a tone completely different from that of the priest's. "Tell me again how it is you speak the language of scholars."

Voice shaking, I said again, "My mother taught me, Your Grace."

"Hmmm. And do you read and write it as well?"

"I do, Your Grace. My mother thought it wise that I learned. We are in the shipping business, and we visit many countries, and . . ."

The queen stopped me with a languid gesture, then tilted

her head. "Oh, Thomas." She gave an amused scoff. "So because this poor child knows the Latin tongue, she must be a spy? I myself speak many languages. I suppose, then, you must arrest me as well. Yes?"

"No," Becket snapped. When Eleanor's eyes flashed dangerously, a blotchy flush bled across his gaunt, pallid cheeks as he seemed to remember who he was addressing. He gave a jerky bow. "No, Your *Grace*. I believe she is a spy because a trusted ally warned me of—"

"And who, Thomas," Eleanor said, imperiously, "is this trusted ally of whom you speak so highly?"

I knew what was coming, knew there was only one person who could have warned Becket against me. And yet it felt like a punch when he said her name.

"The Lady Celia Alvarez, Your Grace. A woman gifted with holy visions. She—"

I snorted at the "holy visions" description. Becket took a step toward me, but Eleanor threw her head back. Her shoulders shook with a full-bodied laugh. "Alvarez? A Spaniard? Oh well, then. We must, of *course*, believe her."

Still chuckling, the queen yawned. She slid around the desk and retook her seat. "So," she mused, watching me thoughtfully. "A merchant's wife who teaches Latin and languages to her daughters. Perhaps England is not the barbaric country I feared."

For an instant, relief began to trickle through me. But Becket's hand snaked forward and fastened around my upper arm. I winced as his fingers dug painfully into my flesh.

"The girl should be questioned, at the very least. By your leave I will take her, Your Grace. I will draw the truth from her myself."

"You will do no such thing." Eleanor shot to her feet. Everyone jumped as the queen's voice resounded through the room. "Let her go. This girl is now under *my* protection."

"Madam," Thomas said. "Surely—"

Eleanor's voice turned to a malevolent whisper. "I said release her."

The priest's fingers burrowed viciously into my skin before he let go. Dropping a choppy bow, he spoke through clenched teeth. "As you say, Your Grace."

Becket backed toward the door, clearly furious. "If that will be all, madam, I shall get back to the king. I'm quite certain he'll be interested in what happened here today."

Still petrified, I wanted to rub my aching arm, but refused to give Becket the satisfaction.

"Ah, yes. I am told that since we've arrived, you are always buzzing in my husband's ear. And that in turn you have a thousand little bees of your own, scattered throughout this city, whom you pay to buzz news of *my* kingdom to *you*. Buzz. Buzz. Buzz." The queen's hand idly caressed her belly as she bestowed a malicious smile on the priest.

At the door, Becket turned and began to stomp toward the door, his earlier arrogant, gliding step forgotten.

"Oh, Thomas," Eleanor called.

Becket's lips were white as he swiveled to face the queen. "You know what they say about bees, don't you?"

Thomas Becket glowered but said nothing.

"Bees," she said, "are ruled by a queen. Not a king."

Thomas Becket jabbed a bow and fled. Dead silence ruled the chamber for a beat, before the tension slowly bled away. Everyone began chattering among themselves, though Eleanor's eyes remained fixed on the door.

Sister Hectare placed a gnarled hand on the queen's arm and whispered to her.

Eleanor blinked hard and shook her head as if throwing off disturbing thoughts. "Yes," she said. "Of course he will. Henry's always taken my view in the end."

The nun mouthed a few more words to the queen that I could not hear.

"Tell me your name again, child?" I startled when the queen addressed me. For a moment, I thought she'd forgotten all about me. But her eyes were fixed on me now with a sharp curiosity.

"Mistress Hope Walton, Your Ma—Your Grace."

Careful. I'd almost said "Your Majesty," a term that wouldn't come into play until the reign of Henry VIII.

"The good sister here informs me you've come searching for your cousin?"

My gaze shot to Rachel, who stood pale and shaking at my side. She nodded, though, encouraging me.

"Yes, Your Grace," I managed. "My cousin Sarah de Carlyle."

"Yes, yes." She waved her royal hand dismissively and picked up her quill. "After Rachel spoke of you, Sister

Hectare made inquiries, I believe. Tell the girl what you've learned, Sister."

The ancient woman's voice creaked like an unoiled door. "All the barons of the land will be here tonight at Your Grace's precoronation feast. Lady Sarah's name is de Carlyle no longer, of course, but she and her husband will be in attendance."

For an instant, all I felt was an overwhelming thrill of exhilaration. Of triumph. My mother. Here. Then the rest of the nun's words penetrated, and I could only blink at her.

Husband? The words tangled in my mouth. "I'm sorry, but my c-cousin is not married, sister. You aren't . . . I mean, you don't have the wrong person in mind, do you?"

"I don't believe so, child," Hectare replied kindly. "Though these old ears could have heard wrong."

Thoughts of my father laughing quietly with Stella Montgomery began to thread through my mind. Shock turned slowly to anger at how easily they'd both given up.

Apparently I'm the only one in this family with any damn loyalty.

I had to go. Had to get out of there before I puked all over the queen of England's pretty bejeweled slippers. I had to think this through. I knew my mom. No matter what kind of situation she'd faced, my mother always, *always* did what she wanted. Sarah Walton didn't compromise. There must have been a reason. A plan.

A servant signaled to Rachel, who tugged on my arm. "We are dismissed."

We backed away from the now-distracted royal. As we reached the door, Sister Hectare scrambled around the table and approached us.

"Mistress Hope," she said, "the queen enjoys interfering with that prying priest. He hates women in general, and learned ones even more. But make no mistake, you've made an enemy in Becket here today, so take heed. The queen's protection extends only so far." The little nun bestowed a sweet, toothless grin to soften her words. Her face folded into a million wrinkles. "In any case, Her Grace would like to extend a personal invitation for you and your family to attend the feast tonight. There, I believe, you shall find the woman you are searching for."

CHAPTER 25

"You're not being fair, Hope." Phoebe's teeth chattered as our rented sled lined up with hundreds of others. Sleds, sleighs, and riders on horseback, filed out the city gate, headed for the Palace of Westminster and its nearby Abbey. "First of all, you don't even know for sure the woman they mentioned is *our* Sarah."

I nodded, though I did know. I knew it in my heart. After we returned to the house and I revealed what I'd learned, I'd sunk into a depression that left me wrung out and numb.

Alongside the procession, hundreds of mounted soldiers bore blazing torches, lighting the frigid night until the fat snowflakes glowed like bits of fire falling from the sky. Shouts and cheers rang out. The smells of horse and ice and burning pitch. The jangle of bells on tack as people's cheeks and fingertips froze.

It wasn't far down the road called the Strand to Westminster that—in this bygone age—still lay a few miles outside the city proper. Based on the sprawling hamlets and great estates we passed, it wouldn't be long before London outgrew its walls completely, and the great Abbey and Palace became the center of town.

I burrowed deeper under the musty furs. Every exhale turned to a cloud of frozen mist that iced my blood in a world gone cobwebby and cold. In the orange haze, Collum rode beside us on a sway-backed mare. He seemed twitchy and anxious. I'd never seen him nervous before. I did not care for it.

Dismounting, we merged with the crowd as they flowed toward the castle's entry. Phoebe's emerald dress—purchased secondhand at market—suited her auburn hair and pale, freckled skin to perfection as she puffed beside me. "Let's just find Sarah and get the story from her, okay?"

My own gown of rich indigo, embroidered in whorls of scarlet, swept down in a cascade of plush wool. With Phoebe's needle, the long, belled sleeves, lined with crimson silk, draped to the ground in swooping elegance.

When I'd come down the steps at Mabray House, my hair braided and pinned in place by Alice's clever fingers, Collum had stared at me for a long moment before mumbling a begrudging "You'll do."

The knot on my forehead from my previous tumble pulsated. The freezing wind whipped at the filmy veil as—for the hundredth time—I adjusted the bronze circlet that ringed my scalp like a torture device.

Phoebe glanced over at me. "You all right, then?"

"Peachy."

People lined up before the torchlit entrance to the

Palace of Westminster, dressed in their glittering, courtly best. Butterflies cartwheeled in my gut as we joined the queue of invited guests.

She's here—I know it. My mother's here and she's married.

Phoebe gave me a concerned look as we crossed the scoured cobbles and mounted the steps. "It'll be okay, Hope. Honestly. We'll find Sarah, and then . . ."

My eyes never stopped scanning the crowd. *Not her. Not her. Not her.*

"Oh," Phoebe said, "so I shagged the groom in the hayloft this afternoon after going to the market. Had to do it. Little 'lady and the stable boy' fantasy of mine. I don't think Doug will mind, do you?"

"That's nice," I said absently. Then her words made it through, and I rounded on her. "Wait. What?"

My friend's eyes crinkled as she exchanged a glance with her brother.

"Paying attention now are we?" Collum said. "We have a mission to complete. Quit whinging about, and get on with the job at hand."

I wanted to smack him, but he was right. Nodding, I picked up the hem of my skirt and entered the Great Hall, determined to find my mom so we could get the hell out of there.

The long, rectangular hall was decorated for royalty. Trestle tables stretched the length of the room, set with pewter plates. Multitudes of candles glowed from deer-antler chandeliers that were twined with ivy and gold cloth. The astringent essence of evergreen wafted down from swags stretched across the sweeping rafters. Cinnamon-and-clove-scented steam boiled up from vats of mulled ale.

The delicious aromas, layered with the reek of stale sweat and dirty hair, made the place smell like Christmas at a hobo's house.

Liveried servants passed among the guests with platters of steaming beef and pork. Spiced meatballs floating in tureens of hearty sauce. A savory, fatty smell flooded the air as trays of roasted goose and ornately decorated peacock were presented. At the head of the room, a dais dripped with scarlet and gold silk, waiting for the king and queen.

"We'll split up," Collum ordered, eyes scanning the crowd. "Cover more ground that way."

At our answering nods, Collum's gaze flicked back and forth between us, before fixing on me. His hazel eyes looked oddly sad as he whispered, "Take care. No matter what happens, get Sarah out, and make sure you're at the glade on time."

"What . . . ?" I started, but he pushed off into the crowd without another word. My pulse thrummed as I gave Phoebe a questioning look. She shrugged, frowning, as she moved off.

As each person passed that wasn't my mother, I grew more frantic. I skimmed the crowd, desperate for the curve of her familiar cheek. The slope of too-broad shoulders beneath colored finery.

"Mistress Hope."

I turned to find Rachel's William Lucie looking resplendent in a blazing azure tunic, yellow diamonds stitched at the cuffs and along the hem. "I wish to thank you."

He took two goblets from a passing servant and offered one to me. "I know what you did for my . . . for Rachel."

"No," I said, "you have it wrong. Rachel helped me."

"I think we both know that's not true."

William captured my distracted gaze. "Rachel is . . . my friend, and Eustace Clarkson tried to hurt her. I shall take that up with him in due time. But that's not why I wanted to speak with you. I came to warn you, Mistress Hope. Warn you that someone's been making enquiries about you."

That did it. I quit searching and gave William my full attention. "I beg your pardon?"

Instead of answering, he took my elbow and turned me toward the dais. A group of churchmen chuckled as they emerged from a side door to seat themselves at the head table. A fat archbishop in blinding white and gold sat down next to one of the thrones. Lounging behind him in humble black was Thomas Becket.

"Becket," William announced quietly, though there was no need. A chill had skittered across my skin when I saw him, features pinched as he scanned the room. "Becket is a priest, yes, but he has eyes and ears everywhere. For some reason, you've drawn his interest."

As if he'd heard us above the clamor, Thomas Becket's eyes stopped roving the crowd and fixed on me. His mouth made a small moue of surprise. I took an involuntary step back. Then trumpets blared from the back of the Great Hall, and Becket's malevolent gaze dropped away.

I thanked William and scuffled back against the wall as feasters scrambled for spots at the long tables.

Henry Plantagenet—second of that name. King of England, Scotland, Ireland, and Wales. Count of Anjou, Brittany, Poitou. Duke of Normandy, Maine, Gascony, and Aquitaine, as the herald announced—was short, stocky, and bowlegged. A russet-haired fireplug of a man who Eleanor topped by half a head. They strolled arm in arm down the wide space between the tables, like graceful ships in the middle of a cheering storm.

The disheveled woman I'd seen idling in her nightclothes was gone, replaced by regal opulence. She stunned in cascades of jade silk embroidered with golden lions that emphasized her round belly. Candlelight sparked off the emeralds set into her gold coronet. Henry looked like a man ready to burst with pride.

As they came level with me, Henry placed a square freckled hand on his wife's belly and crowed, "Another job well done for England, eh, boys?"

The crowd went nuts.

Phoebe wormed her way to my side. "No sign of Sarah yet. But there're a lot of people here. It may take a while."

She was still talking, but her words faded into nothing when I saw something that froze the breath in my lungs.

"Hope?" Phoebe said, "Did you hear me? I said I don't know where Collum went. I think he's up to something. He's disappeared."

Tomorrow, the course of England would change forever, when two of England's greatest rulers were crowned in Westminster Abbey. A dynasty empire was being born before my eyes. None of that mattered, because I'd just caught a glimpse of someone on the far side of the room. A tall woman with athletic shoulders.

"Cripes," Phoebe muttered. "I have to find him. I'll kill him if he does something stupid."

Mute, I grabbed for my friend's sleeve to tell her what I'd just seen, but she'd already darted off. My hand fell slowly back to my side. My attention lasered in on one thing. The spindly pale-strawberry braid that hung limp down the woman's broad back.

CHAPTER 26

SHE LET IT GROW OUT.

It was a frivolous thought. Mom had always kept her hair bobbed to shoulder length, claiming middle-aged women with long hair were trying too hard to hold on to something that was long gone. But here, where only nuns chopped their hair, she'd had little choice, apparently.

Go. What are you waiting for? My snarled thoughts trapped me in place.

When she turned, just enough for me to catch sight of her profile, my body leaned in her direction, until I was poised on my toes.

Move, I commanded my feet. *She's right there. Your mother, your supposedly* dead *mother, is right there. Why can't you move?*

I clenched my fists. Took a step.

"Not yet, child." A gnarled claw, with cracked yellow nails, gripped my forearm. Its strength startled me. I hadn't even seen her approach. *How can someone so old move like that?*

"Hold," the ancient nun, Sister Hectare, whispered as she towed me back toward the wall.

As I started to protest, a man appeared at my mother's side. His greasy bald head barely reaching the level of her chin. His pudgy fingers clutched her elbow.

"Lord Babcock is a venal man," Sister Hectare's rusty voice said. "Though that is only part of his charm. He's also cruel and overproud. And he has the brains of a beheaded fowl, besides. You must not approach until he leaves her side."

"Wait." I blinked as it hit me. "*That's* her husband?"

"Yes. Sarah de Carlyle, now wife of Lord Henry Babcock. In the war just past, Babcock fought on the wrong side. But our new king seeks peace with his barons. Even minor, idiotic ones. He restored Babcock's lands but kept most of the family fortune — such as it was. Did your cousin come with a great dowry, perhaps?"

"No." I still had no idea why this tiny woman was helping me.

"Hmm," Sister Hectare mused. "She's not young. Though young enough, I see. And somewhat comely. Still, Lord Babcock is not known to pick a wife merely because her face isn't pox scarred. 'Tis odd. He does seem taken with her."

"Yes, I see that."

The little toad never took his hands off my mother. Not even when he snatched a chicken leg and began gnawing at it with little gray teeth. Juice glistened in his straggly beard.

The bewilderment I'd felt turned to pity as I watched her husband's pale, protuberant eyes narrow when another man greeted my mother.

What happened here, Mom?

"Ahhh," Sister Hectare breathed.

William Lucie approached the pair. At first, Babcock glared suspiciously at the handsome soldier. But William only gave my mother the briefest of nods before turning to her husband. Babcock's amphibious eyes nearly popped from his head at whatever William told him. He whirled and stared toward the royal table.

"That would be a summons from our queen, requesting to meet one of her most loyal subjects." Sister Hectare chuckled as Babcock growled a command at my mother and followed William like a preening peacock toward the high table. As they passed, William Lucie shot us a wink.

"Best go, child," the nun said. "Eleanor won't be able to tolerate Babcock's company for long, but she wanted you to have a moment with your *cousin.*"

She dragged out the word, her hooded eyes glittering as she looked up at me. She knew something. *But how?*

As if she'd read my mind, she smiled. "Does it matter, child?"

It didn't. Not a bit.

"Thank you," I rasped. "And, please, thank Her Grace for me."

Mom's back was turned to me. I edged forward as if my

feet were mired in quicksand. Now that the time had finally come, I was weirdly reluctant. My mouth dried up, and my lips felt glued shut.

"Mo—" My voice cracked. I tried again. "Lady Sarah?"

She froze, fingers twitching at her sides in a nervous habit I knew so well. Her shoulders rose. She turned slowly. When she caught sight of me, her eyes widened, then closed as if in pain.

"No," she whispered.

A smell of spring wafted toward me. Lilac, her favorite. One hot tear slipped down my cheek. I didn't move as she opened her eyes, though I felt my lower lip tremble like a lost child's.

An instant later, I realized what I was seeing and my mouth fell open in utter shock. My mother's cheeks were too full. Puffy bags drooped beneath her eyes. Even her lips seemed waterlogged.

She whimpered, her eyes scanning the room frantically. She stepped toward me and grabbed my hand, squeezing too tight.

"How?" she said. "How is this possible? I was so careful to keep you out of all this. I don't understand." She took a deep breath through her nose and dropped my hand, speaking rapidly. "Doesn't matter. You have to leave. Now. If she finds you here, I don't know what she'll do."

I didn't say a word. I couldn't. Because my gaze was trapped on my mother's abdomen. Her extremely round, extremely *pregnant* abdomen. A sick jolt rocked me back on my heels as a memory consumed me.

Dad had brought my very pale mother home from a short hospital stay. I was seven, and so excited, because in four months I'd be a big sister. No one spoke to me when they got home, and I wasn't exactly sure what had happened. All I knew was that they seemed really sad and that my mother's tummy looked strangely flat. That night, Dad had perched on the edge of my bed.

Well, kiddo, he'd said, *looks like it's just gonna be the three of us. And that's okay. It's . . . it's fine.*

The scratchy sound in his voice had made my throat ache. And that night, alone in my bed, I heard my mother sobbing from her bedroom next door. I had never, ever heard my mother cry. It scared me so much, I'd huddled under the covers and bawled myself to sleep.

Years later, Dad told me Mom had nearly died when she lost the baby. There'd been a problem, and I'd always be an only child.

"Mom?" I gasped. "I—" God, I couldn't manage to string two words together. I flung a hand at her belly. "When?"

"Soon, I think. They don't exactly have ultrasound dating here."

Her voice was clipped. I answered back in the same tone. "No. Guess not."

I counted back in my head, trying not to show it.

She noticed. "Obviously, I didn't know I was pregnant

when I left," she said. "How could I? The doctors said it was impossible." The muscles in her jaw tightened. "Hope, I don't understand this. How do you even know about—"

Her voice cracked, and she covered her mouth with swollen fingers. I felt myself begin to crumple with disappointment. I'd built this moment up in my mind for so long. Every second since I'd learned she was alive. Now it was here and all I wanted was to run away.

"Aunt Lucinda sent for me," I said. "*She* told me the truth."

"She had no right." Every muscle in her face tightened. "Look, you must understand. I always wanted to tell you. I just . . . I wasn't sure you'd be able to—"

"You know we thought you were dead?" I let the words drop, heavy as a sack of rocks, between us. "There was an earthquake in that city where you were *supposed* to be. A bad one, Mom. Thousands of people died. Hundreds of buildings collapsed, including the university tower that held the lecture hall where you were supposed to be. They never recovered most of the bodies. And since they couldn't find your body . . . they declared you *dead.*"

When she flinched, I felt a throb of something like triumph.

"Oh no." Her hand covered her mouth again. "I was just supposed to be gone for a few days, I . . . All those poor people. The teachers . . ."

My teeth ground together so hard, my ears popped. I suddenly wanted to hurt her. "We had your funeral the other day, you know. Dad buried an empty coffin. He even had a headstone with your name carved on it. It says 'Beloved Wife and Mother,' in case you wondered."

Her lips went white as she whispered, "Sweetheart, I . . ."

When she buried her face in her hands and started to weep, I could only stare in utter and complete astonishment. This wasn't the mother I knew. I'd expected Mom to sweep us all up and take over. Fix everything. That was how it worked. My mother was a warrior. A fixer. And yet, all I felt as I watched her shoulders shake . . . was an uneasy pity.

Her face was blotchy as she raised it and scanned the room. "Where's Lu? I need to speak with her at once."

That's it? I shook my head in disbelief. *That's the extent of our big reunion?*

Numbness crept out from my chest. "Aunt Lucinda, Mac, and Moira came here a few months ago, looking for you. They couldn't find you. Obviously, they aren't here this time. It's just Collum and Phoebe. And me."

"Just you kids? Good Lord, what was she thinking? And *you?* You have no practical training whatsoever. How could Lucinda allow this? It's insane." Her eyes closed for a long moment. When they opened, she looked hard into my eyes. "Listen to me, Hope. The three of you, go and find a safe place to hide until it's time to go back."

"But—"

"No, Hope." Her eyes roved from person to person. "You don't understand. You mustn't let Celia find you here. If she does—"

"Celia can't return to this time," I said, though fear prickled my scalp as she shook her head. "She can't," I insisted. "She was here before, and Lucinda said the Dim won't allow anyone to return."

She flinched at my casual mention of the Dim.

"My sister is wrong." Her hands nearly crushed mine when she grabbed them to jerk me close. Her blue eyes swam with fear as she whispered, "The Timeslippers have found a way to keep this timeline open. I don't know how. But I've seen them here at least three times over the past months, and I know they were here before I came. I don't know what they're up to, but Celia's made some powerful friends here. *She* trapped me. *She* arranged my marriage to that"—she covered her belly with her hands as she growled the word—"monster."

I was breathing hard now, fear making my lungs shrivel like crumpled paper sacks.

"Celia's little minions watch me all the time, Hope. Which is why you must get away from me. They may already know you're here."

CHAPTER 27

THE NEARBY BLARE OF TRUMPETS STARTLED US BOTH. During our talk, I'd barely noticed the series of dignitaries parading toward the dais, presenting gifts to the new sovereigns. Now I followed Mom's gaze as a group of bearded men in yellow hats stood before their king. Henry beamed down as one held up a sheath of shining black leather etched with gold and glittering with precious gems.

"The Jews of London are grateful to our new, and most gracious, king," their leader intoned. "In honor of your coronation and in most humble gratitude for the protection you offer our people, we present you with this dagger."

There was a collective "ahh" from the crowd as the man yanked the knife from its sheath. It gleamed beneath the candlelight, silver and shining and lethal. "May your reign last as long as this legendary stone fixed into its hilt."

The Jewish contingent bowed low as their leader laid the dagger carefully on a marble pillar set before the dais to showcase each gift as it was presented. "God save His

Grace," he said as he went to his knees. The crowd joined in. "God save the king!"

The legendary stone fixed into its hilt.

So, this must be the opal Rachel had mentioned. I couldn't see it from where I was standing, but when I turned back to my mother, I saw her cover her mouth with trembling fingers.

"The Nonius Stone?" she mumbled behind her hand. "That's why the timeline stays . . . but no. It couldn't be, could it?"

When the Jews marched from the room, the feastgoers went back to their meals. Lutes and pipes played as people filled the space between the tables, dancing and chatting. Others began stuffing their faces with meat and downing endless goblets of wine.

"Mom," I said, "listen. I don't care about some ridiculous stone, and I don't care about Celia. We're here to rescue you. But we have to—"

"You idiotic lout!" The shout echoed from the dais.

I whirled in time to see that a servant had just stumbled hard into the pillar. Rocking on its base, the thick marble stand teetered, then crashed over. Shards of stone flew into the crowd. The servant's heavy tray of goblets followed, crimson wine splashing across the rush-covered floor like an arterial spray. The king rose, apoplectic. Angry voices boomed off the rafters as the servant bowed over and over in apology. He leaned down to retrieve the goblets, then began to scurry toward a side entrance.

"Thief!" someone yelled, and I saw that it was Becket. His eyes blazed after the servant. "He's taken the dagger, Your Grace!"

Becket whispered furiously in the king's ear. Henry's hand came up and pointed a beringed finger at the servant, who was now blocked in by two guards. "Seize. That. Man."

The servant zigzagged through the crowd as men tried to snatch hold of his scarlet servant's tunic. I couldn't see much, only the top of his head, and the ripple effect as he shoved through the mass of people.

An awful dread began to build inside me.

The crowd became too thick. The thief leaped up onto the far table, rampaging down its length. Goblets of wine and plates of food flew into the laps of startled guests.

"Oh God," I whispered when I finally viewed the man's face. My pulse doubled and my heart began to cave in on itself.

Next to me, Mom made a strangled noise. "Oh, Collum, no."

Collum MacPherson never slowed as he neared the edge of the tabletop. His muscular thighs bunched as he jumped. He flew through the air, snatching hold of one of the hanging swags of evergreen.

Like a sports commentator diagramming plays for the viewers at home, my mind mapped it all out before he even made the motions. Neon-green lines drew themselves before me in curving arcs.

The first swag. Swoop. The low-slung chandelier. Backswing, then on to the second swag. Another backswing before a vertical drop to the table in the rear. A hop to the floor. Then a sprint out the back door.

Every muscle in my body strained. *Stretch. Swing. Faster. Hurry, Collum.*

"My God," the king of England shouted. "Look at him go."

It would've worked. Mathematically, it *should've* worked. If only the last bough had been stronger. The verdant swag ripped beneath his weight, and Collum dropped to the ground in a tangle of limbs.

All the air left my lungs in a rush. A dozen guards merged on him, a mix of the king's crimson and the black and silver of the city watch. I lunged forward, but someone snagged the back of my dress.

"Hope!" my mother yelped in my ear. "You can't."

A guard went flying backwards. Another tumbled end over end, bowling into the hovering crowd. Collum was up, gladiator sword gleaming as he hobbled toward the open exit.

Phoebe raced to my side, braids flying, chest heaving. "Oh sweet Jesus."

He was almost out. No one had yet thought to block the exit. Collum was hurt—that was obvious. But it didn't slow him as he raced toward freedom.

Only three more steps. Two. Go, Collum! For God's sake, run!

Phoebe already had one of her slim blades pinched between thumb and forefinger. As a burly guard approached her brother from behind, Phoebe's arm reared back as she prepared to throw.

Seeing it, I frantically scanned the mass of guards converging on her brother. In one sweep, I calculated the odds, then snatched her arm down before anyone could notice. "No," I hissed. "Not here. Not yet."

It was the white-haired pig Eustace Clarkson who got him. Just as Collum's foot stepped over the threshold, the brute raised a short nubby club in an overhand swing that bashed across the back of the Collum's neck. He dropped like a chunk of lead. The other guards raced in, and the world narrowed to meaty thwacks as they kicked Collum's limp form.

Bile raced up my throat. Sickened, I held fast to Phoebe. My friend's sweet face had washed to green beneath her freckles as she struggled with me to let her go.

"Enough," the king roared. "Do not injure that man further. He's provided better entertainment than any juggler, by God. And every man in my kingdom shall have a fair trial. Take him to the Tower and see him patched up."

Eustace Clarkson—pretending he hadn't heard the king's command—launched a last, savage kick to Collum's ribs.

Phoebe had stopped fighting and was making a low, keening noise. I wrapped my arms around her tiny, shaking form, though my own chest felt like it had been scooped out with a melon baller.

As two of the guards lifted the slack Collum between

them and hustled him away into the night, Thomas Becket glided across the room and snatched something from the floor. Smiling, he raised it triumphantly in the air. The dagger, all gleaming steel and polished gold. Though I couldn't see the ornamental jewel from this angle, I couldn't care less. We now had much bigger problems than worrying about a stupid stone.

The king settled back onto his throne while the room rang with cheers and the banging of cups. I stared out the door, a heavy weight slamming down on my shoulders as I realized we might never see Collum again.

Henry addressed his subjects. "From this day forward, may every man under my rule know that he lives in a just kingdom." Shouts of "huzzah" slashed the stuffy air. Henry was energized. His voice boomed over the room, sending every eye his way. "And I say, a thief with enough balls to steal my own property right out from under my nose deserves a proper trial! Let no man ever claim I am not a fair ruler!"

"God save His Grace! God save the king!"

They roared it until I thought the roof might cave in.

CHAPTER 28

HENRY WAS RIGHT. I'D STUDIED THIS ERA BACKWARDS AND forward. I knew that by the end of Henry's thirty-five-year reign, the previously lawless kingdom would become a land of peace, law, and stability. When he died, it was said a virgin could walk the length of England completely naked without being touched.

It wasn't something this virgin would try. And though it was great for England, it was a terrible, awful thing for us. Collum had just become the first criminal of King Henry II's reign.

I dashed the tears from my face and whirled to face my mom. "We have to help him."

She didn't answer, only stared at the empty door.

"Mom?" When she didn't respond, panic began to edge my voice. "Mom!" I shook her, forcing her to look at me. "What do we do?"

My entire life, my mother had had all the answers. She'd ruled over our family like a four-star general. My curriculum. Hobbies. Where I went. Who I spoke with. When

I ate, drank, slept. Every hour of my day dictated by her command. And now, when I needed her most, she'd gone practically catatonic.

"Sarah?" Phoebe blinked up at my mom through a storm of tears, only just now realizing that the pregnant woman standing close beside me was my mom. "My God. Sarah, what happened to you?"

Ignoring Phoebe's comment, Mom turned to us. "Girls," she said in a voice flat and devoid of all emotion. "They'll hang him for this."

"Yeah," I said. "I got that. Now tell us how to get him out."

Instead of answering, her blue eyes flicked to a spot over my shoulder. I turned to see her toad-husband marching toward us with William Lucie on his heels.

"Sarah," Phoebe begged. "Hurry, please."

But my fierce, capable mother was curling in on herself, cringing as Sir Henry Babcock brushed me aside and latched on to her arm. "Away to your rooms, wife," he snarled. "In your condition, you should not be witness to such excitement."

I knew by the way his gaze fixed on my mother's low-slung belly that he thought the kid was his. He didn't care about my mother. The baby. That's all that mattered to him.

I shot a frantic look at William.

"Sir Henry," William started, but Babcock ignored him and gestured toward a waiting manservant. "Jasper, take my wife to our chambers."

Without another word, Babcock strolled off and disappeared into a cluster of men who were analyzing the whole event, like reporters after a crime spree. I glanced toward the high table. While Henry was laughing, having a high old time, Eleanor of Aquitaine appeared flushed and exhausted. Frown lines marring her brow, her eyes snagged on me.

Babcock's thuggish guard planted himself at Mom's side. "Let's away, milady."

With a furtive glance in her husband's direction, Mom scrubbed at her face. The hanging sleeves of her ice-blue dress dropped back and I caught a glimpse of raised, angry scars circling each wrist.

I grabbed her arm. "What happened to you?"

It was all too easy to imagine what could've made those terrible mutilations. But she tore away from my grip and began whispering in ragged, desperate Latin.

"Doesn't matter," she said. "Listen to me. We don't have much time, and you must understand something."

"Milady," the guard warned.

Mom sighed then, and placed cold, trembling hands on each side of my head. Tears glittering, she stared hard into my eyes. "They will never let me escape. Trust me, I've tried."

"But—"

The ridge of scars that ringed my mother's wrists chafed against my chin as she pulled me closer and let her forehead rest on mine. "You must leave me here. There's no other way."

I felt Phoebe stiffen as Mom whispered in English, "Get Collum out. If you can."

"H-how?" My voice wavered as the world around me began to shear away in great hunks.

My mother, the one person in my life who'd always had the answers, shook her head. "I don't know."

Behind me Phoebe whimpered. "Sarah . . ."

At Jasper's grunted order, we exited through a side door where flagstone steps led to the upper, residential floors of the palace. The air smelled of lye and old fires. Past the wide, second-story landing, the stairs narrowed, the next levels obviously meant for lower-level guests. There, grime still edged the narrow risers, and a rank, musty stench lingered. As Phoebe and I trailed Jasper and my mother to the stairs that led up to the third landing, Mom stopped and planted her feet. She turned, her face set with a grim finality I recognized all too well.

"Stop," she said. "You can't come with me any further."

"But—"

She held out a hand to silence me. "No, darling. I love you so much. But I can never leave. It's far too late for me, but not for you. Go. Now. Both of you. They'll have taken Collum to the Tower. Get him out. If you can. But you must get yourselves home to Lucinda. That is an order."

With that, she turned away and disappeared down the shadowy hall.

I collapsed onto the bottom step. Phoebe slumped down next to me and buried her face in her knees.

How could Mom do this? She wouldn't even *try* to escape? And Collum . . .

Oh God. Collum.

I leaned against the crumbly wall, scanning through everything I'd ever read about the twelfth-century Tower of London. What I remembered was bad. Very, very bad.

I bolted upright as boots stomped up from the landing below.

"We have to get out of here, Pheebs," I whispered, "go back to Mabray House and figure this out. But we're not leaving either one of them here. I swear it."

I jerked on her limp arm as the footsteps grew closer. "Get up. We can't help Collum if—"

"Mistress Hope, I thought I'd find you here."

Slowly, so slowly, I turned. And oh, I knew that voice, but—

Impossible.

A clutch of men rounded the landing below. I squinted against the glare of a torch. As my eyes adjusted, my hands flew to my chest, pressing hard, to keep my heart from leaping out and flopping onto the floor like a landed fish.

I'm dreaming. This is all just a horrible nightmare.

But my head filled with a roar of white noise when, as he languidly gestured for his men to stay put, Bran Cameron sauntered up the steps toward us.

CHAPTER 29

I STOOD, REELING IN CONFUSION. BRAN FOLLOWED AS I backed up the steps to the landing above. I stared up into his familiar, mismatched eyes. They traced across my face, remote and cold, as if we'd never met.

"Hope?" Phoebe moved unsteadily to stand beside me. "Who is this?"

I couldn't answer as I studied him. Embroidered with a gold crest, his blue-black tunic soaked up the light. Twin curved blades hung from a leather belt slung across his narrow hips. Sleek dark hair curled to his nape. With his sharp jaw and cut-glass features, Bran looked every inch the haughty medieval aristocrat.

"Bran?" My mushy brain began to solidify. Ideas stirred in its depths as it tried to solve this new part of the equation.

Okay, Bran's a Viator.

He must be. Because the only other explanation would rip me in two.

He tutted, and spoke in perfect Norman French. "Mistress Hope, what *shall* we do with you?"

Phoebe stiffened, repeating in a hoarse whisper, "Who.

Is. This?" Her voice grew urgent when I didn't—when I
couldn't—respond. Her fingernails dug into my arm. "Th-
the river," I managed, never taking my eyes off Bran. "I—
we met at the river. Back home." My eyes turned to hers,
desperate. "We went riding together. I thought he was just a
normal guy. But he's one of us, right?"

Bran leaned in, whispering to me in modern English, his
mouth curved in a wicked half smile. "Yeah. Sorry about
that, dove. Just business, you know."

Phoebe got it before I did. With a roar, she launched herself from my side. Before I could draw breath, she'd leaped
into the air, one small foot on a collision course with Bran's
midsection.

"Phoebe! What the hell?"

Bran tossed the torch aside. With no effort whatsoever,
he caught her ankle in his hands and twisted, sending her to
the floor. Phoebe landed like a cat and threw herself at him
again, hands curled to gouge out his eyes.

I watched, completely stunned, as Bran caught her up in
a bear hug and, with a fluid motion, tussled her off to one of
the guards.

"You bloody wanker!" Phoebe screamed. "Hope, he's one
of them. He's—"

A jowly guard muffled Phoebe with a huge hand. She
twisted and kicked at him.

Bran barked the order. "Take that one back to Mabray
House on the South Bank and put her under guard." He
looked at me. "Tie this one's hands. I will question her here."

A huge, low-browed brute frowned. "Them weren't the lady's orders, milord. We was to take them both to her at once."

"Who is in charge here, Smithson?" Bran didn't bother to turn. "Do as I say. Tie her hands."

The foul-smelling guard approached. I tried to run, but he snatched me by the hair. Pain shredded my scalp as he held me against him while another guard wrapped a rope around my wrists and cinched them tight in front of me. When I flailed and kicked at them, they only laughed and shoved me to my knees.

I actually heard the puzzle pieces click together in my mind. *The river. The bluff. I'd told him I was going away. Told him when.*

"He's one of *them*." Phoebe's muffled shout floated up to me. "He's a —" A door slammed shut.

A Timeslipper. The answer burned like a hot coal behind my eyes. *Yes. And I'm a fool.*

I decided to play dumb. I babbled in the Norman French I now knew he would understand. "I can't believe you're here, Bran. But listen, I need your help. My mom is . . ."

He raised a palm and I trailed off, my lips silently forming the final word. "Trapped."

I looked up at his cool expression, and my heart just stopped, as if someone had ripped it out with greedy hands.

"Oh," he said, "you're brighter than that. You must know I'm not here to help you or your mother."

The truth was seeping through. It felt like being slowly boiled alive.

Still, I had to try.

"My mom's husband, I—I think he hurts her, Bran," I whispered. "Please, you have to help us. You have a mother. Surely you can understand?"

Stall. Just keep stalling until you figure a way out of this. So many levels of pain bubbled up and popped inside me, I didn't know which one hurt worse. My mom, Collum, or this mind-bending treachery.

Collum, what are they doing to you? Where are you? I need you.

"Come, now," Bran drawled. "You're too perceptive to believe I'd be swayed by sentimentality. Of course I have a mother. I imagine you've heard of her by now."

An agony too exquisite to touch twisted inside me. I closed my eyes, trying to bear it as the truth settled between us. "You haven't met, but she would like very much to change that."

I knew, then. Of course I knew. Who else could it be? Celia Alvarez. Mother of Bran the Liar. Bran the Spy. Bran the Betrayer. He'd been working for her the whole damn time.

"Bit of privacy, lads?" Bran moved toward me, smirking at the guards as he ran a finger down the side of my neck and across my chest, lingering at the edge of my bodice.

Most of them chuckled and headed down the steps. Only one, balding and with a wrestler's build, stayed in place. He wasn't dressed like the others. Instead he wore a tunic like Bran's, though it stretched tight across his brawny shoulders.

He grumbled to Bran. "Celia gave specific instructions that we—*both* of us, mind—were to bring the girls to her at once. There's no time for this."

His accent wasn't right. It came slow to his lips, as though he was translating in his head as he went. A flick of black poked out above the ratty bandage around his neck. It curved in toward his jaw line. The fangs and forked tongue of a serpent, inked into his skin.

"Who's in charge here, Flint?"

When the guard's face hardened, Bran laughed and clapped the man's shoulder. "Come now, man." Bran spoke so low, I could barely hear. "Surely after all the pains I went to, softening her up enough to reveal their plans, I deserve to have a little bit of fun before we have to turn her over?"

Horror pressed down on me. I clenched my teeth as tears of rage burned my eyes.

No. No! This cannot be happening.

I tried to struggle to my feet, but without my hands I only toppled sideways. I lay there, panting with the futility of it.

When Flint hesitated, Bran pressed. "Come on, I know you want to get back to the Hound and Barrel. To that blond chippy I saw on your lap earlier. Give me half an hour, eh? Bet there are plenty of empty chambers around here, with everyone celebrating below."

Flint licked his lips as his gaze roved down my body.

"Well"—he dropped all pretense, and when he spoke again it was with a strong Australian accent—"bet a pretty little thing like her ain't even been plucked yet, eh, mate?"

Bran laughed. I wanted to scream.

"I'll even keep her hands bound," Bran waggled his eyebrows. "Where's she going to go?"

The man glanced over at me again and chuckled. "Right-o, Bran. See you in a bit, then."

Bran stood listening as the man's heavy tread faded.

I tried to formulate a plan. The second he approached, I'd kick him as hard as I could in the kneecap, then . . .

Before I could even think it through, Bran hurried over, leaned down, and, with a quick jerk of a small knife, sliced through my bonds.

I scuttled back. "Get away from me."

Sighing, Bran picked up the stuttering torch and shoved it into a nearby iron bracket. "I'm not going to hurt you, Hope. But I had to tell Flint something to get him to leave."

I rose, rubbing my wrists.

"Why should I believe a word you say?" I filled my words with every ounce of scorn I could muster.

He ignored the question. "I'll do what I can to get your friend away from the guards, though it may not be possible. My mother doesn't know your entry point, so I'd suggest you go back to wherever you came through and wait until it's time for you to go back."

When he finally turned, shadows emphasized his cheekbones and hooded his deep-set eyes. I stepped back, still wary. The torch flared, and I saw his face clearly for the first time. Odd eyes. Still beautiful, emerald and sapphire. But all light and humor they'd once held were gone.

"Bran," I began, but he shook his head.

"I'll tell my mother you ran," he continued. "That you banged me on the head or something. But you can't go back to that house. She knows where you're staying now. Get yourself tucked away somewhere. I'll try to retrieve your friend and meet you. Tomorrow, perhaps."

"I'm not going anywhere," I snarled, "not without my mother and *both* my friends."

"Your friends," he snorted, and ripped off supple leather gloves, stuffing them into his belt. "If you mean MacPherson, he's done. Finished. After the stunt he pulled, he'll swing for sure. Forget him."

The memory of Collum being dragged away limp and helpless stabbed at me. "I won't leave him."

I realized instantly I'd said something wrong as all emotion faded and the mask dropped back into place. "So Mother was right. When I told her what happened at the river, she said you were cunning, just like your mother. That you knew all along who I was, and that you'd play me for a fool."

"*I* played *you?*" Incredulous, without thought I shoved him. I had none of Phoebe's tactical training. Knew zero about aikido or karate or whatever the hell it was she studied. But he wasn't expecting it, and he tumbled backwards onto his butt. Looming over him, I yelled with all the pent-up frustration I'd stored over the last eight months. "Are you kidding me? Up until a week ago, I had no idea time travel even existed! I was nothing but a homeschooled *loser* without a mom."

He threw up his palms as if to stop me, but I was so not done.

"Then," I continued, my words dripping venom, "I get dragged to Scotland and told, *Oh, by the way, your mom's not dead. She's just trapped in freaking time!*"

"Hope—"

"And, to add icing to my crap cake, just when the world was falling out from under me—again—I meet a guy. A regular guy, who I *thought* might like me. I started to wonder if maybe I wasn't such a loser after all."

Bran got to his feet with an easy grace. Something about the way he moved was oddly familiar. Then it struck me. "It was you in that alley yesterday," I gasped. "You stopped Eustace and that other guy from chasing me and Rachel."

His eyes dropped to his boots.

"Why?" I begged. I was choking on a clutter of emotions I couldn't begin to unravel. "Was it all a lie, then? Everything? The accident at the river, too?"

"Is that what you think?"

"What am I supposed to think, Bran?" I spat. "Why don't you tell me, hmm?"

His response was acrid, sour. "I have *never* let myself get close to anyone, because of the bloody lie I live every day. Okay, so my mother was wrong and you *didn't* know. And yes, I was spying on you, but I was only supposed to take your picture and report back. The fall was real."

I spun away, disgusted.

He crossed in three quick strides and grabbed my arm, twisting me to face him. His voice rasped with emotion. "But you helped me. You were so kind. So concerned. And so damn beautiful. I—I'd forgotten that. Years—*years*—I've waited to talk to you. Then finally . . ."

Realizing what he'd said, his eyes widened. He dropped my arm as though it was a rattler and backed away.

"Years?" I said. "What the hell are you talking about, Bran?"

The river. That moment of strange familiarity.

He refused to meet my eyes as he pulled out the worn-looking silver medallion I remembered and began worrying it between his thumb and forefinger. "Nothing," he muttered. After a long moment, he brought it to his lips, then tucked it back into his shirt.

"There's only one thing I can do for you," he said coolly. "We only just learned where you were staying. If we can get there and grab your friend before my mother arrives, I can tell the guards the orders have changed. I'll escort both of you to an inn I know on the edge of the city. Tomorrow, gather food and water, then go back to wherever you came through until the Dim comes back for you. It's the best I can offer."

I stared at him. The best he could offer? Was I supposed to fall to my knees in gratitude?

"And the others?" I asked in a voice rimmed with frost.

"There's nothing I can do for your mother or MacPherson." Bran snatched the torch and moved down the steps without looking to see if I'd follow. "You have to let them go."

CHAPTER 30

WE DIDN'T SPEAK ON THE LONG RIDE BACK TO THE CITY. Bran set such a brisk pace, I was hard-pressed to keep up on the mount that was waiting for me outside the palace. As we galloped across slick, muddy cobblestones, my veil flew off. My hair came unmoored and streamed behind me. Snowflakes caked in my eyelashes, refreezing on my cheeks as they melted.

Sure, there was a cowardly instant before we reentered the city walls, where I thought of trying to make a run for it. Just take off across the fields. Find the glade. Hide out in the forest until the Dim came for me. The impulse quickly faded when I thought of what they might do to Phoebe. They had my friend, and I would never leave her—leave any of them—behind.

A guard with a massive tangled beard met us at the court-yard gate of Mabray House. Bran dismounted and told him to keep me there, as he'd only be a moment. I huddled in the saddle and tried to rub the ache from my thighs. Beard face leered up at me, grimy teeth showing through the mass of hair. I stopped, feeling a smug satisfaction when I saw blood caked near his split lip.

"Aww," I said, the rage building inside making me reckless, "did my friend do that?" I flicked a finger at his mouth. "You remember her. Little bitty thing. Barely bigger than the fleas that probably live in that mangy beard?"

The man's grip tightened on my horse's bridle. He jerked her head down savagely to get to me.

"Rackley!" Bran barked from the doorway, leading a bound and gagged Phoebe. "Leave her be."

Her hands were tied so tight before her, I could see them reddening even in the bouncing torchlight. Her auburn wig hung slightly askew. Bran, following my stricken gaze, discreetly tugged it back into place.

Phoebe swore through the cloth gag stuffed into her mouth and tried to lunge at him. Bran handed her off to a gangly youth with a lantern jaw, who picked Phoebe up— keeping well out of foot range—and swung her into the saddle.

"You are dismissed," Bran told his men as he swung up onto his own mount, taking Phoebe's lead rein. "I've no more need of you tonight."

Rackley mumbled into his beard but didn't dispute the order. The young guard, though, looked dubious. "Are you certain, milord? The little wench throws a mean punch. And the lady shan't be pleased if aught goes amiss."

"I have my orders," Bran insisted. "Lady Celia has plans for them."

"Yes I do, my son," a female voice called from the gate.

I froze, unable to draw breath as the woman's throaty laugh drifted through the night. I shot a questioning look at Bran, but his face was inscrutable as he stared at her silhouette, backlit by torchlight.

When the riders clacked into the courtyard, the last of my hope floated away with the whirling snowflakes. First came the burly Flint. Bran's jaw tightened at the sight of him, but the man only shrugged as if to say, *Sorry, mate, you don't pay the bills.*

Though she was much older than she'd been in the photo I'd seen in the library, I had no trouble recognizing her.

Celia Alvarez. The elegant features had coarsened from that of the pretty young girl. But she was still lovely, with a heart-shaped face and high forehead. When she saw me, her wide mouth stretched into a satisfied smile.

She chuckled at my expression, a throaty sensual sound that crawled down my spine like a centipede.

"I wondered, you know"—she spoke in a heavy Spanish accent—"what you would look like now." My knuckles whitened on the pommel as she shrugged and moved closer, so that her knee grazed mine. "My son's pictures do not do you justice."

Bran moved his horse to my other side. They hemmed me in, and I felt the familiar tightening begin to swell in my chest.

"You were right," she said to Bran. "She is pretty."

"Mother," Bran started, but someone called out, cutting him off.

"Lady Celia." My head whipped around at the familiar voice. "May we get on with this? I have other duties to attend."

I hadn't even noticed him, all my attention focused on my mother's enemy.

Thomas Becket pursed his lips as he looked me over. "I have a cell ready for her."

"Cell?" Bran asked.

"Yes." Celia clapped her hands, delighted. "Sarah's daughter shall go with the good father." She gestured at Phoebe, who was glaring hard at her over the gag. "I had thought to let Moira's granddaughter go. Then I remembered years ago overhearing her warn her son away from me. So I believe they shall both suffer."

"Milady," Becket interjected, "I have no time for this. I want the girl taken into custody. Now. I must return to His Grace."

Celia's dark eyes flew to his face. "You will get me the Jews' stone, yes?"

"Yes, but the king—"

"No excuses," she snapped. "That was our arrangement when I came to you all those months ago. I gave you the gold to finance your rise, did I not? And I told you of the holy visions, yes? That you would become powerful. The king's right hand? That if you get me this stone, you will rise as high as the king himself. And are these things not coming to pass?"

Thomas Becket blanched. "Yes, milady," he mumbled. "You did. They . . . they have."

"Then take the girl," Celia said. "And get me the stone." Her upper lip peeled back from white teeth. "Or go back to being nothing but a lowly priest. A nothing. The son of a petty knight."

I tried to catch Bran's gaze, but he was staring down at his horse's mane, frowning. As Celia turned away from Becket, her eyes rolled to the sky in contempt.

She hates him, I realized. *She's just using his greed to get to the Nonius Stone.*

I swallowed down the shards of fear and straightened in my saddle. As a plan began to coil out before me, Celia raised a hand.

"Guards," she called. "You may dice for the little red-head. Whoever wins can take her. Do what you will. Pass her around if you wish. I care not. The other will enjoy the hospitality of the good father's prison cell."

CHAPTER 31

Every cell in my body tightened. *Focus, Walton. For God's sake, focus.* Figure this out.

The clamor in my head quieted. I opened my eyes to see the calculated paths of escape forming before me in brilliant neon swoops. I discarded one after the other, until only one route remained.

Celia walked her horse over to whisper with Flint. The guards crouched near the front steps, throwing dice against the cobbles. The dice rattled as they hit the stone. The younger guard groaned and let Phoebe's reins dangle to the ground.

The bearded one chuckled. "Mine."

"Hope, you have to believe me." Bran's whisper brushed against, but didn't penetrate, my concentration. "I didn't know about Becket."

My eyes caught Phoebe's, and I mouthed, *Hold on.*

With one finger, I tapped the high front of my own saddle. Phoebe nodded, and her tied hands moved to grip the squared-off section.

Bran, a horrified expression tugging down his mouth, trotted over to his mother. The two of them began arguing in rapid-fire Spanish.

Slowly, discreetly, I gathered my reins and took a deep breath. "Now!" I screamed at Phoebe, who kicked her horse into motion.

The startled animal leaped toward mine. I pressed my knees into my horse's sides, turning her parallel with my friend's mount. Bending low, I snatched up Phoebe's dangling leads.

"Oy!" One of the guards yelled behind us. "Milady!"

Shouts and a crash sounded behind us. Footsteps pounded. The gate was open, but Celia savagely wrenched her horse around and moved to block our exit. I gathered Phoebe's reins and pulled her closer. "Right through," I said.

Her clenched teeth glowed white as she nodded and hunkered over her animal's neck. Celia drew something from her sleeve. I burrowed my heels into my horse's sides. *Go. Go. Go.*

Celia stood her ground. My horse tried to veer, but I held the reins taut. It was a game of chicken, and from the triumphant leer on Celia's face, I wasn't sure who'd win.

Racing at my side, Phoebe muttered a prayer. My eyes were fixed on Celia. On the knife clutched in her hand. We were on a collision course. She wasn't backing down, but neither was I.

From the corner of my eye, I saw a horse suddenly rear, forelegs flailing at the winter air. Bran's mount leapt forward, plunging into the side of his mother's beast, causing it to stumble out of our path. Moonlight flashed on steel as we surged past. Then we were out the gate and galloping down the street. I had no idea if Bran had done it on purpose or if his horse had simply gone skittish.

Doesn't matter, anyway. He's the enemy. He's a liar.

With her hands still tied, Phoebe reached up and wrenched the gag down past her chin. "Hope," she gasped. "Those bloody bastards stole my bag."

"What does—"

"The extra bracelet," she cried over the pounding hoof-beats. "The one we brought for Sarah. It was inside."

Phoebe's stricken look made my heart plummet. My mom's bracelet was gone. Without it, we didn't have enough lodestones for us all to get home.

"Jesus, Hope, what will we do?"

"I don't know," I panted as the horse pounded beneath me. "We'll figure it out. But first—"

The thud of pursuit sounded on the muddy street behind us. I knew there was only one place we might—*might*—find refuge.

"This way." I kneed my horse, jerking the reins to the left. "We're going to Baynard's Castle. It's our only shot."

We raced, side by side, down one crooked lane after another. At each turn, they gained on us. Cold air that stank of fish and the dank Thames stole my breath as it rushed past my face.

"Good girl," I called to my horse. "Keep going."

"Bloody damn! Hope, they're coming."

"Go," I urged.

"Help us," I screamed to the guards as we thundered toward the gate, playing my only card. "Sister Hectare sent for us, but there are thieves on our tail."

The guards exchanged a look. One shrugged and stepped aside. We plunged through the gate just as the other shouted for the crew behind us to halt.

"What now?" Phoebe asked as we thundered across the courtyard to the front entrance.

"Now we pray Sister Hectare is here," I huffed. "And that she'll help us."

After dismounting, I quickly untied Phoebe's hands. It took every bit of breathless coaxing before the stern-faced guard at the front entrance agreed to send a servant to see if Sister Hectare was there.

He allowed us inside the entrance hall but set a pimply guard to watch us. The castle had an empty feeling. Only a few torches, set at intervals, lit the long hallway as the minutes passed.

Come on. Please be here. Please.

I heard a woman's raised voice just outside the massive front doors.

"Oh crap," I whispered to Phoebe. "I think they got in the gate."

"What is your business here?"

I whirled to find a wimpled servant approaching, one I'd

seen in Eleanor's chambers — *Was it only yesterday?* She was scowling, which didn't bode well for us.

I assumed what I hoped was an imperious demeanor. "It's imperative that we see Sister Hectare immediately."

The servant eyed our soiled, wrinkled gowns. "I assume that the good sister has gone with the queen to the Tower, where she and the king reside until coronation on the morrow. And even if she were here, it is late and I would not disturb her."

Idiot. I chastised myself. *You knew that. Even in our own time, the king or queen traditionally stays at the Tower of London the night before their coronation.*

"Thank you, Wilifred."

My knees went weak as Thomas Becket, still disheveled and out of breath, slithered out from a side door.

Where the hell did he come from? I forced myself not to flinch. Beside me, Phoebe let out a quiet groan.

A malevolent smile played around Becket's mouth. "I'm sorry you were disturbed, good madam," he said to the servant. "I'll see these young ladies returned to their *rightful* place."

"Father Thomas." Wilifred's age-spotted hand rose to her chest at the sight of the priest. Blotches of red spread across her withered cheeks, and I swear she fluttered her drooping old eyelids at him. "You know I would do anything for you. It is so nice to see a decent English face among all these . . . foreigners."

With a last glance over her shoulder, the aged servant mounted the steps. Thomas Becket turned to us with a triumphant sneer.

Ignoring Phoebe, Becket reached forward and grasped my chin in a pinching grip. His malicious eyes bored into mine. His breath stank of old meat. "Lady Celia claims that besides being a spy for the loathsome French, you seek the stone as well. I guarantee, however, that I shall learn your secrets before this night is over." His long fingers squashed my cheeks against my teeth so hard, I tasted blood. "You silly, stupid little girl."

"And yet," a vibrant voice spoke from a darkened doorway, "you seem somehow afraid of her, Thomas. Why is that?"

With a wrench, Becket released me. I spun, then sank to my knees as a round, magnificent figure glided toward us.

"Y-Your Grace," he stuttered, bowing. "What are you doing here? I had thought you abed in the Tower."

Eleanor of Aquitaine ignored the question. She brushed by Becket and waved a pale hand to Phoebe and me. "Get up, get up."

Inserting herself between us and the priest, Eleanor turned to Becket. "The better question, I think," she said, "is why are *you* here, Thomas? Henry was bellowing for you earlier. Why is it that you are not stuck to his side?"

A shadow rippled over Becket's face. He glanced over at a set of steps. From the damp, fishy smell that wafted from that direction, I thought they must lead down to the river landing, where boats could transport people quicker from one castle to another.

"I wouldn't tarry, Thomas." Eleanor's voice stabbed at the next word. "*My* Henry is not a patient man."

With a fierce exhalation and whirl of black robes, Becket lunged down the steps. As Eleanor watched him go, I released a breath that flapped the jewel-encrusted ribbons sewn onto the queen's sleeve.

"Hectare took to her bed earlier this evening." Eleanor turned to us. I could see worry flit across her face before she began to ascend the steps toward the upper chambers of the castle, where Rachel and I'd been the day before. "I summoned the Jewish apothecary and his granddaughter to tend her. She . . . She is dear to me."

Fatigue carved faint lines in the queen's face. She grasped the rail and hauled herself up.

When we didn't immediately follow, she snapped over her shoulder, "Well, come on, then. Hectare insisted the two of you would appear here this night and that I must bring you to her at once."

Phoebe and I exchanged a look.

How? Phoebe mouthed.

I shrugged in answer as we followed Eleanor's train up the marble steps.

CHAPTER 32

SISTER HECTARE LAY BENEATH A MOUNTAIN OF FURS, HER
small form dwarfed by the huge four-poster bed in a chamber that rivaled Eleanor's own. She shivered, despite the
heat from two enormous copper braziers and a crackling fire
in the small open fireplace, the first I'd seen in this time.

Papery eyelids closed, the little nun's cracked voice whispered for Rachel to add more coal. An elderly man brewed
a pot of medicine over the fire as Rachel dumped more coal
into one of the braziers. The moment we entered, Eleanor
rushed to Hectare's bedside. Rachel's tired face transformed
with delight at the sight of us.

I breathed in the scent of simmering herbs and camphor
as we watched the queen take one gnarled hand in hers and
kiss it. "The girls were below, just as you said they would
be."

Without opening her eyes, Hectare smiled. "Thank you,
my child. Now, please, go back to the Tower. Your babe
needs a rested mother. And you have much to do on the
morrow."

"And how many nights did you and Amaria sit at my bedside, nursing me through childhood illnesses? How many nightmares did you soothe after my father died and left my sister and me all alone? How many times did you stand at my side when everyone else in Louis's court turned on me?"

"Yes, child." Hectare's eyes opened. She turned her head on the pillow and fixed her rheumy eyes on the queen. "But you are precious. Your name will last through the ages as a queen of legend, though there is yet great sorrow in your path. You'll bear Henry more children. *Too* many, I think," she said with a chuckle. "Mayhap you'll want to bolt your door from time to time, eh?"

Phoebe and I exchanged a startled glance. *How could she know all those things?*

Eleanor's response was cut off when Hectare's laugh morphed into an alarming cough. It racked the woman's bird-like frame. Between them, Rachel and Eleanor raised the sister up. The old man hurried to the bedside and handed the queen a pewter cup. She placed it to Hectare's cracked lips.

When she'd taken a couple of sips, her breath eased, though the map of wrinkles around her mouth remained a dusky color. "Thank you, kind physician. I wish we had more with your skills here."

The man bowed. His clothes were plain. A clean, but patched, brown tunic. A conical yellow hat slumped on his head. As he approached, I saw Rachel's honey eyes peer out of his leathery face. "I take it you are the friends of my

Rachel, yes?" He gave a quick bow, speaking in a thick accent. "I wish you good eve. I am Aaron ben Yitzhak, and I owe you my thanks for helping my granddaughter. If I may ever be of service, you have but to ask."

Even from our place near the foot of the bed, I could hear Sister Hectare's labored breath. Without waiting for a response, Aaron hurried back to his concoctions.

"You shall not leave me." Tears roughened Eleanor's voice. "I am your queen, and I order you to stay."

"Sweet child," Hectare rasped. "Even someone with your strength cannot tell God when to call His children home. And why have me moved from my own chamber? All this"—her gnarled fingers flicked toward the animal skins covering the floor, the lush pastoral tapestries, the heaps of plush pillows behind her head—"seems rather like setting an old crow into a lark's cage."

Ignoring the comment, Eleanor settled her bulk on an embroidered chair next to the bed and swiped a hand beneath her eyes. "Nonsense. And besides, now you have room to receive your guests properly."

The old woman's gaze shifted in our direction. "Ah, the lost lambs who are so very, very far from their own pasture."

A fierce urge overtook me, to fall sobbing at the little nun's side and confess everything that lay so heavy on my heart. How I'd always been such a coward. How I'd disappointed my mother so many times, and how I was going to fail her yet again. How I was petrified for Collum. How I felt so small, and how badly I wanted just to forget everything and go home. A strangled sob escaped. Though I tried to stifle it, Sister Hectare's gaze lit on me.

With a gesture, Hectare drew Eleanor close and whispered in her ear for a long time. When she was finished, the queen drew back, stunned. Her head pivoted incrementally toward us, her face gone moon pale.

As the queen stared at us in wonderment, Hectare whispered, "Yes. It is as I told you, child. And we must help them return to their rightful place."

CHAPTER 33

"How can this be?" Eleanor whispered.

The smile that crinkled Hectare's craggy face was one of the most beautiful things I'd ever seen. "The sisterhood knows many things, child."

Eleanor stared hard at Hectare for a long time before she nodded.

"Rachel," the queen called, though her voice sounded shaken. "I believe I hear boots in the hallway. That would be Captain Lucie, with word of the girls' brother. Would you kindly allow him entry?"

Rachel's hand tightened around a lump of coal. When she opened the door, the longing on her face was so plain, I wondered that no one else noticed. William Lucie stared down at her for a long time. Then, remembering himself, he hurried to present himself to his queen. He brought the smell of outdoors with him. Smoke and winter air.

"You found where the brother is kept?" Eleanor asked without preamble.

"Yes, Your Grace." William bowed low to his queen, then turned to Phoebe and me. "The city watch took the prisoner to one of the lower cells. They will allow no visitors."

Eleanor grimaced. "I wish I could assist, but even I cannot be seen supporting a thief who stole from the king."

Next to me, I felt Phoebe bridle at the word "thief." I reached for her hand, squeezing to keep her quiet as fear, sharp as shattered glass, raked my insides. When Eleanor and Hectare began speaking in low voices, I gestured William and Phoebe to a spot near the wall, so the queen couldn't overhear.

"There's no chance we can see him?" I asked William in a hushed voice.

"I'm afraid not."

"Will—Captain Lucie?" Rachel joined us. "Are these the cells on the south wall, by chance? The ones with the window at ground level?"

William braced himself before he looked at Rachel. A charged moment passed between them as he stared into her eyes. "Yes. I believe so."

"Mistress"—Rachel turned to me, excited—"I know of these cells. My cousin was held there before he died. There is a small, barred window where you may kneel down and speak with your brother." She frowned then. "Though I doubt the guards would allow you access to the grounds."

She bit her lip in thought, then took William's arm and escorted him to the door. They spoke quietly together. He shook his head, but Rachel persisted. After a moment, he sighed and stared at her, drinking her in as though she was the last cup of water on earth. My mind began to sift through all the sketches I'd ever seen of the medieval Tower of London.

When Rachel returned, she was grinning. "Be near the southwestern corner of the Tower walls at dawn. There is a small gate there, little used. Captain Lucie will let you in."

As Phoebe thanked her profusely, my mind raced. "Rachel, how big is this window? Could a man get through it?"

"Well . . . yes, I think so." In seconds, she saw what I wanted to do. But then she shook her head, sadly. "But there are iron bars set across the opening. It would be impossible."

I gnawed at a cuticle, glancing across the room to where the queen sat, still holding Hectare's hand. Eleanor's head was bowed, and her lips moved in silent prayer.

Iron bars. Iron bars.

Chemical formulas wrote themselves in the air before my eyes. My fingers twitched as I discarded one after the other, growling with irritation.

Not invented yet. Too weak. Too volatile. I hesitated, calculating the odds.

"What are you thinking, Hope?" Phoebe whispered.

I looked to Aaron, who was adding a handful of herbs to his pot on the fire. "Rachel, does your grandfather's apothecary shop carry oil of vitriol by any chance?"

Rachel's brow wrinkled. "Yes, he makes it, then cuts it with water to clean his steel tools. If he makes an excess, he sells it to the blacksmith."

My lips struggled to form the words fast enough. "Does he have any now? Uncut? And could you get some and bring it to the side gate at the Tower?"

The confusion on Rachel's face cleared. "Oh! I see. Yes, of course. Of course I can."

"Would someone please tell me what you're talking about?" Phoebe said. "Because I'm about to pop my bloody—" She broke off, clearing her throat as she glanced at Rachel. "Er . . . I am soon to become quite angered."

I shushed her as Eleanor called for us to join her at Hectare's bedside. "Later," I whispered as we obeyed.

"We shall speak more of this on the morrow," Hectare was telling Eleanor, cutting off her queen's protest. "I give you my solemn vow that I shall still be in the land of the living. Go back to your husband. And for the babe's sake, if not your own, get some rest. In any case, I wish to speak with these girls alone."

When Eleanor sighed in defeat, Hectare placed a hand on her cheek in a sweet blessing that stung my eyes. We both dropped into a curtsy as the queen stood. Eleanor's eyes were bloodshot. She stared down at Phoebe and me as if we were ghosts.

"There is to be a masque at Westminster Palace tomorrow night, after the coronation. I will take chambers there. Come to me before it begins, and I will see that Lady Babcock attends me. And I . . . I would speak with you."

She's going to help us! Mom will have to obey a summons from the queen. She'll have no choice. Then I'll move heaven and earth to get her out, whether she wants me to or not.

"Thank you," I breathed. "Thank you, Your Grace."

The queen crossed to where Phoebe and I knelt, surrounding us with her unique smell. Roses laced with a spice I didn't recognize.

"Rise."

Her intelligent green eyes scanned back and forth between us. "I trust Hectare with my life." She paused, licking dry lips. "But this?" She took a step closer and looked deep into my eyes. Her voice husky with emotion, Eleanor whispered, "I wonder . . . will this world always belong solely to men?"

Slowly, carefully, without taking my eyes from hers, I shook my head. "No, Your Grace. Not always."

Eleanor's eyes closed. A smile edged her mouth as she sighed. "I shall, of course, not live to witness such a thing. But perhaps . . . to help sow the seeds of that glorious harvest?"

I didn't answer, though I knew that in the years to come Eleanor of Aquitaine would endow convents and be as much of a champion for female education and rights as was possible in her era. A thought startled me as I wondered how much of that was due to this moment in time.

Smiling, I allowed all the admiration I felt for the brave queen to shine through.

The queen of England nodded to herself. "Yes," she whispered as she departed. "Perhaps."

"What was that all about?" Phoebe said.

"Dear physician," Hectare called. Aaron hurried toward the bed and bowed low. "I thank you for your efforts," the nun said. "But like me, I believe you'd as soon rest those old bones of yours? If you will but allow your granddaughter to stay? She comforts me."

"Of course, learned sister," the apothecary said. "I shall return on the morrow."

Aaron left, and Sister Hectare asked Rachel to see about getting Phoebe and me a place to sleep for the night. When Rachel shut the door behind her, the nun patted the side of her bed. "Come, come, we haven't much time."

Hectare spoke in a voice like crinkling paper. "One of the few advantages to being very old is that one has seen so many mysteries, one can pick and choose which to believe."

"Sister?" I paused, but my gut was telling me to speak truth to this woman. "You . . . you know who we are, don't you?"

Phoebe's sharp elbow jabbed into my back. *What are you doing?*

"More than fifty years ago, when I was but an eager young novice at the abbey at Saint Evre," Hectare went on as though I'd not spoken, "I met a woman who had come to view one of our reliquaries." The nun's watery blue eyes studied us from behind her veined nose. "I was called to speak to her, as the woman's accent was difficult to understand and the saints had blessed me with an ear for languages."

Despite the overheated chamber, a chill skated up and down my spine. I asked in a quaky voice. "Was this reliquary decorated with a great opal, by any chance?"

I heard Phoebe's sharp intake of breath, but I couldn't move. Every muscle in my body strained for Hectare's answer.

"Yes." She nodded proudly, as if I were her student and I had come up with the correct cipher. "A stone of some repute, if the rumors were true."

Swallowing, I pressed on. "Do you happen to remember what the woman looked like?"

Hectare's grin showed her pale pink gums and creased her cheeks into a hundred wrinkles. "How could I forget?" she answered. "Considering I saw the same woman this very night at the feast. Black hair. Eyes that pierce. A haughty manner. And a face that had aged but little in over fifty years."

"Celia." Phoebe breathed the name.

"Just so," the nun nodded. "That was her name then as it is now. She wanted that stone very much. I could see it in her eyes. To be truthful, the woman frightened me. I recommended the sisters not allow her access."

"Bet she didn't like that much," I muttered.

Hectare chuckled. "No, no she did not."

"Sister," Phoebe asked, "do you know what happened to the opal? Is it still there?"

A flare of hope fired through me. We thought the opal in the Jews' dagger was the Nonius Stone, but what if we were wrong? What if it was still safe in a French abbey?

As if she could read my thoughts, Hectare shook her head. "No, child. The stone was sold off many years ago, before I was even called upon to help care for Eleanor and her sister, Petronilla. I've tried to keep track of it, however. All these years. There was something . . . odd about it. I—I needed to know where it had gone. I think we both know where it is right now: secure in the king's counting chamber."

Phoebe and I sat immobile, stunned. Recently—at least in our own timeline—Celia had traveled back fifty years before this time and tried to buy or steal the Nonius Stone from the nuns. She'd failed, thanks to this amazing little woman before us. I felt an enormous tenderness and grief wash over me. Hectare was fading, and the world would be a sadder place without her.

"Sister." I choked against the lump in my throat. "Why are you helping us?"

Hectare leaned forward and touched first my face, then Phoebe's. "The two of you," she said, "have a light around you that is so bright, I can barely see your features at times. It is a lavender shade that dances and flares from your skin. The black-haired woman also glows with this same light." The wise, ancient eyes turned to me. She laid a too-cold hand on top of mine. "Like this Celia, you do not belong here." Hectare's scratchy voice dropped. "Or am I simply being fanciful in my old age?"

"No," I whispered. Her dear, homely features blurred. "You're not being fanciful."

Hectare let out a deep sigh, and her eyes closed. "Then we must help you to get home."

CHAPTER 34

THE SNOW HAD STOPPED DURING THE NIGHT. OUTSIDE in the predawn, the London streets glowed oddly bright as a new coating of sugary snow reflected the expanse of stars above. Phoebe's black horse and my bay slogged through knee-high drifts toward the Tower of London. I couldn't quit staring up as the horses whuffed clouds of steam into the brittle air.

With no earthly light to compete against, a trillion stars glittered like tiny holes punched into a field of velvet, allowing an unearthly light to filter through.

Twenty-four hours. It's all we have left. Then the Dim will come. And if we aren't there . . . poof.

"Okay. My brain was too fashed when we went to bed, so explain it to me again." Phoebe jounced at my side. "The stuff Rachel's bringing."

"Oil of vitriol," I told her, "is basically sulfuric acid. I had a hunch Aaron might use it. It's common for apothecaries and blacksmiths during this time to keep a diluted form to clean their tools. We are going to use a full-strength version to melt those iron bars and get Collum the hell out of that cell."

"Will it really work?"

"It . . . it has to."

The streets were mostly empty, though we had to duck around a corner when a city guard stomped by, muttering to himself as he pushed through the pristine snow.

"I've been to the Tower before," Phoebe said. "On a school trip to London. There used to be a moat encircling the walls. How will we get over?"

I grinned. "The moat hasn't been built yet. Richard the Lionheart had it constructed. And at the moment, he's not even a gleam in Henry's eye."

Phoebe snickered as our horses ambled along, patiently wading through the powder. I patted my mare's neck. She tossed her head in answer, harness jingling in the stillness.

On the ride over, the crisp air cleaned most of the cobwebs out of my head, and I was able to mull over everything we'd learned. The Timeslippers were after the Nonius Stone. That was clear enough. And who knew what they might do once they had it.

Yet Celia's motives were murkier. I didn't know what had happened between my mom, Celia, and Michael MacPherson, but I was convinced it was key. Why go to all the trouble and risk of trapping my mother here? Of selling her out to the brutal Babcock? That took planning and foresight. No. Something else had occurred that night. Something besides Michael choosing to stay behind.

"There they are." Lost in the puzzle of what could've happened twelve years ago, I startled at Phoebe's alert.

"Yeah." I nodded, shaking it off to concentrate on the task at hand. "Good."

William and Rachel hadn't heard our approach, locked as they were in each other's arms. My heart squirmed as William pulled back and gently clasped Rachel's face between his palms.

"I cannot bear it," he was saying. "Please, do not go to him."

Rachel's face crumpled in agony. "You know I must. My father, he—"

"Damn your father." William seized her arms. "All he cares for is the contract he'll gain if you marry into that family. Tell me it isn't so."

She gazed up into his face, wet eyes sparkling in the low light, like nuggets of gold under a moonlit stream. He pulled her to him. When they swayed together, I could feel the misery streaming off them.

My horse whinnied, blowing steam. Startled, the two broke apart.

"Oy." William sent a final pleading look at Rachel before he stepped away. "There you are. Let's get this done."

After we dismounted, I hurried to Rachel and whispered, "I'm sorry. We didn't mean to interrupt."

Rachel swiped at her cheeks and tried to smile, but it wobbled and faded. "It matters not."

A single tear plopped into the snow as she bent to pick up the handle of a small iron pot. William opened the gate, obviously uncomfortable. He thought we were just going for a last visit. If he had known what we really planned, there was no way he'd have allowed it.

Once we made it through the thick wall and into the snow-packed yard, William spoke. "I'll wait outside and make sure no one comes. But I like this not. Pray you let me come with you."

He glanced at the pot dangling at Rachel's side. "Food for the prisoner," she lied. "He must be hungry, and even a thief deserves a meal."

William's eyes narrowed, though his shoulders slumped in acquiescence. "Hurry. Dawn approaches, and the guards make their round on the half hour. We must away by then." He pointed across a snowy expanse to where several ground-level, arched openings stood black against the paler stone. "Last one, near the back corner."

Once he was safely outside the wall, the three of us plowed across the yard. Our skirts grew heavy, as snow caked us to the knees.

"Is it strong enough?" I whispered to Rachel. "How is it not melting the pot?"

"'Tis lined with gold, which isn't affected by the oil. It's a fresh batch, though, and should attain our purpose."

It had to work. *Had* to. In a little over twenty-four hours, the Dim would come to take us home. And we were going to be there if it killed me. All of us.

"Collum?" I dropped to my knees before the low, barred window. "Collum, can you hear me?"

I pressed my face between the bars. Cold iron burned my cheeks. I ignored it, though I struggled to keep from gagging at the fetid stench. Rancid straw. Stale urine. Old blood. And worse.

"Coll!" Phoebe pushed in beside me. "It's us. Please, Coll. Answer me."

Nothing but black silence. What would it be like to be trapped there? Entombed there? What if Collum was still unconscious? What if they'd hurt him so badly, he couldn't walk? What if . . .

"Phee?" My shoulders sagged in relief.

Alive. He's alive.

"Phee? Hope? Is it really you? Or . . . no . . . I'm dreaming again."

I tried to keep calm, but the resignation in his cracked voice made me want to scream at the sky. "You're not dreaming, Collum." I said. "Listen. We're going to get you out. Can you walk?"

"Aye." A shuffling sound came to us as Collum moved closer to the window. I listened for a telltale clink but heard nothing but boots on reeking straw.

No chains. Thank God.

A pained inhale came from a few feet below us. "You shouldn't have come. If they catch you, I—I don't know what I'd do. Please, just leave me." Desperation infused the plea. It twisted up from that horrible, dark hole and wrapped around me.

Phoebe's nails bit into my forearms. She leaned forward and pressed her face hard against the bars. "Not likely, Collum Michael MacPherson." Her thin shoulders spasmed as she choked back a sob. "You know Gran would tan my backside with that wooden spoon of hers if I came back without you."

She hiccupped and rubbed a shaking hand under her nose. "Just be quiet and stand back. Hope has a plan."

"No!" His voice was fierce with alarm. "I won't risk you two getting caught. You have to go. I'm getting what I deserve, and that's the truth of it. I was stupid and—"

"You listen to me now," I hissed through clenched teeth. "We're not leaving without you. There's no time to explain. Just back away from the window and be ready."

"Don't," Collum begged. "It's not worth it."

"No man left behind," I said. "That's your motto, right? So listen to your own advice and back the hell up."

After a long pause, I heard the swish of hay as he moved aside. I knuckled away an angry tear. "Bring me the bucket, please."

Rachel removed a set of thick lead-lined gloves from a pocket and handed them to me. "Careful," she said as she unlatched the lid. "Do not spill any on you or 'twill eat clear through to the bone."

"Gah." Phoebe reared back as a putrid miasma of rotten eggs enveloped us.

With a quick prayer, I picked up the heavy pot and poured it carefully down one bar after another. Smoke blasted up as the liquid bubbled and foamed against the iron. I kept my face averted, but the fumes scorched my face and stung my eyes.

A miniscule droplet splashed onto the unprotected skin of my inner arm. I whimpered at the pain.

"Hope?" Collum's voice rose up from the pit. "What's wrong, lass? Are you all right?"

My hands shook as the acid burrowed through flesh into the muscle beneath, but I never faltered.

"Hush." Rachel moved up beside me, leather flask in hand. "She's burned herself." Cold water sluiced over my skin, making me moan as I poured the remnants of the vitriol onto the final bar.

The pot empty, I handed it back to Rachel and shook off the gloves. All we could do now was wait. And hope.

Metal sputtered and foamed as the minutes ticked by with agonizing slowness. Above us, the sky lightened in increments of gray. We'd run out of time. I picked up the leather gloves, but Phoebe stilled my hand.

"Let me," she said. "I'm stronger than you."

I stepped back without protest. Despite her tiny stature, Phoebe was nearly all muscle, while I had the upper-body strength of a toddler. Bracing her feet against the stone lip of the window, she heaved at two of the bars. They groaned, and one bowed but didn't break.

Panting, she tried again. "Aiii."

I glanced around. "Shhh," I said. "You'll bring every guard in the place down on us."

She crashed back on her butt as one of the bars snapped from its moorings. She held it up triumphantly. "One down."

A pinkish glow peeked above the wall behind us. *No time.*

Collum's voice sounded close as he spoke. "Phee, tell Mac and Gran I love them. And tell Lu—"

"Tell them yourself." Phoebe's voice squeaked with terror. "Now stand back. We're all going home—together. You hear me?"

"Maybe if we all try?" Desperation pulsed through me. *The guards will be here any moment. Hurry. Hurry. Hurry.* "I'll grab Phoebe. Rachel, pull on my waist. We'll—"

"Won't work," said a voice from behind us.

I whirled, groping for the knife in my boot. When his features came into focus, my throat closed up, but I didn't relinquish my grip on the blade.

Voice flat, I brandished the knife at him. "What are you doing here, Bran?"

Bran Cameron lifted one shoulder. "Out for a stroll." He squinted casually up at the pinkening sky. "Lovely morning, isn't it?"

"Look," I said through my teeth. "Just get out of here. Leave us alone."

He lifted one shoulder. "Could do that," he said. "Or I

could lend you a horse and a rope. As it happens, I have both."

Suspicion twined with a cautious exultation as I remembered him charging his horse at Celia. "Why?" I said. "Why would you help us?"

"After you got away, my mother was . . . well . . . a tad miffed." In the quickly strengthening light, I saw him press a hand to his side. "I thought it best to lie low, as it were, and spent a lovely night outside in a snowstorm, waiting for you to come out of Baynard's. Once I figured out what you were up to, it took me the devil of a time getting inside the Tower after curfew. Had to give the guards most of my gold and my best flask of Tuscan wine, but it won't hold them forever."

He didn't look at me as he brushed past and clicked his tongue. A gray horse stepped out from behind the corner. With quick, economical movements, Bran uncoiled a rope from the saddle and latched the attached iron hook around the bars.

He turned, his eyes intense on mine. "Shall we?"

I exchanged a look with Phoebe. Rage burned in her eyes as she gave a sharp shrug. Rachel just looked confused.

I nodded to Bran. "Yeah. Let's do it."

With an impertinent wink, he turned and spoke quietly into the gelding's ear. "All right, boy. Pull hard now."

We stood back as Bran Cameron hauled at the horse's reins. The animal's muscles bunched. My body strained with it, urging it on. *Go. Go. Go.*

The creak of leather. The squeal of bending iron echoed against the walls.

We're going to get caught. All of us thrown into cells to rot. Or hang.

Already I could feel the dank walls closing in, the scratch of rope around my neck as the gallows dropped.

Hurry!

With a horrible screech of metal, the entire unit of bars ripped from its moorings. One ragged edge slammed into the side of my calf as I leapt out of the way.

Bran didn't waste a second. He unhooked the rope from the bars and tossed it down into the shattered window. "Can you climb, mate?" he called quietly down into the cell. "Do I need to come after you?"

In answer, Collum's blood-caked blond head appeared in the opening. "No," he said as he scrambled the rest of the way out. "And just who the bloody hell are you?"

"Shh." I cringed as Collum's hoarse accusation carried across the snow. Ignoring the question, Phoebe and I clasped him under the arms and helped him stand. "Be quiet. We have to—"

"Oy!" A shout boomed down from an arrow slit a few stories above. Silhouetted against the flickering light, the guard yelled, "You there! Halt!"

"Brilliant," Bran quipped to Collum. "Since you've alerted the guard, I'd say this is no longer a clandestine mission."

With a deft hand, Bran untied the rope, dropped it, and casually leaped into the saddle. His eyes crinkled at the corners as he leaned down and let his knuckles brush gently down my cheek. "I'll meet you on the next block. I've taken rooms at an inn in Cheapside. They're not the most luxurious accommodations. But they're clean enough, and no one will ask any questions. Hurry now."

He kicked his mount into motion, heading around the side of the building as the rest of us fumbled through the snow to the small postern gate. Muffled cries of alarm rang out behind us, but William Lucie was there to open the gate and hustle us through. He frowned when he saw Collum, but at a quiet word from Rachel only locked the small gate and turned away.

CHAPTER 35

WITH A GROAN, COLLUM PULLED HIMSELF ONTO PHOEBE'S horse. His voice was taut with forced control. "Who," he said, "was that boy?"

Phoebe mounted behind me. Neither of us answered as we cantered away, leaving Collum to follow.

Dawn painted the tattered clouds in rose and lilac as Collum trotted up beside us. He hunched over his horse's back, nursing obviously-battered ribs. In the pinkish light, I got my first clear look at him. I groaned inwardly at the sight of his broad face, a ghastly bloody mask of swollen eyes, bent nose, and horrific bruises. Behind me, Phoebe stiffened against my back.

Though she hid it like a trooper, I could feel the shakes rattle her small body as she quickly explained how I'd come up with the plan for the oil of vitriol.

Collum didn't blink. "Answer the question."

"Does it matter?" I said. "He helped us, didn't he?"

Even as I said it, I still wasn't sure of Bran's motives. We could be walking into another trap. But something in his expression when he'd looked at me . . . I *wanted* to believe him.

Collum's scraped knuckles gripped the reins too tight, making his horse nervous. "He isn't from this time. I know what I heard. And though I may be a fool," he said, "I'm no idiot."

"You sure about that?" Bran nudged his gray gelding from a shadowed alley. "I'd say your idiot status is debatable at the moment. After all, who steals from the king at his own coronation feast?"

Collum kicked his horse forward. "Who the bloody hell are you?"

Collum's heftier mount pressed in, causing Bran's slim gray to stumble back. Bran glanced in the direction of the looming Tower, where shouts echoed up into the dawn sky.

"While I'd love to share some serious bro time with you, mate," Bran said, "maybe we ought to hold off until we *don't* have a cadre of the city guard running up our tails?"

Without looking back, Bran raced off. We followed until we were blocks away and the shouts of alarm had long faded. In this poorer area, the houses leaned on each other, as if for comfort. Two by two, we walked our mounts down the middle of the snow-packed street. Above our heads, shutters were thrown open and night soil splashed down onto the new snow.

Collum reined up. "Now," he said, "explain. Where did you come from? Who do you work for? Who are you?"

Bran held up a long, slender finger. "First, your perception that I'm not from this time is accurate, though unimportant to our current situation." Bran lifted a shoulder. In the dawn light, his jovial expression slipped, just for an instant. He kneed his mount closer to Collum until the animals jostled for position. Harnesses jingled, and leather creaked as they scraped together.

"As to your second question, based on recent events, I'd say I'm likely unemployed at the moment."

As his third finger rose, I leaned forward in the saddle. "Bran—"

"Third question." He dipped a short, mocking bow. "Name is Bran Cameron. I generally use my stepfather's name, though I suppose you'd have no trouble recognizing my legal one. In case you haven't worked it out yet, mate, it's Brandon Alvarez. Which—yes—makes Celia Alvarez my mum."

In the moment of stretched silence that followed, I knew what would happen. Knew it like I knew my own name or that the sun would set in the west.

"Coll," Phoebe begged at the same instant I kneed my horse forward.

Too late.

Collum kicked a foot free of the stirrup and lunged. He hit Bran sidelong, hurtling him from the saddle. Both boys tumbled to the snow in a tangle of fists and booted kicks.

"Timeslipper scum," Collum snarled as he pummeled Bran.

Bran rolled away and sprang to his feet at the mouth of

an alleyway. Collum was slower to rise. Already beaten and bloody, he hauled himself to his feet.

"Listen," Bran said, palms up in a conciliatory gesture.

But Collum was incapable of hearing. He darted forward, and before Bran could react, Collum had snatched one of Bran's curved blades.

Sparks flew as the edge of the sword scraped along the wall.

Bran's eyes narrowed. His hand moved to the hilt of the other blade.

"For God's sake," I growled. Bolting from the saddle, I shoved past the staggering Collum to stand between them.

I glared at Bran, whose sword was halfway from its sheath.

Don't.

Pivoting back to Collum, I huffed, "Look, we need Bran's help right now. I mean, I doubt we can totally trust him." I cast a withering glare Bran's way. "Since he *is* a noted liar."

Bran clutched his heart. "You wound me, madam."

I rolled my eyes to the clouds.

Phoebe called out from her mount, "Come on, Coll. If you're finished trying to carve each other up, I say we go with Bran before the city watch shows, yeah?"

Overhead, several heads peeked out of second- and third-story windows, watching the drama play out. Collum hesitated. I knew it must be hard for him to swallow. Rescued by the son of Celia Alvarez.

Well, he'll just have to get over it.

With a disgusted huff, Collum stalked to his horse.

Once he was mounted, Bran looked at me. One side of his mouth quirked. "Charming fellow."

"Bran," I said, wearily, "just . . . stop talking."

True to his word, Bran's inn was clean, if a bit worn around the edges. Collum, Phoebe, and I feared a trap. But when we entered, the first-floor tavern was empty.

The small room boasted a well-swept floor with long oak tables scoured until their scratched surfaces gleamed. A blowsy matron took one look at us and shouted for her rotund little husband to bring food. With a few quick commands, she sent two young maids upstairs with buckets of hot water for baths.

I loved her.

"Eat up," she ordered as steaming bowls of stew and loaves of brown bread were laid before us. "Then it's off to bed."

"If we weren't harboring a felon"—Bran lifted an eyebrow at a morose Collum sitting next to him—"I'd have taken you by the famous London cookshop that supposedly lasted for hundreds of years. It's said to be the only one of its kind. Open round the clock, twenty-four hours a day, cooking any kind of meat you can think of, in any way you can imagine. If you're rich, it's braised lark tongues with honey. Or quick-fried hummingbird in beer batter. Eels sautéed in browned butter, or boar smoked for days in a deep pit. For the poor . . . Well, they don't really discuss the meat's origins. But it's brown and served with thick onion gravy, so no one really cares."

"Hummingbirds?" Phoebe muttered through a mouthful of bread. "The poor wee things. That's barbaric."

"Barbaric? Hmm, perhaps," Bran teased. "But they're tasty little buggers. And afterward you can pick your teeth with the beaks."

Phoebe's brows shot up. I could see Bran's charm beginning to work on her. She snorted, choking back the laugh when she saw her brother frown.

Eyeing the bowl before me, I wondered at the origins of the meat chunks floating in this thick brown sauce. I wasn't hungry. Or so I thought, until the first tender bite passed my lips and I groaned. It could've used some salt, and for a second I actually looked around for a salt shaker.

Stupid. Only the rich could afford salt at table, and even then only for the most important guests. We definitely did not fit either category.

Salt or no salt, we all scarfed it down. Soon, I was sopping up the remnants with a crust of coarse bread.

Before I could ask, the innkeeper ladled another helping into all our wooden bowls. That one I savored, slurping it in long, delicious mouthfuls and washing it down with a crisp ale that sparkled on my tongue.

When we were done and the table cleared, Bran stood.

"I'd like to say something," he announced quietly. "If I may?" All humor erased, Bran's voice sounded grave and almost fragile as he glanced nervously at each of us in turn.

"In my life, I've done many things I regret." He cleared his throat and glanced up toward the ceiling.

When Bran's gaze dropped back to mine, the huge knot in my chest began to unravel.

"But I swear, I never wanted any harm to come to you. And if you could *try* to trust me, I'll do everything in my power to see you safely home." His blue and green eyes flicked to Phoebe, then Collum. "All of you."

Phoebe, Collum, and I exchanged looks. "He did help us, Coll," Phoebe said. "I say we give him a chance."

Collum's tawny head tilted as he studied Bran. "Fine," he said through clenched teeth. "But if you play us false, *boy*, I will kill you, aye?"

Bran's own jaw tensed in reflex, but he nodded. "Agreed."

Slowly, Phoebe and I filled them in on what had happened in their absence. Sister Hectare's tale of seeing Celia Alvarez at her convent, fifty years earlier. How the small nun somehow knew if not exactly *who* we were at least that we did not belong in that time. We told them of the queen's invitation to meet with her before the celebration that night, and how she'd make sure my mom was there.

When we explained how the lodestone we'd brought for my mother was stolen by the guards at Mabray House, Collum's head dropped into his hands.

"With Sarah's bracelet gone, there's no option, then," he said as he raised bleary eyes to mine. "We have to get the Nonius."

To Bran's credit, when we spoke of Celia and the stone, he didn't flinch.

"You must understand," he said, "my mother is obsessed with the Nonius Stone. She and Doña Maria—her grandmother, and the most twisted old bat you'll ever meet—have a master plan. I, however, am most definitely *not* part of their inner circle."

He held up a hand as Collum made to protest. "No, mate, I admit I knew about the visit to the convent. It happened a year or so ago, and Mother was furious. I find it both amusing and ironic that the good sister is here." Bran took a deep breath, visibly bracing himself as he went on. "There is something you should know, however. Recently, my mother and Doña Maria recruited a new chap, a genius, who's been tinkering with Tesla's design. When they noticed the timeline to this place was relatively stable, he conceived a way to incorporate the Nonius Stone directly into the electrical components. Something about encasing the gem inside copper housing. Or at least that is what he claims. I don't know the details, but apparently, the stone would allow us—allow them—to open and close the Dim at will, and go anywhere, to any time, they wish."

"Bran's telling the truth," Phoebe said to Collum. "That matches with what Sarah told us."

Collum nodded, his poor, wrecked face solemn as he murmured, "And with that kind of control, there'd be no stopping them."

"The only thing of which I'm absolutely certain," Bran finished, "is that the Timeslippers *will* go after the stone tonight. The exit point we came through will close about midmorning tomorrow. As for the rest, believe me or not. But my mother has *never* confided in me."

I noticed an almost imperceptible tightening around his eyes when he spoke of Celia. Sure, she was a murderous lunatic, but she was still his mom, and he'd openly defied her to—

Save me.

"Bran?" I had to ask it. The answer might mean everything. "Back at Mabray House, did you push Celia out of our way on purpose?"

When his hand landed lightly on top of mine—warm, callused, strong—I looked up. Our eyes met.

"Do you truly have to ask?"

He said it so simply, so sincerely, that I could only swallow.

At the corner of my vision, I saw Collum lean in, hazel eyes hooded, fixed on the spot where Bran's slender, tanned hand covered mine.

"Well, then." I eased my hand back, ignoring the way the warmth lingered even as I picked up my horn cup. "I think—"

"Hold that." Collum raised a hand, shutting me down as he spun on the bench to face Bran. "Aye, you may've helped us today." He shrugged, mouth pursed, as if the words tasted bitter. "But you're still a bloody Timeslipper."

Bran's hand splayed on his chest in mock offense. "Well, that stings a bit."

"We may need you for the moment," Collum said, ignoring Bran and rising halfway off the bench. "But understand this: *I* am in charge of this mission. In charge of them."

As he flung a hand toward me and Phoebe, Bran reared up, meeting Collum nose to nose. "And a great job you've done so far, yeah? Getting yourself arrested. Leaving the rest of your team to fend for themselves. Was that part of this grand scheme of yours, mate? Top notch, then, I'd say."

"Why, you limey bast—"

"Not again," Phoebe groaned.

"Oh hell no!" I shoved back so hard, I nearly sent her tumbling off the bench. Marching around the table, I planted myself between the two bristling boys. "Sit," I ordered. "Now. Both of you."

To my utter shock and amazement, they did. I'd never ordered anyone around before. I decided I rather liked it.

"We," I said, "are going to work together to get out of this mess. So you two are gonna cut all this machismo crap and stop being such . . . such . . . *buttholes* to each other."

Bran snorted. Then his head fell back, and he howled with laughter. Phoebe giggled, and even Collum's mouth twitched. A momentous accomplishment on my part.

I was offended. Here I was trying to assert the tiniest bit of authority for once in my life, and they were *laughing?*

"What," I spat, "is so freaking funny?"

"A butthole?" Bran wheezed to Collum. "I don't know

about you, but I haven't been called a butthole since I was in primary. I have literally *never* been so terrified. I think we'd better agree, or we're likely looking at big trouble from this one."

I pointed at Bran, pinning him with my sternest look. "I've said it before, and I *know* I'm going to say it again: You. Stop. Talking."

Bleary with food and exhaustion, we trudged up the stairs to our rooms. I mumbled to Phoebe as we climbed, "Shame we can't watch the coronation. To be so close . . ."

"Not me." Phoebe yawned as we entered the small bed-chamber. Her eyes lit on the steam rising from a wooden hip bath. "You couldn't get me to move from this spot for a brick o' gold."

"While you bathe and rest, I'll have the girls brush out your gowns." The serving matron frowned at our near-ruined dresses.

"No need," Bran called from the hallway.

Without asking, he strode in, hefting a trunk. "Before I left for the Tower, I took the liberty of having some of your things brought over. A helpful young girl named Alice packed them for you. Though apparently some shrew of a housekeeper gave my man a bit of trouble."

"Hilde," Phoebe murmured in a drowsy voice. "I almost miss that moldy old hag."

"The innkeeper's wife will tend to MacPherson's injuries

and give him a tincture to help with the pain. He'll sleep for a while." Bran set the trunk down with a bang. "Get some rest." He winked at me as he sauntered out. "I'll see you soon."

Phoebe's eyes narrowed as he closed the door behind him. She wheeled on me.

"What?" I asked, suddenly finding great interest in a row of wooden clothing pegs that protruded from the wall.

"You know very well what," she said as she began unlacing the sides of her filth-spattered gown. "And I get it, I do. The lad's charming and no mistake. And he did help us today. I want to trust him too. I do, but." She paused, until I reluctantly met her gaze. "Just be mindful, Hope. Remember, he's still Celia's son."

As if I could ever forget.

Seconds after her bath, Phoebe was snoring in the narrow bed. I took my time, even though the water was barely tepid. Despite the small, red-hot brazier in the corner, I was shivering by the time I'd dried off and pulled the clean shift over my head.

A soft knock startled me. Dust motes danced in strips of late-morning light as I opened the door to find Bran Cameron staring at me. His eyes ranged from my face down to my bare feet. My toes curled when I realized I was standing there before him in only a threadbare shift.

I crossed my arms over my chest and tried to ignore the way that—even in the chill—I felt his gaze burn like a trail of coals.

"It can't be time to go already?"

"What?" His Adam's apple bobbed. "Oh. No. There's plenty of time. But I thought . . . maybe . . . you might care to see the coronation?" His eyes scanned my face.

I darted a glance at Phoebe, still dead-asleep beneath the covers. "I don't know about that. Collum might be recognized. We haven't even dyed his hair yet."

Bran studied the toe of his boot as it scuffed the floor. "Well, you see, I know a place we can watch the entire event without being seen. The abbey isn't far if we use a shortcut, but there's only room for two. Of course, if you don't want to go without them," he hurried to add, "I'd understand."

I nipped at a cuticle as I studied him. The thought of witnessing one of the most remarkable events in history sent a thrill through me. But though Bran had risked his life to help us, he had still lied to me. About everything.

Yet nearly all the nobility in England would be there. What if Mom was among them?

"I heard you say you wished," he started to turn away. "Never mind. It was just a thought."

"Wait." I reached a hand out to stop him. "I'll go."

CHAPTER 36

THE STONECUTTER'S SCAFFOLDING WAS DRAPED IN YARDS of scarlet silk, disguising our climb.

"Are you sure this thing will hold us?" I whispered as the wobbly wooden structure creaked beneath our weight.

Bran's ash-colored tunic blended with the dappled stone of Westminster Abbey as he spoke from a few rungs above me. "It better," he said. "I paid the mason a fortune to let us have his spot." He frowned, letting his gaze drift down my simple gray gown. "Unless you weigh more than a half ton of granite?"

I punched him in the leg.

He was still chuckling as we emerged onto a narrow platform that butted up against the ceiling. Crouching, we eased over to the edge and settled, arms propped on a rickety wooden railing. Our boots dangled a hundred feet above the floor.

Even at this great height, the sweet melange of melting beeswax and incense wafted up in waves, mixing with the lilting voices of a hundred choir boys. Carefully, Bran parted the rippling silk. I sucked in a sharp breath.

Our bird's-eye view was perfect. Far beneath, the new king and queen of England knelt on the steps of the altar, upon which sat two thrones. One large and sturdy. The other smaller, delicate. As the song faded, the magnificently robed archbishop of Canterbury raised his arms before them. I shivered when the king and queen made sacred vows that echoed up to us, as clear as if we stood at their side.

The priest took a small bottle and anointed the royals with holy oil, then placed the crowns of England on their heads.

Henry helped Eleanor rise. Once they were seated on their thrones, the archbishop lay the scepter and orb in Henry's waiting arms. He turned and threw up his hands as he called, "God save the king. God save the queen."

The roar blew the roof off the place. The reverberation rocked the scaffolding beneath us.

"Can you believe we're actually seeing this?" I elbowed Bran in my excitement. "It's so surreal."

I glanced over to see if he felt it. The sense of wonder at witnessing this incredible piece of history. But Bran wasn't watching what played out below. No. He was looking at me. Watching *my* face, *my* reactions. A fluttery heat skittered across my skin, like butterflies on fire.

"Thank you for this," I whispered.

The smile that lit his eyes left me breathless.

He leaned in, and I could almost taste his scent on my

tongue. Salt and wood shavings. Snow and smoke. And somehow . . . the winey tang of overripe apples.

"Hope," he whispered. His eyes darted from my eyes to my lips and back, as if he couldn't see everything at once. "There's something I need to tell—"

A furious cheer erupted. We both turned to see the royals marching down the central aisle, a long trail of nobles in their wake. I leaned forward, thrilled to see the crabbed, dark figure of Sister Hectare take her place behind her queen.

Standing, I leaned over the waist-high railing, scanning the top of each head to see if I could recognize my mother. There were too many, crowded in too close. Agitated, I huffed and stretched out a little more.

"Come on," Bran scrambled to his feet. "We should probably get—"

The flimsy barrier gave beneath my weight. As if in slow motion, I watched it tumble, snagging against the silk drapes as it plummeted to the abbey floor, the crash lost in the tumult of cheers and song. I had time for one, oddly calm thought before I pitched headfirst off the edge of the platform.

I'm sorry, Mom.

A rip of pain knifed through my hip as I jolted to a gut-wrenching halt. Above me, Bran crouched at the platform's edge, straining as he gripped the gray hem of my skirt and one, booted foot. Blood flooded my brain, filling my ears with the pounding of my own heartbeat.

"Oh God, oh God, oh God."

"Hold on," he growled. "I won't let you go. I swear it."

High above the marble floor, Bran cursed under his breath. His fingers dug desperately into my ankle as I swayed upside down. If anyone looked up, they'd see me, a gray pendulum against scarlet silk. My heart boomed, missing beats. Blood swelled my face as Bran began to haul me up, inch by painful inch. He reached out and grabbed my flailing hand. With a great heave, he jerked. I flew up and landed smack on top of him, nose to nose on the splintery platform.

Quaking with shock, I tried to form a coherent word. "I . . . I didn't . . ."

"You know," Bran panted as he stared up into my face, "If you wanted to get on top of me, you could've just said. No need for such dramatics." The flippant words were all Bran. But he negated them by wrapping me in his arms.

Electric flicks of adrenaline sparked across the back of my tongue, making my teeth chatter. Bran squeezed tighter, and despite what had nearly happened, I began to feel safe. To feel *alive*, as if up until that second, I'd only been pretending to live.

After a long moment, while our breaths synced and Bran's arms trembled with strain and something else, I became acutely aware of the long lines of his body pressed beneath mine.

"So," I answered him, teeth still clacking as I rolled off and rose on jittery legs. "Yeah, the next time you save me from diving off a hundred-foot drop, I'll remember to ask."

I knew immediately I was in a lot of trouble. At the tavern, Collum and Phoebe were embroiled in a fierce argument. Phoebe whirled away from her brother and rushed to me, enveloping me in one of her spine-cracking hugs.

"Crap on a cracker, I'm glad to see you," she whispered. "Collum's pure furious you left."

When I had extricated myself, I turned to face Collum. In the dusk of evening, only a small fire pit lit the empty tavern. It shadowed his features, though I could tell by his stance that he was livid.

"Well," he asked in a deceptively calm voice, "if you don't mind my asking, where in blazes did you go?"

"Bran took me to the coronation," I said. "We—"

"I told you they'd be back, Coll," Phoebe hurried to intervene. "See? Everything's fine, so don't get your breeches in a knot."

Collum brushed his sister aside and moved across the three feet that separated us. Bran started forward, but Collum stopped him with a raised hand as he stared down at me.

"So," he said in a deadly voice, "without a word, you just run off with some stranger?" His upper lip curled as his gaze darted to Bran. "This Timeslipper boy whose own mother wants to give you to Becket? What if it had been a trap?"

"It wasn't—"

"Do you have no thought for your own safety? Or at least for the mission we've come to carry out?"

"Nothing happened," I lied. "Look, Collum, I know we shouldn't have gone. It was stupid, but Mom—"

"'Stupid' doesn't begin to cover it," he roared. "You are my responsibility. I swore an oath to Lu to keep the both of you safe, and I plan on keeping that promise."

Bran grunted at that, but I ignored him as Collum raged. "I cannot believe you'd take a chance like that. Not when we're going after Sarah tonight."

"Oh, *you* have a lot of room to talk," I shouted back. "You're a hypocrite, going all superhero, trying to steal that freaking dagger. Talk about stupid?" I was shaking, all geared up to say a whole lot more. But the words dried in my throat when I saw anguish pinch the skin between his earnest hazel eyes.

"You're right," he said, nodding. "Aye. I betrayed this mission. Lost my wits when I learned the Nonius might be near. It's just that I—I've wanted to find it for so long." Collum dropped onto a three-legged stool, head in his hands as he mumbled. "But look what happened. I failed, and endangered everyone in the process. What do you think would happen to Sarah . . . to Lu . . . if I lost the two of you?"

My cheeks burned as shame wormed through me. After the stunt Collum pulled, how could I have been so selfish? All that mattered was stealing Mom away from that monster, and getting us all home safe.

"I'm sorry, Collum," I said, meaning it. "It won't happen again. I swear."

Standing, he raked his hands through his short hair. "As do I," he said. "So let's put all the nonsense behind us and focus on the mission, yeah?" He looked from me to Phoebe, and finally to Bran.

Bran gave a mock salute. "Aye, sir," he said. "I'm always up for an adventure."

CHAPTER 37

WE REACHED THE PALACE OF WESTMINSTER IN AN EARLY
winter dusk. Fat flakes lazed down to rest on our hair and
shoulders as our horses' hooves crunched and squeaked on
the new crust. The moon peeked out intermittently from
behind high, racing clouds, transforming the falling snow
into a silver rain. From the lights and sounds coming from
inside the enormous building, it appeared the place was already in full-out party mode.

After dropping our horses with the groomsmen, I shivered inside my thick cloak. Admittedly, the deep plum skirts
and ash bodice of my gown were lovely, though the raw silk
was little protection against the cold.

"You realize this is completely insane," Bran whispered at
my side. "Bringing him with us."

I glanced back at my friends following close behind. The
walnut juice we'd used to dye Collum's blond hair and stain
his freckled skin gave him an odd, monochromatic look.
But if they were looking for him at all, on this night of celebration, it would be as a blond, not a brunet. The masks

everyone wore also covered eyes and noses, leaving only the lower half of the face exposed.

Plus, who would imagine someone who'd tried to steal from the king would be idiotic enough to return to the scene of the crime?

I kept stealing glimpses of Bran. Dressed all in black, with whorls of silver threaded throughout his tunic, he looked like a finely made sheath. Slim and supple. Lethal. A circular pin secured his dark cloak at the throat. Crafted of beaten silver, it held an opal the size of my fingernail.

I realized with a little jolt that it must be his lodestone. I hadn't seen it before. I frowned, wondering then when he'd have to get back to his own entrance point. If his mother would be there. If she would try to block him. The thoughts fizzled away when his eyes behind a leather mask fixated on my mouth.

"What?" I swiped at my chin. "Do I have a smudge or something?"

"Yes," he said in a sultry tone that rumbled along my nerve endings. "Right there." He edged closer and brushed aside a wayward curl Phoebe had left hanging by my ear. When his thumb skated along the edge of my lower lip, something pulsed deep inside me, stretching, waking.

The harried guards at the door barely gave us a second look. Revelers tumbled out of the packed Great Hall into the entrance portico. Masks—bedecked and feathered, or with beaked noses and grotesque horns—shielded all the partygoers.

"Well met." A sloppy drunk in yellow hose, purple tunic, ridiculous spangled mask careened over and slapped Collum hard on the back. "God save the King, eh?"

When Collum didn't answer, the man frowned. Staggering a bit, he peered up at Collum, face hidden beneath a plain cloth mask and cowled hood. "Did you hear me, man? I said God save His Grace our good King Henry."

I froze, but Bran didn't bat an eyelash. "God save the King!" he boomed, and plucked the goblet of wine from the man's hand. He downed the contents, belched loudly, and swiped a hand across his mouth before gesturing dismissively to Collum. "You must forgive my brother, good sir. He is naught but a feeble idiot and cannot speak."

Collum's head shot up at that, but the man only guffawed. "Perhaps on Yule Night the king will declare him lord of misrule. Come"—he snatched hold of Collum's arm and tried to tow him toward the Great Hall—"let us introduce him to the king now. Oh, this will be right good fun."

A ball of terror rose in my throat. If the king laid eyes on Collum, it was all over. He'd be cast back into that hole and hung. Collum shoved the drunk away. The man tripped over his own feet and stumbled back, affronted.

"Here, now. What's this?" he thundered, swaying. "Do you know who I am? Why, you bumbling imbecile! I shall have you thrown in chains for laying hands on me!"

My feet felt stuck to the floor. I couldn't breathe. Phoebe, however, was magnificent. Without missing a beat, she inserted herself under the man's arm.

"Milord," she cooed, "surely I am more interesting than some addle-witted fool? Perhaps, if you were to go inside and grab another goblet of wine, we might share it?"

The drunk's angry snarl was immediately replaced by lust as his gaze dropped from Phoebe's upturned face to her low-cut bodice.

Collum let out an agitated rumble. The man's attention wavered, but Phoebe was on it. She rose on tiptoe and planted a kiss right on the creep's wine-stained mouth. His glassy eyes widened behind the mask.

"Aye." He draped an arm around my friend's narrow shoulders. "Right you are, mistress. A cup of spiced wine would go a long way to wet this parched throat."

Phoebe ducked from under his arm but gave him a hearty smack on the butt. "Away you go. Find us a cozy spot, aye? I'll be right along."

Drunkie lolled away, leering.

I gaped at my friend. "Wow. *That* was amazing."

Phoebe gave a saucy wink and with an exaggerated sway of her narrow hips, sashayed toward the steps.

Watching her performance, Bran and I exchanged a grin. When his arm brushed against mine, a little thrill ruffled through me. Collum groaned as he followed after his sister.

"Come on, dove," Bran said, tucking my hand into the crook of his elbow. "Let's go save your mum."

Still smiling, feeling lighter than I had in days, I hurried up the steps toward the queen's chambers.

Eleanor was waiting for us. The moment we presented ourselves, she curtly dismissed her ladies and servants. The high noblewomen of England glared as they filed by in their brilliant courtly best. The servants followed. One, in a plain white wimple, ducked her face as she scurried out the door.

Sister Hectare reclined on a lush divan at the end of the queen's bed, furs piled on her tiny form. Except for two hectic spots on her protruding cheekbones, her skin was ashen.

She looks worse. So much worse.

The cough confirmed it. Queen Eleanor herself held the linen cloth to her mentor's mouth. When she drew it away, it was spotted with red.

"She overtaxed herself." The queen fussed, mopping at the nun's brow. "I told you the coronation would be too much for you. You are ill and should've stayed abed."

"And miss the moment the crown of England was placed on my sweet girl's head?" Hectare croaked. "Not likely."

The queen's regal manner had morphed the instant her ladies left. Now she just looked like a scared little girl. Her voice verged on panic as she muttered, "Where are Rachel and the apothecary with that tisane? They should have been here long ago."

"Your Grace." The words came out squeaky, too high. "Where is my . . . cousin? Where is Lady Babcock?"

Disgust rippled across the queen's lips. "Sir Babcock, that horrible little cretin, claims his wife too ill to leave her chambers. Even at his queen's command." Her thin lips pressed white together. "But worry not, I've sent my man to fetch her. She shall be here anon. No one disobeys my order."

My diaphragm constricted, pressing against my spine. *Too ill?*

The queen scanned the room. Her gaze lingered on Collum, his face shaded by the cloak. "Who is that man? Why does he hide his face?"

I looked to Phoebe and her cloaked, hooded brother, clustered together near the now-closed door.

"He is with us, Your Grace." I so hoped that would be explanation enough.

Eleanor stared hard at Collum for a moment as my pulse pounded in my temples. Yes, the queen had agreed to help us, but I wasn't sure how far that help would extend if she knew Collum was the very thief who'd stolen from her husband.

Hectare squinted blearily at Collum, then came to our rescue. "Never mind him, my girl. It is time. Give them the dagger."

All movement in the chamber ceased. I don't think anyone even breathed.

"It's here?" Bran asked in a reverent whisper.

We'd been prepared to beg. To somehow make them understand how important it was that we took the dagger with us. If that didn't work, we'd have had to steal it. With my mother's bracelet gone, it was the only way.

Hectare nudged the queen with a gnarled hand. Eleanor

stood, then from a nearby table retrieved a carved ebony box. As her ermine cloak glided along the rushes, a delicate scent of summer roses and nutty herbs drifted up.

When Eleanor withdrew the blade from its sheath, a walnut-size opal seized the candlelight and cast it back in blue and green shimmers that sparked across the beamed ceiling and tapestried walls. It was as though someone had captured the moon and imbedded it in the golden hilt.

My hand flew to my chest. Beneath the fabric of my bodice, the lodestone warmed against my skin. Bran reached up to clasp the cloak pin at his throat.

"My bracelet," Phoebe murmured.

From his place near the door, Collum quietly studied the ring on his right hand.

"Yes," Hectare said into the silence. "Our world is not yet ready for such a thing as this. It holds a power the ignorant might use for ill. I think it best that it leave this place. But . . . may I see it for a moment first?"

The queen stared down at the dagger, mesmerized.

"My child?"

The sister struggled upright on her cot, her stern command breaking the dagger's hold on Eleanor. With a grimace, she thrust it back into the sheath and handed it to Hectare.

The nun slid the blade out just enough to examine the hilt. She tilted her head, frowning. "I must have misremembered. I thought . . ." Hectare pursed her lips, and a thousand wrinkles radiated outward. "No matter." She slipped the blade home and held it out to me. "This old memory is not what it used to be. Take it."

Blindly, I snatched the dagger and handed it off to Collum. He stared down at the blade. I saw his shoulders bunch and his head bow as he rubbed a thumb over the stone.

Something was gnawing at me, though. Something about the stone. I tried to focus, but as each moment ticked by, a queasy trepidation began to build inside me.

Why isn't my mom here yet?

"Hectare would speak with the two of you," Eleanor called, waving Bran and me over. The queen looked wrung out, heart-bruised. "Do not tax her," she warned in a voice cracked with grief. "For I think she does not have much time left. I must find out where Rachel has gotten to. It is not like the girl to tarry."

The queen's footsteps dragged as she went to confer with the guard at her door. Bran and I knelt by the nun's cot. When I looked into her face, grief coiled through me at the dusky color around her lips.

"I've given much thought to you since we met, child." Sister Hectare spoke in a crackle. Paper ruffling in a breeze. "In my long life, the Lord has seen fit to grant me many gifts. When I look at those two over there"—she gestured to where Collum and Phoebe spoke quietly together—"it is as though I am seeing them through a long tunnel. It was the same with this Celia."

She coughed, wheezy and weak. Her rheumy gaze switched back and forth between Bran and me. "The two of you now, you are clearer to me." Hectare reached out and clasped my hands between hers. Her palms felt like silk and sandpaper. "The same yet different from the others."

A chill raced across my shoulders. I glanced at Bran, but his eyes were riveted on Hectare.

"None of you belong here." My hands bunched inside the old woman's skeletal grip. Her gaze fixed with Bran's as she finished. "Though you two are not so far away as the others. It is difficult to explain, though I see in the young lord's eyes he knows of what I speak, yes?"

Bran's response was so quiet, I barely heard. "I do, Sister."

Spent, Hectare fell back on the pillows. Exhaustion pulled at her parchment lids, but the corners of her mouth lifted.

I turned to Bran, but he wouldn't meet my eyes. "What's she talking about?"

"Ah," came Hectare's creaky whisper, "the girl does not know."

Bran closed his eyes. "No, Sister," he said. "Not yet."

CHAPTER 38

BEFORE I COULD ASK EXACTLY *WHAT* I DIDN'T KNOW, VOICES sounded outside the door. Collum stiffened, but Eleanor hustled to open it herself. William Lucie rushed in, cradling someone in his arms. She was hooded and cloaked, but I would've known her anywhere. Pain struck low and hard when I saw the coarse ropes knotted around her ankles. The severed ends swayed as she struggled weakly in the soldier's arms.

"No," my mother whimpered. "Take me back. He'll punish me again. I said I'd be good. I swore it. Please . . ."

The queen stepped forward, her voice glacial. "What is the meaning of this, Captain?"

He laid my mother gently on a chair draped with soft animal skins and pulled back the hood and cloak. Her eyes were red rimmed and wild as she slumped there, dressed only in a long white shift.

William dropped to one knee to address the queen, his kind eyes pinched in pity. "I found Lady Babcock in her chambers, as you said, Your Grace. Her guard is dispatched.

The lady had been most ill-used. Bound to her bed and . . ." A disgusted exhale through his nose. "She's been scourged, Your Grace. Her back is naught but a shredded mess."

Phoebe's hands covered her mouth. I wanted to run to my mother, who cringed and huddled over her round belly. But my knees had turned to water and my lungs to empty paper sacks.

Eleanor stiffened in outrage. "What? And she with child? This will not stand! Not in my kingdom."

My mother's weak voice filtered to me. "Celia told Babcock the baby wasn't his. That he'd been cuckolded. She *watched* while he did this to me. If the baby was a boy, he said he'd drown it in the river and lock me in my room until he got another on me. Take me back, please. Don't you see? She'll tell him I tried to run. She'll come after Hope."

Bran, suddenly at my side, gave a moan and dropped his head in his hands.

"Sarah. Sarah, listen to me." Collum's voice was so tender as he knelt down before her. "Hope's here. She's safe. And we're taking you to Lucinda. We're taking you home."

She shook her head violently. "No! If I do as she says, she'll leave Hope alone. She swore it."

Mom rocked forward. The cloak puddled around her hips. And I sucked in all the air in the chamber. All the air in the world.

"No," Bran whispered.

I closed my eyes, but the image was imprinted forever inside my lids. The back of my mother's shift had been ripped to the waist. The pale, freckled skin beneath was scored with dozens of torn, bloody lash marks.

My mother cried out as the air hit her raw flesh. I stumbled across the room and dropped to my knees beside her as Phoebe moved to the other side.

"What do we do?" My gut rolled at the blood seeping from the rips in her skin. "We need Rachel. She'll know—"

The chamber doors burst inward. Collum whirled and stumbled back as Thomas Becket sauntered in. Four members of the black-clad city watch formed a line behind him, dragging the limp body of Eleanor's guard, his chain mail jangling. Hate, white hot and pure, surged inside me when I saw the pale blond head of Eustace Clarkson move up next to Becket and shove a bound Rachel to her knees. Shuffling in at the rear was Wilifred, the old serving woman who'd been so enamored of Becket back at Baynard's Castle.

"It's as I told you, Father Thomas," she said, pointing at me. "The girl is here. And I saw this Jewess and Captain Lucie myself, embracing in the hallway less than an hour ago." She sneered down at Rachel. "Blasphemer."

William's hand was at his sword. He'd had eyes for no one but Rachel since the second they'd entered.

Thomas Becket clapped his hands in delight, then gave the simpering servant a pat on the shoulder. "You may go now, madam. I also thank you for bringing this sacrilege to my attention. A Christian and a Jew in carnal relations. The laws against this are clear, and they will both pay the price."

Eleanor glided across the room, her face flushed with

outrage. "How dare you burst into my chambers, you trumped-up clerk! And you"—she loomed over the now-cowering Wilifred—"you will live to regret this."

The serving woman paled under the queen's furious scrutiny. She bunched her shoulders as if warding off a blow and hustled out of the chamber.

I stared at Rachel, tears prickling my eyes when I saw the fresh bruise that marred her delicate cheekbone. Her yellow veil was missing and blood trickled from a swollen lower lip. Yet she appeared so serene, so poised. When her gilt eyes met mine, I gave a sharp nod, letting her know we'd get through this. Somehow.

"The bloody rat bastard," Phoebe muttered in Becket's direction.

"Enough!"

At Becket's shout, Eleanor advanced on him. "When my husband hears of this . . ."

"Oh, but I suspect he will not hear," he said with a condescending leer. "For if he does, will you not have to explain how two of *your* servants committed treason?" As he skimmed across the floor toward our little group, he pointed at Collum. "And that you concealed a thief under his very roof?"

Becket's men moved up behind him as he flipped the hood back from Collum's face and stepped back. The queen stiffened, but Hectare reached for her sleeve and pulled her down to whisper in her ear.

"And"—Becket's saturnine smile widened as his gaze

sharpened on me—"that you parley secretly with the French as well?" He pivoted toward the queen with a bark of laughter. "Oh ho, milady. I think His Grace would be *most* interested to learn of the company you keep, don't you?"

The queen paled, her mouth pressed into a thin line. Without a sound, Bran moved to Collum's side. With only the briefest hesitation, William Lucie joined them, creating a wall between Becket's men and the rest of us.

"Madam," Becket said, "you have taken an item presented to our king by the Jews of London. A jeweled dagger."

I forced myself not to look at the bag at Collum's waist.

"His Grace doesn't realize the value of the blade. He believes it naught but a pretty bauble. I've convinced him to gift it to the church."

"Oh really?" Bran muttered through clenched teeth. "You claim the dagger belongs to the church. Yet I know you promised it to Lady Alvarez. Which is the truth?"

Thomas Becket studied Bran. "Ah, the traitorous son. Your mother will be most pleased to see you." A fanatical light shone in Becket's eyes. "Lady Alvarez is blessed with holy prophesy. I've seen the evidence myself. This dagger holds an object of great evil. One cursed with pagan magic. Only Lady Alvarez can take it from here and destroy it."

"Priest." Sister Hectare pushed herself up on wobbly legs. The queen rushed to support her old friend. Frail, her back bowed, the little nun shook off the queen's arm. Exuding a magnificent dignity, she hobbled across the floor until she was standing directly before Becket. Her wavering voice gained volume and strength as she proclaimed.

"'Then the Lord saith unto me, the prophets prophesy lies in my name: I sent them not, neither have I commanded them, neither spake unto them: they prophesy unto you a false vision and divination, and a thing of nought, and the deceit of their heart.'"

Fury ignited Becket's gaunt features. With a movement too quick to see, his arm reared, striking the small, fragile nun in a backhand blow to the face that sent her reeling to the fur covered floor. Crossing himself, he hissed down at her prone, crumbled form. "Witch! You dare quote scripture to *me?* Our God has blessed Lady Alvarez with the gift of true sight."

Teeth bared, Bran took a furious step forward. "But you are the only fool who believed her."

Becket glared at Bran for a long moment. Then, lifting his chin, he mastered his rigid control.

He snapped his fingers as the thugs ranged behind him. "Search them, and bring me the dagger. I must away to the king. Secure the others in the Tower, but return Lady Babcock to her chambers." He made a mocking bow in my mother's direction. "I'm sure her husband would have words with her upon his return."

Mom whimpered, cradling her round belly. My jaw clenched so hard, I thought my teeth would shatter.

Eustace Clarkson mumbled something to the priest. Becket glanced down his long nose at the kneeling Rachel.

"Yes, yes," he said, dismissively. "You may have the Jewess for a time. Do what you will. Then she goes into a cell with the others."

A throaty, animal rumble came from William as Eustace stroked Rachel's hair. With a sweeping bow in his queen's direction, Thomas Becket slipped to the door.

"Becket." The queen knelt by her barely conscious friend. When she spoke, her voice sounded raw, dangerous. "We are enemies now, you and I."

"Your Grace," he said quietly, "do we not already walk that path?"

As Becket opened the door, the queen of England slowly got to her feet. "Priest," she called. Regal and brilliant and cold as the moon in her fury she said, "The day will come when I shall see your blood spilled for this, Thomas Becket. This is my vow."

Tiny hairs prickled on the back of my arms as Bran and I exchanged a stunned look.

Had *we* changed history, or only aided in its inevitable outcome? If we had never traveled here, would Henry still one day call for Becket's death? Or had we only changed the catalyst which would drive Henry to murder, pitting wife against friend? I had no time to process this. Eustace Clarkson had dropped the heavy beam across the door. Collum reached for the plain, serviceable blade Bran had procured for him. Bran withdrew his curved blades, while William lunged forward and seized Rachel's tied wrists. With a twist, he wrenched her to her feet and flung her in my direction. I caught her, and in seconds Phoebe had sawed through Rachel's bonds.

William ripped his sword from its scabbard as Eustace Clarkson's eyes followed Rachel. When he yanked a heavy gladiator blade from his belt, the tendons in Collum's neck went tight.

"That sword," he said, "belongs to me."

Eustace grinned, little baked-bean teeth showing between his thick lips. "Then come and claim it, thief."

The world held its breath. Though dozens of candles lit the room, not even their tiny flames dared to flicker. I looked to the queen, who held the barely conscious Hectare in her arms. With a hiss of hatred, William Lucie launched himself at Eustace.

While Eustace parried the blow, Collum and Bran engaged the other guards. Sparks erupted where steel met steel. A table tumbled over. A writhing mass of limbs bashed into one of the large braziers, sending it hurtling to the ground. Red-hot coals skittered across the floor and smoked on the animal skins.

Eleanor dragged Hectare away from the fray, protecting the old woman as she shrieked for her guards, calling for help that would not come.

"Hope!" Phoebe raised my mother to her feet as the clash of blades filled the room. "We have to get Sarah out of here. Now."

"What?"

I ripped my gaze from the fight to see my mother staring at me with terrified eyes. "I'm so sorry."

"What are you talking about, Mom?"

"There's . . . there's something I should've told you," she said.

Too distracted by the battle being waged only feet from us, I didn't have time for confession. I waved her off. "It's all right, Mom."

"No, Hope," she urged. "You must—"

She cried out and bent double, hands white-knuckled on her bulging stomach. Beside me, Rachel made a low hum of distress. Jerking on my arm, she drew my attention to the floor beneath my mother's feet.

I looked down. What I saw nearly sent me to my knees. There, spreading across the flagstones, was a growing pool of pink, watery fluid.

"Mistress Hope," Rachel said. "The babe, it is coming."

CHAPTER 39

No. Nonono. Not this. Not now.

A shout jerked my attention back to the other side, where Bran had just sidestepped one of the guards. With his lithe cat's grace, he spun and brought the hilt of his weapon down on the back of the man's skull. The man dropped like a bag of sand. Collum was slashing furiously at a red-haired giant, who battered at him with superior muscle power.

Bran ran to Collum's aid, and the two of them worked in tandem. The brutish guard leaped forward to smash a chain-mailed fist into Bran's left side. Bran yelped, and dropped to a knee. Seeing his advantage, the giant rallied. Driving toward us, he slashed and beat at Collum, who seemed to be tiring, his movements going sluggish.

Phoebe snarled, struggling to draw out her throwing blades. One arm still around my mother's waist, she flicked one of the knives through the air. It whistled past Collum's ear. The giant stumbled back, then slid down the wall, blood bubbling around the small blade protruding from his throat.

Both boys turned to Phoebe, Bran's eyes wide in admiration. When Collum heaved him to his feet, Bran gave a low whistle and told him, "Remind me not to get on your sister's bad side, mate."

Across the room, the queen knelt near the bed, shielding Hectare's body with her own, while Collum and Bran joined William who was battling the last, ferret-faced guard. They were winning, and I allowed myself a tiny bit of hope that we might get out of here after all.

But I'd forgotten about Eustace, who'd stayed by the door on the edge of the fray. Before I could call out, he dashed around the battling men and bolted across the room to where we stood near the far corner. He wrenched Rachel from our midst. Drawing her back up against him, he set the edge of his sword against her throat.

"Stop," Eustace called out. "Or I slit the Jew's throat."

The boys' attention wavered for only an instant. But it was enough. Like a striking cobra, the final guard bashed the hilt of his sword across William's neck. Before William even hit the ground, the ferret whirled and, with a meaty thwack, buried his blade in Collum's upper arm.

With a furious shout, Bran whipped his sharp curved blade up and brought it down where the man's shoulder met his neck. An arterial jet of jewel-red blood arced through the air once, twice. Then the man's beady eyes rolled to white, and he crumpled sideways to the floor.

Jaw set, Collum wrenched the embedded sword from his own arm. He swayed but didn't go down as Bran helped a staggering William to his feet.

With two of his guards dead and the other still unconscious, Eustace now backed nervously toward us as a united
Bran, Collum, and William advanced on him. His cheek
twitched and I could see the beads of sweat that pocked his
pale scalp as he held the sword across Rachel's throat. Blood
flooded down Collum's arm, dripping off his fingertips. In
the low light, I could see him blinking too fast.

Shock. He's going into shock.

"Coll!" Phoebe yelled.

"Back up, or I swear I'll kill her," Eustace snarled, candlelight glinting off the links of his chainmail.

It was a standoff. If the boys moved, Eustace would kill
Rachel. Of that I had no doubt.

But we'd run out of time. Sunrise was only hours away,
and if we didn't make it to the glade, it was all over.

I had to do something. But what? I skimmed the room
frantically, trying to find a way that didn't involve getting
some of us killed.

*No way out. There's no way out. At the very least he'll kill
Rachel. I can't let that happen. Oh God, what do we do?*

Phoebe edged up beside me, slender blade in hand. Leaning close, she breathed in my ear, "If all else fails, stick them
with your knife."

I nodded my understanding. The guys couldn't chance
him hurting Rachel. It was up to us. And we'd have to do
this together. By itself, Phoebe's tiny blade was no match
against armor and sword.

With a few gestures, she indicated her plan. I shook my

head, still not trusting my own ability with the blade in my boot. Instead, I snatched up the heavy silver candlestick off a nearby table. Scorching wax splashed over my hand as the thick taper fell to the floor and spluttered out.

Phoebe smiled, mouthing, *Even better.*

Eustace was so close now we could smell his greasy hair and the rank oil he used to polish his armor.

A muscle twitched beneath Bran's eye. He saw what we meant to do but didn't take his eyes from Eustace.

With a slow exhale, I raised the heavy candlestick to my left shoulder like a baseball bat.

Just a little closer, you barbaric freak.

Phoebe darted forward, jabbing her blade toward the man's armpit, the one place the chainmail didn't protect. As Eustace jerked and gave a surprised grunt, I swung the candlestick at his skull.

I was off. Too low, and the angle was wrong. Still, the solid mass of metal smashed into the side of his neck and face. There was a sickening crack, like a chicken leg snapped in two.

Eustace went down, crushing Rachel beneath his weight.

As Phoebe crowed in triumph, a clump of bloody hair slimed down and crawled across my knuckles. I shivered and flung the stick aside as cries and the sounds of a struggle came from the other side of the door. Eleanor's eyes found mine. She gestured to Collum and shook her head. I understood. She knew who he was now. And knew what would happen when the castle guards got into the room. There was no way we'd get out in time. The queen would back us up. But even she could do nothing once the authorities recognized Collum.

William dragged Rachel from beneath Eustace's bulk. He hugged her fiercely to him. But at Collum's low moan, Rachel pulled back, patted William's cheek, then raced to Collum's side. She pressed a wad of cloth to his arm. When the blood soaked through too quickly, she muttered under her breath.

"Rachel?" I begged as, out in the hallway, something slammed against the thick door. "What do we do?"

Chewing her lip, she rifled through her supplies. "There's no time to stitch. Only one thing will stop the bleeding."

Our eyes met. Hers flicked to the brazier. My stomach lurched, but I nodded. "What do you need?"

"Take the poker and bury it in the coals. Make certain it is red hot."

Rachel became a whirlwind. Using clumps of something that resembled moss and spider webs, the girl applied pressure to the gaping wound until I returned with the glowing poker.

"Hold him down," she commanded. Eleanor held a lamp aloft as the rest of us arranged ourselves around Collum, each restraining an uninjured limb.

Collum's eyes looked glassy. Sweat poured off him, but he didn't utter a sound. When he nodded at Rachel, she took a deep breath and, holding the ragged edges of the wound together, pressed the poker to his skin and seared the wound closed. Collum reared up, shoulders and heels the only thing touching the floor as his flesh sizzled. The sickening stench of cooked meat filled my nose.

He was gasping and horribly pale as Rachel bound the wound. I stood, my stinging eyes scanning the chamber. From the door came a loud thud. It shuddered, and the tip of an ax appeared through the wood.

Can't go through the door. What do we do? Think, Walton. Think.

The others' worried voices blended together, but I closed my eyes, blotting them out. Summoning the last ounces of concentration I possessed, I opened my mind and let everything I'd ever seen or read about the history of the Palace of Westminster flood in. My head pounded as the words of each article, rare book, drawing, sketch, scrap of paper, innuendo, or passing gossip began to scroll through my mind in glowing green columns. Books flipped open and pages flapped away like a colony of disturbed bats.

I could feel my fingers twitch as I cast off one after the other. *Come on. Come on.*

There.

My eyes flew open. *Got it.*

I turned to William Lucie. "Behind one of those tapestries on the north wall there should be an entrance to a hidden passage."

He started to shake his head, but I urged. "Just try. Please."

The door to the hallway was shaking under the weight

of blows. "All is well here!" The queen was trying to buy us time, but the axe blows kept coming. A crack had appeared in the thick wood. It wouldn't hold much longer.

"Hope," Bran called, "Sister Hectare wants you. I—I don't understand what she's saying."

I hurried to the nun's side and dropped to my knees. Behind me, I heard the grinding of stone on stone and William's shout of surprise. I didn't turn. Sister Hectare's bleary eyes were burning into mine.

Mesmerized, I leaned close as she whispered in a voice weak as wet paper. "We were wrong. It is not . . ." Her eyelids drifted closed. Her mouth twisted. Her head pitched from side to side on the pillow as she struggled for breath. Alarmed, I rested my hand on her forehead, trying to soothe her. The tissue-thin skin burned my palm.

"It's all right, Sister Hectare," I whispered, my words thick with tears. "You rest now."

Sorrow etched Bran's brow as he met my eyes. When he took the nun's gnarled hands in his own, she grasped him hard, pulling him closer.

When she began to whisper, I leaned in but still could barely make out the crackly words. "The lady lies beneath their knees in robes of purest white." A wheeze. "She guards her dark treasure in the deep. Only its children see the light."

Puzzled, I glanced at Bran, but he seemed just as befuddled as I was.

The loud crack of wood beginning to splinter sounded from the door. The muffled shouts grew louder. Hectare blinked rapidly. Her eyes cleared as she looked up. "It is time for you to go now, my children."

"Thank you," I managed as I swiped my wet eyes with a sleeve. "I will never forget you."

"Nor I you, sweet girl." She closed her eyes, a beatific smile lighting her face. "Nor I you."

When we turned, my shoulders slumped in relief. I'd been right. A dark rectangle now mawed open in the stone wall.

Bran helped my mother into the passage. Rachel had secured Collum's arm in a sling. With a last look in my direction, he leaned on his sister and limped to the entrance.

Phoebe called over her shoulder. "Ready, Hope?"

I held up a finger and turned to William and Rachel. Next to the tunnel entrance, William cupped Rachel's face between his palms. "Come with me," he was saying. "We shall flee to the continent and start over. Now that Becket knows, this did naught but decide things for us. 'Tis our chance, my love. As long as you are by my side, we will conquer any trials that come our way."

I grinned as Rachel whispered her answer and melted into his arms. Her eyes shone like gilt when she drew back and returned my smile.

I suddenly realized I'd never see these two remarkable people again. "Rachel," I said. "William. I can never thank the two of you enough for helping us."

"Mistr—" Rachel corrected herself. "Hope. It is I who give thanks. If not for you and your friends, I would never have gained the courage to follow where my heart led." She reached up and, placing gentle hands on my head, murmured a Hebrew blessing. "I wish you long life," she said quietly. "And happiness. And that your journey home is a safe one."

William cradled my hands between his large, callused palms. "Go with God, Mistress Hope."

I watched as they blended into the tunnel's darkness. They'd have a difficult path, I knew. But they'd be together, and maybe that was enough. I closed my eyes and sent up my own prayer that they'd have a happily ever after.

The heavy chamber door was almost fractured now. Queen Eleanor hurried over to me as I entered the passage.

"I will close it behind you, to cloak your escape."

Bowing low, I thanked her. My eyes grazed over the dead and unconscious men in her chambers.

Eleanor caught my look and shrugged. "I am the queen. Who would speak against me? Not that craven priest, now that he's failed. Though I daresay Becket and I shall cross swords again."

I nodded, thinking, *Oh yes, Your Grace. That you will.*

Eleanor glanced over my shoulder to the darkness where my anxious friends waited. "Hectare told me of your strange travels. My friend speaks naught but truth, and yet . . ." When she glanced down the tunnel, there was such longing in her face, I couldn't look away. "If I did not have a duty to my kingdom, I would wish to go with you. There is much I would know, but I shall not ask how my life turns out. That is for God alone to decide. I would ask one question of you, however."

Reluctantly, I nodded. However much I wanted to, I couldn't warn her. Couldn't reveal the pain she would suffer when bitter jealousies arose to warp and ruin her family. But neither would I lie to this extraordinary queen.

"I'll tell you what I can, Your Grace."

Her voice was tentative, and I could see her brace herself for the answer. As she looked into my eyes I glimpsed the vulnerable woman behind the queen, the legend.

"So many queens before me have come and gone, their legacies washed away like sand beneath the tide. In that place to which you return . . . will my name fade as have so many before me? Will anyone remember?"

Against all royal protocol, I reached out and took one of her soft, ink-stained hands in mine. "Your Grace," I whispered around the giant lump in my throat, "your legacy will never fade. You *will* be remembered. Even a thousand years from now, your name will live on."

CHAPTER 40

I MADE SEVERAL WRONG TURNS AS I LED THE OTHERS through the twisting, turning passageways. The musty, damp stone pressed heavier as they followed me down and down. The torches Phoebe and I carried spat flecks of hot pitch onto our gowns, but I beat out the sparks, never slowing. When the walls tightened, forcing us to squeeze through sideways, my heartbeat faltered.

Oh no. Can't breathe. Too tight.

I wouldn't—couldn't—lose control.

Not now.

Claustrophobia pecked at me. Peck. Peck. Peck. An evil bird nibbling away my reason. Collum frowned at me but said nothing as I moved faster through the tunnel. My brain filled with two words. *Get out. Getoutgetoutgetout!*

When the tunnel split into three smaller ones, I nearly lost it.

Oh God. Which way?

Phoebe shot me a scared look as my mother's rhythmic groans grew closer together. We both knew what it meant.

The baby was on its way. And we had to get home before it arrived.

I braced myself against the wall, choking on the sharp, metallic tang of fear and adrenaline. Beneath my palm, I felt a design, grooves carved into the stone. Something buzzed up from my memory, but I shoved it back at Phoebe's shout.

"Oy! I can feel wind. This way."

The torch's flame trembled as a cold breeze wafted against my sweaty face. I nearly sobbed with relief.

Thank you. Thank you.

The tunnels ended at a grated entrance near the back of the abbey. I gulped for air as we emerged into the crisp winter night. Marveling, I realized we'd traveled underground all the way beneath the cobblestoned square to the rear of the cathedral. The large village that surrounded the palace and abbey was dark, all its occupants still abed. But that wouldn't last for long. Dawn was approaching. And we had to be deep in the forest when it came.

Between us, Collum and I kept my moaning, barely conscious mother upright as Bran and Phoebe stole inside a nearby stable, absconding with several horses and tack. Without wagon or sled, we had no alternative. Wrapped in her cloak, Mom curled sideways on the front of Bran's saddle. He held her in place with one arm, controlling the reins with the other.

Snowflakes floated down as we raced through the village, down a rutted road, past sleeping farms, until we reached the treeline. Mom's guttural moans occasionally drifted up like smoke into the frigid air. Galloping at his side, I watched Bran grip her tighter, jaw flexed as he glanced my way. The bluish glow from the snow-covered ground shadowed his eyes and carved his face into a marble statue.

I must've looked worried, because he winked. "Not to worry, preety lady," he panted in an awful Russian accent. "Am strong like bull."

By the time we reached the spot in the woods where we'd emerged three days before, the snow had stopped. The moon peeked between rushing black clouds, illuminating the thick powder.

I jumped down and bolted to where Bran was struggling to keep my mother from tumbling off. I helped her down, keeping her upright while Bran dismounted. She was shivering uncontrollably. With no nearby place to sit but the snow-laden ground, we sandwiched her between us, sharing our heat as she convulsed. My mother's belly pressed into me, high and round. Her knees sagged and her head dropped onto my shoulder.

Bran's eyes bored into mine across my mother's shuddering body. "Hope." My name emerged from his lips in a mist of white that wreathed around us. "There's something I—"

Phoebe skidded to a halt beside us, ice particles spraying from her horse's hoofs. I took on Mom's weight as Bran went to assist Collum, but was waved away.

"Coll's bleeding again," Phoebe said quietly at my side. "It's bad. Can you watch out for him and I'll help Bran with Sarah?"

"I'm not deaf, you know," Collum spat. "And I don't need help. Let's just bloody well get this over with."

"I'll take Sarah," Bran murmured. With a last, troubled look at me, he scooped my mother into his arms and trudged off into the forest.

Phoebe raced ahead of Bran to break a trail. As Collum stumbled after, she called over her shoulder. "Quit being such a stubborn ass, Coll, and let Hope help you."

I drew even with Collum, almost gagging at the strong, mineral waft of blood that emanated from him, corrupting the clean, cold smell of the forest. In the night's bridal shades of moonlight and snow, the liquid streaming down his arm gleamed black as an oil slick.

"I said I'm fine," he muttered.

"Oh yeah?" I countered. "Well, you *look* like a freaking ghost. And if you bleed out any more, you'll pass out and I'll have to drag you the rest of the way. So, please . . . Please just let me help you."

Collum stared at me for a long moment, mouth tucked in at the corners. "You," he said quietly, "have surprised me, Hope Walton. I never expected it of you."

"Why, Collum MacPherson," I kidded. "Is that an actual compliment? Coming from *you?*"

He didn't smile. Instead he inched closer. "Listen," he

said, hazel eyes intense. "We wouldn't have made it out without you. I just . . ." He sighed. "I just want you to be careful around Cameron, aye?"

I looked away. "I don't know what you mean."

"Yes you do," he said. His head jerked as Phoebe shouted from the woods.

"Come on," he said. "We have to hurry."

With that, he allowed me to drape his good arm over my shoulders and together, we navigated after the others.

Breathless and sweating despite the cold, we finally reached the glade, still oddly bare of snow or a single leaf. I looked back at the path of gore and broken branches we'd left. A blind man could've followed our trail. Once inside the eerie circle of trees, Mom slithered from Bran's grip. Phoebe helped me ease a shaking Collum to the dirt. A whine escaped Mom's clenched teeth, and in the inconstant light, her skin looked bleached. Dead.

"How long?" I huffed.

Collum glanced up at the patchwork of black clouds scuttling across the silvered sky. "Not long now."

Mom whimpered as a contraction took her. I knelt and gripped her hand. When the pain subsided, she panted. "Hope, listen to me. I have to tell you something. It's important."

"It's okay, Mom," I soothed. "Not now. It can wait till we get back."

"No," she insisted. "You have to know. It was long ago, but—" Her eyes flew open. Her back arched, and a sound like the cry of a trapped animal ripped from her lips.

"Mom!"

Her lips moved without sound. I leaned closer to listen.

"Something's wrong," she gasped through lips bleached with shock. The hairs on the back of my neck stiffened. "It happened before." When her pained eyes met mine, I sat back on my heels, stunned at the realization.

"What's she talking about?" Phoebe's voice was screechy with fear.

"She lost a baby when I was little," I managed. "It was bad, Pheebs. And that was in a hospital. We have to get her home."

Mom's next cry dragged on until I wanted to cover my ears and scream. Tears welled in Phoebe's eyes.

"What do we do? Is she supposed to be bleeding like this?" She gestured to the blood seeping out around my mother's skirts.

I tried to burrow into my memory, to bring up everything I'd ever read about childbirth, but when Mom slumped sideways in a faint, the words scattered.

"I can't do this." I cradled her head in my lap. "It's too much, Mom. Please wake up. Tell me what to do. I need you."

I hugged her to me, buried my face in her shoulder, and wept like a child.

Shivering, I felt warmth settle next to me. I looked up to

find Bran at my side. Collum moved to kneel beside Phoebe on the other side of my mother's supine body. They didn't say a word, but as they all watched me I could hear them just the same.

We're here. You're not alone.

The back of my throat burned. I'd grown up a mostly solitary being. My grandmother had always, and very deliberately, made certain I never felt like part of the larger family. And though I had my parents, my mother had long ago determined I hadn't the time or need for friends in my life.

Now, as these three people clustered around me, their combined strength bathed me in a warmth I'd never experienced. I'd been weak, a broken and fragile creature. I knew that. But maybe with actual *real* friends beside me, I was learning to be strong.

I nodded and closed my eyes. Years of study began marching through my head in systematic rows. Pain struck in the middle of my forehead, but I ignored it. When I came across a paragraph that matched my mother's symptoms, I flinched and tried to discard it, but it fit too well.

Placenta previa. An abnormal implantation of the placenta at the opening of the cervix. This condition can impede the child's delivery and, left untreated, can lead to maternal hemorrhage. Without immediate medical attention, the condition can cause severe injury and/or death for both mother and child.

My eyes popped open. "We have to get her back," I said. "Fast. There's no other option."

I followed Collum's gaze as he read the sky. To the east, there might've been a hint of gray, but would it come soon enough?

Black blood spread out beneath us on the hard packed dirt. Under my knees, my gown sopped it up like syrup. Mom's freckled face looked ghostly, as if she were already gone. My whole life, she'd guided me. Now, when I needed her most, she was far away. Farther than she'd ever been.

The pendant jolted against my skin. My head jerked up, and I saw that the others had felt it too. Somewhere, a thousand years in the future, Doug was fiddling with the dials of the Tesla device, ready to flip the switch and bring us home. The Dim was coming for us.

Hurry. Hurry. Hurry.

"The Nonius Stone," I gasped. "It has be on Mom when the Dim comes, right?"

With his uninjured hand, Collum fumbled for the dagger in his bag, cursing his own stupidity. Phoebe took it from him and unsheathed it. With the knife in my boot, I slashed through the bottom of my underskirt, making a long strip to secure the blade to my mother's arm.

We're going to make it. Lucinda and Moira will know what to do. We'll—

A twig cracked in the forest. Bran leaped up, the two curved swords instantly in his hands. Collum tried to struggle to his feet. When he fell, Phoebe gestured him back and withdrew her knives. Side by side, Bran and Phoebe peered into the darkness.

CHAPTER 41

"Ah." Her sultry voice preceded her as she stepped through the circle of trees. "It seems we are in the nick of time, yes?"

Celia Alvarez's glossy dark hair poured down on either side of her face. Her forest-green gown blended perfectly with the trees as she surveyed the scene before her.

My eyes fastened on the object in her hand. A very small, very modern gun.

She brought a gun?

Phoebe took a step toward her. "Celia." Hatred burned as she spoke the name.

"No, no." Her wide mouth turned down into a regretful frown. "Get back, little one. I do not wish to kill Michael's child, *mi querida,* but I will if I must." She noticed my scrutiny and examined the pistol in her hand. "Anachronistic, I know." She shrugged. "But a woman must have her useful things, yes?"

With a spatter of displaced snow, the bald Flint slunk from the trees holding another, larger pistol.

Flint grinned when he saw Bran. "Good work, Brandon."

I flinched. Suspicion danced across my mind, leaving rotting pits in its wake.

Good work?

Bran sheathed his swords and ambled toward Celia. "Hello, Mother."

"My son." Celia kissed him on both cheeks. Her victorious smile sent my heart plummeting into my feet. "You've done well. How is your injury? It is good?"

Bran touched his side and nodded. "Fine, Mother."

"Accidents will happen, my son," she said, patting his cheek. "Now get their lodestones and bring them to me. We have a long journey ahead, and time grows short."

Bran nodded. "Of course, Mother."

Oh, no. Not this. Please, not this.

I tried to catch Bran's eye, but he wouldn't look at me. He advanced on Phoebe, ordering her to kneel. She shot quick glares at the two guns, then spit at Bran, plopping down just behind me. Collum had somehow gotten to his feet. Bran faced him.

"Your ring, MacPherson."

"You worthless piece of scum," Collum said quietly. "You'll have to kill me first."

Bran shrugged. With a sweep of his leg, he knocked the injured Collum's feet from under him and kicked the sword from his hand. It skittered across the frozen ground as Collum crashed onto his wounded shoulder with a grunt of pain.

Overhead, the sky brightened imperceptibly. I heard Phoebe's intake of breath behind me as she felt her lodestone twinge. I felt it too.

Bran knelt in front of me, his back to his mother. "Sorry, Hope," he drawled. "It's been fun, love. But I'll need that pendant now. And, Phoebe, your bracelet if you please."

My heart was a mangled thing when I raised my eyes to his. Poisonous words burned on my tongue. But they dissolved as Bran's blue and green eyes seared into mine. He mouthed, *Be ready*.

My chest inflated. Relief thrummed through me as I mimed giving him the necklace.

Phoebe, still not understanding, wrenched the bracelet from her arm. "You bloody rat bastard."

Bran let Phoebe's bracelet drop into my palm, then stood and crammed the imaginary objects into his bag. "Got them, Mother."

Carefully, I eased my hand behind my back and held it there until I felt Phoebe stiffen, then pluck the bracelet from my fist. Pink and orange flared in the east. It could only be minutes now. We just had to stay alive till then.

"Flint." Celia sounded amused. "The Nonius Stone is strapped to dear Sarah's arm. Get it for me, *por favor*."

Impotent rage boiled through me. I wanted to rip her black eyes from her head. I trembled with it as Flint shoved me aside and ripped the dagger from Mom's limp arm. He sheathed it, then handed it to Celia.

"Finally," she whispered. "Finally."

As Celia unsheathed the blade, turning it to the last of the moonlight, she gasped and reeled back. Her head whipped toward me, lips peeled back in fury.

And all at once, I knew what had bothered me about the stone back in Eleanor's chambers. I think Hectare had realized it too. The legendary Nonius Stone was reputedly an extremely large and extremely rare *black* opal. This one was white.

I beamed at Celia. "Oops."

"What is this?" she screamed. "This is not the true Nonius! The Nonius Stone is black as night, with all the colors of the rainbow contained inside. This . . . This is nothing but another lodestone. Bah!"

She slammed the dagger into its sheath and tossed it to Flint. He examined it and whistled a murky white mist. "You're right, boss. It's ancient. Powerful, too. It'll be of use, no doubt. But it ain't the bloody Nonius Stone." He crammed the dagger into his belt, his wrestler's shoulders bunching as he threw his hands in the air and stomped off toward the tree line. Evidently, he no longer considered us a threat. The gun in Celia's hand rose. It swept the clearing as if she couldn't decide which of us to shoot first.

"It won't work, Celia." My mother's voice was a pallid croak as she pushed herself to a seated position. "Even if you find the Nonius Stone," Mom said. "You can't just go back and do whatever you want. You could change history on a fundamental level, and you have no idea what it might do to the fabric of time. You know this."

Celia stomped toward my mother. Her dark eyes scanned the blood saturating the dirt around her. For just an instant, I thought I saw a flicker of regret cross her features. Then her lips peeled back in contempt. "Saint Sarah. With all your degrees and knowledge, you still haven't brought *him* back, have you?"

Collum made a noise, but I didn't take my eyes off Celia.

"It is *your* fault Michael is gone," she spat. "If you hadn't insisted on bringing back these stupid brats, he would never have sacrificed himself like that. If he hadn't stepped in front of the blade I intended for *you,* he and I would be together now." She shrugged. "No matter. When I find the Nonius Stone and my men alter the device, I *will* find him."

Celia paused, head tilting to one side as she noted the horrified glance Mom cast at me.

Celia threw her head back and laughed. "Oh, *es fabuloso.* Do not tell me you never told your precious daughter the truth about herself? At least I did not raise my son on lies. Brandon knows where he came from, don't you, *hijo?*"

"Oh yes, Mother," he said. "You've never let me forget that, have you?"

Celia ignored him, looking from me to Mom. "Look at this girl. How she protects you. And still you lie to her. Your daughter, yes," she said. "But not of your blood."

A kind of nervousness rolled over me as my mother's voice turned querulous. "Celia, don't. Please. Not like this."

"Mom?" The shadows that had always covered my earliest memories began to thin and dissipate. Images edged in at the corners of my consciousness.

"You had no idea my father was there too, looking for the good doctor. You didn't even know John Dee held the Nonius Stone." She stepped closer, whispering the words. "But I did. And I now know who *she* is." Celia swung the gun toward me.

At the sound of the man's name on Celia's lips, firecrackers exploded inside my head.

Smoke and stamping horses. A frozen forest. Thatched roofs on fire. Shouts in the distance as a man rocked me in his arms. His long gray beard tickled my cheek as he whispered fiercely, "You must run now, granddaughter. There are men here who would take what I've been entrusted with protecting. They are hurting these good people who sheltered us, and I must help them. But do not fret, for I will come after you."

Another image came, slamming into the first. *A doll tucked under my arm as I raced through the woods. Someone held my hand, dragging me away from a scene of screams and blood. Cold. So cold. Then blackness consumed me as I screamed inside the rotting trunk of the nightmare tree.*

Someone tore away the huge branches that had trapped me inside. I was wrenched from the darkness. Gentle hands brushed the creatures from my hair, my gown. I looked up, but his face was lost in shadow. The only thing I could see was a small, silver medallion, hanging on a leather thong. "It was my mum's," he said, when I reached out a shaking finger to touch it. "I took it off her after they . . . after they killed her."

My heart refused to beat. Celia laughed, a pretty silver sound that sliced through the glade, sharp as a razor's edge.

"Sarah's daughter. Loved but not trusted. Too pathetic and frail to know her own truth."

"Hope," Mom whispered, but I was beyond hearing.

My savior pressed something into my hand. I looked down to see a small, withered apple resting on my palm. "Here. It's for you."

I cried then, because I was so hungry, so tired. I missed my grandfather, and I'd lost my doll. My Elizabeth. As the boy lifted the meager fruit to my lips, I smelled the familiar, cloying scent. Suddenly, three people emerged from the trees. A man and two women, dressed in fine clothes. The boy stood, a stick thrust out before him, protecting me.

One of the women hurried across the clearing and knelt down. "I won't hurt you," she promised the boy. She called to the others. "They're starving and nearly frozen. They must've come from that burned-out village we passed yesterday. We can't leave them here. They'll die of exposure if we don't do something fast." She smiled. "Don't worry, we're going to take care of you."

When she returned to the others, the dark-haired woman began arguing with her. The man got angry, but the first woman only said, "You take them. I'll stay."

The man shook his head. "Like hell you will."

He pulled her to him, murmuring something that made the other woman furious.

As the three began struggling at the edge of the clearing, I could no longer hold myself upright. I toppled over onto my back and stared up as stars wheeled in the night sky. The boy crawled over and held my head in his lap. He smiled down at me, and I re-membered the first time I'd seen him in the small village. How his face had darkened as my grandfather explained that men were chasing us. He'd held so tight to my hand as we ran through the forest. He never let go, except to put me in the tree, where he thought I'd be safe while he went to search for food. As the moon snuck out from behind the clouds he looked over to the arguing people, and I could finally see his eyes. His odd, mismatched eyes.

I blinked, shaking my head, my breath coming in little huffs.

". . . that your daughter did not come from any orphan-age," Celia was saying. "But was brought back, along with Brandon, from the year 1576."

The images expanded until I thought my head would rupture. A small child's half-formed memories skittered through my mind. The gray-bearded man had been tak-ing me back to my mother. My real mother. The lady with long, brown hair, who'd trained my hands to spin the wool. When the bad men raced into the small village, killing and burning, he'd shielded me with his body as he begged the boy to take my hand and run.

I knew that dear old face now. I'd seen it in history books all my life.

My poppy. My grandfather. Doctor John Dee.

Queen Elizabeth I's most trusted advisor. A scientist and astrologer. Religious fanatics had hated him. Called him a wizard. But he'd only been brilliant and far ahead of his time.

And . . . according to many biographers . . . he'd been blessed with an eidetic memory.

I sat back hard, falling away from my mother.

There'd never been an orphanage. That was my mother's lie. More memories splashed thorough in cyclical waves. A small, snug house with an herb garden out back. A crowded city. Horses. A flash of a scary white-faced queen with orange hair.

The boy.

My gaze locked with Bran's. The pity in his eyes was too much to bear as the earth and sky switched places. Tall, bare trees spun around me like horses on a carousel.

"Hope." My mother's hand clutched at me, but I yanked away. She sagged against Phoebe, spent. "I had no choice. The two of you would have died. I should have told you, but . . ." Her anguished face begged for understanding. A spasm of pain racked her body. When it passed, she whispered, "I need you to know I will never regret taking you from that terrible place."

Phoebe's voice was aghast. "Sarah, you didn't. You brought them back from the past? Both of them?"

"After Celia stabbed Michael," Mom whispered, "he placed the extra lodestones on you children. Then he just ran away. He knew the Dim was coming, so he took the choice from us, you see."

I looked at Collum. If he'd known about this, I didn't know what I'd do. But his mouth hung open in pure shock.

"Brandon." Mom's voice was barely audible. "I wanted to take you, too, to raise you as my own." Bran took a shuffling step toward her and stared down with an unreadable expression. "But when we got home, Celia took off with you so fast. We couldn't stop her."

Celia stepped between the two of them, severing their line of sight. Bran's face had gone pale at my mother's declaration.

Celia's voice morphed into a low hiss. "You took Michael from me. You weren't taking everything. The honorable, loving family and *two* children to love you? *Never.*"

CHAPTER 42

"Now you know the truth." Celia leered down at me. "That your mother is a liar. But the two of you will have much time in this age to discuss it." She glanced down at the blood. "Or perhaps not. Come, Brandon, these people are nothing to us. Without their lodestones, they dare not travel the Dim." She snorted and gave that brittle laugh. "Perhaps Babcock would take you back, Sarah," she said. "And when I bring Michael home, I will tell him you are happily wed."

Bran blinked at me. There was a message there, but I couldn't read it. Celia turned to go, then whipped back, something catching her attention.

An undulating lavender mist had begun to coalesce around Collum and Phoebe. The pendant, still clutched in my hand, twitched against my palm. I looked down to see the same purplish haze shimmering up my arm.

The Dim had come for us. Celia's eyes bulged as she realized that her son had never taken the lodestones from us.

"Traitor," Celia snarled as she swung the pistol barrel at Bran. "I should have left you to die in that forest."

Before he could react, Celia leaped forward and ripped Bran's opal cloak pin away. She danced back, Bran's lodestone — his safety, his only sure way back to where he started — clenched in her fist.

With the gun still raised, she spoke. "I should have known you would do this. You are weak. You are nothing." She tossed her hair back, and gave a haughty laugh. "Eh, It is no loss. *You* are not of my blood. I will train Antonio to stand by my side. He is my only true son."

"No!" Anguish and rage all balled together in one horrible expression skimmed across Bran's features. He took a step in Celia's direction, stopping only when she trained the gun straight at his heart. Hands raised in supplication, he begged, "Mother. Please. Tony's too young. He's not cut out for this. You know that. He'll only get himself killed."

"Then, *querido*," Celia sneered, "you should not have betrayed me."

For one, brief moment I thought she would pull the trigger. That she would kill her own son where he stood. The blood in my veins turned to slurry as the second stretched into an eternity.

Then, with a disgusted huff, she turned and fled into the trees. Bran's hands fell to his sides and his head dropped in defeat.

Beside me, Mom was trying to say something, but the pain and blood loss were too much. Her eyes closed, and she slumped against Phoebe.

"Mom?" When she wouldn't stir, I lightly smacked her

cheeks, then shook her hard. "Mom!" No response. Shaking, I groped for a pulse. It flickered against my fingertips, weak and thready.

A cold wind began to circle us. Back at Christopher Manor, Doug had flipped the switch. The Dim had come to take us home, but something wasn't right. The fractured light that danced over Collum, Phoebe, and me turned a deep violet. But the glow rolling across my mother was a sick, putrid shade of yellow.

Horrorstruck, I remembered what had happened to Dr. Alvarez's son. How he was sliced in two, only half of him returning when he traveled without his lodestone.

"The dagger," I cried. "Celia took it. Without the lodestone to guide Mom, she'll go somewhere else. Or she'll die."

From the corner of my eye I saw Bran, pale and alone, move to the edge of the clearing. At my words, his head came up, and our eyes met. I hesitated for only a heartbeat. Five people. Three lodestones. And though Bran stood outside the glade, that still left four of us.

As I let the pendant spool out of my fist, I said to Phoebe, "tell Mom I'm sorry."

She didn't get it, but Collum did. He tried to tear the ring from his own finger, but the nerves in his injured arm wouldn't cooperate. "Cameron, help me," he yelled. "For God's sake, get this bloody ring off and give it to Sarah. Hurry."

Blood sheeted down Collum's arm and streamed from his

fingers. I glanced from the pendant, then back at Bran. I could see the argument forming on his lips. But we didn't have time and he knew it. Finally, he gave a sharp nod. A silent agreement.

"Aye." Collum nodded frantically as Bran approached. "I can't remove it with this blasted arm. You'll have to do it."

"I'm sorry, Collum," I said. "But you need a doctor."

"What? No!" he cried, ripping at the ring.

I tossed the strip of fabric we'd cut earlier to Bran. He caught it and quickly bound Collum's hands together, then ran over and grabbed Michael MacPherson's sword. He shoved it into the scabbard at Collum's belt while Collum writhed against his restraints and cursed us.

"Make it fast, Hope," Bran shouted against the roaring wind.

The translucent cyclone began to circle higher and higher, whipping dark curls into my face, blinding me. My hands shook so badly that I could barely wrap the pendant's chain around my unconscious mother's wrist. When I closed her limp fingers over the stone, the soft purple light transferred instantly to her. My own skin turned an ugly mustard color. "I love you, Mom," I whispered.

"Come on. We've got to get out of here." Bran hauled me to my feet and rushed me to the edge of the glade.

The instant we passed the tree line, the muddy haze around me faded.

"Oh, Hope. No." Tears poured down Phoebe's ravaged face.

"Get them to the hospital as fast as you can," I shouted. "Tell them it's placenta previa. There's time if you hurry."

I tried to smile, but the muscles in my face had turned to stone. My knees wobbled. Bran's arm came around me, propping me up as he had when we were children when we were lost in the woods so long ago.

"We'll find a way back," I cried. Bran pulled me farther from the cyclonic wind and raging light. "I swear it." My voice broke on a sob. "Tell Lucinda . . . Tell her we'll find a way."

Collum screamed in frustration. Phoebe and I had time to share one horrified look before the air around them ignited in a fireball of violet light.

CHAPTER 43

THE SHOCK WAVE SMASHED INTO US AS THE INEXORABLE power of the Dim wrenched the others back to their own time. Hurtling backwards through the trees, I slammed hard into the snowy ground, the breath knocked from me. Green spots danced behind my eyelids.

They're safe. Thank God they're safe.

Bran crawled over to me, groaning. "Well, that smarted."

"You knew," I blurted as I blinked up at him. Above him, the clouds glowed in a riot of amethyst and topaz. "You knew about us all along, and you didn't tell me."

When he only gazed down at me, I shoved him away and sat up. "How could you? Don't you think maybe, just *maybe*, that's something you might've shared with me?"

He jumped to his feet. "And just how was I supposed to do that, hmm? Sit you down over a pint and say, 'Oh, hey, by the way, you remember when we met as children back in the sixteenth century? Boy, weren't those jolly times?'"

I felt my lips peel back, ready to hurl an answer, but he was faster.

"Or maybe I could've reminded you of the time you and your rich pop-pop, or whatever you called him, burst into my tiny village, a group of men on your tail? Men who killed everyone and burned my home to the ground?" He paced back and forth, his voice growing louder. "Or . . . how I had to forget watching my real mum drop dead from an ax blow to the skull while I dragged your butt through the forest for two *days* before we got abducted by bloody time travelers!"

Bran was panting as he glared down at me.

Furious, I jumped to my feet. "It's better than being left in the dark!"

"Oh, you think ignorance is worse? Worse than being the only person who knows you don't belong in your own fucking time?" he shouted. "Worse than your mother spewing poison and telling you every day that you're nothing but a mongrel who's only alive on her charity?"

"Maybe not, but . . . but . . ." I trailed off at the look of unutterable pain that creased his face. He turned away and slumped down on a nearby log.

I dropped beside him, wondering if he was right. Maybe ignorance *was* better. My mother probably thought she was protecting me. Yes, she was demanding and controlling. But she loved me. I never doubted that.

"I'm so sorry, Bran," I whispered. "About your mother—both of them. About everything."

I felt him shrug. "You don't remember any of it?" he said. "Not even me?"

"Not till just now. But when we first met, I . . . thought I smelled apples."

He smiled at that. "I don't remember that much myself," he confessed. "I was only five. I get glimpses sometimes. My house. My mum. I had a dog named Beaufort."

I put a hand on his arm. "I'm sorry I was such a brat."

He nudged me. "Eh, you weren't that bad."

I shot a sideways glance at him. "I um . . . think Dr. John Dee is my grandfather."

He turned to me, brows pinched in thought. "Yes," he said, nodding. "Yes, I remember now. He'd been to our village before, visiting with our wise woman."

"I think he was taking me home to my parents," I said, realizing as I spoke the words that they were true. "I'd been visiting him in London for a few days. I think . . . I think I did that a lot."

Bran could only shake his head in wonder.

"He must have gotten away, because he didn't die until 1608. I wonder if he came looking for us." My chest ached a little at the thought. "You know," I said, "when I was eight, I found his portrait in a book, and I just started crying. I didn't know why, but when my mother took the book away she kept staring at the picture and then back at me." I kicked at the snow. "I think she knew, or at least suspected."

We were quiet for a long moment before I reached up to touch the leather strand peeping from his collar. "This was your mother's?" I said. "Your real mother's?"

Bran tugged the medallion loose and touched it to his

lips. "It was a St. Christopher, at one time. Though I remember her telling me that our family had long rubbed off the etching." His eyes clouded. "I think she would've wanted me to have it."

"I think so too," I said.

"Moth—*Celia*—claims that when they found us, we were nearly dead," Bran said, tucking the disc in place, but not before I saw him swipe at his eyes. "That we wouldn't have lasted much longer. Not even long enough for whoever stayed behind to get us to another village. She lied, you know. Told me Sarah was the one who stabbed Michael. That she stole his lodestone. She always claimed your mother took you and would've left me behind. That *she* saved me. Can't believe I was stupid enough to buy that."

"I used to dream about them, you know. I thought they were angels."

Bran chuckled. "Hardly. My mother certainly has never exhibited any angelish behavior."

I cocked an eyebrow at him. "Angelish?"

He grinned. "New word. I'm thinking of adding it to the current lexicon. Then, by the time the others reach home, it'll be in all the dictionaries, with our names beside the asterisk."

I blew out a long breath, letting it puff my cheeks. "So . . . then . . . we're, like, four hundred years old? Or . . . minus four hundred, depending on how you look at it."

He turned, giving me an exaggerated once-over. "I suppose. Though you look pretty good for an old gal, I must say."

Halfway to the road, we stopped so I could sluice the blood from my hands in an icy brook. After swallowing all the bright, crisp water we could hold, we sat back on a mossy log to formulate a plan.

"We could make our living as fortunetellers." I tried for a joke, but the words caught in my throat when I remembered the day I'd met Phoebe, and how she claimed I looked like a gypsy girl.

Bran smiled, and plucked a stray twig from my hair. "Though I would be the hottest thing on two legs in balloon knee breeches and a gold earring, I happen to be overly fond of iced macchiatos, hot showers, and films with frequent explosions."

"Plus"—he turned to stare down at the frozen bank—"my brother Tony's not even twelve," he said. "He's a sweet lad. Innocent, you know? I can't . . . I *won't* let my mother use him like she did me. He'd never survive all this."

When his fists clenched in his lap, I scooted closer, until our sides pressed together. Bran's heat bled through the layers, stopping my shivers.

"We'll just have to find another way back, then," I said. "Your mom and Flint, they ran off. Obviously you didn't come through at the glade?"

"No. We used another portal at a site clear across London. I would've had to cross through that one to get home." He squinted up at the sun. "It came and went a while ago, I would guess. On horseback, Mother and Flint would've made it in time."

"Then why?" I cried, shifting so I could see his profile. "Why come with us at all when we left Westminster? You could have just gone back to London. You could've gone home."

His jaw muscles worked, but he didn't look at me. "You needed me," Bran said simply.

Silence fell as I realized the sacrifice he'd made. "Bran—" I started, but he interrupted.

"Doesn't matter. What we have to do now is figure out another way home. However, in case you haven't noticed, neither of us is currently in possession of a lodestone. Clearly you know what can happen if you travel without them."

At my nod, he yanked one of the curved swords from his belt and began digging distractedly in the frozen turf. I watched as the tip of his blade gouged a design in the mud. A figure eight. Three wavy lines bisecting the figure horizontally where it crossed over itself. The sign of the Dim.

I stiffened. Then, taking the sword from him, I drew a straight line vertically down through the center.

He frowned. "Why did you do that?"

"What does it mean?"

He frowned. "It's the sign of a Source. Obviously."

I started to nip at my cuticles, but stopped when I saw my

mother's blood still crusted there. "Since I'm kind of new at this whole time-travel thing, why don't you just enlighten me? What the hell is a Source?"

Bran stretched out his long legs and leaned back against a thick oak that grew just behind us.

"Sources are supposed to be the most powerful and ancient entrances to the Dim," he explained. "That line you drew indicates an original portal, where thousands instead of hundreds of ley lines intersect. Supposedly Stonehenge is one, though there's no way to access it, since it would be deep underground. Also, Avebury, the Great Pyramid of Giza, the Bermuda Triangle, Easter Island, and the ancient ground drawings in Lima. They're all rumored to contain a Source. They're believed to have been sealed or otherwise hidden long ago."

Bran may've been speaking by rote, but my heart had started galloping at his words.

He looked over at me. As I gestured for him to go on, ideas began racing through my mind.

"Theoretically, a real Source would not require machinery, and a powerful-enough lodestone would allow one to travel wherever and whenever they wished." He shrugged. "According to my mother, that is. It's an obscure legend, but she never stops searching for an accessible Source."

I let my eyelids close as I remembered leaning against the damp stone wall of the tunnel beneath Westminster and feeling a design etched beneath my palm. In my panic, it had slipped away. But now I jumped to my feet, pacing as another memory popped to the surface. I'd been swaying, upside down, a hundred feet above the abbey floor. I'd just caught a glimpse. Near the altar, the curve of a design embedded in black and white marble.

"Come on." I tugged him to his feet. "We have to go. Now."

"Where?"

I looked up at him, willing him to trust me. "Westminster Abbey."

Bran's mouth twisted. "Going to pray, are we? God knows it couldn't hurt."

"Well, that's true," I quipped, "But it's not why."

His sigh rose white and steamy in the winter air. "You realize it's a good bet Becket might be about?"

"Doesn't matter."

With a groan, he slid his blade into his belt. "All right, but may I make a suggestion?"

"Sure."

"We might want to change out of these gore-soaked rags before we enter the holiest place in London. I can't speak for myself, but you"—he grimaced, tutting as he gestured at my skirts, which were tacky and stiff with frozen blood—"are a horror."

CHAPTER 44

As we suspected, our horses were long gone, likely thanks to Celia. Fortunately, the roads were still passable, with plenty of inbound traffic, even at that hour of the morning. With a few charming words and a jingle of coin, Bran procured us a ride. Also, the young couple was absurdly grateful to trade their own, musty homespun for our fine silks and wools, no matter the condition.

When the rickety cart approached Westminster, Bran and I tucked ourselves down between sacks of weevily flour, in case someone was looking for us. As I breathed in the bland, homey scent, an image popped into my mind. Moira—steady, capable Moira—hands dusted in white as she kneaded bread in the manor kitchen. She'd know exactly what to do to save my mom, and the baby inside her.

I swallowed hard against the new ache. Ridiculous of course, to feel homesick for a place I'd known for such a short time. And yet the people there had believed in me. Trusted me. Taken me in and made me one of their own.

Spooned behind me, beneath the layer of rough weave,

Bran must've heard my quiet sigh. His arms tightened around me. His breath curled past my neck. As he hugged me to him, I luxuriated in his extraordinary heat. I was beyond tired, and it felt so good to lie there, despite the fine grains that filtered down, somehow lodging into every crease and crevice. A thought occurred to me as I fidgeted inside the rough homespun.

"If I get fleas from these clothes," I whispered as I twitched the plain brown skirt, "I'm going to kill you."

I felt Bran's deep chuckle vibrate through me. "Too cold for fleas."

Just as I'd relaxed, his lips brushed my ear. "If I were you, I'd be more concerned about the lice."

As the wagon rumbled and jolted down the pitted streets, I elbowed him—hard—and started scratching.

A freezing mist encased us as we hurried toward the high stone walls of Westminster Abbey. Every muscle in my body felt used up, exhausted. Hopping over a stream of something vile and steaming, I noticed Bran favoring his left side.

"What's wrong?"

"Nothing. Let's go."

He tugged at me, but I noticed the wince and I planted my feet.

"Raise your shirt."

"Hmm. While I'm terribly flattered," he said, eyebrows raised, "this may not be the time—"

"Cut it out," I said, and when I looked up into his eyes,

I saw they were shiny and glazed. A feverish spot stood out on each cheekbone. Gently, I laid my palm against his forehead, as my mother had done to me when I was a child. I jerked my hand away, gulping back a gasp of alarm. "You're burning up." I said. "And you're limping. What's going on, Bran? Let me see."

I tugged at the rough oat-colored tunic, which smelled of smoke and flour and its previous owner. He grunted with irritation but raised the hem. I sucked in a breath.

A long, angry scab marred his side. Starting just below his ribs, it jagged and disappeared into the tied waistband of the dark, nubby breeches. Red streaks shot across smooth, tanned skin like malevolent spider legs. The black thread someone had used to stitch it had all but disappeared beneath the swelling.

When I pressed hesitantly, he hissed. Dark yellow pus oozed from the scab.

He heaved the shirt down. "See? Like I said. Nothing."

His words might've been dismissive, but I could see pain cinch the corners of his eyes. He'd carried my mom through the tunnels and into the forest. The pain must've been excruciating, yet he never complained.

"Wait," I said, recalling Celia ask about some wound back at the glade. "Did your mother do that to—"

"Leave it, Hope. It doesn't matter."

My horror was instant and nauseating. In the snowy courtyard of Mabray House, when Phoebe and I had escaped, I'd seen the moonlight on Celia's blade when Bran's mount had shoved hers out of my way. This was my fault. We had to get Bran back. To antibiotics and a sterile, modern hospital. If I was right about the Source, we'd at least know we *might* have a way out. Yes, we'd have to worry about locating—and likely stealing—two opals. But the stones meant nothing if the Source wasn't there.

I refused to think about what would happen if I was wrong.

The low, barred grate where we'd emerged from the tunnels only hours before was now sealed. No amount of tugging or kicking made it budge. I yanked on the frosted iron until my palms were ice-scalded. "Gah!"

"Um," Bran muttered, "it appears to be locked."

"You think so, Captain Obvious?"

I gave the grate one, last savage kick for good measure, then let fly a string of curses.

Bran's eyebrows flew up. "Impressive."

When I told him to do something that was anatomically impossible, he only chuckled and took my arm. "Come on. We'll find another way."

"I can't believe it." Bran's eyes scanned across the nave floor to the main altar.

On the road, I'd explained what I'd felt in the tunnel and

seen, dangling upside down from the scaffolding during the coronation. We'd discussed Hectare's cryptic message about a lady in "robes of purest white" guarding "her dark treasure in the deep." But what if she had been trying to tell us there was a Source beneath Westminster Abbey?

Whether the little nun knew what she was saying or not, the clues added up. And since it was our only shot, we had to at least try.

"You know," Bran mused, studying the curves imprinted in the black and white marble floor. "Even if the Source is here and we *happen* to locate some opals, it might dump us in some monstrous dinosaur era. Or even worse"—he shuddered theatrically—"the seventies."

"You think bell-bottoms are worse than velociraptors?"

"Infinitely," he whispered with a grin that made my pulse jump.

Bran had heard his mother and great-grandmother speaking reverently about the mythical Sources, and how travelers could choose their destination, just by concentrating on where they wanted to go. We had no idea if it would really work. But again . . . no options.

The nave lay mostly empty, and the bare floor stretched out toward the high altar. As we wove through the stout pillars that held up the barrel-vaulted ceiling, copper braziers and enormous candles filled the space with smoky layers of spicy incense and melting beeswax.

Rubbing my itchy nose, I whispered, "Okay. The

entrance to the vaults should be behind the altar. We have to sneak by all those little old ladies waiting for confession, and we'll have to be really stealthy, because—"

No warning. I sneezed. Explosively. Twice. The sound blared across the church and echoed against the walls. A flock of geese would've made less noise. A monk in the process of lighting candles frowned at us.

One side of Bran's mouth quirked. "Quite right. Stealth. Got it."

"Ohhh, you're talking again," I managed as I swiped a sleeve across my face.

Bran, eyes wide in mock innocence, closed his mouth and mimed throwing away a key. My face felt weird, and I realized I was grinning at him. Really, truly grinning for the first time in forever.

Would it be so bad if we didn't make it out? If the two of us made a life here together?

I quickly thrust that thought away. "Guess we better get going."

We knelt near the front, heads bowed, just another pious couple. When everyone's backs were turned, we rushed behind the high altar; in this age only a shadow of the spectacular gilt masterpiece it would one day become. Beyond lay a stuffy storage room.

Accoutrements of the mass filled the shelves. Golden cups and saucers. Vials of holy oil. White robes and purple stoles hung on hooks. The heavy aroma of old incense drifted thick from dangling censers.

"Umm," I moved to a dusty corner where an iron ring was set into the stone floor. "I think, at least, I hope, this leads down."

Down a narrow, splintery set of steps lay the dank cellar. Cobwebs cloaked the wine barrels and jumbles of dusty crates. Bran located a pile of very old rushlights. He lit two with knife and flint, and we headed deeper into the vast subterranean vault. When we finally arrived at the farthest wall, an arched and ancient door stood partially ajar. Our light revealed a sweeping arc in the dust where it had recently been opened.

Beyond, a stone tunnel sloped sharply downward. Bran held his torch low to the ground. "Footprints. Recent." he whispered.

I ground my teeth as claustrophobia slithered around my chest. *Tunnels. Why does it always have to be freaking tunnels?*

Unlit torches lined the walls beneath the low, barreled ceiling of the undercroft. The overpowering reek of mold and damp earth made my lungs constrict. Close beside me, I felt Bran tense at the scritch of tiny claws on stone.

"What?"

"Nothing," he said. "Simply not a big rat fan."

I gave an undignified snort that guttered the flame.

"What's so funny?"

"You. Cringing at a few teensy mice."

"For your information," he said, offended, "I wasn't cringing. I was merely worried we'd step on the sweet little fellows. Grind them to red paste beneath our boots."

"Lovely image," I said. "Well, just hold on to me, then. I'll protect you."

A little thrill pulsed through me as his grin gleamed white in the darkness.

The cold intensified as we moved down the endless system of corridors, following the scuff of footprints marring the long-undisturbed dust. When muffled voices sounded around a corner just ahead, Bran doused the torches and led us behind a low wall of stacked barrels next to a small alcove.

"I tell you, it's here," an irritated voice said.

Bran mouthed the name: *Becket.*

We edged closer to peek through the cracks. Thomas Becket's back was to us, barking to two men in black and silver. I stifled a groan when I saw one of them was the odious Eustace Clarkson.

Perfect.

"But, Father," Eustace complained, "Lady Celia said—"

"Lady Celia is gone. And though she claims the stone is not here, I am no longer certain she spoke truth. The old nun, Hectare, made her final confession to Father Jerome, right before she died."

A stab of sadness hit me. Sister Hectare was gone, and the world was a little darker now. Bran's fingers laced with mine and squeezed.

"Since I happen to know a thing or two about some of dear Father Jerome's . . . habits," Becket went on, "he gave me every word of the old crone's confession. Apparently, she believed there is an object down here. Something precious. So, you shall search this place. Inside and out. Bring it straight to me and tell not a soul. There will be a reward for whoever finds it." Thomas Becket hesitated. "For the church, of course."

Bran and I exchanged a questioning look. What could he mean? Not the Source. That was a place, not an object.

Becket swept by us without a backward glance. Eustace Clarkson glared after him.

"Oh, we'll find it, Father," he spat. "And make a pretty penny, too."

"But you heard him," the other guard, all greasy black hair and cretinous expression, said. "The stone belongs to the church."

I reared back, nearly dislodging the stack of crates. *The stone?*

"Bah," Eustace sneered. "You want to live your life bowing and scraping to those above you? Then do as I say. Go that way." He pointed in our direction. "And I'll search down there."

Eustace Clarkson stomped off down the corridor in the opposite direction. The other guard sighed, crossed himself, and headed straight toward us. There was no place to hide. As soon as he passed the barrier, he'd see us.

Bran pivoted. I saw the motion as he silently drew the curved blades from his belt.

"No," I whispered. But it was too late.

Greasy-hair turned the corner. Bran launched himself at

him, knocking him to the ground. The man's sword spun away to land at my feet. I froze as the men growled and grappled in the dust. For a moment, Bran had him pinned, but the larger man shoved Bran away and slithered out from under him, then flipped him on his back and pressed a thick knee down on his neck. Bran's arm's flailed. His face turned purple as he gagged.

I slipped from the shadows, heart slamming as I picked up the guard's sword. It was heavier than I expected, the leather grip still warm. I hefted it in both hands, trying to get the feel of it. But before I could do a thing, Bran's fist came up and slammed into the guard's temple.

The man toppled over and fell away, unconscious. Bran scrambled up, gasping and choking. I ran to his side, peering over my shoulder into the blackness, sure that Eustace had heard.

"We have to tie him up," Bran rasped, hand at his bruised throat.

We dragged the man into a shallow chamber. Bran sliced off several strips of my underskirt and, with deft movements, soon had the unconscious man bound and gagged.

"Hurry," he said. "They'll find him soon enough."

He picked up the guard's stuttering torch and we hurried down the tunnel. When Eustace Clarkson's boot prints veered into a left passage, we went right.

We passed through archways and down damp stone steps. Cobwebs draped the ceiling, and water dripped from everywhere. The passage here seemed much older, cut into the very bedrock of the earth. When the tunnel narrowed until I could touch both sides, fear began to nip at me.

We'd made it to the crypt. Tombs lined both walls from floor to ceiling, like file cabinets of death. The names were mostly worn away, though some showed the carved words. As we moved deeper, twisting and turning, we saw that some of the seals had crumbled away completely, revealing grinning skulls and flashes of other bone.

Finally, we reached a dead end. This time, Bran's frustration showed. He slammed his boot into the offending wall. "Damn! I was so certain this was the right way!"

"It's okay," I soothed. "Hang out here for a second, I'll backtrack and check the other tunnel."

Hurrying back the way we'd come, I saw that the passage we hadn't chosen was also blocked.

I returned, brushing cobwebs from my hair. "Hey, we'll need to double back at least . . ."

Bran's lit torch hung in a rusted iron holder. Bran himself was gone. He was gone. And I was alone.

CHAPTER 45

My voice shook, "This isn't funny, you know."

Silence.

"Bran?"

A crunch from deep in the tunnels. A random chunk of stone? Eustace? Bony fingers crawling from a grave? I yanked the torch from the wall and waved it out in front of me like a sword, pressing my back against the wall.

"Bran," I hissed as the terror ate into me.

"Yes?" Bran's voice said from just behind me.

I whirled, torch raised to strike. He squeezed the rest of the way out—as if from the stone itself. I stared at him, dumbfounded. "Wha—how?"

Then I saw it. A cleverly constructed false wall that folded back on itself. You had to be at the perfect angle to even find it.

I lowered the torch. "Fabulous," I snapped. "But if you ever leave me like that again, I may have to kill you."

Three sharp turns and a descent down four flights of nearly vertical steps took us to another world. At the bottom, the floor morphed from slick gray stone to a mosaic that shone in jewel colors where our footprints dislodged the dirt.

Excited, I tugged on his arm. "The cave under my aunt's house has a floor like this. That's gotta be good, right?"

The torchlight revealed elegant fluted columns supporting a ceiling that swirled in black and white concentric circles.

"Roman?" I wondered aloud. "Or . . . no, I think it's even older than that."

We stopped beside a dust-choked bronze sculpture. Waist high, it'd been cleverly molded into a cupped hand.

"There's some very ancient wood here." Bran peered down into the sculpture's palm. "I think this was for fires."

He set the torch to the dry kindling, and in moments light flickered, revealing the huge statue that dominated the chamber.

She was an angel. Or more likely a pagan goddess. Much, much older than the saints guarding the congregation above. The woman's blank eyes stared down into her own cupped palm.

"That must be her," Bran said. "The lady. The entrance to the Source has to be around here somewhere."

While he searched the perimeter, I puttered around the base of the statue, staring up into the serene face. Curious, I scrambled onto the square plinth, using the statue's marble skirts to steady myself. As I perched next to her, my arm around her slim waist for support, I leaned out to peer down into her hand.

A globe-shaped object rested in it, as if she kept watch over the world in miniature. Reaching out, I touched it. Something flaked off. I scratched at it, and another white chunk fell away. Frantic now, I gouged at the object. Tiny pieces of ancient painted clay crumbled beneath my touch, revealing what was hidden beneath. As the object came free at last, I plucked it from her palm. And stared.

"Bran." Excitement edged my voice. "Come here. Now!" I beamed down at him. "Heads up."

His nimble hands flew, snatching what I knew, without a doubt, had to be the true Nonius Stone. "Bugger me," he breathed. "You found it."

This time there was no question. Even in the low light, the black stone sparked with all the colors of the rainbow, just as Pliny had described. Red and violet. Green, orange, yellow, and blue.

"The lady lies beneath their knees," Bran said in a whisper, looking up at the shadowed ceiling. A smile danced across his lips as he held up a hand to me. "Come here," he said in a smoky tone that took my breath away.

As Bran held out a hand to help me down, his grin faded. I followed his gaze to where the statue's arm met her shoulder. There was a dark seam in the otherwise flawless marble. He helped me down, handed me the stone, then reached up and pulled on the statue's outstretched arm. Her shoulder joint gave way with a loud creak, followed by a horrible screech of stone as the statue began to turn.

When it stopped, it had turned ninety degrees, revealing an opening no more than two feet across. Situated at the base of the plinth, a perfect square of black now marred the white marble. It looked like a mouth waiting to consume us.

As we stared at what could only be the entrance to the Source, I took an involuntary step back. My throat closed, and the phobia I'd experienced since my time inside the nightmare tree roared to life.

That can't be it. No way. It's too small. Too small.

"Nope. Can't do it. It's too tight. I mean, don't you see? There has to be another way. Yes, another way. Just have to keep looking."

Understanding dawned on Bran's face. "That's what happened to you in the tunnels earlier. You're claustrophobic."

"Oh, okay, *Einstein*," I said. "Yeah, that's one way to put it." My voice had gone all screechy and black dots now danced at the edges of my vision. I recognized the sign. The onset of a full-blown migraine.

Bran spared a quick glance over one shoulder. "How about this?" he said. "I'll go in first. Scope it out, so to speak?"

Before I could argue, he grabbed the torch, dropped to all fours, and crawled into the entrance. An orange glow rimmed his body as he moved inside. After a moment, even that disappeared and I was left alone with only the bronze sculpture's dwindling fire for company.

An eternity passed as I paced back and forth in the

flickering circle. With every rotation, I glanced at the hateful square of blackness, praying for a glimpse of light. "Bran?" I whispered.

Nothing.

Is the fire going out? What if he never comes out? What if I end up alone here in the dark? I glanced back at the opening.

Darkness. Nothing. Alone.

I crouched before the entrance and tried again, his name wrenched from my lips in a primal scream. No answer. I closed my eyes and dropped back on my heels. "Where are you?"

Fire blazed up in my face. I yelped and I scuttled backwards—crab-like—damp palms slipping against gritty tile.

"Well," Bran croaked as he crawled out. "That's hardly the hero's reception I was expecting."

Feeling foolish, I rushed to help him to his feet. In an instant I could see that the exertion had cost him. He looked ghastly. Dark circles ringed his eyes, and he was shivering convulsively. I knew by the way his skin scorched my palm that the fever was worse, so much worse.

How's he still standing?

Bran's elegant hands rested on my shoulders. "Okay. It's not *so* bad." His voice was gentle, coaxing, though I noticed he wouldn't quite look me in the eye. "I mean, we probably wouldn't want to summer there or anything, but it opens up nicely once you get inside."

"How far inside?"

He waggled a hand back and forth. "Ehh . . . not that far."

"Bran."

He looked away. "A hundred meters or so."

I did a quick conversion. "You expect me to squeeze through that tiny toothpaste tube of an opening, the length of a freaking football field?" Close to hyperventilating now, I eked out the words between inhalations. "I can't. I'm sorry. I just can't. You go. I'll just stay here. I'll become a seamstress or something. I'll—I'll whore on the streets if I have to. I don't have any personal experience, but how bad could it be? And it's nice here. No pollution. And—"

I stumbled over a fallen column and sat down hard, panting. Already I could feel the walls closing in around me.

Bran knelt before me. "I'd wager you can't sew worth a damn. And as far as whoring goes"—he cocked a half grin—"I hear it's an awful return on one's investment. Especially during this age. You'd end up spending half your money on powdered goat balls, or whatever it is they use these days to get rid of the clap."

"They didn't have the clap in the twelfth century," I rasped

"Syphilis, then."

"Nope." Wheeze. "That didn't start until—"

"Either way," he cut in, "I have to say prostitution wouldn't be *my* first choice in career paths for you."

Wheeze. Pause. One side of my mouth twitched as I met his eyes. "No?"

"No," he said. "Decidedly not."

In the uncertain yellow of the flame, Bran's eyes burned like jewels in a face gone pale as porcelain, with beautiful, gaunt planes. The fever was eating him up from the inside. Without the proper treatment, the infection spreading from his wound would get worse. He'd get sick. He would die.

Die. The word tasted like poison in my mouth. I swallowed hard. Of all people on this godforsaken world, I could not—*would not*—let him die. We were the same, he and I, aliens in our own time.

His voice was fierce as he whispered, "Listen to me. You are the strongest, bravest person I've ever met. With barely any warning, you traveled a thousand years into the past to save your mum. And who do you know that would sacrifice their only way home for someone else?"

"I know you," I said, softly.

"Yes, well . . . aside from my brother, I haven't much to go home to."

"Neither do I."

Bran shook his head, staring hard into my eyes. "Untrue. Besides, no one can come close to matching that lovely brain of yours. You melted iron bars, for Christ's sake." That crooked incisor peeked out. "I think you're a bloody superhero. Of course," he said, eyebrows waggling, "you'll need a cape and some tights."

I tried to scowl, but I couldn't hold it. He wrapped me up in his arms. When his lips grazed my ear, I shivered though I was no longer cold. Not at all.

When he pulled back, I skimmed the pads of my fingertips across his forehead. "Your temp's getting worse."

He stood, smiling down at me. "Then let's go home and get some blasted ibuprofen, shall we?"

When I took his outstretched hand, electrical pulses sizzled along my nerve endings. He cocked his head to the side, studying me.

"What?"

"Nothing," he said. "Just imagining you in those tights. I'm not sure my heart could take it."

A buzz of pleasure shot through me at the lazy look in his eyes. Somehow, I managed to whisper, "There you go with the talking again."

Bran grinned and wrapped an arm around me again, tilting his head to rest against mine. We stood like that for a while, staring into the square of darkness.

"So," I murmured, "crawling into the bowels of hell, huh? That should be fun."

His chuckle rumbled through me. "Loads."

When his knees wobbled, I held him up, giving strength for once instead of taking it.

CHAPTER 46

As soon as we entered, I felt it. That elemental, cell-invading tremor I'd first experienced under my aunt's home. It quivered up the bedrock, through my palms and knees, and across my skin. This was it. The way back.

Just ahead of me, Bran struggled to push the torch out in front of him. He called back over his shoulder, "See? Not so bad, is it? Keep holding on to me. We'll be out of this in a jiff. Just breathe."

The bony skin of his ankle burned my palm as I clutched at it.

Keep going. Don't think about it.

Choking on the dust, I moved one hand forward. Knee, hand. Knee, hand. Grit scraped my palms, but I focused on the dancing light that glowed around Bran's slim body.

Just breathe. It became my mantra. Hand, knee. *Just breathe.* Hand, knee. *Just breathe.*

After an interminable time, I began to think maybe we'd make it.

Then we rounded a bend and the tunnel narrowed. On our bellies, we shimmied through inch by inch. The sensa-

tion of crawling down a monster's throat became more pro-
nounced as I sucked in air as thick as a tomb's. My ragged
nails dug into Bran's ankle, but I couldn't help it. The hot
pulse of full-blown panic started to boom inside me.

Can't do it.

"Bran?" I gasped.

He stopped, called back to me in a hoarse voice, "Almost
there. I'd sing to you, but since my singing voice more closely
resembles a scalded cat than anything else, it would likely
only sour the experience. Learned *that* from the choirmaster
when I was in second form."

The image made me smile. And for a millisecond, I felt
better. Forced myself to think of open spaces. The snow
blowing over us as we stood before Westminster Abbey. The
brutal beauty of the Scottish Highlands.

The press of stone brought me back, and I felt myself begin to shatter, one molecule at a time. I kept my eyes trained
on the yellow glow as Bran squirmed forward. The tunnel curved downward at a sharp slope. Down, down, always
down. Deeper we crawled. And then a prickling feeling hit
the back of my neck, and suddenly I knew something was
behind me.

"Something's back there." My mouth was so dry, I could
barely form the words.

He coughed. It sounded awful. "Nothing's there, Hope,"
he wheezed. "Hang on. Almost there."

Terrified I'd lose my hold on him, I kept going. What
choice did I have?

I have no idea how long it took. How do you track time when you're living your worst nightmare?

Just when I thought I'd die—when I couldn't possibly exist this way for another instant—the light disappeared, and we plunged into a death-like darkness.

I lost it.

Thrashing and fumbling, I shoved, trying to force my back up through the millions of tons of dirt and stone above me and break through to the surface. I was trapped. Choking. I would die here, buried beneath the stone. Buried alive.

Bran's ankle ripped from my grasp. I shrieked and writhed and raged against the sides of the tunnel. I tried to flip over, but it was too tight, too tight. The blackness was a living thing, eating me. I clawed against the stone, my fingernails ripping until my fingers slipped on blood.

I screamed as something grabbed my wrists. I twisted and bit and gouged with shredded nails. "Noooo!"

I thought I heard someone calling my name, but the panic had me. I was lost.

"Hope!" I was wrenched forward. "For Christ's sake, open your eyes!" It was Bran's voice. Bran's voice!

My eyes snapped open in shock. I could *breathe*. And I was wrapped in Bran's arms, lying on the floor of a large, open cavern.

"We—we're out," I said lamely. I looked up to see the hole in the smooth wall where we'd emerged.

"Um, yes." Bran touched a jagged scratch across his jaw. "We are at that."

When I could stand on my own, Bran used the guttering torch to light several others mounted in iron holders.

I recognized the tingle of power against my skin. The pulse of the Dim, but magnified a hundred times. The cave was narrower than that beneath Christopher Manor, but longer. Forty feet across from where I stood — at the triangle's apex — a chill breeze blew from a man-size opening. I crossed the room to peer inside, but could see nothing except unrelenting darkness. Picking up a stone, I tossed it in.

I never heard it land.

I snatched a torch from the wall and thrust it inside, then gulped as my eyes widened. A chasm. A vast emptiness that was so deep and so dark, it seemed to have no beginning or end. The electrical pulses, powerful and ancient, shivered across my skin.

I skidded back, panting, drawing in the scents of earth and long-faded incense. A desiccated, electric flavor skipped across my tongue.

Ghosts.

A shiver ran up my back. "Bran, this opening, it's a . . ."

I trailed off at the sight of him huddled on a stone near the tunnel exit. He curled in on himself, as though his skin was shrinking.

Bran's exhausted smile wavered around the edges. "I'm fine." He gestured with his chin. "By the way, there's your symbol."

Carved into the smooth floor, near the dark opening, was the figure I'd felt under my fingers in the tunnels, and that Bran had drawn in the mud. An elongated figure eight with three wavy lines bisecting it, and a single vertical slash through the center.

"So what do we do now?" I knelt beside him. "Say *abracadabra*? Click our heels together?"

Bran snorted. When he shifted on the rock, though, a quiet moan escaped.

"Let me see."

Unprotesting, he let me draw up the hem of his tunic. I sucked in a quiet breath. The wound had broken open. Dark blood and murky fluids drenched the side of his breeches. The red streaks across his abdomen were now a dark, malevolent purple. When he touched my hair, in question, it was a moment before I could face him.

"Okay," I tamped down the horror and plastered on a smile. "So . . . it's not that bad. But, uh, we probably need to get home pretty quick."

"You," he said, "are a terrible liar."

I opened my mouth to argue, but he brought a finger to my lips.

"When we met by the river," he said, "I had a purpose. Get the information for my mother. Do whatever she said, so she'd leave my brother where he was safe. Then, once he turned eighteen and could leave her, I'd take him away with me. We could go and I'd never be her bloody slave again."

Inside the silence of the cavern, the only sound was Bran's raspy breath as he curled a strand of my hair around his finger.

"But there you were," he said, "so shy and funny, but brave, too. So beautiful and so damn brilliant that everything changed."

He leaned in toward me, his lips hot embers where they touched my cheeks, my lashes, my forehead. His hands scorched my cheeks as they cradled my face.

"I've thought of you every single day since they took us, you know." His voice was husky. It filled me with a need so deep, I couldn't get close enough to him.

He smiled ruefully. "When I was small, and things were so bad at home, I'd pretend you were a lost princess in a tower, and that I'd be the shining knight who rescued you."

I trembled in the cold as tears stung my eyes. "You did." His eyes widened, as I choked out the words. "Don't you know that?"

The kiss was sweet. A blessing. My eyes closed as I leaned into him. When he rose onto his knees, I went with him. His hands burrowed into my hair, his mouth slanting over mine again and again. When he gave a deep, guttural growl, I felt it all the way to my toes. The kiss turned desperate, hungry. Savage. I was soaring, the blood singing in my veins as I twined my arms around his neck, and I knew I'd wanted this since the first moment I'd seen him in the river. Since the instant I'd felt that strange connection between us. I felt something click into place, like two long-lost puzzle pieces finally brought together and made whole.

The muscles in his shoulders bunched as he pressed me to him. We breathed each other. Fire and ice.

CHAPTER 47

I FELT HIM SMILE AS HE MURMURED AGAINST MY LIPS, "I cannot *tell* you how long I've wanted to do—"

A thunk vibrated through me. Bran went instantly limp in my arms and slithered bonelessly from my grip. My eyes popped open, and I couldn't comprehend what I was seeing.

Bran puddled on the cold stone. And behind him, a stout club still raised in his fist, stood Eustace Clarkson.

"Hallo, pretty," the foul guard said, showing mossy teeth.

I scrambled away until my back met the cold stone wall. With an arrogant nonchalance, Eustace dropped the club and bent over Bran, his greedy eyes brightening at the sight of his fine, twin blades.

The side of his face where I'd struck him with the candlestick was purple and swollen. Eustace caught my look and touched the cheek.

"It's time to collect payment for this." His hand moved from his cheek to the ties on his hose.

Disgust twisted my guts. *Think. Think. There has to be a way out of this.*

Eustace lunged without warning, raising me up and slamming me hard against the wall in one motion. My head smacked into stone. Waves of pain crashed through my brain. He was huge, his muscles hard and sinewy. My torn fingernails dug for his eyes. I tried to stomp his instep or kick him in the crotch like Phoebe had taught me. But he was too close, and I only connected with his thigh.

His lips drew back in a snarl, and he slapped me with such force, I nearly went limp. Stars exploded in my vision an instant before the pain arrived.

Bran. Oh God, please, Bran. Please wake up.

But I was alone. And no one would ever hear me scream.

My left eye was already swelling shut from the blow. A trickle of liquid ran from my nose, rimming my teeth with the iron taste of blood. I slapped and scratched at Eustace, but he merely clamped my wrists together in one hand and slammed them above my head. His bulbous nose smashed against mine as wet, flabby lips wormed over my closed mouth. I squeezed my thighs together as he viciously tried to wedge his knee between them.

Weak. Weak. Weak.

"*NO!*" I writhed and twisted, but he was too strong. He yanked at my bodice. My dress ripped down the front like it was made of paper.

Furious tears turned the torches into giant prisms. God,

I wanted to tear out his eyes, his black heart. Black as the inside of the chasm.

The chasm.

My eyes darted to the small opening and chasm beyond. An idea began to form as he slobbered on my neck.

"So," I made myself say, "you're nothing but Becket's lackey, huh? While he's dining with the king, he sends you down here to do his dirty work."

I wasn't exactly sure where I was going with this. But the jealous words Eustace had spat at the other guard earlier had roared up in my memory.

In minute degrees, I forced myself to meet his pale, insipid eyes. "I bet he didn't even mention the treasure."

A glimmer of confusion flickered behind his eyes. He leaned closer, his stubble grating against my cheek as he growled in my ear. "There's no treasure."

I made myself slump in his grip, trying not to wince at the rotted-meat stench of his breath. "You're right. Just do whatever you want, then. I won't fight. But leave me here when you're done." I looked pointedly at the chasm. "I didn't want to share it anyway."

Eustace followed my gaze, just as I'd hoped. His mouth and chin gleamed with bloody spittle. "You lie."

But I saw the indecision on his face, and pressed on. "Don't pretend you haven't heard. Everyone knows about the treasure of the abbey cave."

He studied my face. When his tongue flickered out to

lick my blood from his lips, I clenched my teeth to keep from gagging.

With a final twist of my wrists, he let go and backed away. "All right, wench. What treasure? Where?"

Again, I let him see my eyes flick to the dark opening.

Careful now. Not too obvious.

"Um, I'm not sure exactly."

When he wrapped his fist in my hair, I could feel each individual strand rip loose from my scalp. He forced me to my knees, bending my head back at an unnatural angle. "You tell me where it is," he snarled in my ear as he moved behind me. "Or . . ."

I heard the snick of steel just before the edge of his blade stung my throat. A trickle of blood oozed down my chest.

"Fine." Terrified, I didn't dare breathe. "It's there. Just inside that opening in the stone."

"Show me."

He jerked me to my feet and frog marched me to the entrance of the Dim. As we approached, a cold breath of wind huffed out of the chasm. It smelled of grave dirt and nightmares, and even Eustace took an involuntary step back. When it ceased, the goon's hand flew forward, wrapping around my throat. He lifted me until my toes barely touched the ground.

I heaved, scratching, fighting for breath.

"Tell me where!" he bellowed, tossing me back to the floor. I landed hard on my hip. A stab of pain shot up my side as the Nonius Stone—nestled deep inside my pocket—plowed into my flesh. I rolled over, retching.

When he stalked over, fist raised, I cowered.

"Yes! I'll tell you," I didn't have to fake the sobs. "Please—don't hit me again." I took a ragged breath. "The treasure is in a jeweled case, on a ledge inside the crevice. You have to lean way in to reach it."

I scuttled away until my back met the damp wall, my hands wedged behind my back. My blood-caked fingertips ached against the cool pebbled surface.

Eustace stopped a couple of feet from the entrance, then swiveled back to me, eyes narrowed. "You get it." He snapped his fingers at me, as if I were a dog.

"I can't reach it." I bowed my head, letting my hair curtain the faint gleam of hope in my eyes. "Lord Brandon was supposed to—"

"Shut up," he said, "and stay where you are."

He jabbed the dagger at me in warning and turned back to the chasm. Stroking his weak chin in thought, he moved to the opening.

Turning back, he leered at me. "If this treasure is worth it—and you please me properly—I may let you live. Might even give you a coin or two when we're done."

Laughing, he sheathed the dagger and leaned out over the edge, steadying himself on the wall with his left hand.

I knew I'd have only one shot. If I failed, Eustace would kill us both. And I had no doubt that he'd make my death very, very unpleasant.

"You'd best not be lying to me, wench. If you are, I'll cut your pretty little tongue out of your head." He leered. *"After you use it on me, of course."* He laughed at his own joke, but the chasm ate his laughter. He shot a look over his shoulder, looking uneasy for the first time. "Where the devil is it?" he growled. "Damn, it's cold as a nun's tit in here. And why does it feel so queer in this place? Like ants crawling over me?"

I closed my eyes. Every possible option flooded out before me in a neon-green overlay. In an instant, my brain had calculated the perfect angle, the required velocity, the number of steps it would take. Every muscle in my body tensed, ready. Eustace began to turn, his ugly, battered profile illuminated by the torchlight.

"Higher." I kept my eyes locked on him as I inched to a standing position. "You have to reach up high."

A sudden wind blasted from the chasm. It circled the chamber, sending tiny pebbles skittering. "I feel nothing," Eustance said. "What the hell was—"

I launched myself from the wall, slamming into him from behind with every bit of strength I had left. Already unbalanced, Eustace teetered, arms pinwheeling. His horrified eyes met mine for a split second before gravity won and he tumbled over the edge. At the last instant, he snatched the hem of my skirts. His weight dragged me forward, and my feet skidded over the slick stones as the brute dangled over the seemingly bottomless chasm.

Bracing a hand against the rock face, I jerked desperately

at the fabric. A look of pure terror washed over his snarling face as the material ripped. The sound of it reverberated as Eustace Clarkson tumbled backwards into the abyss.

His screams echoed around me. I clapped my hands over my ears, but it didn't help. There was no cutoff. The sound only grew fainter, until finally it faded away.

CHAPTER 48

I SANK TO MY KNEES, MY LEGS UNABLE TO HOLD ME AS I crawled back to Bran. Wind circled the cavern, casting the pebbles in an endless loop around us. I groped at the side of his neck, praying frantically for a pulse. At first there was nothing. No answering beat.

"Oh no. Oh no. Oh no."

I rolled him to his back and tried again. My fingertips were all but numb. I pressed harder, begging, until finally I felt a weak, threadbare thump of life.

Sobbing with relief, I grabbed his hands and dragged him to the center of the room, into the eye of the cyclone that was building around us. His skin felt like fire beneath my palms.

"Bran," I cried, "wake up. You have to wake up."

The glimmering light played across his pale features and closed eyelids. His breaths were so shallow that his chest barely moved, and no matter how hard I shook him, he still didn't respond. Wincing, I slapped him, twice, as hard as I could. My fingers raised scarlet welts on his cheeks.

Now furious, exhausted, and more frightened than I'd ever been in my entire life, I screamed, "You jerk! How can you do this to me? You lied to me. You spied on me. You followed me here. Your screwed-up mom nearly killed mine. And now you are going to just lie there unconscious while I deal with this alone? Oh hell no. *Hell* no!"

I shook him so hard, his head bounced off the stone. Sinking back, I hugged my knees and rocked back and forth, my face buried in my skirts. I had a sudden, fierce longing for Collum's sturdy presence and Phoebe's cheerful comfort.

I let out a long string of curses, pounding the stone with my fists until they were scratched and stinging.

"Such language." My head shot up at the creaky voice. "And, uh . . . not to abuse the cliché," he said, groaning, "but where am I?"

I threw myself on top of him, darting small kisses on every inch of his face. He winced. "Ow. Why do my cheeks hurt?"

My hair hung down, framing his face as I grinned. "No idea."

His brows drew together. One fingertip traced a gentle line across my cheek. "Your face."

"Doesn't matter."

Nothing mattered, because Bran was alive. He was *alive.* His eyes darted around the room. Though the wind was sweeping around the perimeter of the cave, its velocity growing, it barely touched us. "Do I want to know what happened?"

He struggled to his feet, his hand clutching his side. I glanced away from the dark pool of blood he left behind.

"It was Eustace," I said. Once I started babbling, I couldn't get the words out fast enough. "He hit you from behind. The wind started a few minutes ago. I have no idea if it means what we hope it does. I thought you were dead. Then he . . . he tried to . . . And so I—"

"Did he hurt you?" Bran's voice was deceptively soft, but I could see rage glimmer in his eyes as he pulled the edges of my ripped bodice together and tied it closed. "Did that bastard touch you?"

"No. I mean he hit me, but he didn't—you know—do anything else. He didn't get the chance."

As our eyes met, the realization of what I'd done struck me. "I killed him, I think. Shoved him into the chasm. He screamed for so long, Bran, but I had no choice. He was going to . . ." I slapped my hands over my mouth, trying to hold in the moan. Bran eased them away and cupped my face, forcing me to look at him.

"Listen to me. You did the right thing. The *only* thing. I hope that misbegotten son of a whore is burning in hell."

A weird little hiccup erupted from my throat. "Well, he's on his way. That's for sure."

Bran pulled me to him and held me so tight.

In his arms, I felt the sense of unbelonging I'd lived with

my whole life begin to fade away. The grief at losing my mother. The confusion when I learned she was still alive. It all disappeared as Bran rocked me in his arms while the wind keened and tugged at our cloaks and hair.

He stiffened suddenly. "The Nonius Stone? That monster didn't take it from you?"

"No."

We still had no idea if it would take us both back. Or where we'd end up if it did. But I pulled the walnut-size stone from my pocket. It throbbed against my palm, and immediately my skin shimmered in a lavender light.

I grabbed Bran's hand and pressed our palms together. The mist crawled up his arm, coating him in purple, and the knot inside my chest loosened.

"See?" I said. "It'll work. It's powerful enough to take us both. Now we just concentrate on where we want to go. Concentrate hard, Bran. Think about Christopher Manor. Hold it in your mind as hard as you can."

The wind became a cyclone, and suddenly I could feel pinpricks dancing along my nerve endings. The Dim's pull.

He looked at me then, and I felt cold dread pour over me at the regret on his face.

"Hope," he said, "Listen, I can't . . ."

"No," I tried to protest, but he stopped me, his fingers soft on my lips. "I can't let her corrupt Tony. But I swear I will never let her hurt you again."

The pain when I realized what he was saying was so exquisite, I couldn't even touch it. I could feel myself coming apart but didn't know if it was the Dim or what his words meant. His hand twined in my hair, and he raised my face to his.

When our lips touched, I murmured against his mouth, "Please."

The suction ripped the air from our lungs. We kept pressing the Nonius Stone between our palms and knotted our fingers together, clinging. Desperate. Bran locked his other arm around my waist. As he tightened his grip, I felt no fear. I didn't even worry where we might end up. Either way, I had lost him.

"Hope!" Bran called over the roar of the wind. "I will always—"

But whatever he'd been about to say was drowned out by a sudden roar, and all I knew was the smell of wood smoke and apples as it filled me. As the Dim took us.

The Nonius Stone. It must've been why the journey back was so much easier. At first.

Sublime joy flooded through me, shoving away the sorrow as we soared forward through time. I felt no disorientation, no pain. Saw no rotting faces. Brilliant colors burst from between our fingers, twining around us in a blaze of rainbow light. It fused us together, and I threw my head back and laughed with sheer exultation.

Then I felt him slip. Just a bit. But it was enough. The Nonius Stone slid from our joined hands. Bran's hold on me loosened as he grappled for it. It grazed the tips of his fingertips and dropped away into the shimmering, sparkling ether around us.

Everything changed. Darkness rushed at us. The faces of the dead crowded in, not one at a time but in a churning mass.

I tried to hold on, to keep us bound together, but the Dim ripped him away as I twirled end over end, tumbling and whipping like a leaf in a hurricane. I felt each cell as it tore apart, one microscopic particle at a time.

I landed hard on my shoulder and hip, rolling over and over until my head bounced against stone. My brain imploded in agony, and nausea rolled through me. I forced my eyelids open, but something was wrong. Everything was bleary, as though I was peering through the water of a murky fishbowl.

I can't see.

My lips refused to form words. My mind was sluggish, my muscles as weak as water.

"Bran," I croaked.

No answer. I tried to scrub at my eyes, but lightning bolts of electricity jolted over my nerve endings like my entire body had gone to sleep. My ears felt stuffed with cotton. "Someone! Anyone! Please!"

Muffled noise. Footsteps pounding across stone.

"Bran!" I screamed his name with everything I had left.

A familiar hand grabbed mine. Scalding fingertips traced my cheek for an instant before his hoarse voice croaked, "I'm here."

My head fell back in relief, and the indistinct world around me faded to black.

CHAPTER 49

I PERCHED ON THE EDGE OF MY MOTHER'S HOSPITAL BED, my baby sister a warm lump in my arms. While machines beeped quietly around us, I inhaled the baby's scent. Fresh-baked cookies and newness.

I still couldn't believe it. I had a *sister.*

"She's really beautiful, Mom."

"I know." My mother was beginning to get a bit of color back in her wan cheeks after three days in the hospital.

Misty morning light poured in through the window as the baby stretched out a tiny hand, as though grasping at a dream. She gripped my finger with surprising strength. A wrinkle of concern appeared below the pink-and-white knitted cap. I smiled, recognizing Moira's handiwork.

"Lucinda has contacted your father," Mom said. "All she told him was that you were ill. He'll be on the next plane out. He knows nothing about me." Her gaze flicked to the baby. "Or her. He—he's coming alone."

I looked away. So she knew about Stella. In my mind, I

saw my dad standing next to the quiet, thoughtful librarian. He and Stella shared roots in the same small-town world, and I honestly didn't know what he would do. Dad was a scientist. His life revolved around test tubes and logic. I knew he'd loved my mother, but hadn't recent events proved that sometimes love wasn't enough?

"Hope," she said, "I want you to know that I'm going to tell your father everything. He deserves that. But . . . well"—she pressed her lips together to still the trembling—"I think we both know how that will likely go. I've never been fair to Matt, keeping him in the dark this way. In the end, I just want him to be happy. And if he's found happiness with Stella, I won't contest it. I hope you understand."

The baby let out a squawk when I squeezed her too tight. Her little-old-man features blurred as I nodded.

"Here." My mother held out her arms. "Let me have her."

I handed her back, then tied my own blue and white hospital gown tighter around me. I'd been admitted for observation the day before, the concussion I'd received still making my head buzz and throb like a nest of angry wasps.

After the baby was settled, Mom smoothed a finger absently down one downy cheek. "I wanted to tell you so many times about . . . everything."

My mind flipped to a snowy forest. To the image of an angel holding me in her arms, and a horrifying journey that my young mind had locked away.

"You were so sickly when you were small," she went on.

"Fragile. You caught every illness imaginable, due to your lack of natural antibodies for this time. So I kept you close, thinking it the right way to protect you. Yet I prepared you, as best I could, in case the day ever came. I—I should've never kept this from you. Any of it. I'm sorry."

I reached out to squeeze her hand and felt one of the hundred cracks in my shattered heart begin to mend itself. A slender thread of forgiveness wove itself between us. It was tenuous, but definitely a beginning.

When a nurse entered and began fussing with my mother's IV lines and telling me to head back to my own room for a vital sign check, I stood. "Well, I guess I'd better—"

"I've decided on a name," Mom blurted out.

Guilt stabbed me when I realized I hadn't thought to ask. "Really? What?"

"Eleanor." The name whispered through the room, coating me in memory. "Her name is Eleanor."

"I think"—my breath hitched—"I think that's perfect, Mom."

As I reached for the door handle, Mom's voice rose over the beeping. "Bran came to see me before he was transferred," she called. "He wanted to see you, but you were sedated."

I knew Bran was long gone. Transferred by Celia to another hospital within hours of our arrival. No one knew where. I didn't even get to say goodbye.

My knuckles whitened on the handle. "He could have waited."

"He didn't have a choice, honey," she said. "He explained about his brother. And even with that, I think it was a difficult decision for him."

I looked back over my shoulder at the tiny bundle in my mother's arms. What would I sacrifice to keep her safe?

"Yeah," I said. "I guess it was."

"We were sore worried." Phoebe lay curled next to me on the starched hospital sheets. "When you and Bran just popped in like that."

I nodded, though the motion made my head hurt. Still, it was nothing compared with the sharp throb in my chest, as if my heart had been scooped out and replaced with a tangled ball of needles.

"I was down in the watch room," Doug, his bulk perched awkwardly on a tiny rolling stool, explained, "when suddenly every line on the monitors turned red. That's when I knew you must've found the Nonius Stone. It was the only explanation. I flew down and powered up the machines. There was this enormous blast that rocked the whole house. Then the two of you just . . . appeared."

The glance that passed between him and Collum set my teeth on edge. "What?" I asked. "What's wrong?"

Collum still looked washed out after minor surgery to repair the damage to his arm. He'd be in a sling for a few weeks, but the doctors thought there would be no permanent damage.

"There's a problem with the Tesla device," Doug said. "The diagnostics show some damage. I can't know for sure. I think it'll go for a couple more voyages, but nothing is certain."

Phoebe raised herself up on an elbow and looked at me, her small, freckled face so serious. "Cheese an' crackers, Hope. When you did that—gave up your lodestone—I've never been so scared," she said. "I don't know that I could've done it."

"Reckless." Collum rose and moved to the edge of the bed. "Stupid. Rash." A ghost of a smile flickered over his mouth as he reached down to squeeze my hand. "And the bravest thing I've ever seen."

Lucinda was waiting for me at the kitchen table when Mac brought me home to Christopher Manor.

"Sit," she said. "Please."

Strangely numb, I shuffled over and slid onto the wooden bench across from her. Deep purple ringed her eyes beneath a matching plum-colored turban. Her face seemed thinner, the skin tinged yellow and pulled tight across her broad cheekbones.

Two days earlier, Mac, perched quietly in a straight-backed chair by my hospital bed, had finally told us what was ailing my aunt. "Lu don't want a fuss made, mind," he said, "so keep your opinions to yerself."

Apparently, while on a trip to the thirteenth century, Lucinda had picked up a blood disorder that had no modern equivalent. Akin to a rare kind of leukemia, it did not respond to any known treatment. They'd researched all they could, but there was little information to find. A dear friend of Lucinda's, a doctor in Edinburgh, knew all about the Viators and was doing all she could. But at this point, Mac said, only frequent blood transfusions were staving off the inevitable.

"I want you to know that I was quite impressed with the job you did," my aunt said. "This mission was a success, in no small part due to your efforts. You protected the members of your team. You brought your mother back. And you've kept the Nonius Stone out of Celia's hands." I couldn't be sure, but I *thought* I saw pride skim over her features. "In quite a unique fashion, I must say."

Frowning, I remembered the moment the Nonius had slipped from Bran's fingers and tumbled away into the Dim.

"You must realize, however, that it's likely the stone will reenter the timeline somewhere," Lucinda went on.

I nodded. I'd already thought of that, wondered about it.

"Celia's clever," Lucinda said. "She'll realize it soon enough. And she's brought in some hard men who will stop at nothing to locate the stone. Her mind, you see, is warped by jealousy. We tried to help her once, to make her feel part of us, but she just couldn't accept it."

Lucinda sat straighter in her chair. "Our task now is to

ensure that the Timeslippers never get their hands on the Nonius Stone. For without our interference, I fear they may alter the timeline in ways we cannot imagine."

Silence fell between us as I remembered the little Carlyle girls, lost forever by one thoughtless act. Yes, Celia had to be stopped.

Lucinda was watching me carefully. "Hope," she said, "you have proven your abilities beyond anything we expected. I have spoken with your mother, and though it frightens her, she believes it is your right to make up your own mind."

"About what?"

"We could use someone with your knowledge and unique gifts." Lucinda's blunt fingers gripped the edge of the table. "I'm asking you to join the Viators, Hope."

I stared down at the table. The offer spun before me, tantalizing and horrifying all at once. Could I actually go through that hell again? What kind of insane person would even think of choosing such a life?

Without waiting for a response, Aunt Lucinda slid off the bench. "I'll give you some time to think it over." At the door, she turned. "But might I make a suggestion?" She glanced at the silvery glass of the kitchen window. "The river is especially lovely by moonlight. Perhaps you should consider taking a ride."

❧

Ethel and I were breathless when we reined up at the riverbank. All around me, the Highlands looked like another world. In the daytime, the moors and mountains seemed like a fairyland untouched by time. Now the river had transformed into a brilliant ribbon of light, every leaf of heather and gorse frosted in a million shades of glorious silver, like a child's dream.

The rush of the river. The perfume of heather. The mist that swirled up from the ground. It all matched how I felt. Ghost-like. Insubstantial. One foot in each time, but belonging to neither.

I picked my way to the exact spot where I'd first tumbled down the bank and, closing my eyes, wished I had it to do all over again. This time, I'd tell him I knew his face. I'd make him tell me everything. I'd beg him to stay with us. And if he refused, I'd drag him back to the manor if I had to. Anything to keep him safe. To keep him *here*.

"Ridiculous," I muttered, cursing under my breath.

"Really, Hope." The voice echoed weirdly in the fog. "Such language."

Heart leaping into my throat, I spun in a circle, trying to locate the source. As if I'd conjured him from the mist, Bran Cameron stepped over the edge of the riverbank, leading his horse.

"Hello," he said.

"What are you doing here?"

I wondered briefly if I was dreaming. But the smells and sounds and feel of the moist fog against my skin were too real. Bran led his roan to nuzzle against Ethel and moved toward me, leaving a few feet of space between us.

"I had to see you," he said simply.

When he reached out a hand, I stiffened, and he let it drop. He'd made his choice. And though I understood his reasons, even admired them, it didn't change how much it hurt.

"My mother's agreed to leave Tony in school for now."

"That's good." I choked back the excruciating ache. "I mean, I'm glad he's safe. But I don't understand. Why would Celia agree to take you back, when she knows you betrayed her?"

I had to look away from the cocky half grin. That crooked incisor. "She didn't have much choice, really," he said. "Before I left, I hid all her Tesla research." He winked. "A little insurance policy."

Awkward seconds passed while we stared at each other. He was so close, I could see the condensation from the mist pearling on his cheeks. Yet he might as well have been on the moon. I looked away and began to move toward Ethel.

"Well," I said, "good luck with that."

Before I could take another step, Bran grabbed me, eyes like a starving man's as they roamed my face. "When you rode into my village on the front of your grandfather's horse," he said, "you were the brightest, most beautiful thing I'd ever seen. Like a duchess, with your silks and your little doll." His fingers tightened on my arms. "No matter what happens, don't ever forget that."

I ripped away, fighting back sobs that slashed at the inside of my chest like shards of broken glass. "Then leave her," I cried. "Lucinda could protect your brother somehow. I know it. She's got a lot of influence, and . . ."

Still gibbering like a maniac, I let him pull me to him. Beneath the snug T-shirt, I could feel the bandage wrapped around his slim waist.

I breathed in, wishing I never had to exhale, that I could keep Bran's scent in my lungs forever. My fingers played up the ridge of his spine, memorizing the flex of each muscle, and how the fine hairs on the back of his neck stiffened when my lips grazed his earlobe.

If this was all I ever got of Bran Cameron, I would sear every nuance into my mind. I had a photographic memory, perfect recall for books and maps and arcane knowledge no one had ever cared about. But I was terrified I'd forget how he felt against me.

He murmured into my hair. "I can't take that chance, Hope. But I will *never* let her hurt any of you again." He pulled back to look down at me. "I'll do everything I can to ensure my mother never gets her hands on the Nonius Stone." His eyes shuttered. "I've agreed to feed information to the Viators. It's all arranged."

Lucinda. That's how she knew he'd be here tonight.

"No." My fists bunched in his shirt. "Bran, if your mom finds out you're helping us, she'll kill you. You know that."

He planted a kiss on the end of my nose and stepped back. "Then I shall have to be very clever, won't I?"

He gave that Bran Cameron smirk and walked over to withdraw something from his saddlebag.

Grinning, he returned with a bulky object wrapped in a scrap of aged fabric. He placed it in my open palm and backed up, worrying at the silver medallion at his neck. The only thing left from a life that was taken from him. Robbed, because of me.

"What's this?"

"Just open it."

The silky material fell open at my touch. All the air left my lungs as I reached out a trembling finger to touch her hair, the delicate silk of her faded gown.

You must take good care of your Elizabeth until I come for you, sweet girl, my grandfather had told me.

But I hadn't. I'd lost the doll in the nightmare tree.

I looked up into Bran's eyes. Sapphire and Emerald. The only points of color in a silver night. "You kept her? All this time?" My intake of breath was quick and shallow. "Why?"

He tucked a stray curl behind my ear. "Don't you know?" he whispered. "Haven't you always known?"

There comes a moment in every person's life when fate wheels on the head of a pin and changes their destiny forever. For me, that instant came when a little boy, with blue and green eyes, handed me an apple.

I flew to him. When Bran Cameron pulled me close and began to murmur the words that would send my heart soaring and shatter it in one fell swoop, I shook my head and touched his lips with shaking fingers.

"Bran," I said through pain and joy that mixed to scratch my voice. "Just . . . stop talk—"

His mouth came down over mine, stopping my words, crushing me to him in a kiss we both knew would have to last us for a long, long time.

TO BE CONTINUED

ACKNOWLEDGMENTS

I DON'T KNOW HOW ANY AUTHOR CAN EVER BEGIN TO thank all the people who were involved in helping her write a book. But I'm going to do my best.

First and foremost, I want to thank my husband, Phil. My love, best friend, and sweetheart since that Halloween party when we were seniors in high school. (You know what I'm talking about, baby.) Day after day, he's my biggest fan, my strongest cheerleader, and the one who's talked me off the ledge more times than I can count. This book would not exist without him.

It also wouldn't exist without my book-loving mom, Nena Butler. My mom is my alpha reader, my traveling companion, and the one who put a book in my hand when I was three years old, teaching me how the little squiggles on the page could carry you away into a million different worlds. Thanks, Mom, for reading all the terrible first drafts and telling me each one would be a movie someday. To my sweet daddy, Duck, who's so very proud of me, and to my beautiful sister, Jennifer, and my gorgeous nieces, Hannah, Kayley, and Ava—who let me use her middle name for my main character.

A humongous thanks goes to my incredible rock-star agent, Mollie Glick. Mollie, you never gave up on me or on Hope. You recognized something in my little time-travel story, then whipped me beyond the boundaries of what I thought I could do. Thanks also to her fantastic assistant, Joy Fowlkes, who fielded a million emails from me and never got tired.

Thank you to my fabulous editor, Sarah Landis. Sarah's my guru, my sherpa, and the keenest editorial eye I've ever known. Thanks also to Mary Wilcox and Christine Krones, for taking me in hand while Sarah was off being fecund. My brilliant publicist, Rachel Wasdyke, and marketing sage, Ann Dye, and all the wonderful folks at Houghton Mifflin Harcourt for believing in this story.

To Heather Webb, author extraordinaire, leader of our writing group, and the best friend/sprinting partner in the world. Huge hugs to all the girls in the SFWG writing group — Susan Spann, Candie Campbell, Julianne Douglas, LJ Cohen, Marci Jefferson, Amanda Orr, DeAnn Smith, Arabella Stokes. Together we've become better than we ever dreamed.

Love to all my Arkansas friends. My BFF since third grade, Kelley Riggs Nichols (yes, you can come with me and dress me on book tour), Linda Gayton, Yolanda Longley, and Lynette Place (whose talent made my author picture look halfway decent). Michelle Buchanan; her brilliant daughter, Marlee; Barbara Varnon. Thanks to my DFWcon writer friends, Jenny Martin, Dawn Alexander, Kate Michaels, and Lindsay Cummings.

I'm forever grateful to Diana Gabaldon, for making historical time travel cool. And to my experienced guides through this crazy biz—Joelle Charbonneau, Leigh Bardugo, Rysa Walker, Kendare Blake, Alethea Kontis, Danielle Page, Brenda Drake, CJ Redwine, and Rachel Caine.

A huge thanks to my new "posse," the Sweet 16s. I couldn't get through the day without WAY too many texts, IMs, emails, frantic phone calls flying between me and Marisa Reichardt, Shea Olsen, Shannon Parker, Catherine Lo, Kathryn Purdie, Ashley Herring Blake.

The most massive "I love you" goes to my brilliant, hilarious sons, Phillip and Parker, who keep me in line when I try to be cool.

And finally, in loving memory of Parker's beautiful girlfriend, Katherine Palludan, who loved books as much as I do, and whom we lost so tragically last year. We love you, Katherine.